STAY

Hilary Wynne

(#1 in the Alexa Reed Series)

Publisher's Note: This is a work of fiction. Names, characters, places, and incidents are a product of the author's imagination. Locales and public names are sometimes used for atmospheric purposes. Any resemblance to actual people, living or dead, or to businesses, companies, events, institutions, or locales is completely coincidental.

Ordering Information:
Quantity sales. Special discounts are available on quantity purchases by corporations, associations, and others. For details, contact the "Sales Department" using the contact form above.

Interior formatting by www.standoutbooks.com
Cover Design by Daliborka Mijailovic
Any people depicted in stock imagery provided by Shutterstock are models, and such images are being used for illustrative purposes only.
Certain stock imagery © Shutterstock.

Stay/ Hilary Wynne. -- 1st ed.
ISBN 978-0-9960294-4-5

CHAPTER 1

The traffic on the way to Ellen's office is horrible, and now I'm about fifteen minutes late. I tried to call and let her know, but the answering service always picks up when she's in session with a client. I know she won't care, but I'm upset because I need the whole hour today. Getting stuck showing units to a customer who I knew wasn't a serious buyer was a total waste of my afternoon and kept me from leaving the office on time.

I bound up the stairs, as much as one can bound in four-and-a-half-inch platform heels, and burst through the door to her small office. Nobody else is in the small lobby area, and I notice the door to her office is open. I peek in and see Ellen flipping through a magazine.

"I'm so sorry I'm late. I got stuck with a lookie-loo, and traffic was awful." I plop myself down on her couch and take a drink from the water bottle I'm holding in my hand. I'm totally frazzled and need a second to calm down. Unfortunately, I have already wasted enough time.

"No worries, Lexie. Take a second and catch your breath."

I've been seeing Ellen Berger for close to a year now. I found her on the Internet after my sister, Jill, convinced me I needed professional help. Ellen's practice is close by work and home, she was taking new patients, and she accepted my crappy insurance. I felt an instant connection with her, and pretty soon I was pouring out my whole life story to her—well, most of it anyway. My main reason for coming was to work through my feelings about Brady's death. I thought I would have gotten in and out of here in a couple sessions, but no such luck. I ran through my maximum appointments covered by insurance within about six months, but Ellen knew I needed to keep coming, so she offered me a deeply discounted rate and worked out a payment plan with me. She is a godsend and worth every dime I have charged on my credit cards.

"Why are you so agitated today?"

"I don't know. You're right though. I *am* agitated. I guess it's the time of year. A lot of memories are coming up right now. Plus, it's Luke's birthday on Saturday, and everyone wants to go out to dinner and then to Stellar afterward. I don't want to go at all, but I can't say no. It's stupid to be having anxiety about going out, but I can't stop thinking of ways to get out of it."

"It's been a long time since you've gone out and had fun."

"I know. That's what everyone keeps telling me. I'm just not sure if that's really what I consider fun these days."

"Hanging out with your friends, having a drink or two, and dancing *is* fun, and it's okay to want to do those things again. You're allowed to be the old Lexie again."

I have divided my memories of my adult life into three phases: pre-Brady, during Brady, and post-Brady. Ellen doesn't think it's a great idea for me to compartmentalize my life like that, but the demarcations are so obvious that I can't help it. She constantly reminds me that all of my experiences have made me who I am, good and bad, and I'm just the person I'm supposed to be as a result. The issue is that even after close to a year, I haven't told her about all the experiences Brady and I shared. Right now she's suggesting I try to be the pre-Brady Lexie. She didn't know me then, but I have shared a lot of what I was like before I met Brady. I like that girl much better than the girl I am now, and I wish I could go back and find her again. That girl was confident and funny and opened her heart to people. She trusted others and let those same people rely on her. That girl was hopeful about love. That girl was whole.

"Have you had any nightmares lately?" Ellen is referring to my recurring nightmares. The one I have most often is where I'm frantically trying to get a hold of somebody so we can talk before something really bad happens. It's almost that vague. The characters are different. It can be a friend, coworker, or family member. Once it was a stranger. I run around from place to place, trying to find the person. I call and text and e-mail, and nobody will respond to me. I'm racing against a literal clock in the dream. I never actually find anybody in my dream, and I always wake up before the time expires, usually in a cold sweat and panicked. Last night's version had me chasing my sister, Tracy, all over South Beach. I woke up with an impending sense of doom, and I haven't been able to shake it all day today. I tell Ellen about it.

"I'm convinced I'm always going to have this dream. I really am. I wasn't able to get closure with Brady, and now it's going to haunt me forever." I know I sound a little melodramatic, but I really feel that way.

"The guilt you have, the one where you feel you had control over what happened, will tear you apart if you continue to let it. You can forgive Brady right now if you want to. He doesn't need to be here. You can forgive yourself too. You need to remember, forgiveness is a one-time act. When you choose to have resentments and hang on to the guilt, you have to do it every day. Which one is harder?"

"It's all hard, Ellen. It's all really hard."

CHAPTER 2

If I'm being honest, I pretty much agree with my friends and family that I need to get back out into the real world. And by *real world*, I mean the one where I socialize and date and enjoy my life. The irony is not lost on me that if anyone was looking through a crystal ball at my life, they would think I have it made. I have a great job and an even better group of friends. My family is a little dysfunctional, but they do love me. I live in beautiful South Florida where the sun almost always shines, and I can wear sandals almost year round. The only thing that's really missing in my life is a boyfriend, and most of the time I'm okay with not being in a relationship. I actually prefer it. My relationship with Brady changed everything about the way I feel about love. Now I think it's not worth the pain that inevitably comes with giving your heart to someone. My friends seem to understand my reluctance to open myself up to someone and haven't pushed. They do wonder how long I plan to go without sex though.

I think about all these things as I get ready to go out tonight. It's Saturday, and it's Luke's twenty-seventh birthday. Luke is one of my best friends, and there's no way I'm getting out of this. We celebrated his twenty-first doing the "Tennessee Waltz" in Tallahassee, his twenty-fifth barhopping in Key West, and last year's clubbing with a huge group of friends in South Beach. Memories of that night are bittersweet. It was a good night. Brady was good. I was good. But soon after that night, it was anything but good.

This will be the first time in almost ten months I have set foot in a nightclub, and my anxiety is high. You would think I was going on a job interview instead of out to dinner and dancing with friends. I used to be a party girl. I have loved going clubbing since I got a fake ID when I was seventeen. I was the one who was always up for going out. Now I'm worried if I start living like that again, all the painful memories I've been trying to forget will just come flooding back.

A voice interrupts my mind's trip down memory lane, and I hear my roommate and best friend, Marissa Delgado, yelling at me from down the hall. "Lexie, seriously, if you don't hurry up, we're going to miss our reservation."

"I'm almost ready. Give me five more minutes."

Everyone else is ready and waiting on me in the living room. I peek at my watch and realize it's already seven-fifteen. Crap. If we're going to make an eight o'clock dinner reservation, I really do need to get going.

I'm a typical girl; the better I look, the better I feel. I guess that's why I'm putting in all the extra effort here. I've been in the bathroom for an hour with my glass—okay, second glass—of Pinot Grigio and my music, trying to calm my nerves and get me in the mood. My iPod is set on my dance playlist, and I can't help but move around the bathroom as I get ready. Music is my thing and the one constant that has always made me feel better and helped me express myself when I can't find the words. There is nothing more comforting than hearing lyrics to a song you could've written yourself. The fact that another person did means someone else in the world knows how you're feeling and that you're not alone. I don't play any instruments, and I can't sing a decent note, but I love listening to music. I feel if I was ever to write a book about my life, I would divide the chapters by songs. The title would be *The Soundtrack of My Life*. Unfortunately, if I were to start writing my book today, it would be filled with a bunch of depressing stuff. That thought starts to bum me out, so I file it away and concentrate on putting the finishing touches on my makeup.

I glance at myself in the full-length mirror behind the door, and I have to admit I look good. I probably have more makeup on than I usually wear, but it still looks tasteful and not trashy. I'm wearing black, skinny pants with multi-zippered pockets that end just above my ankle. I'm really excited to wear them because I just bought them in a size smaller than I usually wear. I have dropped about fifteen pounds in the past few months, and it's showing in my clothes. I have been running a lot, but if I'm being honest, the weight loss happened because I've been a little depressed, and my appetite is not what it used to be. At least something good has come out of all this drama. I'm not a skinny girl, but I'm not heavy either. I have an athletic, fit body that's toned from years of playing soccer and tennis. The loss of the fifteen just helps me look leaner. I pair the pants with a black-and-white, multidirectional, striped, fitted bustier that really shows off my shoulders, breasts, and collarbone. About a half inch of leather circles the whole top and adds a bit of edginess to the look. There is a little V cut in the front that dips down between my breasts and gives a sneak peek of my ample cleavage. A long, silver, exposed zipper runs down the whole length of the back. I'm wearing brand new Michael Kors black, caged, leather ankle booties with four-and-a-half-inch heels that add height to my 5'5" frame and make my legs look longer. I'm not sure they're a great idea for a night out dancing, but they totally help make the outfit. I add a skinny, silver, tube necklace and slip on my signature silver hoop earrings. I have blown out my wavy, dirty blonde hair and pulled it into a messy, poufy ponytail. I feel edgy and sexy, which is the look I'm going for.

I'm thankful my roommates and I are all about the same size because we can share clothes and shoes. We all love fashion, but none of us can afford to dress the way we want to all the time. I have somewhat of a shoe addiction, an expensive shoe addiction. I think it stems from when I was a freshman in college and some random guy in a bar told me I had the sexiest feet he'd ever seen and that I wasn't treating them properly. He said it all with a straight face too. I was wearing cheap flip-flops at the time. He told me I needed to dress my beautiful ladies up and show them off. Talk about odd pickup lines, right? He was hammered, and my roommates and I laughed our asses off about it all night. We still talk about it years later. I have actually pictured that guy's face a couple times during a few of my shoe shopping sprees. My roommates are always giving me crap about my shoe thing, but they sure don't mind borrowing them every chance they get.

We're going to Stellar after dinner. Stellar happens to be one of the hottest clubs in South Beach and where Luke is currently working as a bartender. It's Saturday night, and I'm sure it will be packed and everyone will be dressed to impress. One more quick glance in the mirror, and I decide for sure I feel good about my outfit choice. I down the last sip of my wine, gloss my lips with nude lipstick, unplug my phone from the charger, and head out into the living room. I'm hoping my outward appearance will mask my inner feelings of discomfort.

"Finally," says Marissa. She's not used to nagging me to hurry up because I'm usually the first one ready to go anywhere, and I always make it a point to be on time. When we were at FSU, I used to wait a full hour after she started to get ready before I even got in the shower. She always blames her lateness on the fact she operates on Cuban time. Tonight, she was ready before me and looks awesome. She's a beautiful girl with long, straight, brown hair, huge brown eyes, and perfect skin. She's wearing a white, lacy, mini dress that shows off her natural tan along with a pair of flesh-colored L.K. Bennett sandals she borrowed from me. My other roommate, Shannon Garrett, a pretty blue-eyed blonde, and her boyfriend, Cory Davis, a very tall, very big, ex-college football player, are going out with us too. I love this little group. They have been so supportive of me. Add Luke, and I couldn't ask for a better group of friends.

I roll my eyes at her. "Whatever. Let's go."

I grab my little cropped, black leather jacket from the hall closet on the way out the door. The club we're headed to has a rooftop bar, and that's where Luke usually works. It can get a little chilly at night in April and we'll probably be spending time outside. I plan on getting all of my drinks from Luke, so they'll be free. We're all in our mid-twenties and well into career mode, but none of us has tons of extra money. My job as a marketing and sales consultant for a major property development company pays me pretty well, but I work for commission and only get paid once a month. I have to budget my money so it lasts. Dinner tonight will not be cheap, but we always try to treat each other well on our birthdays.

The plan is to catch dinner at Havana Nights, a popular restaurant in South Beach. After dinner, we are heading over to Stellar. Luke began bartending at Stellar about five months ago and has been asking us to go ever since. The others have been there. I haven't gone. Luke has to work tonight, so we're meeting up with him at the restaurant and catching dinner first. A text I got from him earlier today said he's bringing a date. It's a typical Luke move to show up with a new girl out of the blue. He hasn't changed much since college and is always surrounded by pretty girls.

I used to be one of Luke Miller's girls. Well, sort of. The first time I saw him, he was behind the bar at Bullwinkle's in Tallahassee. He was the guy all the girls wanted to give their drink order to—as well as their numbers. I think I ordered seven beers that first night just so I could keep talking to him. He was a total flirt, and I'm sure he made a killing in tips. Luke is tall, about 6'1", with jet-black wavy hair, ocean-blue eyes, and muscles in all the right places. His handsome boy-next-door face kept the girls lining up night after night. My friends and I would go to Bullwinkle's every Thursday night for nickel-beer night. After a few months of going and many, many cheap beers later, Luke and I struck up a flirty friendship. I learned he was a junior majoring in business, VP of his frat, and serially unattached. We talked about his family, friends, and school, and I could see he was a smart and driven guy. I felt like I was getting to know him pretty well even though we didn't spend time together outside of the bar. We kept in touch through texting, and at least a couple times a week I would get some funny, random text from him. I started to look forward to getting them, and pretty soon I admitted to myself I really was interested in being more than friends.

So when Luke invited me and my girlfriends to a party his frat was having, we went. I was very excited and was totally hoping we'd hook up. The party was the first time we had really ever socialized outside the bar, and I was curious to see how Luke would act toward me. He had texted me a few times throughout the day to make sure we were going. There were a couple of other things going on that night, so we ended up showing up late. It was a huge party and totally in full swing when we arrived. When I finally saw Luke, it was obvious he had been drinking heavily. He was very excited to see me and came right over and kissed me on the lips. I remember thinking the kiss was an awesome start to the night and that clearly I wasn't misreading the signs Luke was interested in being more than friends. We talked for a few minutes before Luke pulled me out into the middle of the floor where everyone was dancing. Well, it wasn't actually dancing; it was more like bumping and grinding. Our hands were pretty much all over each other, but we didn't kiss. To this day, I know Luke is not big on PDA, but that night I thought it was pretty obvious we were together. Obvious to me at least. Our "togetherness" didn't stop several drunken girls from coming up and pulling at him, trying to get his attention. He stayed pretty focused on me, but he did seem to enjoy the attention and never really told any of the other girls he was there with me. Because this was our first time out together, I didn't make a big deal about it, but it didn't make me happy.

After a few hours of dancing and drinking, I found myself with Luke in his room. He told me he brought me back there so we could "hang out and talk where it was quieter". Yeah, okay. I was a little buzzed, and although I knew he was pretty hammered, I still wanted to be with him. At first it was a little awkward being alone with him, but when he leaned over and started kissing me, the awkwardness disappeared. He was an amazing kisser, which I had expected. We kissed for a while, and soon were lying on his bed. When he took my shirt off, I didn't stop him. When he took my jeans off, I didn't stop him. When he failed to be able to produce a condom, I stopped him. I'd seen all the girls that surrounded him both at the bar and here tonight, and I wasn't going to sleep with him without protection. I was glad I was sober enough to be responsible. Surprisingly, considering his drunken state and my state of undress, Luke didn't try to change my mind. He said, "Okay," and everything happening between us just kind of stopped. All of a sudden, Luke seemed a lot more sober and appeared uneasy with what was going on between us. I was thoroughly embarrassed and disappointed as well. I quickly got dressed and tried to salvage some of my pride. We left his room and went back out to the party without saying much to each other. I left not too long after that, and I couldn't find Luke to say goodbye. Then again, I didn't really try very hard. When I woke up the next morning, I turned my phone on and saw there were five texts from Luke. I could see they had come in very early that morning, and as I scrolled through them, I wondered if he was still drunk.

Luke: *hope you are home ok? Didn't say bye*
Luke: *can't stop thinking about kissing you and touching you*
Luke: *can't do it again*
Luke: *you are too good for me. I'm an ass*
Luke: *see you Thurs?*

I had woken up feeling embarrassed and was happy to see the texts. I was still being blown off, but it was done in such a "nice" way. I didn't hear from him the rest of the week, and I didn't reach out either. When Thursday night rolled around, I really didn't feel like going to the bar. I got a text from Luke at about eight o'clock.

Luke: *you better come tonight or there will be consequences*
Alexa: *you don't scare me*
Luke: *plz come*

I didn't respond to his last text but did decide to go. We got to the bar at ten-thirty, and when Luke saw me, he flashed me a huge smile. I immediately felt at ease and not at all awkward. He came out from behind the bar, kissed me on the lips, and gave me a huge hug. He looked me right in the eyes and asked me if I would be his best *friend*. Yes, it was odd, but I decided to go with it. The rest is history. Over the years, the question about why we're not more than friends has come up many, many times. Luke always makes a joke about it and says I'm too good for him. When that happens, I tell myself that one day I'm really going to talk to him about that night and ask why things didn't go further. But honestly, I think I'm scared to hear the answer because it's been six years and I still haven't asked.

CHAPTER 3

Thanks to Cory's Indy-style driving, we manage to get from Coconut Grove to South Beach in time to make our eight o'clock reservation. We park in a lot that's between the restaurant and the club and head to dinner. Luke has been texting me for about fifteen minutes, so I know he's already there and waiting.

Luke: *Where r you?*
Alexa: *On way. Chill*
Luke: *Hurry the hell up. I'm hungry*
Alexa: *Eat some peanuts at the bar*
Luke: *allergic-remember? Trying to off me?*
Alexa: *Parking. And no offing tonight. It's your bday*

After I type the text and hit send, I realize how totally inappropriate those texts are. Have Luke and I come so far that we're making jokes about dying?

Luke has made arrangements to get to work a little late tonight, but he's still rushing us. My anxiety level is still pretty high, and being rushed makes it worse. We find Luke at the bar, sitting next to a pretty, petite redhead. He immediately introduces all of us to his date, Krista, and I wonder where she came from because he hasn't mentioned her before.

"About time you guys got here," he says to all of us while looking straight at me. I walk over and give him a big hug and kiss on the cheek.

"Relax. It's your birthday. You're old now, and we can't have you getting all worked up and stroking out on us."

Luke swats me gently on the butt and whispers in my ear that I look sexy as hell. I see Krista is a little confused and uncomfortable with our interaction. Most new girls are. This won't be the first time I've had to explain our relationship.

I look directly at her and smile. "Luke's my best friend; has been for almost seven years. We sometimes act like an old married couple, but we're *just* friends."

Krista thanks me with a smile, but I can tell she isn't totally convinced.

We only have to wait a few minutes before the hostess comes and leads us to our table. Luke sits down next to me, and Krista sits on the other side. I'm sure she would have rather been farther away from me, but I'm not surprised he chose to sit there. The food and drinks begin to arrive at the table, and we're all talking and laughing and having a great time. I hate to admit it, but it feels good to be out. I'm really enjoying myself. Salsa music is playing in the background, and there's definitely a festive atmosphere in the restaurant. I can't keep from dancing in my seat, and I'm starting to look forward to getting to Stellar to dance. I order my second mojito and notice I'm definitely not anxious anymore. Actually, I'm pretty buzzed. I feel Luke grab my hand under the table, and I look over to find him staring at me. There's tenderness in his eyes I know he doesn't share with many people.

He whispers in my ear. "You look so happy tonight. It's the best birthday present ever."

I smile a real smile and squeeze his hand back. "I feel happy." Wow! It's been a long time since I've said that and actually meant it.

We order dessert and a round of café con leches. We sing "Feliz Cumpleaños" to Luke and toast his twenty-seventh.

It's getting late, and Luke tells us he really needs to get to work. He told his manager he would be there by ten o'clock. The restaurant isn't far from the hotel, but it will take him about fifteen minutes to walk there. Marissa asks him if his manager will get pissed if he's a few minutes late, and Luke says he doesn't think so, but that the owner of the club is going to be there tonight instead of the manager, and he doesn't want to cause any issues. At the mention of his boss, Marissa, Shannon, Krista, and I give each other knowing glances and start gossiping like high school girls.

Julian Bauer is Luke's boss and the owner of Hotel Del Marco, the boutique hotel where Stellar is located. He's also the eldest son of the family that owns Bywater Properties. Bywater is a direct competitor of Wilson and Mitchell Investment Group, the company I work for, so I've also heard about him in work circles. Their properties are located all over South Florida, and they have a small property next to the one I'm working at on South Bayshore Drive in Coconut Grove. I've never seen Julian in person, but I've seen pictures of him on the Internet, usually with a model on his arm. Julian Bauer is young, rich, gorgeous, and single. Did I mention gorgeous? I'm sure women all over South Beach go to sleep at night dreaming of him. He's *that* guy. Luke has mentioned him a few times since he started working at Stellar but generally seems reluctant to talk about him. I gather from what little Luke has said that Julian seems like a pretty cool guy, but that he's a player and is always leaving the club with a different woman. When Luke described Julian to me that way, it made me laugh.

"Oh, so you two have a lot in common," I teased.

"If you exclude the filthy rich part, yeah, I guess we do."

On paper, Luke and Julian do seem to have a few things in common. Luke is also very good looking, young, and single. The main difference is Julian owns the bar, and Luke works at the bar. I suspect that's one of the reasons Luke might be a little jealous of Julian. Luke comes from a family with a lot of money. Both of his parents are big-shot attorneys in West Palm Beach. They had expected Luke to follow in their footsteps and go to an Ivy League school. He opted to stay in Florida and decided early on in college he wasn't lawyer material. He has an entrepreneurial spirit and wants to own a bar someday. It hasn't been a career choice that's gone over well with his parents, and they aren't very supportive of him. They think he's all about the party and nightlife. I know for a fact Luke works his ass off and has been saving his money for years. I don't doubt that someday in the not so distant future he'll open a place of his own. Getting a gig at Stellar was a huge deal for him. It happens to be one of the hottest bars in South Beach right now, and the jobs are very coveted. He says the tips are great and the whole club/bar/hotel seems to be really well run. I know he hopes to move into a management position soon, so I understand why he wants to impress the boss.

I won't lie. I'm a little excited at the prospect of seeing Julian tonight. What a perfect distraction. I'm not the type of girl Julian Bauer goes for, but it might be fun to spend the night fantasizing about a man like him.

We tell Luke it's cool to take off and say we'll take care of the check. He gets up, gives each of us girls a kiss, and shakes Cory's hand. We invite Krista to stay and walk over with us, but she says she's meeting some friends there and will see us later. I'm sure she really just wants some more alone time with Luke. She seems pretty cool, but it's never easy being the new girl in a group of close friends.

"Thank you all so much for dinner. I can't think of a better group of people to celebrate me with." Luke is all about celebrating his wonderfulness. We finish our coffees and settle up the bill.

It's a beautiful night, and I'm stuffed from the huge meal I just ate, so I'm happy to walk to the hotel. My feet, clad in four-and-a-half-inch heels, are not in agreement and are protesting loudly along the way. It's ten forty-five by the time we get to the door, and there's already a long line to get inside. Stellar isn't the only reason people flock to the hotel. The whole property has undergone a major renovation in the last year, and the quality of the venues here draws large crowds. I haven't been here since the place has been redone, and I'm anxious to get inside and check it out. The rooftop bar where Luke usually works, Orion, has a stunning ocean view, private cabanas, and a huge fire pit that attracts people even in the chillier months. According to Luke, it's crowded all week long. There's a tapas restaurant named Ursa's on the property that has one of the hottest chefs in South Beach serving up great food well into the night. We would have eaten there, but we couldn't get a reservation, and the wait on a Saturday night would have been ridiculous. The pool area outside the hotel houses two other smaller bar areas, and there's usually live entertainment either at Orion or downstairs by the large pool that overlooks Ocean Drive. The whole place has a great vibe, and you can feel the energy as you walk up.

Luke texted me while we were still at the restaurant to let me know he put our names on the VIP list and that we just need to walk to the front. We tell the bouncer our names, show our IDs, and head in with no wait. The bouncer waves off the cover charge too. Having connections definitely has its perks. I'm in a hurry to get inside because I need to pee, and I need to sit down for a few minutes because my feet are killing me.

After a quick pit stop at the ladies' room near the entrance, we head up to Orion to find Luke and get some drinks. Luke wasn't exaggerating. It's very crowded up here, and it's not easy to get to the bar. We all make our way to the corner of the bar, and I try to get Luke's attention. I immediately see Krista on a stool, front and center at the bar. She's looking at Luke with puppy dog eyes, and I feel kind of sorry for her. She seems like a nice girl, and if she wants to stay around for more than a few days, she definitely needs to play a little hard to get. Luke never stays interested in girls who are clingy or needy. After a few minutes, Luke notices us and heads right over. It's definitely an advantage to know the bartender. He knows what we all like to drink and gets our order turned around quickly. I'm going to stick to mojitos tonight. This is my fifth drink, and I probably should stop after this one. My nice buzz doesn't need to turn into a bad hangover.

Marissa and I hand everyone's drinks over, and we all go our separate ways. Shannon and Cory want to spend some time alone, so they head off toward the fire pit in the middle of the bar and find some open seats on one of the white couches nearby. Marissa and I head off to dance.

I follow Marissa as we walk down the stairs to Stellar. There are a few people in the stairwell, and I really should be paying attention to where I'm going. I'm walking slow, because I'm a little buzzed, and looking down, because my damn feet are killing me, when I literally run headlong into someone coming up the stairs. Seriously? This would only happen to me. I look up and find myself staring into the deep green, mesmerizing eyes of Julian Bauer. I quickly look away. He's big, like big-beautiful-muscle big, and I sort of bounce off of him. Luckily I'm able to grab the stair railing before I fall on my ass. My face comes up to the middle of his well-defined chest, and I notice I've spilled half my drink on him. I'm so mortified I can't even look up at him again. I mumble a quick, "I'm so sorry," under my breath and take a little step to the side to try to move past him. Marissa looks back at me and tries her best not to laugh at the horrified look on my face. The only thing that stops her is that she's also mesmerized by him. I think I'm home free when I feel a hand reach out and lightly grab my elbow. The touch sends sparks throughout my body, and I grasp the railing tighter. This touch on my elbow just set me on fire. What the hell? I stand still for a few seconds and then spin slowly around to acknowledge this man holding on to me.

I find myself staring at one of the most gorgeous men I've ever seen in my life. Julian's hair is brown with natural golden highlights mixed throughout. It's cut short on the sides and back, and the top is a little spiky and unruly. I can't decide if this is a look that takes time to create or if this sexy "I don't care" look is what he looks like when he wakes up in the morning. Either way, it totally works for him, and all I know is I want to run my fingers through it. His sun-kissed skin gives a nod to his Latino heritage. His eyebrows are full, and he has a small scar running through the left one. I can't help but wonder how it got there, and I have to restrain myself from reaching over and touching it. His piercing green eyes are big and framed with thick, black lashes, and something I see in them speaks to me in an indescribable way. His sculpted cheekbones and upper lip are lightly covered with what looks like a few days' worth of stubble. This adds a bit of an edge to a face that's otherwise almost too pretty. He's tall, about 6'1", with strong, broad shoulders and the muscular arms of an athlete. I can see the definition of his chest through his fitted gray shirt, and I again have to restrain myself from reaching over and running my hands over it. Holy hell, do I want to touch this man. *Everywhere.* I imagine most women feel the same way when they see him, but I'm unnerved by my visceral reaction to him. He's so close I can smell his cologne, and I take a deep breath and inhale the delicious scent. I'm so dazzled I don't notice anyone else in the stairwell.

"Are you okay? You ran into me pretty hard." Julian's beautiful eyes sparkle with amusement, and I hear the teasing in his voice. He's smiling in a flirtatious way that's making me weak in the knees. His lips are full and look both soft and powerful at the same time. He gives me a smile, and I get a glimpse of two rows of perfectly straight, white teeth.

I can hardly look at him. I swear it's like looking into the sun. When I hoped to run into Julian tonight, this is so not what I had in mind. I imagine Julian can see how uncomfortable I am, and he lets go of my elbow.

"I'm fine, but I'm so sorry I just spilled my drink all over you." I swear the words come out garbled and know I sound like the teacher on the Peanuts cartoons. My mouth has become dry while staring at him.

"No worries, it's an occupational hazard. I get drinks spilled on me at least once a week." I totally appreciate that he's trying to make me not feel like such an idiot.

"I'm sure you're also used to women throwing themselves at you at least once a week too." I follow his lead and try to make this a less embarrassing situation for myself. I let go of the railing, and as I'm finding my balance, my breasts gently brush up against Julian's chest. My body is once again assaulted by the shock of our bodies touching. Does this stuff really happen? Am I the only one who felt that? I look up at Julian to see if he felt anything.

He's no longer looking at me with amusement in his eyes, and my question is answered. His eyes are blazing with desire. Now I can't stop staring at him, and I feel like a spaceship caught in a damn tractor beam. I see confusion in his stare, and I immediately sense his discomfort with this "thing" that's happening between us. After a few moments, he looks away. He doesn't look at me again and turns to head upstairs.

"Come find me when you need another drink." I hear Julian's offer as he walks away, and I respond in my head. *Hell yes!*

I walk down the stairs as quickly as I can without falling again and find Marissa waiting for me at the bottom. I exhale and realize I've been holding my breath. She's laughing at me, and I can't help but laugh back.

"Oh my God that was embarrassing. Of course he's the guy I run into and spill a drink on. Think I made an impression?"

"Oh, you made an impression all right. I doubt he'll forget the girl who almost knocked him over in the stairwell and spilled a drink all over him."

"Just trying to stand out in a crowd." Seriously though, embarrassing as that was, he probably won't forget me.

"I keep telling you not to wear such high heels. You're always doing shit like that." It's true. I have a fascination with really high heels, like four inches or higher. The problem is I'm only good in them for the first few hours. After that, it's a guarantee I'll either be complaining because my feet hurt or I'll trip on something because I can't walk anymore. Being buzzed certainly doesn't help.

"Well, if I'm going to fall into anything, at least it was Julian Bauer. Did you freaking see him? He's better looking in person than he is in pictures. At first I could hardly look at him, and then I couldn't stop staring. It was like some Jedi mind control thing he was doing to me."

Marissa laughs and nods in agreement. "He's definitely one of the best-looking guys I've ever seen in person." This observation is serious coming from Marissa. She never really comments much on guys we see out. She's engaged, and although she looks sometimes, she's totally into her fiancé, Kevin. Kevin is in the army and stationed overseas for the next eight months. I feel bad for her that he's away because I know how much she misses him. But I'm also secretly glad I've had her to myself the last few months. These "girlfriend" moments keep me sane.

"Right." I say it in agreement rather than as a question. We laugh and joke as we head out to the dance floor. Marissa is smiling at me, and I ask her what's up.

"It's nice to see you like this again, Lex—flirting and drooling over a hot guy. It's like old times."

I definitely was drooling. Geez. It has been a long time since I've had sex, and although I miss it, I haven't made any effort to meet anyone. Right now it's all I can think about. Julian Bauer is one hot man.

I'm sure I'll be replaying this scene over and over in my head for the rest of the night, but for now I just want to get on the floor and dance. We head out there and dance for a little while. Well, until I start complaining about my feet hurting. I decide I'd rather drink than dance, and because I spilled half of my drink on Julian, I'm out. I debate going back upstairs to Luke because I'm not sure I want to run into Julian again, literally or figuratively. I played off the whole encounter when Marissa and I were talking about it, but to be honest, something happened in that stairwell that made us both uncomfortable and excited. There was an instant, powerful connection between us, and I really felt like I was being drawn to him in an inexplicable way. I manage to convince myself I imagined the whole thing and decide I want a free drink. Marissa stays in Stellar with Shannon and Cory, who joined up with us a few songs ago.

I head up to Orion and find an open stool at the end of the bar. My feet thank me for finding a place to sit down. Damn shoes. Luke is all the way at the end of the long bar, and I realize I might be here a while. It's very crowded, and I can see Luke is busy. Another bartender comes over to me and tries to take my order. I'm pretty sure his name is Jordan. Luke has told me about a guy he's been working with, and this guy fits the description: multiracial, tall, dark, and handsome. Being hot is definitely a prerequisite to work here. I have yet to see an ugly employee. I tell him I'm waiting for Luke, and he says he'll let him know I'm down here. I sit there people watching while I wait for Luke, and before long, I see Julian headed my way. He has seen me, and although I'm tempted to get up and run away, it would be so obvious I'm trying to avoid him. I actually don't want to avoid him, but all of my alarms go off when he's nearby, and I know in my gut he's not the type of guy I need in my life.

Before Julian reaches the corner where I'm sitting, he stops and makes himself a drink. I contemplate my getaway at that moment, but I'm unable to pull my eyes away from the great view of his hot body. As he moves around the bar, I'm treated to the full display. I've already experienced his chest and arms up-close and way too personal in the stairwell. Now I get to peruse the whole package. His legs are long, and his black slacks are just the right amount of tight to show off the muscles in his thighs. His ass is, well, it's perfect. My heart's beginning to beat faster, and feelings of longing have started coursing through my body. I feel my nipples tightening. Seriously, Alexa? Get a grip.

I'm totally ogling this man, and I can't stop. I'm sure he's used to it, but it's not something I make a habit of. As a matter of fact, I've made it a point over the last nine months to pretty much avoid men. I've tried not to attract any male attention since my relationship with Brady ended, and that means not flirting or staring or doing any of the things I can't stop myself from doing right now. I try not to be obvious as I gawk at him, but the sly smile I see on his face when he turns back toward me tells me I'm totally busted. He knows I'm checking him out, and he seems to be enjoying it.

Julian sets his drink down in front of me on the bar, and I can't help but notice his Patek Philippe watch and the David Yurman dog tag that hangs around his beautiful neck. Everything about this guy screams expensive. His clothes, his jewelry, the fact he owns this place, all confirm he has money. Yet he doesn't come across like some of the spoiled, "I'm better than everyone else because I have money" type of guys that are all over South Florida. There's a tiny bit of Julian's confident aura that reminds me of Brady, and I can't help but think about him for a moment. Brady came from money, and when I was with him, he didn't hesitate to spend it or share it with everyone around him. But it wasn't his own money, and because he didn't work for it, he really didn't appreciate everything he had. Through him, I lived a very flashy and fast lifestyle for almost a year. It was really fun and exciting at first, but I never was really comfortable with the pace and excess. It was my discomfort that made me start to pull away.

Thankfully, Julian's voice breaks through my thoughts and brings me back into the now. "Do you see anything you like?" Julian's voice is flirty and teasing. I'm a little embarrassed but also excited to hear him talk to me in that playful tone again.

I just smile at him, not knowing if I should actually answer his question. Because, boy do I ever see something I like. This guy really should be a model. I wonder quickly if he actually is, or was. He's stunning. It's more than just the way he looks though. There's this powerful, confident, all-male energy that just radiates off of him. I wonder if all the cocktails I've consumed have helped me conjure up this beautiful illusion, like an oasis in the desert. Guys this good looking don't really exist, do they? And if they do, they certainly don't make a habit of flirting with girls like me, right?

My doubting his interest in me isn't a reflection of my self-esteem. It's more of a reality check. I know I'm a pretty girl. I'd say a solid eight on a ten-point scale. My long, naturally wavy, dirty blonde hair, dark green eyes, ample breasts, and athletic body have definitely attracted my share of admirers. But most of those men were all in the eight range on the scale, like me. I'm definitely more comfortable and secure with those types of guys. It sounds superficial, but when I've been with a guy who's more my equal as far as looks go, I feel less insecure he'll be looking to find someone better. If I had to rank Julian, he'd be like a fifteen on that same scale, and I'm sure there are no shortage of models in South Beach who would be more his type.

I kind of laugh at myself for even thinking anything happening between Julian and me is a possibility.

"Can I get you anything …?" He leaves the end of his question open for me to fill in the blank with my name.

"Alexa."

"Alexa." He says my name with a Spanish accent, and it sounds so much more beautiful than when I say it. He doesn't introduce himself, and I assume that he assumes everyone knows who he is.

"A beautiful name for a beautiful woman." Oh, flattery will get him everywhere.

"Gracias."

"Eres Latina?"

"No, soy una gringa," I respond in my best Spanish.

Surprise lights up his face, and he flashes me a sexy smile. "Eres una gringa que habla muy bien el Español."

I didn't think it was possible for him to sound sexier, but he does when he speaks Spanish, and I can hardly focus. I decide I'm not ready to continue a conversation in Spanish with someone who I'm having a hard time even speaking English to.

"Thank you. And in answer to your original question, yes, I do see something I like."

I get the sexy smile flashed at me again, and the butterflies in my stomach start fluttering like crazy. I swear he uses his smile as a sexual weapon.

"That mojito Luke just made looks like just the thing I need."

Julian chuckles and shakes his head. "Not exactly the answer I had in mind, but one mojito coming up."

He calls down the bar to Luke. "Luke, this beautiful lady likes the look of your mojito and would like the taste of one on her tongue."

I swear the words roll off his tongue like *hot, sweaty sex*. The drink is not the only damn thing I want to taste on my tongue, and I'm sure Julian has figured that out by the way I was visually assaulting his mouth just moments ago.

Julian has no idea I know Luke because Luke has not acknowledged me since I sat down at the bar twenty minutes ago. Luke turns around, sees Julian is talking about me, and hurries over to the end of the bar where I'm sitting. He leans over and gives me a quick kiss on the lips. He turns and flashes his own signature smile at Julian.

"Coming right up, boss. This beautiful lady can have *anything* she wants from *me*."

I love Luke. He always knows just the thing to say and do. It's part of the reason he's such a great bartender and an even better friend. I'm not sure Julian hears the possessiveness in Luke's voice, but I hear it. I also catch the warning in his eyes as he turns to make me my drink. Julian has been looking at me like he wants to rip all my clothes off, and Luke must have noticed. I want to tell him not to worry, mainly because there's nothing to worry about. Please. Nothing is going to happen between Julian and me. He should know better than anyone his boss probably dates supermodels. And he also knows I'm not going there, with anyone. This is just some harmless flirting. Right?

I shift slightly on my stool and bring my gaze back to Julian. When my eyes meet his, I do not miss the darts his eyes are throwing at Luke's back. He looks ... well, jealous?

"You two know each other?" It comes out as a statement rather than a question. I decide to have fun with this. I mean, of course we know each other. The man just kissed me on the lips. With as straight a face as I can manage, I respond.

"Know him? No, I don't know him."

"He just kissed you," Julian practically hisses. Wow … he *is* jealous. Really? I'm flattered and enjoying this immensely, so I decide to continue teasing him.

I hold back a smile as I try to look both nonchalant and confused. "I know he did. And he has the softest lips. Mmm. Delicioso. I wonder if having soft lips is a requirement of all of the bartenders here."

Julian is looking at me like I'm totally crazy. He can't tell if I'm serious or not.

"I think this bar has the best customer service policy. A kiss with each drink. Let's see, that's my third drink tonight. So three kisses for me tonight … wait." I pause, purse my lips together, and start counting on my fingers as if I'm trying to recall the missing kiss. "I've only been kissed two times tonight, and I know I've had three drinks. I've been ripped off. Someone needs to get fired!"

I say the last sentence, and I can't help but laugh when I see the expression on Julian's face. He's also laughing now, and it seems I've successfully broken through his surliness. I turn in my stool so I'm facing him completely head on.

"Of course I know him. Luke is one of my best friends."

Julian continues to smile. Wow! He is beautiful.

"Thank God. I'm very glad to hear it. I was beginning to think a sexual harassment lawsuit would be on my desk in the morning."

His lighthearted response makes me smile and giggle. He has a great sense of humor and seems very down to earth. He leans over and whispers sexily in my ear. I can feel his hot breath on my neck, and it sends shivers down my spine. The sweet smell of whiskey mixed with peppermint on his breath coupled with his delicious cologne launches an assault on my senses. If this were a black-and-white movie, I swear I'd be swooning.

"But if you really are looking for that kiss you missed out on, I would be more than happy to personally provide you with the most excellent customer service Hotel Del Marco offers. The type of stellar service only the owner can provide."

I think I gasp, and Julian snickers under his breath. He knows exactly what kind of effect he's having on me. So much for me pulling off calm, cool, and collected.

"Well, it may be nice to know your name before we get that up-close and personal," I whisper back. I'm a pro at snarky banter, and this man brings out my sarcastic nature without even trying.

Of course I'm teasing, but Julian looks like he doesn't really know if I'm serious or not. I'm not sure he even realizes he hasn't bothered to officially introduce himself to me. My comment brings a big smile to his face, and he concedes he skipped that step.

"My bad, Alexa. I'm Julian Bauer. It's very nice to 'officially' meet you. I guess our *run-in* in the stairwell doesn't count as *up-close and personal* then?" Julian is pretending to act all proper and polite and extends his hand as a means of introduction. I look down at his hand and reach out and put my hand in his. His large hand is soft and strong and completely envelops mine. The second we touch, a jolt of electricity shoots through me. His touch really is like an electric shock to my system. It's the third time we have touched, and each time I've gotten the chills up and down my body. I look up at Julian after we touch, and it's totally obvious he feels it too. His playful demeanor completely changes, just like it did in the stairwell. His gaze is burning. I'm practically rendered speechless, but I manage to push a few words out.

"Well, Julian Bauer. I'm Alexa Reed, and it is nice to 'officially' meet you."

Thank goodness Luke walks up when he does and sets my drink down in front of me. He looks at Julian, then at me, and back at Julian again. He has a smile on his face, but I know it's the bullshit one he flashes when he's not happy. He knows something is going down here.

"There you go, Lex. You should stop after this one. Don't want you to be hung-over tomorrow and ruin our whole day."

Seriously? How embarrassing. I can't believe he just said that, and I'm not sure what the hell he's talking about because we don't have plans tomorrow. I don't want to make a scene, so I settle for rolling my eyes at him. I'm ready for him to walk away so I can finish my conversation with Julian. But he just stands there like he has nothing else to do. I shrug my shoulders at Julian as if to say I have no idea what Luke is up to.

I guess Julian decides he's had enough of this little pissing match. As he turns to walk away, he looks me dead in the eyes. That smoldering look is still there.

"Just let me know ... A-lex-a." He's talking about the kiss.

Fuck. This guy is trouble with a capital T.

I swing my head around to look at Luke, and he's standing there with that same fake smile plastered on his face.

"Don't go there, Lex. Nothing good will come of it."

I know he's just looking out for me, so I lean in and give him a hug. "I'm good. Really. Just having some fun."

"Julian Bauer is not someone to play games with. Please try to remember that."

"Go to work, Luke. There are girls dying of thirst over there who need you." I nod toward the other end of the bar where a few college girls are trying to get his attention. Luke finally walks away, and I turn to leave to go find my friends. Out of the corner of my eye, I see Julian standing off in the shadows, and although it's dark, I swear he's staring right at me.

I go back downstairs to the club and find my friends dancing. I pull them off the dance floor to tell them what just happened upstairs. I'm feeling all giddy like a teenage girl with a crush on the captain of the football team. It's sort of ridiculous. I'm a twenty-five-year-old woman who has been flirted with before. Maybe not like that though. I tell them verbatim what Julian said and explain how Luke got all possessive. They're excited for me and don't seem at all concerned that Julian is the big, bad wolf Luke is making him out to be. They encourage me to flirt with as many guys as I want to—especially ridiculously hot ones like Julian Bauer. Shannon starts to give me an earful on how I need to explain to Luke that he's not my boyfriend or my dad. My girlfriends are good friends with Luke too but have, on more than one occasion, questioned me about his *real* feelings for me. I remind them, for the millionth time, Luke and I are *just* friends. Maybe I do need to remind Luke of that too.

I don't talk to Julian for the rest of the night, but I see him several times. I'm sort of avoiding him because every time I do get a glimpse of him, he's surrounded by beautiful women. I've convinced myself he was just messing with me earlier. I came out to have a good time with my friends, and hooking up with anyone, let alone someone like Julian Bauer, was not on my agenda. I do find it a little suspicious though that despite the fact the hotel has several different venues, he never seems to be too far away from where I am.

Time flies by as we all drink and dance and enjoy a great night. I hate to admit it, but it really does feel good to be out again. Dancing makes me feel alive, and it's something I miss doing. I run into a few old friends I haven't seen in forever. They ask me how I'm doing, and it feels really good to be able to honestly answer that I'm doing well. None of these people know about Brady, so they really have no idea how bad things were for me for a while. That life is finally starting to feel like it's in the past, and I grab another cocktail and toast with my friends to new beginnings.

So now I'm officially really buzzed. Okay. I'm drunk. I haven't been out drinking in a while, and I'm basically a lightweight anyway. I look at my watch and realize it's almost one o'clock in the morning. It's time to call it a night.

Everyone agrees to leave, and I tell them to hang on a second while I go say goodnight to Luke. I know if I don't he'll start blowing up my phone the second he gets off work. Right now all I want to do is go home and go to sleep. I unsteadily walk up the stairs and head over to Luke's bar. I wait there for a few minutes before I get his attention. He eventually spots me and raises his finger, giving me the wait-a-minute sign. I turn and lean shakily against the bar as I wait for him. I need the support because my feet are killing me and because I really am pretty dizzy. I think about Julian and our earlier conversation and wonder where he is. I'm drunkenly lost in my thoughts when I sense someone behind me. I can't see Julian, but I swear I can feel his presence. I can also smell him. He smells so yummy. He slowly runs his thumb across the length of my shoulder in a way that is possessive, sweet, and sexual all at the same time. I'm not sure if he's extending an invitation or just trying to get my attention. Who cares, right? Once again, I feel a jolt of electricity shoot through my body. I take a deep breath and slowly turn around. I'm met with Julian's seductive smile. I try my best to hide the fact I'm drunk.

"So we meet again, Corazón. This seems to be our spot. Maybe I should've hung out here more tonight so we could've talked. It would have been more fun than just watching you from across the club all night. You were never alone."

Um okay. Is this guy for real?

"Neither were you," I say seriously, the alcohol making me brave.

Julian chuckles. "I would've been happy to make myself available to you tonight. I told you to let me know."

"Hmm. My bad. Does your offer have an expiration date, Julian?"

Seriously, I think to myself. Because if it does, I'm totally calling in that kiss right now! I stare at his lips and imagine them all over my body. If he can almost electrocute me with his fingers, I can only imagine what his lips and tongue will do to me.

Before Julian can answer, Luke walks over and stands in front of me and looks back and forth between us. This is the second time he's caught us whispering in the corner, and he doesn't look happy. I flash him the smile I know he loves and reach over the bar to give him a hug. I go on the offensive to deter him from saying something that will either embarrass me or piss Julian off.

"We're heading out. Just wanted to say goodnight and tell you we're leaving."

He hugs me back as best as he can over the bar and whispers in my ear, "Go home now."

I shake my head and laugh at him. He's acting more protective than I've seen him since the one night during my junior year in college when one of his drunk-ass frat brothers wouldn't keep his hands off of me during a party. Luke was this close to getting in a fight that night, and looking back, it really wasn't that big of a deal. If I didn't understand why he was acting this way, I would be so annoyed. But Luke knows better than anyone what I've been through the last year, and I can't help but understand why he's acting a little crazy. He obviously really thinks I need to stay away from Julian. The problem is I'm not sure I want to stay away from him, or that I'll be able to.

I look over at Julian, who's still standing there watching us. He doesn't look like he has any intention of being the first one to walk away this time. Julian is Luke's boss, and I'm sure Luke can sense Julian and I both want him to walk away. So he does. But not before giving me that "be careful" look.

"Happy birthday," I call playfully as he walks away. He doesn't turn around but does put up his hand to acknowledge he heard me. Yep, he's not happy with me, and I know I can expect a lecture later.

As I turn back around to face Julian, I see Marissa heading toward me, motioning that it's time to go. I know they've been downstairs waiting for me, but right now the last thing I want to do is leave. But, I also know with everything inside me, I need to. I put my hand up to Marissa, telling her to stop, and mouth the words, "I'm coming". At least I mean to mouth the words.

I turn to look at Julian, and he's laughing. Shit. I just basically screamed, "I'm coming" right in front of him.

"Sounds promising." Oh my God, I could die right here on the spot.

"But maybe we should get to know each other a little bit better before we get all up-close and personal." Again, I'm speechless.

He leans in so close to me that his face is right next to mine and says seductively, "In answer to your earlier question, yes, there is an expiration date on my offer. The sooner you take advantage of it, the better." His words and closeness make me even dizzier than I already am. Before I have a chance to come up with a witty response, Julian gently kisses me on the cheek.

His lips feel so warm and soft. Yes, I feel this kiss too, all over my body and especially between my legs.

"Goodnight, Alexa. I hope to see you again really soon." Julian winks at me and walks away down the bar.

CHAPTER 4

I don't talk much on the ride home. I'm concentrating hard on not getting sick. Damn. Why did I have that last drink? Now every time I close my eyes I get the spins. I also don't feel like talking about my night in front of Cory. I tell the girls we can talk about it in the morning.

It's late, I'm drunk and tired, and I need to go to bed. I slip into a tank top and pair of boxers, wash my face, and crawl under the covers. I'm ready to be alone with my thoughts, my thoughts of Julian. I fall asleep picturing his lips on mine.

Damn! I forget to turn my phone off and I'm woken up when my phone buzzes repeatedly indicating I have a new text. I know it's from Luke even before I look at it. Nobody else I know would be texting me at three in the morning. I knew he would want to talk about what happened at Stellar.

Luke: *You up Hooka?*
Alexa: *Um. Am now* ☹.

Luke: *He wanted to know if you were single*

Alexa: *?*

Luke: *Julian...you know...The guy who wants in your panties*

Alexa: *And?*

Luke: *Said yes...single...but that you're a lesbian*

Alexa: *haha. Seriously?*

Luke: *You're seriously a lesbian?*

Alexa: *Haha. Stop. You said that?*

Luke: *No sweets. Said single. Should've lied. STAY AWAY.*
  Bad for you

Alexa: *No worries. Not his type.*

Luke: *You are every man's type A. ttyl. Dream big.*

Alexa: *You too. xoxo*

I turn the phone off and put it back onto my nightstand. I can't help but smile. I smile because Luke always makes me feel good about myself. I also smile because Julian was thinking about me.

My blaring alarm doesn't help the pounding in my head. I am officially really hung-over, and it sucks because I have to work today. I haven't had that much to drink in forever, and I'm feeling it today. I roll over and look at the clock and realize the five hours of sleep I got last night are going to make for a rough day. I usually have no problem working on the weekends because I haven't been going out at night. Today, I mind. Unfortunately, there's nobody to cover me, so I roll out of bed and head to the shower.

As the warm water cascades over my tired body, I think about my night. Hangover aside, it couldn't have gone better. I had an awesome time with my friends, and meeting Julian Bauer was certainly an unexpected bonus. Holy hell, he is hot. Our flirting was hot too, and I wish it hadn't ended so soon. I could've stayed there bantering with him all night. I'm sure it was a one-time thing, but it did show me the old Alexa still exists in me. The whole night gave me hope that maybe I am ready to get back out there and start living a little again. I hardly thought about Brady at all.

I haven't left myself much time to get ready and get to work. We don't open until ten, but it's already nine. I don't have time to blow out my hair, so I leave it curly and quickly apply my makeup. I slip into a black-and-white tie-waist dress, BCBG black wedges, and head into the kitchen. Nobody is up yet, and I assume my roommates will be spending the day in bed too. We all had a few too many cocktails last night. My stomach is resisting the idea of food, so I grab a banana and throw it in my purse. I take two Advil and wash them down with a whole bottle of water. Ugh. I need to bring in the big guns, so I plan to stop at Starbucks for a very big, very strong cup of coffee. Crap. This is going to be a long day.

Work turns out to be okay. There is a steady flow of traffic, so the day passes quickly. Before I know it, it's five o'clock. I check my phone before I leave. There's a text from Luke.

Luke: *You feeling ok today? Hung-over?*
Alexa: *Better now. Rough morning.*
Luke: *Are we on tonight?*
Alexa: *Of course. Hope I can stay up.*
Luke: *I'll bring Chinese. See you at 8.*
Alexa: *K. Lo Mein plz*
Luke: *K*

Luke and I have a standing Sunday date. We started watching True Blood together when it came out a few years ago, and we haven't missed an episode. This is where he got the nickname Hooka for me. We alternate bringing food or ordering in. I usually look forward to it all week long, but I could have skipped it tonight. I'm exhausted.

When I pull into the driveway, I notice Marissa is the only one here. I'm sure Shannon is at Cory's. She really doesn't spend much time here anymore. Cory has his own place, and I see them moving in together before long. Kevin, Marissa's fiancé, will still be gone for another eight months, so I'm not too concerned about my living situation at the moment, but I see it changing in the not so distant future as they both move on with their lives. I bet they're both married within the next two years. The thought makes me sad because I can't even see marriage in my future anymore.

When I met Brady two years ago, I was ready to find the guy I was going to marry. For the first few months of our relationship, I even thought Brady might be that guy. One of the reasons I fell for Brady was because he was so free spirited, and I liked that he brought out a more playful side in me. I grew up in a house where I was expected to be perfect, and as a result I've always been the responsible one among my group of friends. In college, I made sure the bills got paid, that nobody drove drunk or went home with ugly guys from bars or parties, and that everyone got to class on time. I partied and had a good time, but I never really lost control, and I always knew when to stop. I was like the mom, and I know my friends loved and appreciated me for it. I took care of them then, and I think that's why they try to take care of me now. Brady made me feel like the twenty-three-year-old I was. He had a friendly and engaging personality that drew people to him. He was always on the move, laughing and making plans.

Brady was also very good looking, smart, funny, and totally into me. He was also totally into partying. At first it was fun, but after about six months, I knew in my heart I wasn't going to have a future with him unless he stopped partying so hard. Drugs and alcohol became part of our everyday life, and I became increasingly uncomfortable with the way we were living. Unfortunately, Brady didn't think he partied too much, and neither did most of his friends.

Luke was the exception. Luke and Brady Richards had known each other their whole lives and had grown up together in West Palm Beach. Brady had gone away to college at Georgetown, and Luke had stayed local at FSU, but they kept in touch. I met him out once before in a club when we were all home on winter break. I had a boyfriend at the time, and he was with a girl. I remember thinking he was hot, but to be honest, he didn't really make that big of an impression on me because I was all into the guy I was dating.

I didn't see Brady again until after we graduated. I was out with Luke and a bunch of other friends at a club in Ft. Lauderdale when we ran into Brady. He definitely made an impression on me this time. I was immediately attracted to him. He had dark brown hair and hazel eyes that were friendly and warm. He was always smiling, which showed off his dimples. He shared that smile with everyone and was totally the life of the party. He was the kind of guy people wanted to be around because he made you feel like you were his best friend. He bought round after round of drinks, leading me to believe he had money. I knew Luke's family was well off, so I asked what Brady did for a living. Luke told me Brady had just taken the bar exam and was working part-time at his dad's firm until he got the results. But yes, his family was loaded, and Brady was an only child who got everything he ever wanted. Normally that would be a turn-off for me, but Brady didn't act like a spoiled, rich kid.

We all hung out, danced, and drank, and although Brady talked and flirted with me, he didn't give me any real signs he was interested until the end of the night. As we were getting ready to leave, the song Call Me Maybe by Carly Rae Jepsen came on. We were saying our goodbyes, and Brady leaned in to give me a hug and sang the words into my ear, "Hey, I just met you, and this is crazy, but here's my number, so call me, maybe?"

I totally thought he was just messing with me and being cheesy, and I laughed when I pulled away. When I looked at him, he was smiling and told me he was serious and that he wanted to take me out. I asked him for his phone, programmed my number into it, and told him to call me maybe. And he did. Luke encouraged the relationship. He thought his childhood friend and I made a good couple, and at first we did. Things were great in the beginning. Brady was an attentive boyfriend, a good lover, and got along with everyone. We started spending all of our free time together. I fell hard and fast. What Luke failed to realize was Brady wasn't the same person he grew up with. Yes, they had partied together in high school and when they saw each other at home over school breaks during college. But because they didn't see each other often, Luke had no idea Brady was into a lot more than pot and beer. By the time either Luke or I noticed Brady had a serious cocaine problem, it was too late for me to get out easily. Everything in my soul told me to run. But I stayed. I thought I was in love, and I thought I could save him. I've never been so wrong in all my life.

CHAPTER 5

I called Luke on the way home and told him to come early. I haven't been able to eat all day, and now that I am feeling better, I'm starving. I take a quick shower when I get home, change into yoga pants and a T-shirt, and assume the position on the couch. It feels awesome to lie down.

Marissa comes in and sits beside me. "I'm going to my parents' for dinner. Do you want to come?" I love her parents, and her mom is an awesome cook. But I have plans with Luke later, and I really don't want to move off the couch.

"No thanks. Luke is coming over in an hour, and I'm done for the day."

We talk about the fact both of us drank a little too much last night and that she didn't get out of bed until after noon. We also talk about Julian. We have a good laugh when I tell her how I screamed, "I'm coming" right in front of him.

"You made quite an impression on him, Lex. I wonder how things will go down next time you see him."

"I'm not sure there will be a next time."

"Why do you say that? You do know we're going back there next weekend, right?"

"No, I didn't know *we* were going back, and seriously, Mari, you saw him—right? I'm not exactly his type. It was fun, but I'm not counting on it happening again." I don't admit I really believe we had some kind of inexplicable connection because, now that I'm sober, I'm not sure it wasn't just in my head.

"What's not happening again, ladies?" Neither of us heard Luke come in. It seems he has heard the tail end of our conversation. I wish he hadn't, and I feel a lecture coming on. I start to tell a little white lie, but Marissa jumps in and tells Luke exactly what we were talking about.

"Lexie doesn't think she's hot enough for Julian, and I'm telling her we're going back to Stellar next weekend to prove her wrong."

I can't see Luke's face because I am lying down on the couch, but I can hear the annoyance in his voice when he responds.

"Why are you encouraging her, Marissa? It's totally a bad idea." Ugh. Not this again.

Marissa loves to get into it with Luke. They get along, but both consider me to be their best friend, and jealousy sparks between them from time to time.

"Why? Because he's hot, rich, and by all accounts single?" Her voice is dripping with sarcasm.

"Why, Marissa, I didn't know you were so superficial. And yeah, I don't think he's in a committed relationship, which is the point. He has many, many, many girlfriends. Lex doesn't need that." Luke has walked around the couch and is standing in front of us now.

"So do you, Luke, and I think you're an okay guy. And Lexie does need to get laid, so back off."

I can't believe Marissa just went there. These two are talking about me as if I'm not even in the room. I jump in before this friendly banter turns ugly.

"Hey, guys, I'm right here. Luke, I appreciate the concern. I know Julian is popular with the ladies, but I'm a big girl and can handle it. I don't want a relationship, not that it's even an option, with Julian or anyone else, so chill out. Mari, thanks for your concern over my sex life. I'm okay in that department too. Probably not for much longer, but I am okay. So you two need to focus on yourselves."

They're glaring at each other, but both break into smiles when I finish my speech.

"Okay, all good now. Luke, where's the food? I'm starving."

Marissa gets up and gets ready to leave for her parents'. She likes to get the last word, so I'm not surprised when she looks back over her shoulder and says, "We *will* be going to Stellar on Saturday night, Luke, so put your big-boy panties on and deal with it. Lexie is going to look hot, and Julian will be forgetting about all the other ladies."

Well I guess she told him. Luke just looks at me and shakes his head. He smiles a little, but I know him, and he's really not happy with this topic. I want to ask him more details about the conversation he had with Julian regarding me, but I decide it would be a bad idea. I'm tired and hungry and just want to spend the rest of the night relaxing, so I let it go.

The Chinese food Luke brought is delicious. We sit and eat and catch up on each other's week and fall into our normal, comfortable Sunday routine. I'm happy. As Luke and I lie next to each other on the couch and watch True Blood, any thoughts of Julian are far away.

I am woken up by a soft, warm kiss on my lips that lasts a little longer than it should. I slowly open my eyes and see Luke staring down at me. I sit up, feeling confused. I look at the clock and see it's after midnight.

"Sorry, I tried to wake you up but couldn't." My first thought is, *So you kissed me?*

I'm half asleep, but there's a little nagging part of me that senses something is different. I've fallen asleep here before, and Luke usually just leaves me on the couch. I'm not sure why he woke me up this time.

"Why didn't you just leave me here like usual?"

"I wanted to say goodbye." Um, okay, also not normal.

I get up and wrap the blanket around me. Before I can say anything, Luke wraps his arms around me and gives me a long hug. Too long. This is all feeling very weird, but it's late and I don't want to get into this. Actually, it could be eight in the morning, and I wouldn't want to get into this. Deep down I know this has something to do with Julian, and I can't understand why Luke is acting so off. I walk him to the door, and he hugs me again. We're always affectionate with each other, but this feels different, and I don't really like it.

I get into my bed after he leaves and fall into a deep sleep.

CHAPTER 6

When I wake up, I feel good. I needed to catch up on the sleep I missed this weekend. I'm glad I'm off today because I have a ton of stuff to do. I call my mom, and she talks me into coming over for dinner. I haven't been over in a few weeks, and they're starting to get annoyed with me blowing them off. I go for a five-mile run, hit the grocery store, dry cleaners, and do three loads of laundry before five o'clock. I love days like this where I feel super productive.

Dinner with my parents is something I'm not really looking forward to. I get along well with them, but they've been really overprotective since Brady died and constantly want to talk about how I'm feeling. I try to tell them I would be better if they would stop bringing the bad stuff up all the time, but they get all hurt and tell me they're just worried about me. I think most of their worry actually comes from the fact I'm going to be twenty-six soon and I don't have a boyfriend. I'm the youngest of three girls, and my sisters are both happily married.

My oldest sister, Tracy, is thirty and has already been married for four years. Her husband, Carl, is a dentist. I have twin nieces, Darby and Darcy, who are two. They live in Atlanta in the perfect house in the perfect neighborhood. I don't see them often. My sister, Jill, is twenty-eight and has been married for three years. Her husband, Derek, is an engineer. They live in Tampa in a not-so-perfect house but one that is acceptable to my parents. My parents, Frank and Claire, have been married thirty-one years. They met in college and got married when they were twenty-three. I'm definitely not doing things the Reed way, and I know it stresses them out.

I grew up in North Miami Beach and had a "picture-perfect" childhood, as my mom likes to call it. My dad is an architect and has his own firm. My mom was a stay-at-home mom. My dad comes from a well-to-do family and has always made good money. We lived an upper-middle-class privileged life, and we never wanted for anything. We were that family. You know the one who everyone thinks is perfect. My mom worked hard at maintaining that image, and my sisters were happy to go along with it. We are all pretty, we excelled in school and sports, and we never got into any trouble. Well, at least none my parents ever knew about. I was always a bit of a rebel. I was the sister who got a fake ID, snuck out to go to clubs, and dated a few guys who were too old for me. I've also never really cared about money, which is unlike anyone else in my family. I watched it make a whole lot of people in our country-club circle miserable and decided early on that it doesn't make people truly happy.

My mom and dad were thrilled when I brought Brady home. They thought he was a great catch. He totally fit the mold of what they wanted for me. He was handsome, came from a wealthy family, was educated, and was going to be an attorney. On paper he was perfect. I never told them anything about the real Brady—the one who was always high, the one who failed his bar exam twice, the one who managed to get two DUIs in two months but had his father make them go away. I never told them about the Brady who shattered their daughter's heart. I told myself I never shared any of that with them because it would upset them, but deep down I know I kept it to myself because of what it says about me for staying with him.

Dinner follows the same script as usual. They ask about work. They ask about my friends. They ask if I'm feeling okay. Then they ask if I'm dating anybody. I answer no and brace myself for the lecture.

"Lexie, you know you're never going to meet anybody if you never go out." It only took her thirty minutes to get to the point. I think it's record time.

"I do go out, Mom. We all went out for Luke's birthday on Saturday."

"That's another thing. You're never going to meet a man if Luke is always around. Most men aren't going to be understanding about your relationship." She's kind of right about that.

My parents like Luke and even encouraged me to take our relationship to the next level until they found out Luke wanted to be a bartender. I tried to explain he really wants to own a bar someday, but that's not really a solid career choice in their eyes, so they stopped that matchmaking campaign.

"I'm good, Mom. I'm going out and meeting people. I promise you I will be married by the time I'm thirty-five." I'm totally joking, but my mom doesn't find my humor funny at all.

"You know, if you wait too long, all the good ones will be taken. And you're not getting any younger. I had two kids by the time I was your age. You do want to have kids, right?"

"Good God, Mom. Stop. Tracy has given you two grandkids already, and I'm sure they're good for a few more. Jill should be popping a kid or two out in the next few years also." My good mood is gone. I try to be patient with them, but it's always the same thing. I'm over everyone telling me what I need to be doing with my life. I've been spending a lot of energy just trying to be okay. I don't need this shit. I get up and bring my plate to the sink. I hear my dad saying something about a young, single guy they just hired at his firm. Really? Now my dad thinks he needs to set me up?

"Mom, Dad, I love you. I really do. But I'm not going to come over again until you two agree to stop with the pressure. I will find a man when the time is right, and I will have a family when the time is right. Right for *me*, not you. And I do not need my dad setting me up. That's creepy. How about being proud of me for being awesome at my job. Or just for being a good person. I'm not like Tracy and Jill, and if that's not okay with you, then I'm not sure what to tell you."

I manage to make my mom feel like shit, and I don't exactly feel bad about it.

She actually has tears in her eyes. Great. "Oh, Lexie, we just want you to be happy. We love you, sweetheart. We just want you to have as great of a life as we've had."

I do know my parents love me and want the best for me. They just don't get that I don't want their life. I know my parents love each other, but I've never seen any real passion between them. My sisters married great guys and seem to be happy, but I don't want their lives either. If I could use one word to describe my family, it would not be *perfect*. It would be *boring*.

As I drive home, I think about my parents, my sisters, Brady, and even Julian. I come to the conclusion I really don't have a clue what I want. I just know that after the horrible year I've had, I want to feel alive again, and I realize that's how Julian Bauer made me feel. He was like a drug that woke up my senses, and I can't help wanting more.

I'm changing into my PJs when Shannon and Marissa come into my room. "How long did it take for them to ask if you had a boyfriend?" Shannon and Marissa made a bet before I got home. Marissa said an hour, and Shannon said thirty-five minutes.

"Thirty freaking minutes. Can you believe that? I told them I wasn't going to come over again until they stopped with this crap. They act like I'm an old maid."

"Why didn't you tell them about Julian? That would have shut them up for a few minutes." Shannon has no problem telling it like it is.

"Yeah right. Can you imagine that conversation? Mom, Dad, I met this really hot guy who basically propositioned me at the bar he owns. He usually dates supermodels but was slumming a little that night. I think I'll fuck him once or twice and see if I can get him to hang around."

We all laugh when Marissa replies, "It would definitely get them to back off."

I'm getting into bed when I get a text from Luke.

Luke: *Your parents give you crap about not being married yet?*
Alexa: *You know it*
Luke: *Tell them I will marry you if you aren't married by 35*
Alexa: *Get a real job and I will* ☺
Luke: *Anything for you Lex*

CHAPTER 7

My Tuesday and Wednesday are pretty status quo. Work is a little slow these days as we wind down the project. I've been so busy the last eight months that this is a welcome change. I'm starting to get anxious about where I'll end up next. I'm hoping to move to the new project in South Beach. It would mean a longer commute for me but would be a good change of pace.

Exercise has been a big help in keeping me balanced, so Marissa and I catch a yoga class on Monday night, and I get up early and run a few miles before work on Tuesday. Luke stops by on Tuesday night, and we go out and grab dinner. I'm feeling pretty good when I get to Ellen's office Wednesday after work. Aside from the not-so-pleasant visit with my parents, I've been having a good week.

"How's everything going with you?"

"Pretty good. As I was driving over here, I was thinking I might not have much to talk about tonight. I'm pretty drama-free at the moment."

"That's good to hear, but you do know that you don't need to be in the middle of a crisis for us to be able to do some good work."

Work. Exactly. This is work.

"I do know that. I'm just usually falling apart for some reason or another."

"Lexie, you need to give yourself some more credit. You're not even the same woman I met eight months ago. You're so much stronger now. You need to believe that."

I know I'm not the same as I was eight months ago, and for that I'm really thankful. But I'm not as strong as Ellen thinks. I'm just a pretty good actor. I know I need to give her something to talk about with me or else we're going to end up talking about Brady, and I really would rather we didn't tonight.

"I went to my parents' house for dinner Monday night." Ellen knows all about my family dynamics and knows these visits are often upsetting for me.

"How did that go?"

"Same as usual. My mom is still stressed I don't have a man in my life. Hell, my dad even tried to set me up with someone who works for him. They don't say it, but they think I'm pathetic in the love department." I tell her about my conversation with them.

"Although I don't necessarily agree with their methods, it really is normal for your parents to want you to have a special person in your life. They really just want you to be happy."

I ponder that for a minute, and Ellen changes the subject. "How was your night out Saturday? When I saw you last week, you were anxious about it."

I smile at the memories of Saturday. "I had a great time. It felt so good to be out, and it surprised me I had so much fun." I laugh aloud, and Ellen asks what I'm smiling and laughing about.

"I ran into—and I mean literally ran into—the hottest guy I've ever seen, and we flirted all night long. I'm not making a big deal about it because I'm sure nothing will come out of it, but it was just like riding a bike. I was good at it."

I tell her the story about meeting Julian and some of the things we talked about. She's smiling back at me the whole time I'm talking.

"What's with the huge smile, Ellen?"

"I've never seen you this animated when telling me a story. You're glowing, and it's awesome to see. By the way, I do know who Julian Bauer is, and I understand the attraction."

Of course she does. I forget he's someone people know. We talk about the night a little more before time is up. As I get ready to leave, Ellen has one final thing to say.

"You need to keep doing whatever you're doing. It's working for you."

Okay, I think to myself. I would love to keep "doing" Julian Bauer. I'm just not sure he really has any interest in doing me.

CHAPTER 8

By the time Saturday rolls around, I'm excited about going out, and really hope I see Julian again.

I take a long time getting ready. I picked out what I was going to wear earlier in the week, so that part was easy, but I want to look as perfect as I can in case I run into Julian again. I spend an hour on my hair. I'm wearing it loose and wavy. I do my makeup a little different and create a more dramatic look with black eyeliner and metallic eye shadow. I'm wearing a sleeveless, jersey, black dress with a plunging neckline and a revealing cutout back that hits mid-thigh. It's simple, form fitting, and sexy. I put on big silver hoops and several silver bangles. I slide my feet into Rachel Roy strappy, black leather sandals with silver spikes and double-buckle ankle straps. They have sky-high heels, and I know they won't be easy to wear all night, but they look great.

Marissa and Jenna Stewart, another college friend, are waiting in the living room for me. We valet when we get to the hotel. I had texted Luke that we were coming, and he put us on the VIP list again. We get in quickly and head up to Orion. It's not very crowded yet, so we grab stools at the bar and order drinks from Luke. Jenna, who just got her light brown hair cut into a cute bob, and is dressed to impress in a red mini-dress, says she wants to go look for Bryan, the guy she's been texting with since they met here a few weeks ago. I want to stay at the bar because this is the last place I saw Julian. I give Marissa a look, and she understands I want to stay here.

Luke brings our drinks and heads off to take another order, and the girls get up and leave. I'm sitting on the same stool in the corner of the bar I was at last week when I first really talked to Julian. I find myself thinking about our conversations, and I'm really hoping he shows up tonight. After an hour I conclude it's not looking very promising. Luke did tell me Julian doesn't come into the bar every night, so maybe I won't get to see him. I push away the feelings of disappointment and remind myself I hardly know this guy.

I'm getting off my bar stool when I hear Julian's distinctive voice behind me. "Someone needs to stop putting baby in the corner."

I'm glad he can't see the huge smile plastered on my face. He runs his hand gently down my arm as he walks past me on his way behind the bar. Goosebumps pop up all over my body. He looks down at my glass, sees it's almost empty, and goes about making me another drink. I'm not sure how he knows what I'm drinking, but when I see him mixing a Vodka Cranberry with a splash of Sprite, I know he has been paying attention to what I like.

I flash him a smile. "So now you've moved on to old movie quotes? Did you use up all of your good pickup lines earlier this week?"

"Ouch, Alexa, that hurts. I only use that line on the special ladies. It's a classic." He's smiling back at me, and I realize how happy I am to see him. I'm also flattered he remembers me. I hate that I'm feeling so insecure, but all of the Internet "research" I've done this week has only confirmed there is no shortage of women vying for his attention.

"Thank you," I say as he slides the drink over to me.

Julian leans down and places his forearms on the bar. All of the muscles in his chest and arms bulge out from under a tight, khaki-colored T-shirt. He looks so hot, and something tells me he knows it. I'm taking it all in when I notice a small tattoo on his left wrist. It's barely peeking out from under his watch, but I can see it's in a script font and appears to be a name. I'd love to know what it says, or whose name it says, but I don't feel comfortable asking. He sees me looking at it but doesn't offer any explanation. I wonder if it's the name of a former, or current, love.

As I ponder this, Julian slowly reaches up with one hand and gently runs a finger through one of my curls. "Better," he says quietly as he twirls it slowly. He doesn't look away, and neither do I.

"Better?" I pick up my drink and take a sip. I need something to cool me down. My whole body starts to overheat when he touches me.

"I prefer your hair this way. Se te ve muy sexy." He keeps twirling.

Um. Okay. This is seriously hot. I love when he speaks to me in Spanish.

"I'd rather take this woman to bed than the one with the ponytail. I can picture you straddling me, and I can see your beautiful hair floating across my chest as you make your way slowly down my naked body."

I'm in the middle of taking another sip of my drink when he says this to me, and his comment makes me choke. Holy shit! What a visual. And so quickly too! We've only been talking for a few minutes, and he's already talking about getting naked? Apparently he thinks my "discomfort" is funny and laughs out loud.

"Something wrong with your drink?" he asks through a sly smile.

I try to recover by putting my lips seductively on the straw and taking a slow sip. "Mmm, no, it's perfect."

He arches his brow at me, intrigued by my not-so-subtle response. Hell, I can play this game too. This is fun.

"Good, because I always try to give it the way it's wanted."

"I bet you're very giving, Julian."

He pauses, narrows his eyes, and looks serious for a moment. "You have no idea, Alexa." I love the way my name rolls off of his tongue. He caresses it when he says it.

His eyes are locked on mine and the way he is looking at me is making me squirm in my chair. I think we are both imagining "giving" something to each other. I try and break the tension with some more teasing.

"Do you give this hard of a sell to all the ladies?"

Julian chuckles and shakes his head slightly. "Oh, Alexa, you're the only lady I want to give anything hard to at the moment."

Well, he's definitely not shy or sexually repressed.

We're talking pretty quietly, but I still look around to see if anybody else heard him. This conversation has taken an X-rated turn. The couple sitting next to us at the bar are totally engrossed in the beginning stages of a hook-up and seem oblivious to anything around them. Nobody else is paying any attention to us either. I look down towards the other end of the bar and catch Luke staring intensely at me. He's shaking his head. I'm not sure if Julian sees him do it, but I don't want Luke to come down to where we are. His presence last time caused Julian to walk away, and I don't want that happening again. I nod and smile at Luke and give him a little wave to say *I've got this.* He scowls at me but doesn't come closer. I turn my focus back to Julian and take another sip.

"Okay, Julian, I'll play this game with you."

"I assure you, Corazón, this isn't a game."

"Really? You're not just trying to see how much you can shock me?"

That makes him smile. "Well, unless you have a really good poker face, I haven't shocked you very much yet."

The truth is I do have a pretty good poker face. I *am* a little shocked by how "descriptively" he talks to me. I've never met a man who is more overtly sexual. It just oozes through his pores. He's incredibly sexy and confident without being creepy. No doubt he has been perfecting his craft over the years.

I'm doing my best to play it cool because I like how he's talking to me, and I don't want him to stop. But I also don't want him to think I'm "that girl"; the one who makes a habit of picking up men in bars. I don't want him to think I'm a prude either. I tell myself to get a grip. I can't believe I'm so concerned with what a guy I don't even really know thinks about me. How did this happen? I try to play it all off and give him a fake, shy smile.

"Oh, I'm a little shocked ... and kind of scandalized."

"Only a little?" Julian shakes his head. "I guess I need to up my game."

His comment makes me laugh nervously. If he ups his game I'm in serious trouble.

I look down at my drink for a moment and swirl my straw. When I look up, Julian is staring so intently at me it sends shivers through my body.

"I thought this wasn't a game."

Julian has been leaning up against the bar the whole time we've been talking. He straightens up and takes a step backward. I can feel my eyes widen. Wow. It is impossible to miss the erection straining through his jeans, and I can't help but stare. I bring my straw up to my lips to take a sip. I'm suddenly feeling very hot all over again.

With a tone that is serious rather than cocky he asks, "Still look like I'm playing?" Oh my God, he is shameless.

I continue to look at his crotch and shake my head. "Nope, looks like the real deal to me."

"Oh, Alexa, it's very real. Let me know if you need any more proof."

I'm seriously so flustered right now I don't know what to say. So, I do the only thing a respectable girl can do in a situation like this. I thank him for my drink, get off the barstool, and turn to walk away. I can feel his eyes on my body, and I hear the laughter under his breath. Damn. Round two definitely goes to Julian in a knockout.

I'm running away in a weak attempt to stop myself from doing something stupid. I wonder if he'll come find me or just watch me from afar like he did last weekend. Something tells me we've crossed that imaginary line already and that it's only a matter of time before something more than dirty talk happens between us. I keep telling myself I don't want this and that this is a bad, bad idea for me. Oh, who am I kidding? If he keeps pursuing me, I'm going to let him catch me. I'm so completely drawn to this man I need a whole nightclub and a few hundred people between us to keep me safe. I find my girlfriends downstairs at Stellar. I put my drink on a table and join them on the dance floor.

I'm seriously wound up. Horny would be another appropriate adjective for how I'm feeling. I try to relax and start dancing. The DJ spins Taio Cruz's Higher, and I put my arms up in the air and let myself go.

I can't get enough, I can't get enough.
This is taking me now.
It's taking me higher, higher,
Higher off the ground.

The dance floor is crowded, and we're surrounded by guys and girls enjoying the music. A good-looking blond makes his way over and begins to dance with me. He's attractive in a beach bum kind of way and has a really nice smile. He keeps getting closer and closer, and pretty soon he has his hands on my waist as he sways his hips behind me. I let him for a minute, close my eyes, and pretend it's Julian touching me.

"She's with me." Julian's tone is very matter of fact, and his statement doesn't get questioned. The guy who was dancing with me turns and makes his way anywhere that is away from me.

Julian is standing behind me in the middle of the dance floor, and he just laid claim to me. The imaginary line definitely has been crossed. Julian's energy is pulsating off of him, and I feel a jolt of sexual energy run the length of my body. He hasn't even touched me yet, and I feel him all over. He leans down, nips the top of my ear, and whispers my name seductively. I turn around to respond, and I'm rendered speechless. Julian is looking at me in a way no man has ever looked at me before.

There is no doubt in my mind this gorgeous man wants me. His next words confirm my thoughts.

"There is not a chance in hell that guy is getting the benefits of me turning you on earlier."

He's right. I am turned on. Very. And I have been since he told me he was hard because of me. Seeing the proof through his pants just intensified my longing. I know at this moment I'm not going to be able to stay away from him.

Julian grabs my hand in a possessive yet gentle way and leads me off the dance floor without saying another word. I walk quickly behind him, allowing him to guide me through the throngs of people on the floor. Although Julian walks slowly, there's nothing causal about his demeanor or gait. He's a man on a mission. A mission I'm sure is designed to get me alone. The music is blasting, and there are lights and sounds all around me, yet the only thing I'm aware of is Julian's hand gripping mine. It's the first time he's really touched me for an extended period of time, and the feeling is so erotic it's almost painful. I'm not sure where he's taking me, but I'm sure I need some more time to try and calm my overstimulated senses. I feel completely out of control around this man, and my body seems to be moving without my conscious participation. Julian's energy just draws me toward him like a magnetic field.

A body slams into me as a tipsy girl swings her hands up in the air and twirls around. *Bam.* It's just what I need to snap my brain back into focus. I need to slow him down. Slow me down, slow *this* down. Whatever *this* is. We don't even know each other.

I attempt to yank my hand away, causing Julian to turn around and scowl at me. He doesn't let go. He takes a step closer to me so we're just a few inches apart. We're standing in the middle of the dance floor as bodies gyrate all around us, but

Julian looks at me as if we're completely alone. He seems confused and a little annoyed by my attempt to deviate from his plan.

"Dance with me." I sway my hips playfully, hoping to distract him.

"*Dance*? You want to *dance* with me?"

"You do know how to dance, right?"

Julian chuckles and tilts his head slightly to the side as if confused by my question. "Yes." He nods. "I know how to dance. I happen to own a nightclub, and I also happen to be Latino."

"Well, Julian," I answer in the same sarcastic tone he used on me, "I doubt all the people who own circuses know how to juggle. However, the Latino thing does give you a little more credibility." My jokes are lame, but I've distracted him.

Julian flashes me a seductive smile, his look of annoyance gone. I love this playful, flirty side of him.

"You sure have a smart and sexy mouth, and I would prefer to get to know it better rather than dance, but a challenge is a challenge." He pulls me close to him, and I can feel his erection on my leg. "You want to dance, do you? Vamos a bailar."

It turns out stopping and asking Julian to dance with me as a sexual deterrent is a very bad idea and has the exact opposite effect. He actually was doing me a favor by skipping the dancing part of the night. I've always been turned on by a guy who could move, and Julian is an amazing dancer. He moves so fluidly in front of me, around me, against me. He's like a tiger stalking his prey, and he never takes his eyes off of me.

Rihanna's Don't Stop the Music comes on, and Julian holds me close as he pushes his hips into me and mouths the words. He mimics the lyrics of the song with his body movements. This is hot.

Do you know what you started?
I just came here to party,
But now we're rocking on the dance floor, actin' naughty
Your hands around my waist ...

I'm also a good dancer, and I'm sure Julian and I make a sexy pair on the dance floor. I let go and just let the music take over my body. If I could focus on anything but him, I would notice people are watching us. I forget he owns this club and that everyone knows him. I briefly wonder if he does this often and realize I honestly don't really care. He's dancing with me, and I'm going to freaking enjoy the moment. I feel so alive. We keep bumping and grinding against each other to the sounds of Pitbull's Give Me Everything. Julian keeps singing to me.

And I might drink a little more than I should tonight,
And I might take you home with me, if I could tonight
And, baby, Ima make you feel so good tonight
Cause we might not get tomorrow...

I'm not sure if it's the alcohol or the feeling of Julian pressed up against me, but I'm suddenly a bit lightheaded. I place my head lightly on his chest, and I feel his heart beating rapidly. His desire for me is both literally and figuratively obvious. We are a little sweaty from the dancing, but he still smells so good. I take a deep breath and inhale his scent. That doesn't help with the lightheadedness. Julian Bauer is positively intoxicating. I pull away slightly and look up at him. He looks a bit like how I feel—raw and disheveled. His eyes are gazing down at me with fire in them. He puts his hands on the sides of my head and pushes my hair off my face. It's a gesture that is both gentle and possessive at the same.

"Ready to stop *dancing* now?"

I nod my head and give him a faint smile. It's all I can muster. I no longer have the strength or the desire to resist him. Julian takes my hand and leads me off the floor. At the back of the bar, Julian leads me down a short, dimly lit hallway. At the end of the hallway, we round a little corner. There's a door in front of us, one that I assume leads into his office. I'm surprised that instead of taking me behind the door, he stops, turns me to face him, and presses my back against the wall. He spreads my legs with one of his and keeps it there. I'm straddling his leg, and my dress has crept up my hips, leaving the lower half of my body pretty exposed. Julian holds my hands down by my sides and gently begins stroking my thighs with his long fingers. The feel of his touch on my bare skin is almost more than I can handle. He is so much taller than me that I just come up to his shoulders, and once again my face is in his chest. Being in this position makes it easy for me to avoid his burning stare, yet I can *feel* how he's looking at me. It's like he's trying to see the deepest parts of me. I should feel scared, but I don't.

I take a deep breath, and once again my senses are overtaken by the faint smell of peppermint on Julian's breath coupled with a heady mixture of sweat and cologne. Julian shifts slightly, and I feel the top of his leg hit just the right spot between my legs. I immediately begin gently grinding against him. It's shameless, but I can't help myself.

"Mmm," Julian whispers huskily in my ear. "That's it, baby. Feel me between your legs." Between my legs? I'm feeling him everywhere.

The way we're positioned allows me to feel the heat and power of his erection against my leg, and it turns me on even more if that's possible. I'm so wet that I'm certain he can feel my dampness on his leg. Sensing my desperate need for release, Julian flexes his leg muscle and pushes into me, making it easier for me to rub myself against him. Aside from the sound of our heavy breathing, it's quiet. I push into him, and I can feel how much Julian wants me. Still, he remains restrained and lets me use his body for my pleasure. I'm desperate to touch him, but he refuses to let go of my hands. It will not take much for me to orgasm because I've been turned on for hours and my body is ready to explode. If Julian would just put his lips on mine, something he has yet to do, I will get the release I crave. Here I'm about to come for this man, and he has not even kissed me yet. I'm in so much trouble here.

Once again he appears to read my mind about what I need and want from him, and he finally touches me with his beautiful mouth. But Julian doesn't kiss my lips. Instead he puts his mouth on my neck just below my right ear and slowly runs his tongue all the way down my neck to my collarbone. Chills course through my body, and all I want in this moment is to grab his head and force his lips to mine. But I can't because my hands are still pinned to my sides. I attempt to pull them away again. He tightens his grip and gently shakes his head no.

He whispers seductively in my ear, finally breaking the silence. "What do you need? Are you wet for me? Are you going to get off by grinding your sweet self into my leg?"

I respond affirmatively by grinding into him more forcefully, my dress riding even further up my hips.

"Yes, I know you're turned on, baby. I can feel you on my leg. And it's so okay with me because I can't think of anything sexier and more beautiful right now than you being so turned on that I don't even have to touch you or kiss you to make you come. Can you feel me? Can you feel how turned on I am, how hard? I might come in my pants too. That's how sexy you are, how beautiful."

I'm so close already that his words push me over the edge. I grind my hips hard into his, squeeze my inner thighs as tight as I can, and grip his hands with everything I have. I lean my forehead against his chest and shamelessly let my orgasm shudder through me as I moan softly.

"Mmm, that was so hot, Corazón." Julian exhales into my neck. I didn't realize he was holding his breath.

I keep my head against his chest and can feel how hard his heart is pounding. This is a man who must be close to the edge himself. I try to catch my breath and compose myself before I pull away. I don't want him to see the surrender in my eyes. We stay in this position long enough for both of our heartbeats to slow back down to normal. I murmur a small "Gracias" in an attempt to lighten the moment.

Julian lets go of one of my hands and brings his hand up to my chin. He tilts it up and forces me to look at him. I fully expect my eyes to be met with the same lustful, fiery gaze he's been looking at me with the whole night. I expect a racy, sexually explicit comment is not far off as well. But I'm so wrong.

Instead, Julian is looking at me with reverent eyes and a tenderness I haven't seen from him before. Huh? Here we just had this totally hot, carnal moment, and now he's looking at me with softness that should be reserved for someone he has feelings for, not a girl he just let grind against him in a dark hallway. Maybe it's the lighting and I'm imagining what I see. Well, I think, if he isn't going to say something raunchy, I will. I'll say anything to get him to stop looking at me like that.

I open my mouth to make a snarky comment about what just happened, and I'm stopped as he lowers his mouth softly to mine. Julian's hand is still on my face, and his thumb is stroking my jaw tenderly as he slips his tongue in between my parted lips. I let out a small gasp when I feel the soft silkiness of his tongue as it strokes and caresses the inside of my mouth. Our mouths are connecting much in the same way our bodies did on the dance floor, fluidly and like one. This. Man. Can. Kiss. I can tell by the way he keeps deepening our connection that he's falling into me as much as I am into him. He pulls his tongue out and slowly traces my lips with it. He gently nips at my lower lip before he plunges his tongue back into my waiting mouth. I'm basically pinned to the wall by his hard body, and he's still holding one of my hands at my side. I use my other hand to reach around and grab the back of his head, pulling him deeper into me. I catch his tongue with my lips and suck gently. Julian moans and thrusts his tongue deep into my mouth. A rush of feelings stream through my body. I feel him on my lips, on my skin, between my legs, and in my heart. Fuck! In my heart? As intense and passionate as our kisses are, they do not feel purely physical, and all of a sudden, an overwhelming sense of panic begins to engulf me, and my body starts throwing up red flags. *No! No! No!* I scream internally. *No emotions allowed, Alexa; this is just supposed to be about sex.*

Somehow I'm able to break my lips away from Julian, and I put my free hand on his chest and gently push him away. Julian pulls back and looks at me; his eyes wide open and questioning. It's as if he was somewhere else while he was kissing me, and now he can't believe I'm standing in front of him. His expression is serious, and in this moment I feel completely vulnerable. Again, it's as if he can see everything I'm thinking and feeling.

He groans softly and tries to slow his pulse down by taking a deep breath. I can hardly breathe, and my heart is beating out of my chest. His voice is raspy and laden with lust. "I'm about twenty seconds from ripping all of your clothes off and making love to you right now and I *never* do things like that here."

He takes a small step backward, lets go of my hand, and breaks the connection between our bodies.

"And although the idea of taking you right now against this wall sounds like the best idea in the world, I never mix my business with pleasure. I've already crossed way too many lines with you tonight."

He says this but then steps in closer again and puts his hands on my waist. He seems unable to make up his mind about what he should do.

"But, my God, I want you."

My mind is still stuck on his words from a minute ago. *Make love*? Did he just say make love? Where did *that* come from? The whole night has been filled with dirty talk. Now he's talking about making love? If I were to be honest with myself, which I don't like to be in these emotional situations, I would be acknowledging that I do understand why he's acting the way he is. I felt the shift happen too. I knew the second he put his lips on mine that our connection meant so much more than two people just casually hooking up. But I'm not even remotely close to being ready to go there or admit this is anything other than a one-time thing. I quickly convince myself Julian is just caught up in the moment too. I can play this off. Here it goes. Someone needs to get a hold of this situation. I arch my brows, look up at him, and put both of my hands on his chest. I can feel his heart pounding again. I push him back gently.

"So," I said, "make love? The only thing I'd *love* for you to make me right now is another drink."

How lame am I? I cringe as the words come out of my mouth, but it seems to do the trick. My stupid comment about wanting a drink breaks the spell we have been under since he found me on the dance floor.

Julian quickly backs away from me, and suddenly everything snaps back hard into focus. I internally agree with him, we have crossed way too many lines tonight, both sexually and emotionally. But although I agree with Julian, I can't help but be uneasy about his sudden mood swing. He seems to vacillate so easily between wanting to pull me close and wanting to push me away. I have no idea what he's actually feeling. His eyes are now devoid of anything resembling an emotional connection. The man that just had me coming apart with his words and touch is gone, and I'm looking into the eyes of a stranger. I'm reeling, but I don't want him to see how much his indifference is affecting me. I need to get away from him. I step around him, pull myself together a little bit, and start walking back toward the bar. A huge part of me wants him to stop me. I want him to grab my hand and pull me close like he has done all night long. I want him to say something dirty or something funny. All he says is my name.

"Alexa."

His voice is so quiet I can't tell if it's a question or a command. I keep walking, and I do not turn to ask. I hear the door to his office open and then shut gently behind him.

What the hell just happened?

I find my friends, and Marissa agrees to leave. Jenna isn't ready to go, so we take off without her. I'm quiet when we're waiting for the car, and Marissa knows something is up. She waits until we get in the car to ask.

"So are you going to tell me what happened or should I guess?"

"We hooked up, and then we said our goodbyes. There's not much to tell."

I can't see Marissa's face because she's driving, but I know she's rolling her eyes at me.

"Spill it and give me details, Reed. I've been waiting all week to see how this played out."

"Fine. We made out and did a little bump and grind in a hallway by his office."

"And?"

"And what? You want details?"

"Um, yes. I just said that."

I laugh a little. I've always told her everything. We talk openly about sex, so I'm not sure why I'm being so coy.

"He pinned me against the wall and made me come without even touching me. We made out, and I left. Is that graphic enough for you?"

"Holy shit! What the hell are you in a bad mood for then? That sounds awesome."

"It was until he got all weird on me."

Marissa turns her head, and I see her expression has changed. She thinks he did something to hurt me. "What do you mean? What did he do?"

"He told me he wanted to make love to me and got this whole emotional vibe. Crazy, right? I was grinding against his leg, and he gets romantic. It was weird, so I said goodbye."

Marissa looks at me again and shakes her head. "He told you he wanted to make love to you, and you freaked out? Lex, when a man that hot tells you he wants to make love to you, you say yes, please, and thank you."

I can't help but laugh at her comment, and I shrug my shoulders. She knows why any type of emotional feelings would make me uncomfortable. She does ask me if we made any plans to see each other again.

"Nope." I breathe in deeply and exhale. There's nothing I can do about it now, so I just let it go. I'm going to have to find a way to get Julian Bauer out of my head.

CHAPTER 9

My life returns to its normal boring routine. The irony is that until my encounter with Julian I was pretty content. Now I feel restless. I spent all last week thinking about Julian and what it would be like to see him again. I had forgotten how it felt to crush on someone new. I played out scenarios of how things would go down, and I even got butterflies when I replayed our conversations in my mind. My fantasy ending was nothing like what happened in reality, and when I think about how I reacted, I feel sick to my stomach. I totally blew it with Julian, and now I need to figure out how to forget about him. I'm sucking at that too.

I have lunch with Luke on Tuesday, and I want to ask him about Julian but sense it's not a good idea. He doesn't bring anything up about Saturday night either. He usually shares information about women he's dating, but relationships seem to be a totally off-limits topic today.

When I have my therapy session with Ellen this week, we talk about my little hookup with Julian. I don't share all the details but give her the basics. When she asks me why I think I had the reaction I did, I express my concerns that I don't think I'm good enough for him.

"Why would you think that? Everything you've told me suggests Julian thinks you're good enough for him. I'm not sure what that even means. What about you isn't good enough?"

I don't need Ellen to get all shrinky on me. I don't need to hear about how pretty, smart, and strong I am. I know Julian and I travel in different circles. I try to cut her off at the pass.

"Maybe good enough isn't the right way to put it. I just don't think we're a good fit."

I throw the lie out there and hope it sticks. The irony in my statement is I've never felt a stronger connection with a man in my life. I know Julian was feeling it too. I just can't convince myself it wasn't only a one-time thing. That thought snowballs into another, and I cringe when I think about how I behaved. It's been forever since I acted that way and just let myself go. I'm feeling a little slutty.

"Lexie, I could sit here all night and tell you tons of reasons why you're good enough for anyone. But you already know it, so it's a waste of my time. I can't really speak to you fitting with Julian because I have no basis for that opinion except what you've told me. But honestly, from over here it seems like you're a perfect match. You need to remember you're a twenty-five-year-old, single, beautiful woman, and it's okay for you to have fun and enjoy your life as long you're safe about it."

It all sounds really logical, and if I tried really hard, I might be able to convince myself what she's saying about me is true. Unfortunately, at this moment in time, the bad stuff is just easier for me to believe. Since Brady died, I've tried to find a balance between the fun and the responsibility, but I'm not quite there. I still feel like it was all the "fun" we were having that made everything turn bad.

We wrap up the session with Ellen telling me she won't be able to see me next week. It will be the first Wednesday in eight months I haven't met with her. She's going out of town on vacation. I promise her not to have any crises while she's gone.

Luckily for me, the next week proves to be uneventful. Nothing exciting is happening with work, my parents are out of town in Atlanta visiting my sister and therefore off my case, and I don't have any more run-ins with gorgeous strangers. It's a good thing Ellen is out of town. For the first time in months, I really don't have anything to talk about.

CHAPTER 10

It's been two weeks since I've seen Julian, and because we left things so awkwardly last time, I'm not sure how I'm going to feel when and if I see him again. We shared a totally intimate encounter and haven't spoken since. I tell myself I haven't heard from Julian because we didn't exchange phone numbers, but I know if he really wanted to contact me he could've asked Luke for my number. After repeatedly processing the whole scenario in my head, I've almost convinced myself what happened was a one-time thing and that I probably shouldn't be concerning myself with Julian Bauer.

I've also convinced myself I don't really even want to go to Stellar tonight. The problem with that is I've made plans to go out with a big group of girls. My coworker, Lauren Hendricks, is going with Marissa, Shannon, and I, and we're meeting Jenna and two of her friends. It's a girls' night out, and I'd be an asshole if I bailed. I tried talking them into going to another bar, but that didn't work. They all want to go to Hotel Del

Marco. I think it's because they want to see Julian, and I can't blame them. I'm actually feeling kind of stalker-ish because I have no idea if he'll even be there, and I'm planning my whole evening around seeing him. So much for me *not concerning* myself with him. I'll be totally bummed if he's not there, or worse, if he has no interest in me. This night has the potential to be a total disaster.

If I crash and burn tonight, I'm going to look good doing it. I spend about an hour trying to decide what I'm going to wear, and when I finally pick out my outfit, my room looks like a bomb has gone off in it. There are clothes and shoes everywhere. I've decided I won't be wearing a dress tonight. It ended up around my hips last time, and I'm not planning a repeat of that. I've put on a pair of tight white, skinny, cropped pants and a black silk, draped, sleeveless top that has a plunging V in both the front and back. The front has a lacy, sheer overlay in the V area that keeps it from being completely open like the back is. The material in the back is light and flowing. It's a very flattering top that shows off my boobs and back. I bought it months ago but haven't worn it yet. It took me a while to find a backless, strapless, plunge bra that worked. I'm excited to wear the new Brian Atwood turquoise sandals I found on sale for $250 last week. They're normally almost $500 shoes, so I couldn't pass them up. At least that's what I told myself. The heels are four inches high, and I know they're not good dancing shoes, but as usual, it's fashion first. Besides, they totally make the outfit. Because Julian has told me he prefers my hair down, I spend a long time on it, trying to create a perfectly tousled beach-hair look. I keep my makeup pretty natural and add just a hint of shimmery blue eye shadow. I think I'm pulling off a very casual, sexy, confident look.

Marissa comes into my room and asks me if I'm ready to go. She laughs when she sees the mess I've made and teases me about trying so hard to impress Julian.

"Just tell me something, Mari. Does my butt look big in these pants?" She starts laughing when she hears me asking our standard going-out question. "Nope, Lex, your butt looks hot, but you know you're asking for trouble with those shoes, right? Or are you hoping to fall into Julian again tonight?"

"I should be so lucky."

What a difference a couple weeks makes. When I went out for Luke's birthday, I was anxious just to be going out. Now I'm just anxious about seeing, or not seeing, Julian.

Marissa volunteers to drive, and we take her up on the offer. I don't want to drive because if things go badly, I'm going to start drinking, and if things go well, I hope I won't even be coming home. Right when we get in the car, I get a text from Luke. It's the first time I've heard from him today. He's been spending a lot of time with Krista, and I haven't seen him since we had lunch last week. He always does this at the beginning of a relationship, and then after a few weeks, he gets bored and moves on. I try to lay low when he's in this honeymoon phase in hopes he'll find a girl he really likes and have her stay around for longer than a month. Not all girls are cool with our friendship, so I'm trying to keep a low profile. I do miss him when we're not talking though, so I'm happy to hear from him.

Luke: *what's up Hooka? You coming tonight?*

When I spoke to him a few days ago, I mentioned we might be. I realize now I forgot to ask him to put us on the VIP list. Pete Vaughn, a very popular local indie singer, is playing at Orion tonight, so it's probably going to be really crowded.

Alexa: *yes. On way. Can you get us on list? Plz*
Luke: *how many?*
Alexa: *7*
Luke: *whole posse huh?*
Alexa: ☺
Luke: *I'll give your name + 6*
Alexa: *thanks. Owe you. See you soon.*
Luke: *I'll add it to my tab*
Alexa: *you keeping tabs?*
Luke: *nah. Lost count*

I'm about to write something about the tab I'm running for him when another text comes through.

Luke: *I'll let him know you're coming*

I thought we covered he'd let the bouncer know we're coming.

Alexa: *yeah…7 of us.*
Luke: *doubt Julian cares 7 of you're coming*

I'm confused.

Alexa: *??*
Luke: *Julian asked me if you were coming. Said I didn't know*
Alexa: *ok*

Holy shit! He's there and wants to know if I'm coming. My heart starts to beat faster, and I can't keep from smiling. Lauren sees me texting and asks what's up.

"Just texting Luke to ask him to put our names on the VIP list."

"Text him and tell him I'll be his VIP tonight."

Lauren is constantly trying to hook up with Luke. With her shoulder-length, dark brown hair, big hazel eyes, and killer curves, she's totally Luke's type, but I've asked him multiple times to stay away. She's looking for something serious, and Luke isn't that guy. The fact that I'm doing the same thing with Lauren that Luke is doing with Julian isn't totally lost on me either. The difference is I've had front-row seats to Luke's dating life for years now, and I've seen many nice girls come and go. If I'm being honest, it's not just his reputation that makes me warn him off Lauren. I'm okay with him being with other girls but know if he was with a friend of mine it would bother me. I worry about losing a friend when things blow up like they always do. I nod at Lauren, but I don't text Luke back with her message.

I go into game mode in my head on the drive over. I think about how I should act and what I should say if I see Julian. I come up with all these different scenarios and am even creating dialogue in my head. I've become that crazy girl. I take a deep breath and remind myself all this planning is a big waste of time. The reality is things just happen when Julian and I are together, and I've already seen I have very little control over it.

We pull up to Hotel Del Marco at about ten-thirty, and Marissa valets. The other girls are waiting outside when we walk up. Shannon had texted Jenna to tell them to wait for us. It's totally crowded again, and the line to get in is long. I've been spoiled the few times I've been here and glad to be able to skip the line this time as well. I walk up to Marty, the bouncer who is working the door. I introduced myself last time I was here, and he remembers me. He unhooks the rope barring the entrance and lets us through. As I'm walking in the door, I hear him on his walkie telling someone, "She's here." I wonder if Julian told him to look for me or if he's talking to Luke.

We pit stop at the ladies' room before going to Stellar. The girls all want to dance, so I think we'll be hanging there most of the night. I plan on heading up to Orion for my free drinks and recon mission to find Julian first though. Or not. We haven't been there for more than five minutes when I see Julian across the bar. Because he is tall and so gorgeous, he's easy to spot in a room, even a crowded one. He's dressed in a lilac-purple, button-down shirt that fits his muscled torso beautifully. He has on gray slacks and charcoal Gucci loafers. With his body, it's doubtful Julian looks bad in anything, but each time I see him, I'm more in awe of how good looking he is. He is clean-shaven tonight, and I can't decide which look I prefer. I'm trying not to stare at him and even turn my back so it isn't obvious I've seen him.

Jenna sees him headed our way and gives me a heads up. "Incoming, Lexie."

Nobody moves because they're all dying to see how this is going to play out.

My heart starts to race, and even if Jenna didn't tell me he was coming, I would have felt his presence. Just like before, my body starts to react to the energy that emanates from him. I feel him behind me even before he touches me. Because my top is wide open in the back, there's a lot of skin showing. Julian takes advantage of this and lightly touches my bare back with his fingertips. The feeling is electric, and heat spreads throughout my body.

"Hola, bella," Julian whispers in my ear. He is leaning over my shoulder, and as he pulls back, his lips graze my ear and then my cheek. My knees go weak. I melt inside when he calls me beautiful.

I slowly turn around, and Julian is *right* there in front of me, totally up-close and personal. He pushes all of my buttons so hard that I prefer a chance to get used to his presence, but he has no concept of personal space between us. I take a step backward to give myself a little separation from him. Undeterred, he takes a step toward me. Whatever worries I had about him not being interested in seeing me again have disappeared. He once again moves like a lion stalking its prey. He's smiling down at me with the same hungry look I saw in his eyes during our hallway tryst.

"Hola, Julian. Que bueno verte otra vez."

I'm hoping I sound more relaxed than I feel. His smile broadens when I answer him in Spanish. The truth is I do speak Spanish pretty fluently. I've grown up in South Florida, and I took classes all through high school and college. I have a lot of Spanish-speaking customers, and I find myself using it almost daily.

He switches to English. Maybe because he wants to make sure I comprehend what he's about to say. "I was hoping you would show up tonight, Alexa. I was disappointed when I didn't see you last week. You and I have some unfinished business to attend to."

I look over at my friends. They're totally trying to pretend they aren't paying attention to Julian and me, but I can tell they're enjoying this little exchange.

"I'm not sure what you're referring to. I think our business came to a satisfactory end a few weeks ago."

I place an emphasis on the word came. It amazes me how we instantly fall into a playful and, yes, sexual banter. I'm comfortable with the physical aspect of our interactions. Now as long as things stay that way, I'll be fine.

The girls keep looking back and forth between Julian and me like they're watching a tennis match, and I can tell they're entertained.

"If that was satisfactory to you then I'm afraid you have very low standards. Our business together hasn't concluded at all, and the part that was conducted a few weeks ago didn't end in a satisfactory manner for me at all. I intend to remedy that tonight."

His eyes are sparkling and totally challenging me to say something smart back. My whole body clenches at the implied actions behind Julian's words. I can only hope that whatever "business" we conduct tonight ends up with both of us naked.

Julian takes his eyes off of me for a minute and finally seems to notice my friends are all standing there and hanging on his every word. He addresses them before I have a chance to respond to his last comment.

"Hello, ladies."

He flashes them his sexiest smile and I swear a couple of them swoon. Oh, he's good at this. I wonder if his business cards say hotel owner and professional flirt on them. He sticks his hand out and introduces himself to my friends one by one. I watch to see if any of them have a physical reaction to Julian's touch like I do, and I'm relieved when I see nothing that worries me. He tells them he hopes they have a great time tonight and to let him know if he can do anything to make it happen. I'm not a fan of his choice of words because, friends or not, a few of these girls are drooling over Julian, and I'm sure they would love some personal attention. These girls are all used to getting hit on by good-looking guys, but Julian is kind of in a class by himself, and I can't blame any of them for being mesmerized.

Luckily it seems he only has eyes for me. He asks them to excuse us for a minute, takes my hand, and leads me off to the side so we no longer have an audience.

"I was serious about having unfinished business. I'm not happy with the way we ended things last time, and I'd like to do things a little differently tonight."

Okay. I'm game. Now I'm hanging on his every word.

"I have some actual business I need to take care of, but I should be done in about an hour. I'll come and find you. Do *not* leave."

"Yes, sir." I'm totally playing with him and say it with a smile. His look is serious.

"Alexa, you left me with no way of getting in touch with you last time, and I haven't been able to stop thinking about you since. That isn't going to happen again."

I want to remind him he could have gotten my information from Luke. I also did tell him my full name, and I have a Facebook account. There were ways he could have gotten in touch with me, but he chose not to. I don't point it out because it really doesn't matter now. I have absolutely no intention of leaving here before I find out what Julian's definition of "unfinished business" is.

Julian leans into me and presses his lips against my cheek. His lips are hot on my skin.

"Hasta luego."

As Julian turns and walks away, I feel an uneasiness creep up inside my chest. I'm already missing him. This man I do not even know has already found his way into my heart. I turn to walk back to my friends and push those thoughts from my mind. Within seconds, a flood of questions and comments come barreling my way.

"OMG—he is unbelievably hot!"

"What did he say to you?"

"Are you sure you two didn't sleep together already? That man was looking at you like he's seen you naked."

"Or like he wants to."

"Does he have any friends? Or a twin?"

I assure them Julian has not seen me naked but that if he wants to I'm fine with it, on the condition I get to see him naked too. We all laugh, and I'm sure a few of them run with that idea and try to picture Julian naked. I change the subject because I really don't want to share more of the conversation I just had. It feels too personal.

We all head up to Orion to see what's happening upstairs. It's a beautiful April night, and it feels nice outside. The place is crowded as usual, and we have a hard time getting close to the bar. After about twenty minutes, I'm finally able to get Luke's attention. He comes down to where we're standing and takes the credit card I'm handing him to open a tab for us. I know he won't charge me for all the drinks, but I'm not comfortable asking for free drinks when there are so many of us. He gives me a kiss on the cheek.

"You look hot tonight, Hooka." He's in a good mood.

"Thank you. I try." I feel good, and the compliment just reinforces the feeling.

He gets right to the point. "Did you see Julian?"

"Yes, I ran into him on the way in."

"I'm sure it was no accident." Now happy Luke is gone, and annoyed Luke is front and center.

"Why ask if you don't want to hear the answer?"

I keep my tone playful, but Luke knows me well enough to know I'm taking issue with his crappy attitude about Julian.

"I just don't like the way he looks at you. Like you're something he wants to own. When I told him you were coming tonight, he just got this creepy look on his face, and it bugged me."

I almost laugh out loud. I can't imagine Julian ever looking creepy, and what Luke saw was probably Julian's "good, now we can pick up where we left off" face. I still haven't told Luke what happened the last time I was here. I usually tell him everything, but because I know he doesn't approve of anything happening between Julian and me, I just keep my mouth shut and change the subject.

"I guess things with Krista are going well? I haven't seen or heard from you all week."

I'm not possessive with Luke at all because I know he'll always be there for me if I need him. He has shown that many times.

"Yeah, things are cool. She's a good girl."

I can already hear the indifference in his voice. Typical. He'll be moving on soon if he hasn't already.

"Is Lauren with you?" Well, I guess that answers that question.

Although I've asked him nicely to stay away from her, he's always asking about her.

"Yes, but you're not going there, remember?"

"No, I don't remember. Remind me why I'm not allowed to show interest in one of your coworkers? You're showing interest in my boss."

I really am not in the mood to get into this conversation with Luke. He's trying to pick a fight with me, and it's so unlike him. I give him a big, fake smile, take my drink, and turn to leave. Marissa, Shannon, Jenna, and Lauren are ordering drinks, and I motion to them where I'm headed. As I walk off, I hear Luke start to flirt with Lauren. I know he's doing it loudly and on purpose to piss me off. Whatever. Let them work it out. I walk over to the back of the bar where Pete Vaughn is playing. I've seen him play a few times around South Florida, and he's always so good. I was excited to hear he'd be playing tonight. He writes his own music and plays a lot of acoustic stuff. I'd be happy to sit and listen to him all night, but my friends would probably rather go to Stellar and dance. I glance around and notice most of the people up here tonight are couples. I wonder where Julian is and wish he were sitting here by me, next to the fire, listening to music. My daydream is interrupted when my friends sit down next to me. They tell me Lauren is still at the bar flirting with Luke and the others have gone back to Stellar. Jenna asks me how I feel about Luke and Lauren.

"I've tried to keep them away from each other, but they won't listen. Luke will end up loving and leaving her, and she's going to be all mad and hurt. It's what always happens. But this time I'll be in the middle, and there will be all kinds of drama. But whatever. They're grownups."

"Yeah, he's never going to find a girl who compares to you, Lex."

Marissa is looking straight ahead when she says this.

"Seriously? You guys keep going on and on about how he wants me. I've been right here for almost seven years now. I think he would have said something by now."

"Whatever. You just don't see what the rest of us do. It's weird. He looks at you like he's in love with you. I'm just saying."

I'm not having this conversation with them. It's wearing me out lately. We're just friends. I change the subject by talking about Marissa's finance, Kevin, and Jenna's new guy, Bryan, and pretty soon Luke isn't a topic of conversation anymore. We sit and listen to a whole set. I'm totally enjoying the music, but

I'm distracted and hoping Julian will come find me soon. To be honest, it's really why I've wanted to stay in one place. I want to be easy to find. It's been an hour and a half since I saw him, and with each passing minute, I'm less convinced we will be hooking up again tonight. The girls are ready to go back to Stellar, so we start to head downstairs. I notice Lauren still sitting at the bar and walk over to tell her where we're going. I tell the others I'll meet them in a minute.

"Are you going to be pissed if I stay here?"

I look over and see Luke looking at me with a challenge in his eyes. He was annoyed before, but now he looks mad. What the hell is wrong with him? I look back at Lauren.

"No, Lauren. I'm not pissed. I just don't want to see you get hurt. Luke is one of my best friends, but he's a total player, and if you're okay with that, then go for it. But if not, it's not a good plan."

I've already told her a version of this same thing several times, and I can see in her eyes she doesn't really care what I think about it. She thinks it will be different for her. I look up at Luke, and he's still staring at me with a totally shitty look on his face. I walk over to where he's standing behind the bar and ask the two guys sitting there if I can squeeze in for a minute. They look at me, smile, and make room for me. I motion for Luke to come over. He walks up to the bar with his fake, "I think you suck" smile on his face. I never get that smile, and I'm kind of taken aback.

"What's up? Come to give me a lecture on who I can and can't flirt with?" His voice is low and comes out like a hiss.

"Can you come and talk to me for a minute?"

I ask in a way that lets him know I need to talk to him. I was just going to say something about Lauren, but now I'm wondering what's really going on with him. He's mad at me, and I honestly don't know why. He tells Jordan, the other bartender, he'll be right back and walks toward the end of the bar. We walk a few feet to a little corner that's semiprivate.

"Why are you pissed at me? Don't say you aren't because it's very obvious, and you're acting like a total asshole. What happened in the last hour, because you were fine when I got here?"

"I'm not mad, Alexa, I'm just disappointed."

His tone could not be more condescending, and I know he's mad because he rarely calls me Alexa. It's usually Lex, Lexie, or Hooka.

"Disappointed? What did I do to disappoint you, Luke? Flirt with Julian?"

"Flirt? Ha! Is that what they're calling it these days? And don't even say it's not true, because I can read you like a book."

"I can't deny anything, because I have no clue what the hell you're talking about." I'm trying to stay calm, but he's starting to raise his voice, and I'm getting madder as the words come out.

"I'm referring to your little public bump and grind session. And to answer your question, I'm disappointed because one, you did it, two, you didn't tell me yourself, and three, I just had the pleasure of hearing the gossip from a coworker. Supposedly I'm your best friend, and I looked totally stupid for being the only one who didn't know you and Julian hooked up *two* weeks ago. But, oh snap, guess what. I'm not the only one who looks stupid. Right after I heard the story, I had the pleasure of watching Julian walk right by here with a gorgeous woman all up on him. I'm assuming it was his next conquest and they were on their way down the hall."

He just keeps going, and I can't respond. I'm not even sure how to respond. I can't believe Julian told anyone what happened between us. But then again, I don't even really know him, so anything is possible, and I'm not sure how I can defend him right now. Maybe someone else did see us in the hallway. I was so into Julian I wouldn't have noticed if a marching band came down the hall. Maybe whoever told Luke this saw us on the dance floor where we were bumping and grinding and just assumed something more happened. No, that can't be it. Luke said something about the hallway, so either Julian said something or someone saw us. Whatever. Something did happen, and I don't need to feel bad about it. The shit about the other girl is just a low blow, and if Luke was trying to make me feel insecure, he succeeded. Luke has never intentionally tried to hurt my feelings in all the time I've known him, and I'm so shocked by his attitude. I really don't know what to say to him.

"You have no idea what happened, and I didn't tell you anything because you act crazy when it comes to Julian. And I have no idea why. What did he ever do to you? And why did you send me that text about him wanting to know if I was coming if you have such an issue with him and me seeing each other?"

"Because he's asked me about you several times, and I kept blowing him off. I like my job and thought it would be a bad idea to let my boss know I think he's a dick."

"A dick? Really? Why, because he dates a lot of women?"

"Dates? Ha! How about fucks a lot of women."

"Well if that makes him a dick, then you must be the president of Dickville."

I'm so mad I can't even speak anymore. I just turn and walk away, and Luke doesn't try to stop me. I brush away the tears that threaten to spill out of my eyes and walk downstairs. I try to process what just happened, and I can't. Luke has never treated me like this. Never. I try to push all of the bad shit out of my mind and focus on the one good part where Luke said Julian had been asking about me. He had been thinking about me. My mood brightens a little.

It doesn't last long.

As soon as I walk into the club, I see Julian. What shitty timing. He's standing in a corner not far from where I am, having what looks to be a serious conversation with a very tall, very gorgeous woman. I'm sure it's the one Luke just told me about. They're standing extremely close, and she has her hand on his chest, and his hand is on hers. I can't hear what they're saying, but she looks upset, and he looks agitated. I try to move past them before he sees me, but he turns his head at the exact time I'm walking by. He doesn't say anything to me, but the look in his eyes says enough. He looks guilty, and I know I've caught him in the middle of an intimate conversation with either a current or ex-lover. I'm hoping it's the latter. I keep walking as fast as I can and try to disappear into the crowd. All the confidence I felt earlier this evening is long gone. That woman has to be a model and is exactly the type of girl I'd picture Julian with. Hell, they even looked perfect together. She's tall with mile-long legs, a perfect body, and beautiful long, straight, blonde hair. I feel my eyes sting with tears again, and I start to beat myself up for even thinking anything was going to happen between us. As soon as I get across the club, I duck into the bathroom and text Shannon and Marissa to come meet me there. They find me pacing back and forth.

"Are you okay?" Marissa sounds sad for me. I explain what I saw, and they don't even try to tell me they're sure it's not what I think. We have an honesty policy when it comes to men.

"Yep. I'm just an idiot. I really don't feel like trying to compete with that. Not that I could anyway."

Shannon asks what I want to do. Do I want to stay or go somewhere else? I say I'd rather go somewhere else than stay here, and they agree to leave. I know they don't want to go yet, and I appreciate the offer. It's a big place, and I probably could manage to avoid Julian all night, but I'm in a shitty mood now and would just rather leave. My argument with Luke just makes the night suck more. Damn! It started out so good. I need to get my credit card from Luke and tell Lauren we're leaving. I tell them I'll be right back down. We make plans to meet by the front, and they're going to find Jenna and the other girls we have lost somewhere in the club. There are two ways to get upstairs, and I go the opposite way from where I just saw Julian. I'm determined to get out of here without seeing him again. I know I didn't see him doing anything that should have me so upset, but the image of those two beautiful people together like that just keeps reminding me I'm out of my league. I make it to Luke's bar unnoticed. He sees me right away but ignores me. Really? I get Jordan to close out my tab and give me my credit card back. I see Luke walking toward me, and I hurry up and sign the receipt. He opens his mouth to say something, and I just turn and walk away. I hear him call my name, and I just keep going. Fuck him! Crap. I forgot to get Lauren. I decide to just text her.

Alexa: *we're leaving. Are you coming?*
She responds right away.

Lauren: *no. See you later.*

I assume she's going home with Luke. Oh well, I tried.

I stop by the bar on the other side of Orion for a minute. I'm shaking I'm so upset. I'm pissed at Luke and Julian and also sad and disappointed. The bartender sees me and asks me if I need anything. I'm about to say no when I notice two very blonde, very drunk girls next to me doing shots. I change my mind.

"A shot of Patrón Silver please."

"Do you want to start a tab?"

"No, I'll pay cash."

He brings the shot over and sets it in front of me. I pick it up and glance at the girls sitting beside me. They're hammered.

"Hey. Wait for us. We can do a shot together."

One of the girls is looking right at me. Ah, female bonding at its finest. Next they will ask me to go to the bathroom with them. I don't wait and do the shot quickly instead. I immediately feel shitty because the girl that was talking to me looks totally offended.

"That was so not cool." Yep, she was offended.

She shakes her platinum blonde head at me. I honestly feel bad for being such a bitch. I had no intention of doing any shots tonight, let alone two, but now I feel I need to do another with them. I motion to the bartender I want another. I know this is probably not a good plan. Last time I did shots was with Brady on his birthday. He was turning twenty-six and started talking about how he was going to do twenty-six tequila shots himself. We managed to convince him we should do twenty-six shots collectively instead. There were five of us there, Luke included, so we all went around in a circle and did a shot until we reached twenty-six. I did five in like twenty minutes. I was so drunk and so sick that I didn't drink anything for weeks. I haven't had a shot until tonight, and surprisingly it went down easily. Hopefully the second will as well.

The bartender sets my second in front of me. I hold it up to toast with my new friends.

"Here's to saying fuck off to guys who make you feel like shit."

I toss it back and set my glass down on the bar. The girls repeat what I said and do their shots. I hear them saying something about us girls needing to stick together when I feel my phone vibrate. Marissa is texting me.

Marissa: *hurry up*
Alexa: *coming*

Shit. I forgot they were waiting. I'm a freaking mess. I hurry down the stairs as fast as I can in my four-inch heels. By the time I get all the way near the front, I'm feeling the alcohol. I see Marissa and Shannon waiting for me. What happens next is like a movie. I'm just about to make my escape when at the last second I'm noticed and my get away plan is foiled. As I'm walking toward the girls, I feel a hand grab my elbow from behind. I hear Julian before I see him.

"Donde vas, A-lex-a?" He always drags the syllables out in my name when he's emphasizing a point. He says it almost scoldingly, like a mom would say it to a child who's misbehaving. It annoys me. Right now, *everything* is annoying me.

I spin around quickly and paste a big fake smile on my face. I also pull my arm away so he isn't touching me. I can't think straight when he is. He tilts his head and frowns as I step away from him.

"Leaving. We're heading over to Reign." We're actually probably going home, but I don't want him to know he ruined my night, so I lie.

"I thought we decided we would be spending some time together tonight."

"Change of plans." I say it with my fake smile still plastered on, but I sound like a total bitch, and I know it. The tequila is making me brave, and my defensives are on high alert. Not only was I anxiously waiting around for him, but watching his interaction with the supermodel has me feeling like a loser.

"Qué pasa? Why are you pissed at me?"

He knows I saw him with her, and he knows I've been waiting around for him. He wants to play this game, and I'm not up for it.

"I'm not pissed." And the truth is I'm not mad at him. He really didn't do anything wrong. I tell him the truth.

"I'm just over this thing, whatever it is, or was."

I say the words resignedly and gesture back and forth between us indicating there's something between us. Well, I may as well have waved a cape in front of a bull. Julian steps to me and pulls me to him with one hand around my waist. I'm pressed up against him and feel his heat everywhere. Damn it. He leans down so his mouth is on my ear.

"This 'thing' is so far from over, Alexa, and you know that."

I try to pull away, but he flexes his arm and holds me close.

"I'm sorry I kept you waiting. I had a few things I needed to take care of first so I could give you my undivided attention."

I don't say anything, and when he pulls back a little, I see confusion as well as a hint of hurt in his eyes. "You were seriously going to leave without telling me?"

I look around and notice we have an audience. We're near the entrance/exit of the hotel to Ocean Drive, so most people coming and going pass through here. I see my friends as well as other nosy people staring at us, watching this crazy scene unfold. Julian only looks at me, not caring that a bunch of strangers are watching his every move. He's still holding me close, and he isn't letting go.

"I just saw you. You looked to be taking care of some *other* unfinished business. Here's a little piece of information about me, Julian. I'm not a fan of mixed signals."

The look he gives me is hard and serious. "Do you feel me against you right now?" He's referring to his erection, which I definitely can feel. "Is there anything 'mixed' about that signal?"

I shake my head. I don't question his attraction to me. I can literally feel it against my leg. I'm just not so sure now that I'm the only one he's feeling it with tonight. I'm also not sure I'm up for this game anymore. Julian is trying very hard to pull me back in, and I'm trying to decide if I want to follow.

"Please don't act this way." His tone is pleading.

"What way?" I know exactly how I'm acting. Jealous.

"Like you have anything to be jealous of. I haven't been able to stop thinking about you since the moment you ran into me in the stairwell. Solamente en ti."

Only me? I so want to believe that. I haven't stopped thinking about him either. He still hasn't let me go, and I realize I've stopped trying to get away. My body already feels addicted to his touch, and I can't deny how much I want to be with this man.

"Please stay and talk to me."

"Okay, I'll stay." I say it softly, and obviously I convince him I'm not going to make a break for it because he finally relaxes his hold on me. I tell him to hang on, and I walk over to where my friends are waiting for me.

Shannon is the first one to speak. "That looked intense. What did he say?"

I don't feel like sharing the whole conversation. "That he wants me to stay and that he isn't with that girl."

"So I guess we're staying?" Marissa doesn't sound surprised or mad.

I shrug my shoulders and apologize. "Yes. Sorry."

"No worries, we'll stay too." Shannon smiles at me. "Go do your thing and text us later."

I turn around and start back to where Julian is waiting for me. He's leaning against one of the bar tables and smiling at me. It's so hard to be mad at him. He says and does all the right things. I'm still upset about seeing him with that woman, but he's here with me now, not her. He takes my hand when I get close enough and leads me away. I'm not sure where we're going, and I don't ask. I just hope it's somewhere private. I really want to be alone with Julian. I'm all over the map with my thoughts and feelings, and I'd like to just get back on solid ground with him. We wind our way through the crowds and end up inside the hotel. He leads me to an elevator and uses a special key to get us access to what appears to be a private area. He doesn't let go of my hand when we're in the elevator, but he doesn't make any other moves to touch me. This is the first time we have been alone since the time in the hallway, and to be honest, I'm ready for him to touch me, really touch me. I find myself staring at his lips and imagining them on mine. We're both silent, and I'm dying to know what he's thinking.

CHAPTER 11

The elevator opens into a little lobby area with smoked glass doors in front of us. Julian walks toward the doors and swipes a key to open them. We walk out onto a small private patio that looks like something out of a magazine. We're at the top of the hotel facing Ocean Drive, so we have a beautiful view of the water and the sky. There's a small, white sectional couch and matching chair with big, blue pillows and a dark wood frame that look similar to the ones at Orion. A beautiful, blue-tiled mosaic table with a small, built-in gas fire pit sits in the middle of the patio. It's lit, and the flickering flames throw light and shapes off the smoked glass walls that surround the patio on the other three sides. There's a very Mediterranean feel to this space, and I imagine this is what it must look like in Greece. It's crazy to feel this secluded when there are thousands of people around us in the hotel and on the streets. I notice two bottles of wine and two glasses on the table, and I hear soft jazz music playing in the background. I'm not sure if I've ever been in a more romantic setting. My mind goes dark for a moment as I wonder if Julian gets romantic with women up here on a regular basis. Damn, why can't I be happy and just enjoy this moment? I piss myself off. Thankfully, his soothing voice snaps me out of my unpleasant thoughts.

"I was up here trying to get this ready so I could bring you here tonight. I didn't have much notice you were going to show up. I asked Luke when he first got here around eight, but he didn't let me know until almost ten. He said he couldn't get ahold of you."

I'm not surprised. Luke didn't even try to get ahold of me until ten. I keep that information to myself.

"It's beautiful. It feels like we're the only two people in the world."

"Really? That's awesome to hear because that was the plan when I designed the space."

I hear the pride in his voice. "The patio is private, and only people who rent either the honeymoon suite or the royal suite have access. Luckily for us, neither of those rooms is rented tonight."

"That is lucky, but I'm sure you'd rather have the revenue from the rooms being rented."

He looks at me with a shy smile. "No, Alexa. I'd rather be up here with you than make money off it tonight." That's what I mean about Julian always saying the right thing.

We are still standing, and he takes my hand and leads me to the couch to sit down. We sit very close, and he continues to hold my hand. It feels like we're on a first date, and considering how we have interacted so far, this feels so normal. We have definitely taken a few steps backward, but in a good way.

"I thought maybe we could do things a little different tonight. When I realized I never even got your phone number, I knew we had some backtracking to do. And as hard as it has been all night for me to keep my hands and mouth off of you, I'm determined for us to get to know each other a little better."

I giggle a little when Julian mentions he wants his hands and mouth on me. I totally feel the same way, and I honestly would rather skip the get-to-know-you-better part of the evening. But because Julian has gone to all this effort, I decide to enjoy this little seduction game.

"I already know a lot about you."

"Really? Such as?"

I recite some of the stuff I've read on the Internet using my best announcing voice.

"Introducing Julian Bauer, the thirty-year-old Cuban owner of the Hotel Del Marco in beautiful South Beach, Florida. The Bauer family owns and operates Bywater Properties, one of the largest property development companies in South Florida. Julian has one sibling, a younger brother named Daniel who is twenty-seven. Mr. Bauer graduated from The U where he was a standout baseball player headed for the pros until he decided to join the family business. He is currently one of south Florida's most eligible bachelors and always surrounded by a flock of beautiful women."

Julian is laughing, really laughing at my description of him. "Someone has really done her homework. You know you shouldn't believe everything you read on the Internet."

"I know that, Julian. If I did, I wouldn't be here now."

I'm totally teasing him. I really could not—and I tried to— find any dirt on Julian. The worst things to read were all about how he surrounds himself with beautiful women.

"That bad, huh? I try not to read stuff about myself."

"Did I get any information wrong?"

"You may have reported a couple inaccuracies like the fact that I'm actually half Cuban, half Argentinean, but overall that was a pretty good dossier you compiled on me. The only problem now is that you seem to have me at a disadvantage."

"And why is that?"

"You know so many personal things about me, and the only personal things I know about you besides your name is how you look and sound when you're about to come."

I swear he does it on purpose. He tries to shock me when he says stuff like that, and he just did. I thought we were staying away from the sexual stuff for a while. I clear my throat so I can respond, and Julian senses my embarrassment.

"There's no reason to be embarrassed. It was a beautiful thing, watching you come against my leg. Next time I'd like to feel you come against another part of my body."

This was supposed to be a get-to-know-you conversation, and so far the only thing I know is that we're both still thinking about fucking.

I decide to fight fire with fire. "Well if that's the case, I think I'm the one who's at a disadvantage because I still have no idea how you look or sound when you're about to come."

Julian is very close to me, and I swear I can feel the heat coming off of his body. If he started ripping my clothes off right now, I would not be surprised.

"Dios mío, Alexa. You're something else. Keep saying things like that to me, and I promise the talking portion of this program will be ending very soon."

I meet his gaze with the same intensity he's directing at me. "Promises, promises. I just hope you're not all talk."

Julian leans into me and puts his face right in front of mine. I look at his lips because I can't look him in the eyes anymore. I slowly lick my lips in invitation because I'm sure he is going to kiss me now.

"Like I said earlier, I'm determined to get to know you better before I fuck you tonight. If I even start to kiss you or touch you, both of our mouths are going to be too busy pleasing each other to do any talking. So stop trying to make me harder than I already am and tell me if you prefer white wine or red wine."

He pulls back without kissing me, and I'm left trying to catch my breath. Literally. I swear if he had touched me right then, I would have orgasmed. I'm that turned on.

I choke the word out because I can hardly talk. "White." I've already had those two shots of tequila and a Vodka Cranberry earlier, but suddenly I do not feel buzzed at all anymore.

Julian moves away and reaches for a bottle that's sitting on the table. He opens the white and pours us both a glass. He hands me my glass and raises his in a toast.

"To getting to know each other better."

I repeat the words. His toast is much more eloquent than the toast I gave upstairs a little while ago.

"Do you prefer white, because I would've had the red?"

"I'm not a big wine drinker at all, so either is okay."

"I haven't seen you drink much at all actually."

"I don't drink much, and hardly at all when I'm at work."

I guess I look surprised, and he notices.

"Why does that surprise you?"

"Because you own a hotel with a nightclub and several bars. Alcohol is always around, and I'm sure it's a big part of conducting business."

"That's all true, but I choose not to indulge much. It's a personal choice, but I clearly support people having a good time."

He doesn't offer more, but I know there's more to the story. I don't pry. My thoughts shift to Brady, and I think how great it would have been if he had never chosen to indulge. Every night out with him was a party, and I should have known from the very beginning he had a problem. After going through that, I would have no problem if Julian told me he didn't drink at all.

"And you, what do you like besides white wine, Mojitos, and Vodka Cranberries?"

"I'm actually not a big drinker either. Although it doesn't seem like it the last few times I've been here. I seem to drink more when I'm around you than I normally do."

And it's true. I really haven't been drinking much over the last year. I partied hard the year Brady and I dated. Too hard. And when he died, I couldn't stop feeling guilty about my part in his disease. Drinking and doing drugs were things I wanted to get far away from. Julian asks me a question that brings me back to the present.

"Why is that, Alexa?"

"Because you make me nervous, Julian, and when I'm nervous, I sometimes find a drink calms me down."

He scoots even closer to me, if that's possible. "Why do I make you nervous?" He's actually playing with me and trying to make me nervous now.

Oh my God. Really? I want to scream, "Because you're so fucking hot I can't think straight around you," but I don't. I don't answer that question at all and change the subject.

"What else do you want to know about me?" I think I want to stick to the basics here.

"Todo, Alexa, todo." I'm not sure how to feel about that. He wants to know everything? It makes me feel great and freaks me out at the same time. That's the problem here. I love hearing him tell me how much he wants me and how beautiful he thinks I am, but at the same time it scares the shit out of me. I can't seem to keep my guard up for very long when he's around me, and I don't want to get hurt by him. I already know, judging by my reactions tonight, he has the power to hurt me, and that isn't a good thing.

"Well, let me even the playing field out a little, Julian." I start to recite my own information in much the same way I did his.

"Introducing Alexa Reed. Alexa is twenty-five and will be turning twenty-six in June. She was born and raised in South Florida. She has two older sisters, Tracy and Jill. She is a Seminole, which is kind of an issue because Mr. Bauer is a Cane." Julian laughs out loud at that. "She is employed by Wilson & Mitchell Properties, which is one of Bywater's largest competitors, as a sales and marketing consultant. She is currently working at the Bayview Towers property in Coconut Grove, where she also lives with her two best friends, Marissa and Shannon. She loves music, all music, and loves to sing even though she can't carry a tune. She played soccer and tennis in high school and was a good athlete, but not good enough to go pro. Oh, and she speaks enough Spanish to know if someone is talking about her."

I'm trying to make this playful and light, and I'm winded by the end of my speech. I thought I was being funny, but serious Julian is staring intently at me.

"And Alexa is single?"

That makes me laugh. "Um, yes, isn't that obvious?"

He doesn't say yes. "And Luke?"

Luke? Where in the hell did that come from?

"And Luke is another one of Alexa's best friends. He has been for years."

For some reason, I sense Julian doesn't believe me, and I wonder what the hell was said between them tonight. I don't want to talk about Luke, so I change the topic. I decide this is the perfect opportunity to ask about the woman I saw Julian with earlier.

"And the supermodel with mile-long legs?"

I try to say it jokingly, but it doesn't come out as playfully as I want it to. His response isn't playful either.

"Her name is Caroline, and she's someone I went out with a few times."

Translation: someone I slept with a few times. He offers a little more information, which I'm grateful for. "She isn't happy I'm no longer interested in going out with her and wanted to share that with me tonight."

Yeah, I'll bet she's unhappy, and I'd also bet she doesn't get turned down much. I haven't even slept with Julian yet, and I feel connected to him. And possessive.

Julian gently pulls me toward his chest and wraps his arms around me; I start to really relax for the first time tonight. It may be the wine (and tequila), the beautiful night sky, or just the fact that Julian is making me feel so comfortable. I even feel relaxed enough to put my feet up on the couch.

"Those shoes are hot by the way." I smile at the compliment.

"Thank you. I just got them."

"You like shoes, don't you?" Um, yeah. What girl doesn't?

"Yes, why?" I'm sure I sound defensive. I'm always justifying my shoe addiction to someone.

"Because all three times I've seen you, you have been wearing very sexy, very high, expensive shoes."

Wow. Did a man just tell me he's paying that much attention to my shoes? Ramon, one of my coworkers, is gay, and he always notices my shoes. We actually go shoe shopping together. If Julian had not used the word sexy in his description, I might be concerned. I swear Julian can read my mind because the next thing out of his mouth is, "No, I'm not gay. I just happen to like nice shoes myself, and yours have been hard to miss."

I giggle and respond. "Well Julian, we just may be a match made in heaven."

I'm totally referring to our shared love of expensive shoes, but I don't think Julian is when he softly replies, "We just may be, Alexa, we just may be."

We sit like that for a while just listening to the music and enjoying the beautiful night and each other's company. Julian is holding one of my hands, and when I shift a little, I see the hint of the tattoo I noticed earlier peeking out from under his watch. It feels like it would be okay to ask what it says now. I rub my fingertip over the part I can see.

"What does your tattoo say?"

Julian takes a deep breath and exhales before he answers. I'm already regretting asking because I'm sure he's going to tell me it's the name of an ex-girlfriend.

"Isabelle," he says softly. "My sister. She died of cancer when she was sixteen and I was twenty-one. She also would have been twenty-six this June."

I squeeze his hand. "I'm so sorry." I quickly realize my comment about him only having one sibling was also not completely accurate. I don't want to sound uncompassionate, but I really don't want to start talking about people who have died. Brady's death isn't even a year old, and the anniversary is quickly approaching. I wait for Julian to say something else about it, but he obviously doesn't want to stay on this topic either.

"How long have you been working for W&M?" Good. Work. A safe subject. He obviously knows the company well enough to refer to it by its acronym.

"About a year and a half. I kind of fell into the job through Shannon's uncle, and it's been great. I love working there."

"They have a good product. Not as nice as ours, but still good." Julian's voice is light again.

"What do you do for Bywater?"

"I'm on the board of directors and head up acquisitions, but I try to stay out of day-to-day operations. The hotel is my main focus."

"Are the hotel and condos run separately?" I hope I don't sound too nosy. I'm in the business and genuinely interested.

"I own the majority share of the hotel myself, so it's my baby. The rest of the company is wholly family owned."

He's thirty and owns the hotel himself? I figured it was part of the Bywater portfolio.

"Impressive."

"Impressive?"

"To be so young and have accomplished this. This hotel is fantastic." I hope he can hear the sincerity in my voice. I think he does because his face lights up, and he starts talking about it.

"It's been in my family since the fifties. My great-grandfather, on my mom's side, bought it when there was nothing down here. He was Cuban and owned one in Havana as well. Her family all came over right after the revolution, and this was all they had left. It was pretty run down and mismanaged for years. My dad's family is originally from Argentina. They're wealthy and have been involved in some pretty big property development and real estate businesses both in Argentina and here for years. My mom is an only child, and my grandparents gave the hotel to my parents as a wedding present. The Bauers kept trying to convince my mom to sell the hotel, but my abuelito had never wanted it to leave the family, so she honored that. He always believed South Beach would become what it is today and that it would be worth a fortune one day. It caused a lot of issues between my parents because it hasn't always been a sound business investment. I spent a lot of time here growing up, and it's full of great memories for me. I've always loved this place, and when I 'officially' joined the business after college, it was with the intent to make this one of the hottest spots in South Beach. I had some of my own money, borrowed the rest, and convinced my mom to sell it to me. Some members of my family backed me, and that's why Bywater owns 30 percent. The rest is mine."

I watch Julian as he talks about the history of this place. I see so many emotions cross his face as he talks about the different members of his family. There are definitely stories there. I also hear and see the pride he feels for fulfilling his grandfather's vision.

"Has it always been called Hotel Del Marco?"

"No, that was my idea. It was called Las Palmas before I took it over. Marco was my abuelito's name." It's so obvious Julian and his grandfather were very close, and I'm touched he would honor him that way.

"And the names of the bars and restaurant? Do they have special meanings too?"

"Are you sure you want to hear all of this? I feel like I'm doing all the talking."

"Yes. Aren't we getting to know each other here?" I think to myself it would be fine if he wanted to stop talking because I can think of a hundred other things he can do with this mouth.

I keep my naughty thoughts to myself though. He smiles and continues.

"My abuela loved looking at the stars. I think if she would've had an opportunity to get a college education she would have studied astronomy. Orion and Ursa are constellations, and I remember her telling me about them. I really think she would have enjoyed sitting outside on the rooftop looking at Orion. I named the nightclub Stellar for two reasons. The first is because it relates to stars, and second because my abuelito used to tell me that when businesses provide stellar service, they're successful. I honestly think it was a word he heard when he was first learning to speak English, and he liked the way it sounded. He used it all the time."

"Wow, Julian. You've honored your grandparents beautifully." I mentally add sentimental and family oriented to my growing list of Julian's good qualities.

"We finished all the major renovations a few months ago, and everything turned out perfectly. It's finally the place my abuelito envisioned." He stares off into the distance, and I imagine he's embracing a memory of his grandfather.

"I haven't seen the whole hotel, but what I've seen is awesome." I mean every word. "The vibe here is great."

"I'll have to give you a full tour."

"I'd love that." I have no idea when this tour may happen, but if it's tonight I'm kind of hoping it starts and ends in one of the bedrooms. I'm not gonna lie. I'm totally enjoying this get-to-know-you portion of the program, as Julian called it, but I'm dying for Julian to put his hands on me. It feels like forever since he's kissed or really touched me.

I glance at my watch and can't believe it's already a little after midnight. I reach to get my phone from my wristlet and notice I just got a text from Shannon. I forgot I had put it on silent. Good thing I checked.

Shannon: *What's up? we're ready to go.*
Alexa: *Gimme a sec*

Crap. I'm not ready for this night to end. Julian reads my expression.

"Everything okay?"

"Yep. I didn't drive tonight, and my friends want to go."

I don't say much more because I'm hoping Julian doesn't want the night to end either and will offer up a solution.

"Tell them I'll take you home."

"Are you sure? I live in Coconut Grove."

He flashes me a small, "I'm up to no good" smile. "Totalmente seguro. Our night's not over yet."

Thank God.

Alexa: *Julian will bring me home.*
Shannon: *u sure?*
Alexa: *yes.*
Shannon: *have fun. Be safe. Btw Luke looking for you. He's really upset. WTH happened?*

I realize Julian intercepted me before I had a chance to tell them what happened with Luke.

Alexa: *He's being a dick about Julian and I told him so. He'll get over it.*
Shannon: *haha. ttyl*

I look again and see three missed texts from Luke. He must be feeling bad. They were all sent in the last hour.

Luke: *Where are you at?*
Luke: *C'mon Lex, come see me*
Luke: *Seriously? Are you ok?*

I'm still mad at him, and I'm going to be a bitch and not respond. I know he's worried, and I don't care. He'll text Shannon or Marissa, and they'll let him know I'm okay. Jerk.

I turn my phone off and give my attention back to Julian. He's standing up. I'm not sure if I should get up or not.

"All good?" I know he's wondering what I was texting but doesn't ask.

"All great." That makes him smile.

"Are you interested in getting out of here? I've been here since ten this morning."

I have no idea where he wants to go, but I'd go anywhere with him. I'm hoping our next location has a bed.

"Where do you want to go?"

"My place."

I nod.

"Good. I need about thirty minutes to check a couple things out before we leave. Are you okay waiting here for me?"

I really don't want him to leave me again, but I don't want to seem needy.

"Sure, just don't forget me. I'm not sure how to get out of here."

I'm joking with him, but his reply is serious. "If I could forget you, I'd have done it by now. I haven't stopped thinking about you since you fell on me in the stairwell."

Before I have a chance to respond, he leans over and gives me the sweetest little peck on the lips. His lips are full and soft, and I immediately feel the warmth from his kiss spread throughout my body. I want more, but he pulls away.

"I'll be right back."

I lie on the couch and stare at the fire. I feel like I'm in a dream. Despite the situations with Luke and the supermodel, this night has turned into something special. And it's not over yet. The best part is I can't imagine it's going to end before Julian and I are naked. I close my eyes and visualize us together. Just the thought of him kissing me and caressing me sends shivers down my spine, and I tingle with anticipation. Relaxed as I am, my senses are all totally heightened. I quickly conclude it was probably not a great idea for Julian to leave me alone with my thoughts. I'm absolutely in a tug of war with myself. My body and my heart are being pulled toward Julian in a way that hasn't ever happened to me. I've been in love before, and I certainly have been in lust, but there's something different about the intensity and depth of what I'm feeling now. My head keeps sending warning flares into the mix, telling me I'm on dangerous ground with this man already, and I briefly consider leaving before he comes back. But I can't get my body to cooperate, so I remain still.

I'm lost in my thoughts when Julian comes back to get me. I hear the click of the doors opening, but I don't move or open my eyes. I'm sure it looks like I'm asleep, and for a moment I stay still as I imagine his gaze on me. I hear his voice above me.

"Estas tan hermosa."

I open my eyes, and Julian is staring down at me with that same reverent look he had in the hallway a few weeks ago. The same one that had me looking for an escape. The same uneasiness I felt then passes through me, and I can't figure out what about his stare is making me so uneasy. I'm going to fight through it. I push myself up to my feet and stand in front of him. I turn my face up to him and thread my fingers through his.

"Kiss me, please."

I say the words softly and pleadingly. I'm aching to feel his lips on mine, and I'm searching for a way to bring the physical aspect of our relationship back into the dynamic. It's feeling too emotional between us, and I'm uncomfortable. I half expect him to tell me no. He has withheld himself from me all night and has proven his restraint. I would've let him have his way with me the moment I saw him in the lobby earlier had he tried. I don't want to wait for this anymore, and I'm not feeling shy about it.

I'm not sure if it was the way I asked him or the fact we're touching, but something has helped him decide we're past the just-talking portion of the program now. Julian leans down and brushes his lips against mine. He starts to pull back, but I just can't let him. I let go of his hand and reach up around his neck. I pull him to me and press my mouth to his. Hard. I open my lips and slide my tongue into his mouth. What happens next can only be described as something similar to a dam breaking. All of the lust and need we've been holding back tonight races through our bodies, and we hold on to each other as if we might drown in these feelings. Julian's lips and tongue find their way to my neck and my face, and he marks me with his longing. His mouth is hot and wet on my skin. Our tongues are battling as each of us tries to control the tempo and pace of our kisses. I can feel his muscles tighten as desire courses through him, and I melt into his strong body as he pulls me to his chest. I'm on fire, and nothing could keep me from this man in this moment. Julian takes a step back and sits down on the couch. He pulls me down onto his lap, and I spread my legs so I'm straddling him. We both groan loudly when his erection makes contact with my sex. We're fully dressed, but heat radiates through our clothes, and I can't help but grind into him. Our mouths never lose contact. I lift myself on and off of him in my own rhythm, teasing and apparently torturing him with my simulated fucking. His hands are on my waist, and he fights me to control the rhythm. He lifts his own hips and thrusts up into me, mimicking a move I'm hoping he will be using on me soon.

"My God, Alexa. What are you trying to do to me?" Julian's question comes out in short gasps. It might be a rhetorical question, but I answer anyway.

"Turn you on, I hope." That I'm able to make this strong, powerful man lose control is positively exhilarating.

"I couldn't be more turned on right now. I want you so much it actually hurts. But I want you naked in my bed, not here."

And with those words, he lifts me off of him and sets me next to him. We sit there for a moment as we each try to catch our breaths and come back down to earth a little. Julian stands first. He is right in front of me, and his massive erection is right there on display. I can't help but stare. I want to reach over and unzip his pants and take him in my mouth. And, as if he can read my mind, he takes a step back. I look up at Julian and see nothing but unadulterated lust in his eyes.

His voice is a raspy whisper. "Yes, please. Later."

I'm in serious trouble. He. Is. So. Fucking. Sexy.

He offers me his hand. I take it, and he pulls me up to him. He holds me close for a minute before he turns and walks toward the doors. I grab my purse and let him lead me wherever he wants to take me. We're quiet in the elevator, and Julian only barely holds my hand. I now know my touch does the same to him as his does to me. We're both hanging on by a thread here. Our craving for each other is intense and unfulfilled. We exit the hotel out a back door. I'm thankful because I don't want any more deterrents on my way to his bed. I'm pretty sure he lives in Sofi, in one of the Bywater properties, but there are two, and I don't which one. We walk toward Collins, and I wonder where he parks his car. He answers my question before I ask it. That keeps happening, and it's freaking me out.

"I live on South Point Drive. I don't always drive here, and today I went for a run and came straight here. You may not make it in those shoes. I'm going to grab a cab."

I smile at him and nod appreciatively. We're on Twelfth, and that's at least like fourteen blocks. Not only will my feet not make it, but the quicker we get to Julian's the quicker we'll be naked in his bed.

"My feet thank you."

Julian winks at me, and my heart melts.

Despite the fact it's almost one o'clock in the morning, we have no problem getting a cab right away. The driver even knows Julian, and I darkly wonder if he's used to picking him and a date up on a regular basis. I hate that I keep letting negative, jealous thoughts enter my mind, but I can't seem to help it. I'm having all these new feelings, and I really don't want to be just another notch on his belt. Unfortunately, my negativity gains a little traction, and the warm, relaxed comfortable feelings that embraced me just moments ago are being pushed into the shadows. I straighten up and shift slightly away from Julian. I even try to pull my hand from his, but he doesn't let go. I can't even look at him as I try to fight these little demons off. My God, this is exhausting. I wonder if Julian can see the high-speed thrill ride my emotions are on.

Up, down, twist, turn, fast, slow. He's been able to read me all night, so it's really not a surprise when he squeezes my hand.

"Mírame."

I don't want to look at him, but he forces me to by putting his hand on my chin and turning my face toward him. He's leaning his head back on the seat, and he looks so peaceful. He has been so attuned to my body I'm sure he senses my discomfort. I expect him to say something reassuring to me, but he doesn't. He just slowly shakes his head, telling me no, not to go wherever I just did in my mind. It's the perfect gesture, and I'm amazed at how well he responds to my needs. All of them. I offer a small smile and lean back into him. He exhales deeply.

CHAPTER 12

Ten minutes later, we pull up in front of a large condo building. The Bellavista, aptly named for its beautiful ocean, bay, and skyline views. I've been in this building once before but only in the lobby and in one of the meeting rooms. It was about six months ago, and I was here for a marketing South Beach sales professionals meeting. I was as in awe at the beauty then as I am right now. It's the crème de la crème of properties in South Beach. I love the property I work at, and W&M builds a good product, but this is at a whole other level. My company is getting ready to break ground on a similar building a few blocks over from here, and my dream is to end up working there.

Julian greets the doorman and a few others working in the building as we walk in. It's pretty quiet at this time of night, and we're the only non-workers in the lobby. Julian notices me taking everything in and asks me what I think.

"It's stunning in here. I've been here once, for a meeting a few months ago, and I thought so then. But now, when it's empty, you can really see the amazing architectural details."

I point out several things I like, and Julian seems impressed with my knowledge.

"Those are great compliments coming from the competition. You're totally selling this place, and we're only in the lobby. Maybe we need to steal you away from W&M."

"It'll never happen, Julian. Working together would be dangerous. You don't want a sexual harassment suit filed against you, do you?" I think about one of our earlier conversations when I joked about his bartenders offering kisses with each drink. It seems so long ago.

"Have I been sexually *harassing* you?" he asks in a seductive tone.

He gets his desired effect as tingles run through my body. "Not yet, but I can dream, can't I?"

He laughs as we walk into the elevator. I notice there are only a few floors listed on the call buttons. I've heard the Bellavista has certain floors where the units are so large there are only a few of them. I assume Julian has a primo unit, but then I wonder if he would have such a large one seeing as he's single and lives alone. I quickly realize that I actually don't know if he does live alone. I'm pondering these questions when I feel Julian's lips on my neck. He had been standing behind me. He's obviously a person who doesn't like to share his personal business in public. As in no PDA. But the minute we're alone, he lets loose. He spins me around, and within seconds of the doors closing, he's all over me. His lips, his tongue, his hands. I feel his touch everywhere. He takes my breasts in his hands and caresses them firmly. I moan into his mouth as he sweeps his fingertips over my swollen, erect nipples. We stumble into the wall, and he pushes his erection into me. I grab his ass and pull him toward me. I'm so turned on that I'll fuck him right here if he wants. I don't want to wait anymore. This foreplay has been going on for hours now, and I'm more than ready for the real deal.

I hardly register the bell going off and the elevator doors opening. Julian pulls himself away from me, and I instinctively grab him and pull him back toward me. I run my hands up and down his sides, needing to feel him beneath my hands. With a moan and a little peck on my lips, he pulls away again and exits the elevator. I follow him out, grabbing at his hand so I can continue to touch him.

There are three doors in the little lobby we have entered into. Julian walks toward one and opens it with keys he pulls from his pocket. He leads me through two large, dark cherry doors into a large foyer. The floors are white, travertine tile, and there's a dark, wood entry table off to one side where Julian sets his keys. Straight in front of me is what I'm assuming is the living room. There are floor-to-ceiling windows that overlook the water. The moon is shining brightly and cuts a swath of light across the tile floor.

"I'd give you a tour, but I really can't wait any longer to get you naked."

Julian gives me a sweet kiss and picks me up into his arms. I wrap my legs around his waist and he carries me the short distance down the hall and into his bedroom. He doesn't say anything and doesn't try to kiss me again. His gaze is hot and full of longing. He's holding me tightly against him, as if he's afraid I'll try to get away. I don't want to go anywhere except wherever he's taking me. I officially lost any desire to fight these feelings of doubt I had the minute he kissed me in the elevator. For tonight, I'm his, and I don't want to wait anymore. His heart is beating rapidly, and his breathing is heavy. I can sense he's also through waiting.

The room we enter has no lights on, and Julian makes no motion to flip the switch that's next to the door. I quickly see it isn't really necessary because the moonlight and the lights of the city glitter and shine through the floor-to-ceiling glass windows that also make up one whole wall of this room. I'm amazed by this incredible view, and I want to see it up close. I unwrap my legs from around Julian's waist and wiggle out of his arms. He seems hesitant to let me go and does so slowly. I move toward the window to get a better look. It's literally breathtaking. We're thirty stories high, and it's almost like being outside under the open night sky. I can see for miles.

"Opened or closed?" He's referring to the blinds on the windows.

"Open." I want to see him in the moonlight.

I'm scared to say anything else, and I sense Julian is as well. Our usual conversations are filled with teasing and sarcastic banter. Those words don't fit this setting. The air is thick with our need for each other.

Julian walks up behind me and gently turns me around so I'm facing him and moves me closer to a solid wall. I'm thankful he doesn't press me against the glass. I look up at him and see his eyes are filled with desire. The sheer intensity of his stare makes me take a small step backward, and I feel the wall behind me. This isn't the first time Julian has towered over me in this position, and my mind races back to the night in the hallway at the club. His presence makes me feel protected, and once again I'm amazed by the different feelings he inspires in me. Julian places one of his hands above my head on the wall, bracing himself over me. His other hand starts to work on the button on my pants. We're just staring at each other, lost in each other's eyes and barely touching. I'm in awe of his restraint. I'm fighting everything I have inside me not to reach out and touch him. Something in his eyes tells me he needs to be in charge and that he needs me to understand and respect his dominant nature. I'm dying for his lips to be on mine. They're still swollen from our earlier make-out session, and I've been aching for him to kiss me since we walked out of the elevator. I tilt my head further up to meet his and lick my lower lip as an invitation.

"Mmm, Alexa," he murmurs as he bends down and softly runs his tongue between my slightly parted lips. He stops there and pulls back, never taking his eyes off mine. That isn't exactly what I had in mind, and the ache in my body intensifies.

Once he has the button on my pants undone and the zipper pulled down, he slips his hand in and lets his fingers graze lightly over the silk of my panties. We moan simultaneously. I feel a rush of heat fan out from between my legs, up through my stomach and into my aching breasts. My nipples are so hard they actually hurt. I know he can instantly feel how wet he has made me.

He's barely touching me, and I'm trembling. I feel his touch everywhere. As sexually intense as things have already been between us, it was nothing compared to what I'm feeling now. I feel *consumed* by my need for him. It's too intense. I'm falling apart in front of this man, and I don't want him to see it. I feel completely naked even though I'm still fully clothed. I try to avert my eyes.

"Please, baby, look at me. The want and need in your eyes drives me crazy. I know you can see what you're doing to me. Por favor, mírame a los ojos." He's begging me not to look away. How does he always know the perfect thing to say?

I keep my focus on him but try to concentrate on something else besides these intense emotions that are grabbing me. Julian's hand under my panties and his fingers on my sex do the job. He leans down for a minute and runs his tongue up the V in my shirt, leaving a hot trail of his breath between my breasts. His touches are so deliberate and so powerful, yet so slow and gentle. He strokes his index finger gently up and back through my cleft. I'm so wet that his finger glides effortlessly through my slickness. He pauses momentarily each time he gets to my clit and pushes down a bit harder. He slips his finger just inside me with each pass too. I can't help but sway my hips back and forth to his rhythm. Each time I rock into him, I feel his erection, and I'm aching to touch him. I bring my hand forward to caress his dick, and he quickly pulls his hips away.

"Not yet. Just feel me touching you."

Um, Okay. I'll go with that.

Julian is enjoying owning and controlling my desire and is keeping himself completely focused on me. He still hasn't looked away. I feel so taken care of. He still keeps his hips and his dick away from me but bends his head down so that his lips are right next to my ear.

"Mmm, that's it, baby. You're so wet for me. So soft. So tight. I bet you're so sweet. As soon as I make you come with my fingers, I'm going to do it again with my tongue and then again with my dick. I want to taste you. I can't wait to be inside of you."

That makes two of us.

His seductive tone matches his touch and his voice is so smooth he makes his X-rated words sound like poetry. He's a conductor, and he's orchestrating my pleasure tonight much like he did the first night at the club. As much as I'm enjoying it, I want and need to be more in control. And I need to come.

"Then make me come already," I growl as I slip my hand inside my pants and grab his hand. Wow! I know I'm beyond turned on, but I had no idea how wet I am. I can feel my juices on my fingers as I try to force his hand to stay on my clit.

He chuckles at my impatience. "Okay, bossy girl. I promise I know what I'm doing, but it's sexy as hell that you want to help me get you off. Because you seem so determined, I'll let you help me tonight. And one day really soon I'm going to sit across the room from you while you sit in a chair naked, and I'm going to watch you get yourself off."

Oh my God. What a visual.

With those words, he guides two of my fingers inside my channel and pushes my palm down on my clit. His hand is firmly cupping mine. Of course I've touched myself before, but it was nothing compared to the feeling I get as Julian guides my fingers in and out of my sex and over my clit. "Yes, Julian. It feels too good. I'm so close, so close," I murmur breathlessly.

Julian rubs my fingers hard against my clit. "Come for me, baby, that's it. Let go."

And I do. I shudder and close my eyes as the waves of my orgasm race through me like molten lava. My knees buckle. Julian keeps our hands on my sex until the last ripple of pleasure rolls through my body. He slowly pulls our hands out together and places my hand down by my side. I grab at a table near me to help me keep my balance, and I lean back into the wall to try to keep from crumpling to the ground. Holy hell, that was fucking incredible! I open my eyes and look at him from under heavy lids, my eyes reflecting the intensity of the orgasm he just gave me.

"Wow, if you're going to keep giving me orgasms like that, I can't be standing. It's becoming hazardous to my health." He smiles and responds by putting the fingers that were just in me into his mouth and licks them. Holy shit, that's sexy.

"Now I want to really taste you." I must look either shocked or embarrassed as he tries to put me at ease.

"Don't be embarrassed, baby. You taste so sweet. I knew you would."

Julian takes my hand and finally leads me over to his huge bed. It's a good thing. I need to sit or lie down. My legs are like Jell-O. He sits me down on the edge of the bed and kneels in front of me and begins to unbuckle my sandals. He has gotten quiet again. One minute he's whispering dirty nothings in my ear, and the next he's like a mute. It intrigues me and scares me because I have no clue what he's thinking. As he slips off my sandals, he caresses my feet tenderly. He has pulled his own socks and shoes off as well. Julian runs his hands up my legs to my waist. I lift my hips up as he tugs my pants off. When he reaches up to the hem of my shirt, I stop him.

"Uh uh. I want to see you too, and I've been very patient."

A low moan comes out of his mouth as I slowly unbutton his shirt and slide it off his shoulders. I run my hands over his smooth, muscled chest and flat stomach, tickling him with my fingernails. My god, he's beautiful. I've been picturing in my head what his naked torso would look like for weeks now, but the reality is way better than my fantasies. He clearly works out.

"My turn now." Julian grabs the hem of my shirt and pulls it quickly over my head. He deftly reaches around and unhooks my bra, leaving me naked except for my panties.

"You are so beautiful, Lexie. Tan hermosa." That's the first time he has called me Lexie. He's using my nickname now. I'm not sure why I notice and why it matters to me, but it does.

What's happening between us is definitely intimate, but he's made everything seem so much more personal.

He places his hands on my rib cage just below my breasts and fans his long fingers across them and over my aching erect nipples. He kneads my heavy swollen breasts gently, and I instinctively arch my back in pleasure. My stomach and my sex clench as a jolt of electricity shoots through me. I've dreamt of his hands on my breasts for weeks.

"My turn," I say teasingly. This undressing scene is unfolding very slowly. This is some of the best foreplay I've ever engaged in. I reach over and unbuckle his belt, excited that I'm moments away from finally being able to touch him. I put my thumbs into the belt loops and gently pull upward, indicating I want him to stand. Julian is so tall that when he's on his feet in front of me, his crotch is directly in front of my face. I take a deep breath as I look at the outline of his erection straining against his pants. I've yet to touch him there, and I'm dying to. As I unzip his pants, my fingers gently graze his dick. He gasps loudly and shudders. When I look up at him, I can see the passion burning in his eyes. He has been holding back for hours now and is definitely a man on the brink of losing control.

"You are unraveling me, Alexa."

"That's the plan," I say as I yank his slacks down. He steps out of them, and I literally am left with my mouth hanging open. Surprise! Julian is naked under his pants. His big, beautiful, hard dick is now free and right in front of me. Before he has a chance to move away, I reach over, wrap my hand around the base, lean forward, and guide him into my mouth.

"No. I want to taste you first."

Julian makes a halfhearted attempt to pull away, but I grab his ass and pull him deeper into my mouth. He's bigger than anyone I've ever been with, and I'm not sure I can take all of him in. I swirl my tongue across his plush head and down around his shaft. I keep pumping him with one hand and gently knead his balls with the other. He growls and grabs my hair. His excitement spurs me on, and I take him in deeper. He needs more and gently pushes my head down until I've taken him all the way in. I want to give this to him, so I ignore the burning in my throat. I feel a small spurt of pre-cum on my tongue, and I suck harder. I don't want to rush him, but I'm eager to feel him explode in my mouth. I love how in control sucking him off is making me feel. He's been in charge since day one, and now I'm the one with all the power.

"Your beautiful mouth feels so good on my dick. You see how hard I am, how hard you make me. What are you doing to me?" Julian moans and pushes his dick deeper into my mouth. I know he must be about to come, so I suck harder. But despite my best efforts, he doesn't come. He abruptly stops and pushes me away instead. What the hell? I'm giving the best head I've ever given, and he's stopping me?

Julian answers my unspoken question. "The first time I come in you, it's going to be in you. As good as your mouth feels, that's what I've been dreaming about and waiting for."

I have no chance to argue as Julian pushes me back further onto the bed, climbs over me, and positions himself between my shaking legs. He has pulled the comforter down, and the exquisitely soft feel of what I'm sure are very expensive sheets caresses my body. He stares down at me like he's admiring a piece of expensive artwork, and I'm thankful for the approval I see in his eyes. Overall I'm pretty comfortable with my body, but I know Julian has probably had many models with perfect bodies in this exact same position, in this bed. His next words put me totally at ease, even if they aren't entirely true.

"You are so beautiful, Alexa. So beautiful. I can't wait to sink myself into your perfect body." Yeah, well that makes two of us. I grab at Julian's shoulders and try to pull him up toward me. I need his lips on mine. He resists and sits back on his heels. Uh-oh. He looks serious.

"Are you on the pill?"

Oh, here comes this conversation. If I could think straight, I would have brought this up first, and I definitely wish we would've discussed this sooner. It always seems to be a mood killer.

"Yes, I am. But you still need to use a condom. *Please* tell me that you have one."

I'm pretty much begging. My thoughts quickly go to the time when Luke didn't, and I remember the absence of a condom derailed a promising night of sex. That better not happen now. I need this man inside of me, and there isn't a chance I'm agreeing to not using one. After Brady, I had myself checked, and I know I'm clean. I imagine Julian is the type of man who is careful too. I'm sure he sleeps with a lot of different women, and aside from catching a disease, I would think he worries about some woman trying to trap him with a baby. But I'm not interested in taking any chances.

I expect Julian to tease me about the pleading, desperate tone I'm using, but he remains serious. This isn't good. "I have condoms. I'm not happy about using one, but I will. My dick has been aching to be inside of you for weeks, and I need to feel all of you."

How in the world did he make that statement sound romantic? "Once we prove to each other we're both clean, I promise you'll feel me, bare, in every part of you."

I let his words sink in, and my sex clenches at the promise of additional nights of fucking Julian. I'm so in. I know Julian meant that comment purely sexually, and it did turn me on to think about him being in every part of me, but what Julian fails to realize is that I have already started to feel him in every part of me, emotionally, and I have since the night we met. I'm uncomfortable with that mental admission and decide to keep those thoughts to myself.

Julian gets up and walks to a nightstand next to the bed. He takes a few condoms out and places them on the bed next to him as he gets back in between my thighs. He's kneeling there and looking at me hungrily. I tell him I want him to wait until he's ready to be inside me before he puts one on because I want to feel his bare dick in my mouth again.

He groans. "Keep saying shit like that to me, and it won't be long." I feel so empowered when I see how much I affect him. The feeling is heady.

Julian kisses his fingers and reaches up and puts them on my mouth. My lips are already slightly parted, and I stick my tongue out and lick them. I can taste myself on him; it feels so intimate. He moans deeply and runs his fingers slowly from my mouth, down my throat, across my chest, and between my aching breasts. His fingers stop when he reaches my belly. He leans over, softly kisses my belly button, and runs his tongue inside of it. He blows gently on my skin with his warm breath, and a shiver runs all the way down my body. Julian is completely naked, and I feel his rock-hard erection against my leg. My panties are still on, but I feel the heat from his body pressing against my sex and reaching all the way to my core. I'm thoroughly enjoying his slow descent down my body, but I'm overwhelmed by the anticipation of him being inside of me. I really can't wait anymore.

"Please. I want you so badly." I'm so aroused I don't care that I'm begging for him.

His voice caresses me. "You have me, Alexa. I'm right here. I'm going to take such good care of you, baby." Julian says this as he runs his finger back and forth across my stomach just underneath the elastic of my panties. He does that for a few minutes, and pretty soon I'm trembling beneath his hand. I want his hands on my sex. Or his tongue. I *need* him to really touch me.

"Please," I whisper again.

Julian reaches his other hand up and pulls my panties off in one swift move. His mouth is on my dripping sex in an instant. I'm so wet. His tongue is moving slowly up and down my cleft, and he pauses to put pressure on my clit with each pass. I'm writhing in ecstasy, and I literally can't lie still. Every muscle in my body is clenching in delicious anticipation for the orgasm I know isn't far off. I reach down to grab the back of his head and lift my hips into his mouth. I hear groans, and I realize they're coming from both of us. Julian is licking me with such intensity that I know this is turning him on as much as it is me. Oral sex is one of my favorite parts of sex, and until this moment I believed my past lovers had been good at this. Yeah, not so much. Right now Julian could be teaching a master class. His tongue is amazing, and I find myself actually holding back from coming because I don't want it to end. He knows exactly how hard to lick, how fast to lick, where to lick, and he continues to taste me until I just can't hold back anymore. Julian pulls my clit between his lips and sucks, then lets go and flicks his tongue rapidly over my bundle of nerves. That's it. I push his head hard into me as I come apart from the most intense orgasm I've ever had. After the shudders run through me, I release my grip on his head and try to squirm away from his mouth, which is still on me. My clit is so sensitive now from my back-to-back orgasms that it almost hurts to be touched. He looks up at me from between my legs and gives me a slow smile.

I'm sure my massive orgasm proved to Julian how good he's making me feel, but I still need to tell him. "Oh my God! That was amazing! Sorry about the death grip. I didn't want you to stop."

"Don't ever worry about me stopping. I'll always take care of you, baby."

His use of the word *baby* for like the fifth time tonight both touches me and throws me off balance. I'm not his baby, and he needs to know that, right? Should I remind him this is only about sex and that he needs to keep the terms of endearment to a bare minimum? I'm not ready to be anybody's baby or sweetheart or angel. As those thoughts short circuit in my brain, I realize I'm acting a little crazy. This gorgeous man is doing everything he can to satisfy me and is calling me baby during the heat of passion. He doesn't mean anything by it. I mentally tell myself to get a grip.

I watch as Julian reaches for one of the condoms he has laid beside him on the bed. He quickly rips the package open with his teeth and skillfully rolls it on over his hard shaft. I watch his every move, admiring his dick with my eyes. He sees me watching him and strokes himself slowly. Seeing him touch himself is a total turn on for me too, and I tell him so.

"One day soon I'm going to sit across the room from you and watch you play with your big, beautiful dick until you come." I hope he's as turned on by the visual as I was when he said it to me earlier.

Apparently he is. I watch as his eyes get bigger and hear his desire as he lets out a small groan. As I watch him stroke himself from the head of his shaft to his balls, I begin to feel a little apprehensive about him being inside of me. He's really big, and after all the restraint he's been showing, I'm no doubt in for a hard ride. He doesn't take his eyes off of me and once again seems able to read my mind. "Don't worry. You're so wet that you'll have no trouble taking all of me inside of you."

Before he enters me, he begins to kiss his way back up my body. He gently caresses each of my breasts and drags his tongue across and around each of my nipples. I know if he stays there longer, I'll be coming again in no time at all. After a few minutes, he resumes his upward journey, and when he reaches my mouth, he slips his tongue just inside my parted lips. He's wet with my juices, and I'm so incredibly turned on by his desire to share that with me. I grab his head with my hands and deepen the kiss, never taking my eyes off of him. Every move he makes is so carnal and so raw, and he seems so intent on making this experience as satisfying for me as it is for him. I've had lovers in the past that were all about taking care of their own needs over mine, so I'm enjoying every second of pleasure Julian is giving me. I find myself wanting to reciprocate in every way.

Julian is so hard, and I'm so wet that he slips easily inside me. I'm completely filled by this beautiful man, and it feels amazing. He pulls away from our kiss, closes his eyes, and lets out a deep moan. He's been so controlled during every sexual encounter we've shared up until this point, and I sense he's finally about to really let go.

"You feel so good." The words come out in a tortured hiss. "I'm so deep inside of you, baby. Can you feel me?"

The answer to that would be a big *yes*. I can feel every inch of Julian's hard penis as he grinds it into me. He has settled into a steady rhythm that perfectly suits my need to be taken. His balls are heavy, and I feel them slap up against my sex with every thrust. I reach up and run my hands all over his chest, across his nipples, and down his arms. He has a beautiful physique, and his skin is smooth and warm to my touch. I want to wrap my whole body around his and melt into him.

Julian briefly slows down and wraps his arm around the back of my thigh. He gently pushes it up toward me. The shift in position allows him to go even deeper inside of me, if it's even possible. It seems as if he can't get deep enough to satisfy whatever craving is consuming him, and I have a gut feeling he's fighting his own emotional demons. I'm completely wide open for him, and he looks down admiringly at my sex. I look up at him, and he slowly licks his lips in an incredibly erotic gesture. He's leaning forward, and I feel the weight of his strong body pressing hard into mine. As our bodies, slick with sweat from our passion, fuse together, I'm lost in the sense of how incredibly right this feels. His free hand finds mine, and he threads his fingers through mine and holds it tight. Every time Julian takes hold of my hands, it's with a possessiveness that suggests he's afraid I'll try to get away. He has made me feel so taken care of tonight that I want to give him the reassurance I think he needs.

"I'm here, right here," I say tenderly.

"Good, baby, because I need you to stay with me." Julian is looking at me so intensely I have to close my eyes before he sees every feeling I'm experiencing.

Oh shit.

If I had thought we had crossed some imaginary line before tonight, I was totally clueless. Now we're *really* over the line. I feel powerless to stop this speeding-bullet-train of a ride we're on, and I want him to take me to places my body has never been before.

With each thrust, Julian is breaking through the hard shell that has been wrapped around my broken heart for the last year. And although he's setting my body ablaze with his pounding rhythm and touch, it's the feelings he's igniting in my heart that are overtaking me. I can sense Julian is close to coming, and I delight in the moans and sounds of pleasure that are coming out of his mouth.

"I'm so close. I don't know if I can hold back much longer, and you haven't gotten off yet." Julian sounds apologetic.

"I'm so good. You've made me feel so good tonight, and I don't need to come again right now to feel amazing. You make me feel amazing, and I feel you everywhere."

I want him to believe me because it's true. I want him to let go and pour himself into me. He doesn't argue, and I start to feel the trembling in his body as his orgasm races through him.

Holy hell!

I'm not sure if it's what I just said to him or if it's just the rush of his orgasm, but when our eyes meet at the moment he starts pumping into me, the emotional connection between us tightens, and it feels as if all the air is sucked from my lungs. We have been using our eyes to communicate since the moment we met, and right now I'm able to see so many things in Julian's eyes. I see release. I see desire. I see need, and I swear I see something that resembles love. And I know, if he's looking closely, he's seeing the exact same things in my eyes. I truly feel like a piece of my soul just slipped into his soul and vice versa. He lays his body gently on mine and lets the last little bit of his orgasm fade. I realize I'm trembling as Julian finally pulls himself carefully out of me. As he gets up to throw the condom away, he asks me if I'm okay and if I need anything.

No, I think quietly to myself. *I'm definitely not okay. And yes, I do need something. I need to get the hell out of here.* I feel a panic attack coming on, and as he walks back toward the bed, I frantically start to think about what I need to do to get out of here. I don't want to even look at Julian now. I feel so vulnerable and raw, and I have no clue how to handle these feelings. I know in my gut this night is going to end very badly because I'm about to do something stupid. Julian seems a little bit oblivious to my discomfort. He lies down, pulls me tightly to him, my back to his front, and pulls the comforter back up over us. He finally notices I'm still shaking, and his hold on me tightens. He leans in and kisses my neck softly.

"Are you okay, Alexa? You're literally shaking." His tone is laced with worry.

Great, now it's obvious I'm flipping out. I can add embarrassed to the list of adjectives describing me now. I feel pathetic. Nothing bad just happened. Well, unless you count feeling *love* toward someone you hardly know as a bad thing. I've decided I'm not going to acknowledge what just happened between us. No freaking way.

"I'm great. We just fucked hard for hours. I'm worn out." I try to sound cool and collected, but I don't think I'm pulling it off. I really just sound lame. A flash of heat rushes through my body, and I feel suffocated by his embrace. I pull myself away and scoot off of the bed.

"I just need to get home and go to bed."

"Get your sexy ass back here in my bed. We can rest a little while before round two, or is it three?"

I'm not looking directly at Julian, but I can hear the playfulness in his voice, and I know he's smiling. "This game is over. I really just want to go." I say the words quietly yet with determination.

He reaches over to grab my hand, and I step quickly out of his reach. Julian sits up and looks at me like I'm crazy as I start putting my clothes back on. I turn my back to him so he can't see how shaken I still am by what just happened between us.

"Well this is kind of a first," he says to me in a tight voice.

"What, you bringing a chick home and fucking her thoroughly?" I desperately try to change the energy between us to something way less intense. Sarcasm usually works well for me.

"No," he hisses. "I've definitely brought a 'chick' home and fucked her thoroughly before. I'm referring to the part where you get up and run away right afterward. I mean, the 'chicks' I fuck thoroughly usually can't walk right afterward, never mind run. I'm usually kicking them out, not begging them to stay."

Wow, mission accomplished on the mood-changing plan. He sounds pissed and obviously doesn't like my choice of words. There is no going back now. "Well," I say weakly, "I'm not like most girls, and although my legs are a little shaky, I think I'm okay to walk."

I sit back down on the other side of his enormous bed. I can't even look at him as I slip on my sandal. I'm shaking so much I'm having a hard time buckling the strap, but I know it isn't from the sex.

I'm sitting here on the bed with my back to Julian, and hundreds of thoughts are running rapid fire through my brain. I wish I had the guts to tell him what's going on with me and why I'm acting like such a head case. I want to tell him this is the first time I've had sex since the last time with Brady, and considering how that went down, I'm handling this pretty well now. I want him to know this isn't about him at all. I want to tell him how amazing he makes me feel. I want to take my clothes back off and climb back into his warm bed and have him wrap his arms around me again. I want to not be scared.

Instead, I say nothing as I pick my wristlet up off the floor and stand up.

Julian's voice breaks through the clutter of my thoughts. He sounds cold and detached.

"That's true. You definitely are not like most girls." I take a deep breath and turn to face him but have a hard time looking directly at him. I really need to get out of here. It hits me all of a sudden I have no way to get home. Shit.

"I didn't really think this whole thing through very well. I didn't drive to the club so I need to call a cab to come pick me up."

He looks at me incredulously. "You're really leaving. Now? Like this?"

"Yes," I say to the ground.

Julian's tone is hard. "En serio, Alexa? I've been *in* you the entire night, and now you can't even look at me. Increíble." I note that when Julian gets really turned on, excited, or mad, he often slips into Spanish.

He gets out of bed and walks around to where I took his pants off an hour ago. He slips them on quickly and then does the same with his shirt. He walks over to what I'm assuming is his closet, goes inside, and comes out wearing a pair of flip-flops. He's all rumpled and looks so good. If he wasn't so pissed, I would mention it. I really didn't intend for him to get so mad. But he's definitely mad.

I assume that because he got dressed he's planning on taking me home himself, and to be perfectly honest, I'm not sure I want to be alone in a car with him. I have no grip on my emotions right now. I consider calling Marissa or Shannon but then decide against it. It's the middle of the night, and I don't want them out driving around. I also briefly consider calling Luke but quickly remember we're in a fight. Shit. I'm stuck.

"Julian," I say as nicely as I can. "It's really late. You don't need to take me all the way to Coconut Grove. I can catch a cab. It's really not a big deal."

I expect him to say something sarcastic about him not being the kind of guy that sends girls home in cabs, but he doesn't say anything at all. His silence is definitely worse. He just walks out of his bedroom and down the hall toward the front of the house. I have no choice but to follow him. There are a few dimly lit lights on around the house, but it's mostly dark, and I'm having a hard time reading his expression. Julian grabs his keys off the table in the foyer, opens the door, and walks out. He doesn't even hold the door for me.

Okay. So that's how it's gonna be.

Thank you very much, Julian, I think to myself. *It's easier for me to be bitchy and cold when you're acting like an asshole.* I know I'm justifying my actions, and a small spark of guilt runs through me. I did this. I made him act this way. Crap! I start to feel panicky again. This is exactly the kind of bullshit I've been trying to avoid. I don't want to feel guilty about anything and certainly don't want to be responsible for anybody's hurt feelings. Damn it! Now I'm mad at me too. How did I let this happen?

We stand there in silence and wait for the elevator. When the doors slide open, Julian steps in front and moves to the side. He won't even look at me. I get in and move toward the back. I stand behind him, and I can see how tense he is. His shoulders are tight, and he has a death grip on his keys. I think back to a few hours ago when we were in this elevator and his big soft hands were all over me. Wow. What a difference.

After what feels like forever, the doors open, and Julian walks out into a parking garage. I'm still following him like a scolded child, and I'm pretty pissed now, at him and at myself.

Fuck, I just wanted to go home. I have a hard time keeping up with him because one, he has really long legs and is walking quickly, two, my legs are still shaky from the awesome sex I just had, and three, these freaking sandals look great but aren't really comfortable. He stops next to a shiny, black convertible F-Type Jaguar, presses his key fob to open the doors, and gets in. I don't know why I'm surprised that he doesn't open my door, but I kind of am.

"I need your address," he says dryly as he leans over to program his NAV.

He backs out of the space carefully and heads toward the street. Once we're outside, he turns the volume up on the radio. I'm assuming it's so we don't have to talk. The drive to my house will take about twenty minutes at this time, and I welcome the sound of music, anything to break through the uncomfortable silence that's enveloping us. He looks straight ahead.

I look around the car. It's as sleek and sexy as the man driving it. Jaguar must have had this man in mind when they designed this car because it looks like it was made for him. I want to tell him how good he looks driving it but seriously don't think he's in the mood for any compliments from me. I look out of the window and watch the scenery fly by. He has the top up, but it's chilly at night in April. The tension in the car isn't helping either. I could talk, but I'm really freaking stubborn, and by this point I've convinced myself I didn't do anything wrong. So I say nothing. I wrap my arms around myself and try to warm up. Julian sees me out of the corner of his eye and pushes a button to turn the heat on.

"Thank you," I say quietly. He just nods.

I suddenly realize how tired I am. It's almost four in the morning, and I'm physically and emotionally exhausted. I lay my head back, close my eyes, and listen to the music. Wow. Tears form in my eyes, and I realize just how *not* okay I am. I thought I had come so far since everything happened with Brady. I realize now I'm still a mess. I also realize what a mess I've made of this night. I open my eyes and look over at Julian for the first time since we've gotten in the car. I quickly realize we have pulled up in front of my house. He is staring at me, and he doesn't look mad anymore. He actually looks sad and disappointed. I don't blame him. I'm certain this will be the end of us, so I decide to be brave and tell him what I'm feeling. I open my mouth to say how sorry I am for ruining a perfect night.

"Julian, you don't understand. Please let me explain—"

"Goodnight, Alexa." His tone says it all. I get the message loud and clear.

"Goodnight, Julian," I say softly. "Thanks for the ride."

I get out of the car and head up to my house. I don't look back, but I know he'll wait until I'm safely inside. I hear him pull away as I shut the door behind me and slide to the floor. Tears stream down my face. I totally fucked this up.

CHAPTER 13

I wake up around eleven on Sunday. What little sleep I got last night was fitful. I decide I'm going to spend most of the day in bed because I'm exhausted and because I'm avoiding my roommates. It's also raining pretty hard, so it's the perfect day to do nothing. I'm not on the schedule to work this weekend, which turns out to be a great thing. I've had close to no sleep and don't think I could sell a life jacket to a drowning man today. I feel like total shit. I can't believe I'm back here again. I have a one-night stand go bad, and I totally fall apart. According to Ellen, I've come so far since Brady's death. Not.

Marissa and Shannon are in the kitchen when I try to sneak in for a cup of coffee. They didn't know I was home and immediately want to know why I am and what the hell happened. I know they'll automatically think Julian did something to me, and I need to let them know he didn't do anything wrong.

"*I* happened, and I don't want to talk about it." I say it forcefully so they understand I'm serious. We've been friends for a really long time, and they both know me well enough to know when I say I don't want to talk about something, I won't.

I'm really not in the mood to be analyzed. I've been doing that to myself since I jumped out of Julian's bed last night and made him take me home. I can't stop thinking about every detail. It seriously was one of the most intense, passionate nights of my life, and I'm so disappointed in myself that I flipped out.

Shannon walks over to me and gives me a quick hug. "Cool. But you do know you're allowed to be happy, right? You deserve for good things to happen to you. Just saying."

Marissa adds, "If you change your mind, we're here to listen."

And I know they are. But that's part of the problem. As close as we are and as much as I trust them, I still haven't been completely honest with them about everything that happened between Brady and me right before he died. I haven't been honest with Luke either, and I pretty much tell him everything. I haven't even shared everything with Ellen. I think she knows I'm hiding stuff, but so far I've held her off. Sneaky me. I have my secrets, and I know they're tearing me apart. They have been for almost a year. I think about what Shannon said about deserving to be happy. I hear that from everyone. I wish I believed it were true.

Marissa tells me Luke texted her last night to see if I was okay. I knew he would. I haven't even turned my phone on since last night. I knew Luke would be trying to get ahold of me, and I'm not ready to deal with him. I'm still pissed. I'm also sure he went home with Lauren, and I really don't want to hear about that either. The realization hits me that once again

Julian and I didn't exchange contact information. I'm pretty sure I won't be hearing from him again after the way I acted last night, so I convince myself it really doesn't matter anyway.

I ask Marissa what she told Luke. "I didn't know what to say. I asked him why he was texting me, and he said you were mad at him and ignoring him. I figured it had something to do with Julian, so I just said you were fine and didn't want to talk to him. I guess I didn't lie."

I tell them about the fight we got into. They both look at me like they're not surprised at all. They also think he's uncharacteristically acting like a dick toward me and tell me to keep ignoring him until he apologizes.

"If I don't talk to him, he can't apologize." As soon as those words come out of my mouth, I feel sick to my stomach. It makes me think about how I wouldn't listen to Brady's apology. I get up and walk into my room to get my phone to call Luke. There are five missed calls from him and several more texts. They all basically say the same thing. *I'm sorry, please call me.*

Alexa: *Stop blowing up my phone*

He answers immediately.

Luke: *Answer it and I wouldn't have to*
Alexa: *I'm fine. Still mad though.*
Luke: *Figured. Sorry. Really. Don't want to be president of Dicksville*
Alexa: *haha. Ok, ur impeached.*
Luke: *TY. Dinner & Vampires tonight?*

Crap. We've been watching True Blood together almost every Sunday since it started. I just can't deal with Luke today.

He'll know something's wrong, and I'm not discussing this with him.

Alexa: ☹ *Sorry. Tired and cranky and just want to go to bed early. Early day tomorrow.*
Luke: *Really?*
Alexa: *Let's get a drink/dinner after work tomorrow or Tuesday.*
Luke: *K. But are you sure you're ok? Still mad?*
Alexa: *No. Not mad. Just tired. Call me tomorrow. Xo*
Luke: *Ok Hooka. Have a good day. Call me if you change your mind. Off tonight.*

I know he doesn't usually work on Sundays. I feel a little guilty blowing him off, but he's the one who's gone on the attack as far as Julian goes, and as much as I don't want to discuss this, I also know he won't want to hear about my passionate night and horrible aftermath. The whole thing makes me sad. I feel like I need to hide my feelings from Luke, and I haven't done that since the beginning of our relationship when I was totally crushing on him and didn't want him to know. I even used to tell him about what was happening between Brady and me. I try to cheer up by telling myself that after a few Julian-less days we'll be able to put this behind us and move on. Deep down I'm not so sure though.

I do exactly what I said I was going to do today. I lie in bed and feel sorry for myself. I turn off my phone after I text my sister and my parents that I'm alive and well and too busy working to call. More lies. Shannon and Marissa pretty much leave me alone after I finally tell them an abridged version of what happened last night. They just listen and don't really say much, sensing I don't want to analyze it anymore. They try to help by ordering Chinese food like we always do when one of us is feeling down. I have no appetite, so I just pick at some Lo Mien. I watch *True Blood* in my room. I dream about Sookie, Bill, and Eric all entangled in a bloody love triangle.

CHAPTER 14

My week at work starts out pretty slow. For one reason or another, Luke and I have been unable, or unwilling, to meet up for lunch or drinks. To be honest, I haven't made a real effort, and he says he's been busy. Lauren and I have been on the schedule together Monday and Tuesday, and we've had plenty of chances to talk about Luke. We haven't though, and that's fine with me. Things are okay between us, but I do feel some new tension, and I wonder how much Luke told her about our fight. I also wonder what really happened between her and Luke. But I won't ask. She tries to get information about Julian out of me, but I just tell her nothing happened. I don't trust she won't tell Luke before I have a chance to. That was supposedly one of the main reasons Luke was pissed at me, and I don't want it to happen again. I try to keep myself busy so the days pass quickly, but it's difficult. We only have a few units left to sell, and the constant rain we've had the last few days has kept traffic light.

The rain has also made it impossible to run, but I do manage to make it to the gym on Tuesday evening. I take a yoga class and try to center myself. It only helps a little. I basically want to be alone as I work through my feelings, and my roommates know me well enough to give me space. By Wednesday, I'm crawling out of my own skin, and I know I *need* to talk about how I'm feeling about Julian and about Luke even if I really don't want to. I have my normal Wednesday appointment with Ellen. I think about cancelling it but force myself to go. I know the reason I don't want to go is because I'm avoiding discussing why I freaked out at Julian's.

The minute Ellen sees me, she knows something is up. The reality is no matter how hard I try to hide my feelings, I really am an open book. The people close to me know when I'm upset no matter how hard I try to hide it. The problem is I won't admit it and don't share my feelings. I think it frustrates everyone.

"What's going on? You look very agitated." I guess she's just going to cut right to the chase.

"Well, everything is all fucked up, and I have myself to thank for it."

"Everything?" Okay. So I'm a little dramatic.

"Well, okay, not everything. But my love life, for lack of a better word, is pretty messed up. And Luke and I got into a fight, and it's totally messing with my head."

She decides to address the Julian issue first. "I take it you've seen Julian?"

"Yes, I saw Julian. I slept with Julian, and I fled his house like a thief in the night." I'm being serious, but Ellen can't help but laugh a little at my description. She probably just got a visual of me sneaking out through a window or something.

"Did something happen that caused you to *flee*?" She's poking fun at my choice of words.

"Yes. Something did. We had a great time. It was amazing, and he was amazing."

"Well then, I totally see your need to flee." I know I sound stupid. I've already played the night over and over in my head a million times, and it sounds ridiculous to me too.

"It was too intense, and it was way too emotional. It was just way too *everything*." I know when I say it like this Ellen will understand what happened and why I freaked out. She knows my capacity for emotional closeness is limited. "I just met this man, and I feel like he can look at me and see everything I'm thinking and feeling."

"I understand why that scares you. Did he say something that upset you?"

"No, and that's part of the problem. He says *all* the right things. If I could write a script of how I wanted a man to talk to me, it would have all the things Julian said to me on it. And it isn't even really what he says anyway. It's how he looks at me. How he touches me. How drawn I am to him." As I'm saying these words, I'm thinking about Julian touching me, and I feel an ache at the thought it may not happen again.

"Did you have this kind of connection with Brady? Maybe that's what's making this so intense and hard for you to handle."

"No, Ellen, and that's another issue. I didn't feel this way with Brady. Not at the beginning, not in the middle, and certainly not at the end. I thought I loved him, I really did, but I was always searching for this kind of connection with him. I searched for a year, and I turned myself inside and out to find it. And it was *never* there. I thought I loved him, but he didn't ever give me what I really needed."

Wow. Where did that come from? As the words pour out of me, I come to the shocking realization that I'm feeling more intense feelings for Julian after a few weeks than I did for a man I spent a year with. I'm confused by this epiphany. I look up at Ellen, and she's smiling at me.

"Lexie, I'm not going to get all shrinky on you, but you have no idea how proud I am of you for realizing that and admitting it out loud, even if you didn't mean to." She knows me so well. It all came out before I could stop it. I shift away from Brady and bring the discussion back to Julian.

"How can this be happening?" I want her to tell me it's possible for me to have already developed this intense connection to Julian and that I'm not imagining it. I want to know this stuff really does happen. Love at first sight. I know she won't though. She'll spin it and give me something to think about.

"I have no idea what your connection with Julian is like. But despite your unwillingness to admit it, you're a good judge of character and you do know the difference between reality and fantasy. You need to trust yourself. That's all. Just trust yourself."

"I'm trying, Ellen. I really am."

"I know you are. Keep it up." We sit there quietly for a minute as I absorb my revelation.

"Do you want to talk about the fight you and Luke got into? You've never mentioned fighting with him before."

"Because we never fight. We've always gotten along. We can get on each other's nerves, but we've never tried to hurt each other before." I tell her the whole story from beginning to end, and she just listens and nods her head a little. When I finish, I totally expect her to be on my side and see things exactly like I do. I don't expect her to justify his actions.

"Has it really never occurred to you that Luke's feelings for you are more than friendly and that maybe he's acting this way because he's jealous of what he sees happening between you and Julian?" The way she says it makes me feel like she thinks I'm a blind idiot. I want to say no, he was just being a dick, but I don't.

Okay, I'll try to explain this again. My response is defensive.

"Everyone keeps bringing this up lately. Aside from the first time we hooked up, *six* years ago, Luke has never tried to change the nature of our relationship. Actually, he was the one who decided we were going to be *just* friends. He's dated a million girls, and he introduced me to Brady. If he wanted me, why in the world would he just not say so? I've been right in front of him for years now."

"I can't answer that, but from everything you've told me about Luke and your relationship, it's obvious he has very real, very deep feelings for you. I'm just taking a guess, but I think he might be feeling threatened by what he sees happening between you and Julian. He might be thinking he's going to lose you. You and Luke have been through a lot together, and I imagine he feels a bit protective of you."

I look up at the clock before I answer and see my time is up. Good. I think we have covered enough ground here today. I get myself ready to leave, and Ellen offers more food for thought before I walk out the door. She knows I'm deep in my head right now and processing all of this. This is a great opportunity for her to plant another seed.

"You're going to have to reconcile this soon. You're not going to be able to ignore it, no matter how much you want to. It appears you're having very strong feelings for two men, and if you don't get honest about how you feel about it, and them, you're going to end up without either." I think about that for a minute and want to say she's wrong. Julian isn't in the picture anymore. She cuts me off.

"And, Lexie, Julian isn't out of the picture either. He'll be back." Good God. Can everyone read my damn mind?

I think about everything Ellen and I discussed today and have a restless night of sleep as a result. I wake up tired and cranky and with an impending sense of doom. I decide I'm going to force Luke to talk to me today. I can't or won't do anything about the Julian situation, but I can try to fix what happened between Luke and me. I remember he did apologize and offer to talk on Sunday and that I was the one who said no. I wasn't ready then, and I'm still not sure I am now. I can't see how I'll be able to avoid telling him about what happened with Julian, and I don't want to discuss it with him. He's made no real other attempt to get together this week, and we've only texted a few times. We didn't say much. I sense he's avoiding me the same way I'm avoiding him, and it makes me sad. This has to stop now. My plan is to guilt him into meeting with me tonight. I know he worked last night, so I wait until a decent hour before I text him.

Alexa: *Callahan's for a drink before work tonight? 6:30? Plz.*

Luke always has his phone in his hand and replies immediately.

Luke: *Ok. Miss you*
Alexa: *Miss you too. See you later. Have a good day.*
Luke: *You too Hooka*

That's my Luke.

CHAPTER 15

The weather has cleared up by Thursday, and because I've had some drop-ins, the morning has passed pretty quickly. Right before lunch, two of my bosses come and find me and ask if they can take me to lunch. Mark Sullivan is W&M's regional VP, and Andrea Lewis is the director of sales for South Florida. I tell them I have a follow-up appointment with a serious buyer at one thirty, and they suggest we stay close by. I also remind them I'm the only salesperson in the office today because Lauren and Ramon are at a sales seminar downtown. We decide to go to Arnie's Cafe in the building adjacent to ours. I grab my purse, and as I follow them to the elevators, I start feeling anxious about lunch. This is probably only the third time in a year that I've had lunch with either of them, and the other two times were with a large group of people. They're great to work for, but they're definitely not on my level, and I never see them socializing with their staff. I give myself a pep talk on the ride down. I've been kicking ass at work though, so I figure it can't be about anything bad. They both seem like they're in great moods and are really chatty as we walk the short distance to the little café. Because it's a little before noon and the lunch crowds have not all come out yet, we're able to grab one of the few tables outside. We all comment on how great it is to be outside after spending the last four days inside. It rains plenty in South Florida, but not so hard and not for so many days in a row. We all order our drinks and meals, and Mark gets right to the point.

"Alexa, Andrea and I wanted to tell you what a great job you've done in Tower Three. We know you probably know what the numbers are, but you've sold the most units by far in that building." I do know the numbers and feel great I'm being recognized for my hard work.

"You've been getting tons of great feedback from your clients, so it isn't just the numbers talking." Andrea is more the people person, and Mark more the numbers guy, so it doesn't surprise me she's the one to point this out.

Andrea continues. "We think we should be closed out here in the next six weeks, and it looks like The Promenade will be ready to start selling by mid-July."

I know the company has been working around the clock to get the building ready to sell starting in July, and I'm happy to hear it's going to happen. I've secretly been hoping I'll be moved to The Promenade when the sales office opens. I love working so close to home, but the property in Sofi is going to be so beautiful. The units are total luxury, with some being designed to sell for several million dollars. I could sell half as many units there and make three times the money I'm making now. I'm embarrassed to admit it, but my mind flits quickly to the thought of how many new pairs of shoes I'll be able to buy.

"We want to send you over there. This is a huge opportunity for you. You're so young and relatively new to the company. We tried to figure out a reason why we shouldn't send you over, but we couldn't come up with a valid one." She's smiling at me as she talks.

I smile back. This is awesome! "Thank you both. I know what a great opportunity it is, and I promise you it won't be a mistake. I'm ready to do this."

Mark speaks up. "Good, then it's decided. We want you to go, and you want to go. It's a win-win situation for all of us. You should plan on going in the near future. We'll send you over some specifics about compensation and schedule in the next few weeks. We're still ironing out all the details." That's Mark. Short, sweet, and to the point.

They start talking about the property, and I'm getting more excited as lunch goes on. I listen intently and ask a lot of questions. My mood, which has been crappy since the weekend, is definitely changing for the better. Work can do that for me. Even when things were falling apart with Brady, I was able to focus on work and do a great job.

My happy mood slowly starts to disappear as quickly as it came the minute Andrea brings up the Bellavista II, the newest Bywater development. She starts talking about the competition and how our product will stack up against theirs. I'm lost in my own thoughts for a minute, thinking about my last, and probably only, visit inside a unit there when Andrea's next comment yanks me back to reality.

"Speaking of our competition and Bywater, here come the Bauer brothers now. What a strange coincidence."

Oh no! Did she just say Bauer brothers? Maybe it's Julian's dad and uncle. Please! She is facing the opposite direction from me at the table, so I would have to turn to see who she's talking about, and I'm not about to draw any attention to myself. Well, it turns out I don't need to turn around to see which Bauers she's referring to. I feel Julian's energy as he approaches the table, and I smell his scent before he reaches us. I don't know if he knows it's me, and I'm freaking out about how he's going to react when he sees me. My mind is racing, and I'm feeling hot and itchy. I wonder if he'll acknowledge he knows me, or if he'll pretend we don't know each other. Andrea and Mark both stand up and greet Julian and his brother, Danny. I stay seated and don't turn around. I know it's rude, but I really don't care. I'm not able to pull off calm, cool, and collected. I stay silent until Andrea introduces me, forcing me to stand up and turn around.

"Julian and Danny, this is Alexa Reed, one of our top salespeople at The Towers. We were just telling her we're sending her over to The Promenade soon so she can steal some of your prospects away." Well that was kind of an overshare. I haven't even processed this new job situation yet, and Andrea has already shared it with Julian of all people.

And just like that I'm face to face with Julian. He's standing a few feet away from me, but my physical reaction to him makes it feel like he's *on* me. I mentally will my body to stay put and not fling itself into Julian's arms like it wants to. I'm so drawn to this man. He looks hot. He's dressed very causally in jeans, khaki-colored Salvatore Ferragamo loafers, and a form-fitting, sea-foam-green Polo shirt. As usual, everything fits perfectly and shows off his beautiful body. I quickly think about how I look and am glad I'm wearing what I am. I'm dressed like I'm happy and in a good mood. Maybe he won't see I've been miserable since he dropped me off a few days ago.

I have a coral-colored pencil skirt on that hits my leg mid-thigh. It has cute, lace, circle patterns on it and is very figure flattering. I'm wearing a crisp, white, sleeveless oxford shirt on top and Tory Burch nude wedges. My hair is loose and flowing. It's a very different look than anything Julian has seen me in, and I see approval in his eyes as he sweeps them over me. When his gaze reaches my feet, I see a small little smile flash across his face. He's checking out my shoes. They're high and sexy and expensive. I love it that I know what he's smiling about. It makes me feel close to him. When he looks up, I'm almost knocked over by the searing look in his eyes, and I wonder if anybody else sees it.

"Hi, Alexa. It's nice to see you again." Okay, so he is going to acknowledge he knows me. He doesn't reach out to shake my hand though and doesn't offer up how we know each other. I wonder if he avoids touching me because of the reaction it causes in both of us. It may be hard to hide. "This is my brother, Danny." Danny sticks his hand out and flashes me a smile that clearly is genetic. He's almost as good looking as Julian, and the family resemblance is strong. You can immediately tell they're brothers. I find myself wondering what Julian's parents look like. They must be gorgeous to have produced two such beautiful sons.

"It's nice to meet you, Alexa. Congratulations on the new job. Hopefully you aren't too good at it; we have a lot of inventory to sell." His smile is friendly and warm, and I can tell Danny also shares his big brother's witty conversational skills and flirtatious nature.

"It's nice to meet you as well, Danny." Julian glances down as I put my hand into Danny's, and I want to scream at him that I want *him* to be touching me. "I plan on selling out The Promenade in record time, but I'm sure there are plenty of customers to go around." This gets a laugh from all of them.

As Danny is talking to me, I notice Julian reaching into his pocket and pulling out a card case. He opens it and hands each of us one of his cards. I'm impressed with his quick thinking. We're finally going to exchange contact information. The fact that he has been inside of me and still doesn't have my number is a bit unnerving, and I'm thrilled he seems to want to rectify that. This means he wants to talk.

"Do you have a card, Alexa? When you get down to the beach, we can meet, and I can introduce you to condo life on Sofi." I just nod my head. I'm shaking a little as I reach into my purse and pull a card out. Our fingers touch when he takes the card from my hand, and as usual I feel the touch everywhere. By the look in Julian's eyes, he does too. That is why he didn't shake my hand earlier. It's such a giveaway. I'm glad he's taken my card; I didn't want to be the one to make the next move.

"I don't know if I like that idea, Julian. You wouldn't be trying to take her away from us, would you?" Andrea is totally joking and has no idea there's a hidden meaning in Julian's response.

"I don't think you need to worry, Andrea. Something about Alexa tells me she doesn't do anything that she doesn't want to." Everyone laughs, and I see a little smirk on Julian's face that he isn't even trying to hide. *Really? What a smartass.* I just smile and don't say much else. The rest of them wrap up their conversation, and Julian and Danny say goodbye and apologize for interrupting our lunch. Julian doesn't make eye contact with me as he starts to leave. He's deliberately messing with me, and I question what his next move will be.

Fortunately, I only have to wait a few hours before that question is answered. I just get back from a very promising showing and check my phone to see if I have any missed calls. I'm hoping there's one from Julian now that he finally has my number. There are no calls, but there's a text from an unknown number. I'm excited to see a text but would've rather heard his voice. I read it, and my heart melts.

Julian: *It's Julian. You can explain now.*

The first thing I do is program his name into my contact list. Then I reread his text. I understand its meaning immediately. One of the last things I told him on Saturday was that I wanted to explain my actions. He wasn't ready to hear anything from me then, and that's a reaction I can relate to. Unfortunately, now I'm not sure I can say the words. All of my reasons and justifications for running away from his condo seem immature and overly dramatic. I'm not sure what I want to say. I know I better say something though. Because he texted instead of called, I feel it's appropriate to write my feelings down instead of saying them. I know I can't send everything I want to say via text, so I open my computer and start to compose an e-mail. I write down how I was feeling that night and what was going on in my head. After I write a few lines down, I realize none of the words are coming out right. I'm having a really hard time articulating the reality that what happened between us invoked the most intense emotional response I've ever had. I want to tell him I'm afraid I'm already falling for him and scared he could never possibly feel that way about someone like me. But, that sounds way too revealing. It also sounds a little desperate, crazy, and pathetic. Shit. What the hell am I going to say?

I sit and stare at my blank screen for about ten minutes before I finally decide I'll just send him the lyrics from a song that sums up my feelings perfectly. I know if I do this I'm allowing myself to be extremely vulnerable, but I feel like I have no other options. I'm getting a second chance here, and I don't want to blow it. I haven't been able to stop thinking about Julian, and I really need to see if I can salvage whatever was happening between us. This is a huge step for me. I reply to his text first.

Alexa: *Are you sure?*
Julian: *Claro que sí.*

Of course he does. He wouldn't have asked, right?

Alexa: *Check your email in a few minutes. Too much to text.*

I get his e-mail address off of his card and cut and paste the lyrics to Again by Need to Breathe and highlight the words that mean the most. I hear Ellen's voice in my head, "Just trust yourself, Alexa," and I hit send.

To: Julian Bauer—JPB@BWproperties.com
From: Alexa Reed—AReed@W&Minvestmentgroup.com
Subject: Sometimes I have a hard time saying the words ...
This says it perfectly for me.

I don't want to stay, I don't want to fall.
I don't want to take; I don't want to lose it all.
Maybe I'm a fake, maybe you're a lie.
Maybe our last chance died with last night.

ALEXA

About ten minutes pass before he responds by text. I know because I'm watching the clock.

Julian: *Got it. We need to talk.*
Julian: *Or should I respond in kind?*
Alexa: *Sure.*
Julian: *Check your email.*

I'm dying to see what he sends, and I'm freaking out because the lyrics to Again were pretty serious. As I'm thinking about all the songs he could send that deal with a crazy chick, an e-mail from Julian pops up.

To: Alexa Reed—AReed@W&Minvestmentgroup.com
From: Julian Bauer—JPB@BWproperties.com
Subj: My Deep Thoughts

When I walk in the spot, this is what I see
Everybody stops and they're staring at me,
I got passion in my pants, And I ain't afraid to show it (show
it, show it, show it)
I'm sexy and I know it ...

JULIAN

I can't believe he just sent me lyrics to the song I'm Sexy and I Know It by LMFAO. I have to admit it's pretty funny, but I'm disappointed because I was being totally open and serious, and clearly he thinks this is a joke. I pick up my phone to text him back. There's no way I'm going to let him know I'm upset by his response. Obviously he wants to keep this conversation light.

Alexa: *you're sexy. Glad you know it.*

Julian: *Not funny? Thought it would make you laugh.*

Alexa: *It was funny.*

Julian: *But?*

Alexa: *But nothing. It was funny.*

Julian: *You sound disappointed.*

Alexa: *I'm texting. How do I "sound" any way at all?*

Julian: *Maybe I want you to be disappointed.*

What the hell is Julian doing? I'm not sure where he's trying to steer this conversation, but if he wants to keep it light, I'm going to do the same. I've already played my vulnerability card, and I'm no longer in a sharing kind of mood.

Alexa: *Why would I be? it's a good thing to have a healthy self-esteem.*

Julian: *?*

Alexa: *You think you're sexy …*

Julian: *You don't?*

Alexa: *Think you're sexy? Yes Julian, I already conceded that point. Read text above.*

Julian: *you're trying to change the subject.*

Alexa: *What subject?*

Julian: *last Sat.*

Alexa: *You changed subject with song choice.*

Julian: *Guess I did. Tried to lighten the mood. You don't do "feelings" well.*

Ouch. That kind of hurts. It's true, but I'm not sure how I feel about him calling me out on it.

Alexa: *Mission accomplished.*
Julian: *Mad?*
Alexa: *No.*

I'm not giving into him. I'm an idiot. Why did I send that damn song? I need to send another to counteract the damage I just did to my pride.

Alexa: *Glad we got that all cleared up. Gotta get back to work. Nice to see you today.*
Julian: *Cleared up? I'm more confused than before. We're not finished here yet.*
Julian: *Sorry I didn't respond the way you wanted me to.*

Now I'm getting mad. Does he really need to make me feel more stupid?

Alexa: *Really? And you think you know what I want?*
Julian: *I had no problem figuring out what you wanted last Sat.*

Ugh. I don't know how to respond to that, so I don't. I'm not feeling witty at the moment, and this isn't going the sexual route. A minute or so passes before he responds.

Julian: *Hello?*
Alexa: *Yes.*
Julian: *The song you sent was great. Didn't respond in kind.*
Julian: *I have no problem telling you how I feel in my own words. Do you want to hear it?*

My heart starts to beat rapidly, and I swear my palms start to sweat. Do I?

Alexa: *I guess.*
Julian: *Stop freaking out. It's all good, baby. Let's talk. Tonight. Face to Face.*
Julian: *I actually hate texting. You say where.*

How does he know I'm freaking out? Damn. I can't even hide my feelings from him over a text.

Alexa: *My place. 8. Need address again?*
Julian: *7? Dinner? No to address.*
Alexa: *Can't...Have plans. 8*
Julian: *Plans? Date?*

It is obvious Julian doesn't like to be told no. I'm sure he's used to getting his way, and I'm sure women have no problem changing their plans for him all the time. I'm not going to. As much as I'm dying to see Julian, I don't want to seem too anxious, and I also really need to talk to Luke.

Alexa: *Plans. See you at 8...my house*

The fact he's so anxious to see me has me feeling so much better. He's also being rather bossy.

Julian: *Cancel plans.*
Alexa: *Bossy much?*

I'm not going to tell him I'm meeting with Luke for a quick drink. Julian has no clue what happened between us, and I'm not going to tell him either. I've never kept Luke separate from other men in my life, but something deep inside tells me I need to now.

Julian: *Yes. Used to calling the shots. You know that. Plans must be important.*

I do know that about him, and I find it incredibly hot. I want to tell him that nothing feels as important as seeing him, but I do also want to see Luke, and I already made plans. But, I don't say any of that. When I don't respond right away to his last text, Julian must get the message that I'm not going to give him any additional information about my plans.

Julian: *See you at 8 then.*
Alexa: *Hasta luego, Julian*
Julian: *Hasta luego, Corazón.*

Well that went pretty well. Now I just have to figure out how not to freak out for the next four and a half hours. I get back to work, but to be honest, I don't get anything done. I can't stop thinking about Julian coming over tonight. I told him to come to my place because I want to feel like I have some control if things go badly again. Translation: if I freak out.

I text Luke to tell him I'll see him at Callahan's at six-thirty and also send a group text to Marissa and Shannon to let them know I'm meeting Luke for a drink and then Julian at our house after. I'm so caught up in my man drama I forget to even tell them about my promotion.

Shannon: *Busy girl. Sure you can keep all your men straight?*
Shannon: *Have fun, cya later. btw at C's tonight.*

Marissa: *K. I'm going out too. Be home late.*
Alexa: *Crap. I'm going to be alone with him?*
Shannon: *You will be ok. Relax.*
Marissa: *Have fun!*

It looks like Julian and I will have the house to ourselves. I can't decide if that's a bad or a good thing. All I know is that I have massive butterflies in my stomach.

The afternoon flies by, and soon it's six o'clock and time to go. I've been waiting for an e-mail from a client, so I check my messages one last time before I go. I see a new message from Julian in my inbox, and I can't click on it fast enough. He sent me the lyrics for the whole song, and like me, highlighted the most meaningful part.

To: Alexa Reed—AReed@W&Minvestmentgroup.com
From: Julian Bauer—JPB@BWproperties.com
Subj: Until I get to say my own words

When I first saw you standing there,
You know, was a little hard not to stare.
So nervous when I drove you home,
I know, being apart's a little hard to bear.

"All or Nothing"—Theory of A Deadman

BTW, you looked hot today. Love the shoes. See you soon.

JULIAN

I can't keep the huge smile off of my face. Could this really be possible? Julian seems to really just *get* me. He took the time to find a song that would help me see how he's feeling. I can't ask for anything better. Before I shut my computer down, I reply so he knows I saw this.

To: Julian Bauer—JPB@BWproperties.com
From: Alexa Reed—AReed@W&Minvestmentgroup.com
Subj: 100% Perfect . . .

BTW you always look hot. Curious what the P stands for? Tell me at 8.

ALEXA

I shut everything off, lock up, and head out the door. I text Luke on my way to my car.

Alexa: *Just left, be there in 25.*
Luke: *K. Just got here.*

CHAPTER 16

Callahan's is a restaurant and bar located in between our houses. Luke lives in Coral Gables, and we're in Coconut Grove. We found this place a year ago and hang out here regularly. The bartenders and staff all know us, and the food is pretty good. On my way there, I realize how hungry I am. My stomach was so nervous after seeing Julian that I didn't finish my lunch. I see Luke's car when I pull into the parking lot. I also see Lauren's. I can't believe he invited her here tonight. He obviously doesn't want to talk about what happened the other night even though we really need to. He did apologize for being such an ass, but there's definitely still tension between us. He's using Lauren as a buffer, and I'm kind of pissed now. Not only is there tension between Luke and me, but this thing with Lauren is making me not feel so warm and fuzzy toward her. We're pretty good friends and coworkers, and we really need to get along. Well, at least for another month until I move locations. That's another thing. I wanted to talk to Luke about this promotion, but I'm not ready to share it with Lauren. She's great at her job, but she may not be as excited about my new opportunity as I am. I push all those thoughts aside, put on my happy face, and head into the restaurant. This has been a great day so far, and I don't want anybody or anything ruining it.

It is pretty quiet for a Thursday evening, and I see Luke and Lauren at a table near the bar right away. They have their backs turned and can't see me. They're sitting very close to each other, and their body language tells me they have crossed over the "just friends" line. All of a sudden, I feel like an intruder and like I'll be interrupting them if I walk over. I'm struck by how unfamiliar these feelings are. I've never felt uncomfortable around Luke and any of his girls, ever. I duck into the bathroom before they see me and try to decide if I'm going to stay or send a text, sneak out, and cancel the plans. I choose the latter and walk quickly to my car. I pull out of the parking lot and around the corner before I send the text.

Alexa: *Change of plans. Something came up. Sorry. See you this weekend?*
Luke: *Really? What?*

I'm not surprised that he's questioning me. I know my behavior toward him isn't the norm either. What surprises me is how easily I'm lying to him. I feel justified though. He chose to change our plans when he knows we need to talk. I try to think of a quick, believable response. I can't say it has anything to do with work because Lauren might figure that out. I don't want to say I don't feel well either because I was fine a half hour ago. I go with the next thing that pops in my mind.

Alexa: *Marissa just texted. Needs me to bring something to her parents' house for her.*

Luke: *Um ok. Can't wait until after? I have to be at work by 9:00. Can't stay long.*

I'm not sure why he's making a big deal out of this, unless he wants me to see him with Lauren. He clearly was not interested in any kind of alone time with me. I decide I'm probably right, but I can't let him know I know she was there.

Alexa: *Nope. Sorry. Going now. ttyl*
Luke: *Ok.*

That's it. Just okay? He never responded to me asking about hanging out this weekend. Oh. Whatever.

My next text is to Julian.

Alexa: *Plans cancelled. I'm heading home. Come by earlier if you want.*

His reply comes right away.

Julian: *Glad you realized I'm more important. I'm nearby. Have you eaten?*
Alexa: *haha. No, haven't eaten. Starving too.*
Julian: *I'll feed you. Cuban ok?*
Alexa: *I love Cuban (s)*

I can't help myself and threw that in there.

Julian: *hmm ... Sounds promising. What do you want?*
Alexa: *Ropa Vieja and a café con leche. Por favor.*

Julian: *Got it. See you in a few.*

I have no idea what Julian is doing so close by, but he pulls up less than a half hour after I told him to come over. With food. It's only seven-fifteen, and I haven't even had a chance to change out of my work clothes yet. I'm sifting through my mail when I hear the doorbell ring. My heart starts to beat rapidly, and I start feeling anxious, as if I'm meeting a blind date. I open the door and see Julian standing there with a few bags in his hands. He has a huge smile on his face. He has changed into a cerulean-blue T-shirt, loose-fitting khaki shorts, and Reef flip-flops. He looks so young and relaxed, and I love seeing him like this. It immediately puts me at ease. I almost forget that we're planning on having a serious conversation tonight.

"Come in. Food smells great." I step to the side and let him enter. He leans down and kisses me on the forehead as he walks by. It's a friendly kiss and not exactly the contact I'm craving. I guess we have some stuff to work out first. I lead him toward the kitchen, and he puts the bags down on the counter.

Julian starts to take the food out of the bags and turns his head toward me. "Paul."

"Paul?" I have no idea what he's talking about.

"You asked me what the P stood for. Paul."

I smile brightly at him. "Sorry, I forgot. I was distracted by the food." And by his hotness I might add.

"Just the food?" Julian is acting so relaxed and playful and already looks at home in my kitchen. I stop for a moment and let the warm feeling settle in. I'm going to try my very best to enjoy his company. I raise my eyebrows at him and shrug my shoulders. He knows he's a huge distraction to me.

I get some plates and utensils out and bring them to the table. We have an eat-in kitchen, so the table is right there. I grab the food Julian has taken out and bring it over as well. I notice there's only one coffee there and ask him what he wants to drink.

"We have beer, wine, water, Diet Coke, milk ..." He laughs at my waitress impression.

"Just water please." I grab two bottles out of the refrigerator and sit down. He follows me.

"Do you have a middle name, Alexa?"

"Rose."

"A beautiful name for a beautiful girl." Julian looks up from his food and smiles at me when I thank him for the compliment. It's the same thing he said to me when I told him my name the first night we met.

"I've heard your friends refer to you with different nicknames. Which do you prefer? Alexa, Lexie, Lex, Alex?" I'm impressed he's paid attention.

"Well, Alexa always works. I'm kind of picky about who calls me Lexie or Lex, and nobody that knows me calls me Alex. I think you need to really know someone before you call them by a nickname. It's a personal thing." As I ramble this off, I realize I'm making it sound like I'd rather Julian not call me a nickname.

And that's exactly the way he takes it. "Okay, Alexa it is."

"You can call me anything you want. We have definitely gotten personal."

I try and play it off, but I can see he's a little offended. I change the conversation, and pretty soon we're talking about our favorite Cuban dishes and which restaurants we think make the best food. As the time passes, I'm less and less anxious and actually start to believe I can undo the craziness that happened last weekend. I wonder if we're even going to talk about it at all. We finish eating, clean up the kitchen, and go into the living room. Julian sits down in one of the two armchairs there. It's the one place I can't sit next to him, and my heart sinks when I decipher the meaning. He doesn't want to be close to me. I ask him to give me a minute so I can go change out of my work clothes. Plus, I need a minute to regroup. I change into a pair of khaki, drawstring shorts and a black, V-neck T-shirt, take a few deep breaths, and head back out to the living room.

I sit down on the couch opposite the chair where he is and tuck my feet up under me. I've made sure I'm as far away as possible. My walls are up, and I'm sure my posture is defensive. I can feel the tension seeping out of me. He lifts his eyebrows and shakes his head but doesn't move or say anything about where I'm sitting.

"This is a nice house. How long have you lived here?"

"Shannon, Marissa, and I moved in about a year and a half ago. Shannon's uncle owns it, and when the last renters moved out, he offered us an amazing deal. I actually feel bad because I know he could get so much more than we pay. It's the perfect size and location for us, and we all love living here."

He asks me about Shannon and Marissa, and I tell him we were roommates in college and have been best friends for years. We make small talk about where they work and if they're single, etc. I'm not sure he really cares about my friends, but it's pleasant small talk. For the first hour, I was okay with the slow pace of our conversation, but as time passes, I'm finding I want to talk about us. I'm still unnerved by the fact that Julian is sitting across the room instead of next to me.

After about a half hour, Julian gets up and asks me where the bathroom is. I point to the hall and tell him it's the first door on the left. When he comes back, he finally sits next to me on the couch. He's closer, but not close enough, and aside from the kiss on my forehead when he walked in, he has not touched me. It's been close to 130 hours since he's touched me. I counted when he went to the bathroom. What's bothering me most is that he doesn't seem to need to touch me like the first two times we were together.

He stares at me intensely. "Your eyes are so beautiful. They kind of remind me of my own." I can't help but smirk as he says this.

"Hmm. That's an interesting compliment."

"You know what I mean; the color, it's the same as mine." As I stare back into his eyes, I do see they're the exact same color as mine. They're a dark, forest green and virtually absent of any other shades. His lashes are longer and thicker than mine, which is just totally unfair. I tell him that I noticed the similarities the first time I met him.

Julian closes his eyes for a minute, takes a deep breath, opens his eyes again, and then really, and I mean really, fixes his gaze on me. In his eyes, I see an invitation and a dare. He's daring me to really see him. It's like he's opened himself up to me and is giving me a quick peek into his soul. I try to take it all in and memorize everything I see. I see lust, and I see the desire and determination of a man who's used to getting what he wants. I see the skepticism and wariness of someone who has a very hard time trusting people. I see the pain of someone who has been deeply hurt by someone he loved. I see the same things I saw the night we slept together. I feel like I'm looking into a mirror, and I wonder if he sees the same emotions reflected back. I'm drowning in his eyes, and I have to look away.

I hear Julian sigh and think to myself, *Here it comes.* Time to get down to business. At once I can feel the whole direction of the evening change and set out on a different course. It's the proverbial shifting of gears.

"Are you ready to talk now? Because we don't have to, if you really don't want to."

I don't think I've done anything tonight that has indicated an unwillingness to talk, and I tell him so.

"Maybe not. But it's so obvious to me you become extremely uncomfortable when the energy between us becomes emotionally charged. Can we talk about that?"

"What is there to talk about? You're right, and there's no reason for me to deny it. You have witnessed my "uncomfortableness" up-close."

"Why?"

"Why what?"

"Why are you so uncomfortable around me? Or is it me? I'm assuming it is, but maybe it's just the way you are." I want to tell him yes, Julian, it's you and these intense feelings you're stirring up in me that are freaking me out. Oh yeah, and it's also because I'm a little screwed up in the emotional department too. But I refer to the song I sent him instead.

"I thought you understood why I felt the way I do. I sent you those lyrics to help explain." I think about the song for minute and wonder if he really got the meaning like he said he did.

"Those lyrics tell me you're scared of getting hurt. Have I done something to make you think I'm going to hurt you?"

"No, Julian. You've been great. Really. But I don't know that the average person sets out to intentionally hurt another person. It just happens, and I've been hurt enough to last a lifetime."

That last part slips out, and I want to kick myself. Fuck! Fuck! Fuck! Why did I say that?

Julian tilts his head and asks quietly, "Who hurt you so badly, Alexa?"

I think about my words carefully before I spit them out. I know I can say enough to satisfy his curiosity without letting him in too close. I'm super good at doing that. "An ex-boyfriend. It started great, and it ended very badly. But that's a story for another time. We were talking about us."

The look in his eyes tells me he isn't at all satisfied with my answer, but he doesn't press me further. Bullet dodged.

"Plus," I continue, "You did tell me you were going to let me know how *you* were feeling."

Julian leans his head back on the couch and looks straight ahead. "Do you know that I haven't touched you tonight because I can't focus on anything else when I'm touching you? Do you know I haven't been able to stop thinking about your lips and your tongue and your beautiful body since Saturday? I had to will my body to stay still and not pick you up and hold you when I saw you at lunch today. I didn't even trust myself to shake your hand. I'm aching to be close to you, to be inside of you. This physical connection between us could consume me."

Okay, that's one of the most erotic things a man has ever said to me. My stomach flutters, and I feel a simmering heat rising up slowly through my body. I want to tell him I feel the exact same way and that I want nothing more than for him to touch me, but I sense he's trying to make a point.

"I'm not really sure what it is, but something about you makes me feel like I've known you forever, and I know you know this thing that's happening between us isn't just physical. And I think that's what's freaking you out, and to be honest, it's freaking me out a little too. It's very intense, and I'm okay admitting to you that I'm a bit overwhelmed by it all. I just wish you would have stayed and talked to me about it. About how you were feeling."

As I sit there and listen to Julian give me his take on what's happening between us, I'm in awe of his ability to be so honest and put himself out there. I draw on his strength and try to reciprocate.

"I'm sorry I left the way I did. I regretted it the minute I told you I wanted to leave. But I couldn't talk about what I was feeling then, and I'm not sure I can now either. Again, that's why I sent you that song. But you need to know it was an incredible night for me, and it was wrong of me to ruin it for both of us."

He's looking at me now, and instead of averting my eyes, I keep looking at him and continue. I'm doing pretty well here. "I have a very hard time letting people get close to me, and the walls I've built around my heart are very high and very strong. You have to decide if you want to deal with that because I'm not sure I can let you in."

He answers immediately. "I have no choice but to deal. I saw that this week, when I was away from you. You need to decide if you really want me to get in, because I will. I have to. I want you in my life."

Julian didn't lie when he said he had no problem expressing his feelings, and I'm so moved by his words. I just told this amazing man I had some serious trust issues, and he responded by telling me I needed to get ready because he was going to change all of that. I'm not even sure what to say, so I don't say anything. Instead I lean over and place my lips softly on his. The kiss that follows is tender, sensual, and all lips. At first Julian keeps his hands at his side, but it quickly becomes too much, and he pulls me in close by putting his hands on the side of my face. I open my eyes and see that his are closed. His brow is furrowed as if he's concentrating really hard on something. His breathing starts to get heavier as he slips his tongue inside my mouth. He licks the inside of my mouth and gently sucks on my tongue. I feel my core tighten, and the warm sensation that he elicits from my body takes flight and spreads its wings. I return his kiss in the same manner. It's a passionate, deep, searching kiss and one that feels like it's asking a question. Julian wants to know if I want him. This time I feel like I can read his mind.

I pull back from him just a bit so he can see my eyes. I nod softly and stand up. I reach down for his hand. He threads his fingers through mine and stands up. I take the lead and walk toward my bedroom. He shuts and locks the door behind us and leads me to my bed. It was done very subtly, but it's obvious to both of us that he's in charge now. He just needed me to say it was okay.

Julian slowly pulls my shirt over my head, drops it on the floor, and runs his hands down my back. He unhooks my bra on the next pass. He runs his tongue along my collarbone and shoulders as he slips the straps off. My bra falls to the floor, and Julian embraces me tightly. I pull away a bit and reach down to grab the hem of his shirt. I'm dying to feel his skin against mine. He lets me try to pull it over his head and laughs softly when I can't reach. He does it for me and drops his shirt on the floor next to mine. He pulls me close and smashes my breasts to his chest. His skin is warm and soft. I reach up and wrap my arms around his neck.

"This is the first time you've been barefoot around me. You aren't so tall, are you?" It's funny, and I giggle back. Each time we've made out while standing up, I've been in four-inch heels or higher. The height difference between my 5'5" frame and his 6'1" frame is very noticeable now.

"Well at least I can add this to my list of reasons why I need to wear such high heels."

He just laughs and kisses my neck. He lowers his hands and gets busy working on the drawstring of my shorts. Once he gets it untied, he grabs the waistband and pulls them slowly down. I help him undress me and step out of them. I'm naked now except for a black, satin G-string. Julian slowly looks me up and down, and instead of feeling exposed, I feel appreciated. There is nothing better than having such a beautiful man look at my body the way Julian does. He leaves my panties on and runs his hands over my bare ass. He cups my cheeks and squeezes as he pulls me into him. He groans into my mouth as he begins to kiss me again. His hands make contact with my aching nipples, and he rolls them in his fingers and pinches them gently. He breaks his mouth away from mine and places it on one of my breasts. He nibbles and licks at my nipple, and with every touch a jolt of arousal shoots through my body. I feel myself getting wetter, and I know for sure it will not take much for me to orgasm.

While he's enjoying my tits, I get started undressing him. I don't do it slowly. I don't have the same level of control Julian does, and I want him badly. I tug at his button, lower the zipper, and yank his shorts down in a fluid motion. He looks up at me and sees the determination and lust in my eyes.

"Mmm ... that's sexy, Alexa. Can't wait anymore, can you? I know how you feel. I've been dying to touch you all day."

And he isn't kidding; his erection is massive. Julian isn't wearing underwear again, and I decide this is another thing I really appreciate about him. It gives me easy access to his hot, hard body. I reach around and grab his bare ass and pull him tightly to me. He has started kissing me again, and when his erect penis makes contact with my body, he groans louder and catches my lower lip between his teeth. It's just this side of painful, and an involuntary "ouch" comes out.

"Lo siento, Corazón. That's your fault for grabbing my ass and pulling my dick into you." He licks my lower lip and then kisses it gently.

He pulls my panties off and finishes undressing me. We climb onto my queen-size bed, and Julian quickly gets me underneath him. One of my arms is above my head, and he nestles himself against me. This position allows him to lean his chest into me. He props himself up on one side and starts running his fingers up and down my body lazily. His fingertips slowly circle my nipples. He runs his hand underneath my breasts and caresses each one firmly. It tickles me and arouses me, and I arch my body up involuntarily, asking for more. I run my fingers through his thick hair and tug on it in response to the sparks shooting through my body.

"Te gusta, Lexie? I love the way your body responds to me. It's like you were made for me to touch."

Hell yes, I like that! "Yes. Please don't stop." I know I don't have to ask. I know Julian will make sure I'm taken care of in every way. I see him shake his head before I close my eyes and let the feeling of bliss ripple through me.

He continues his slow, delicious tactile assault on my upper body, and I start to squirm beneath his hands. The best part is that he hasn't even really gotten started yet. Because this isn't our first time together, I know what to expect and what I want. I can't wait for his mouth to be between my legs. I hunger for him to be inside me. But what he's doing feels so good that I don't want him to stop that either. He hooks his leg around the leg of mine closest to him and pulls back, gently causing my legs to spread wider. He lowers his fingers and starts caressing the inside of my thighs. Up and down, up and down. He stares at me while doing this, watching me with lust in his eyes, and I start to tremble beneath his touch. I'm feeling so needy. I want to come so bad. I reach down with my free hand and attempt to direct his fingers to my wet, pulsating with anticipation, sex. If he just touches my clit, I'll come. He intercepts my hand before I make any progress and brings it up over my head like the other. He lets out a little chuckle.

"Not this time. I don't need your help with this. I know what I'm doing, and I promise it will be worth the wait, baby. I'm going to give you what you need." He presses his hand into mine, leaving me unable to really move or touch him. "Can I let go? Can I trust you to let me do my job here?" His voice is teasing, but I sense Julian's serious about being the one in control.

I nod my head. "Yes, you can trust me to lie here and let you pleasure me. Sorry for interrupting. You may continue now." I'm a smart woman. I quickly realize that the longer his hand is holding my hand down, the longer it's away from my overheated body. "But I'd appreciate it very much if you would hurry up and get to the point." Julian flashes me a wicked smile and goes back to stroking my inner thighs gently and slowly. Good God, I'm dying here.

Not only is Julian taking his sweet time making me come, but I'm in a position where I can't really touch him. I feel his hard-on against my leg, and I really want to stroke it like he's stroking me. "You do know the sooner I come, the sooner I can touch you too, right?"

"Alexa, you're shameless. Are you trying to bribe me?"

"Is it working? Because, if not, I can provide more details on what I plan on doing to you."

"Are you that desperate? You really can't wait any longer?"

I shake my head no, and I'm being serious. I need him to make me come before I explode.

Julian's problem, if you can really call it a problem, is that he's a patient, slow, unselfish lover. And in any normal situation that might be okay. But with me, it's not. *My* problem is that the second he touches me, my body ignites with desire, and I just need him to be inside of me. The full body contact that comes from him being deep inside of me is the only thing that completely soothes the ache I feel. I know what he means when he says the physical connection between us could consume him. It's consuming me right now. I'm starting to wonder how I ever survived without his touch.

I guess Julian decides to take pity on me because the next thing I feel is his hot tongue on my hypersensitive clit. He moves so quickly that I don't even have enough time to brace myself for the onslaught of his skilled mouth. He begins feasting on me as he runs his tongue up and down my wet sex. The gentleness with which he was touching me before is gone. I asked for it, and he's giving it me. My clit is so sensitive I find myself flinching every time his tongue presses down on it. It only takes a few minutes before the orgasm I've been longing for rips through me like a freshly lit fuse. It's hot and burning and leaves a scorched path in its wake.

He keeps flicking his tongue over my clit after I come, and I'm forced to push him away and beg him to stop. I can't take anymore.

"Now you want me to stop? You need to make up your mind." He's teasing, but he stops. He knows he just rocked my world. He moves out from between my shaking thighs and rolls over on his back. I immediately see an opportunity appear before me, and I take a page from Julian's book and move quickly to straddle him. He looks up at me, startled and with a burning heat in his eyes. He runs his hands through my hair, and I quickly remember our second conversation when he told me that he wanted to feel my hair floating across his chest as I was straddling him and making my way down his body. I'm happy to oblige. But first I need to address the protection issue.

"Do you have any condoms? Because I don't." And I'm sure of that. I did have some here but threw them away a few months ago after I convinced myself I would never be having sex again. Wow, I really was a mess. I know neither Marissa nor Shannon use them either.

"In my wallet. In my shorts." He's breathing hard, and I feel his dick twitching steadily against my sex. I know if I just moved up a little, Julian would easily slide right in. After that orgasm, I'm wet and ready for his long shaft. I think he knows it too and lies very still, waiting to see what I'm going to do. I can tell by his expression, if I let him, he would gladly forgo the condom. But, as much as I want him inside of me, *al la natural*, I just can't do it. I roll off of him and walk to the other side of the bed to grab his wallet out of his shorts. He watches me as I move across the room.

"Don't move." I issue the order to Julian playfully as I pull his wallet out. He nods his assent that I can get the condoms out of his wallet myself. "I don't need your help with this. I know what I'm doing, and I promise it will be worth the wait. I'm going to give you what you need." I repeat the words he said to me just before he unleashed his tongue on me.

I'm rewarded with a big laugh. "I don't doubt that for a second. Just hurry the hell up because now I'm the one who can't wait anymore."

"Hmm. Maybe you'll remember that the next time you think about torturing me." If I was looking at Julian, I would see the big smile on his face. Instead, I'm momentarily transfixed on the Louis Vuitton wallet stuffed full of hundred-dollar bills that's in my hand. I also notice an assortment of elite credit cards. I don't often think about the fact Julian is wealthy. I'm really not that impressed with money. But when it's literally in my face, it's hard not to acknowledge how well off he obviously is. I refocus and pluck the two condoms I find out of the little pocket in the back. I put the wallet back in his shorts and turn to him, holding the condoms up in the air triumphantly. I notice he has moved up and is lying in the same spot I was when he went down on me.

As I make my way back to him, I decide I'm totally in love with the way this evening is unfolding. We talked, we were open with each other, we're about to have amazing sex, and I haven't freaked out. It's all so normal.

As I climb back on top of Julian, I reach over to put the condoms on my nightstand. In this position, my breasts are right over his face. He takes advantage of this opportunity and grabs them with his hands and mouth and starts to suck on my nipples. My sex clenches tightly, and I feel the familiar stirrings of another orgasm brewing. I think Julian was right when he said my body was made for him to touch. I've never responded to another man this way.

I let him suckle for a few minutes before I reluctantly pull myself away. I gently sit back down on Julian and feel his very hard dick press against my wetness. He moans at the contact and lifts me slightly off of him.

"Do that again, and I'm going in without protection. I want my bare dick inside of you so bad I can't stand it. Don't give me any more opportunities."

I lift my hips off of him and place my mouth on his. I run my tongue over his soft, full lips and slip it slowly in. He doesn't kiss me back, which I find hot. It's his way of giving me control. This is going to be awesome. I start thinking of all the naughty things I want to do to this man's body as I start making my way down. I move over to his neck and run my lips slowly up and down the side. I nip at his ear and dip my tongue inside, which draws a deep moan from Julian. I kiss my way down his chest and take a little pit stop at his nipples. His pecs are hard and defined like the rest of his muscular body, and as I run my tongue over the hard, little points, I hear his approval through his soft moans. His eight-pack abs are flexed and sexy as hell. I spend a little time running my tongue over the muscles that prove he spends serious time at the gym. He keeps reaching out and running his fingers through my hair as it floats over his body. I hope this reality is better than the fantasy he told me about when we first met.

"Sí, Alexa, se siente tan bien. I want your mouth all over my body." Him telling me how good it feels only fuels my desire to please him like he pleased me. I plan on putting my mouth all over his body.

The further down I go, the closer Julian's penis is to being between my tits. And he knows it. He's moving his body in a way that tells me he's trying to facilitate that happening. I press my chest down, and he lifts his hips into me and groans. He makes a few thrusting motions and I think it turns me on as much as it does him. I want him to be thrusting like that inside of me.

I slide back a little and get on my knees so I'm looking down at Julian's very hard, very erect penis. I've reached my final destination. As I slide my tongue up the underside of Julian's long shaft I hear a deep, guttural groan come out of him. It's such an erotic, sensual sound, and my whole body tenses in response. I'm spurred on by the noises he's making and quickly take him in my mouth. I pull him in as deep as I can, and when I lick the pre-cum I find off the soft head of his dick, it sends him over the edge. He reaches down and presses my head down so I can't pull back. It's uncomfortable for me because he's so big, and I can't help but gag as his shaft touches the back of my throat. He hears me gag and immediately pulls his hands away and tries to pull away from me. I literally wrap my hand around him and make him stop.

"I'm so sorry, baby. You can stop. I didn't mean to do that to you. You just suck my dick so good that I can't get in deep enough."

"Oh I'm not stopping. I'm good. And by the way, I'd appreciate it if you'd just lie there and let me pleasure you."

His reply comes out in a whisper. "Yes, please."

I bring my mouth back down onto his dick and resume my blow job. I'm so turned on that he's so turned on, and I want to give this to him. I run my tongue up and down his shaft. I lick the head. I take him deep and suck hard. I suck softly. I gently massage his balls as I flick my tongue over them. Julian lets me dictate the rhythm for a while, but soon it's obvious he needs to control the pace as his orgasm approaches. His hips start moving faster, and he's thrusting harder into my mouth.

"I'm going to come in your mouth if you don't stop. And I fucking want to. But if you're not okay with that, it's fine. You. Just. Need. To. Stop." His words come out jagged and raspy. I'm not going to stop, and I'm totally okay with him coming this way. He didn't come in my mouth last time we were together, and I want to taste him this time. I don't tell him though. I just suck harder and pull him in as deep as I can.

"Alexa. Oh my God." His words trail off as he totally lets go and releases himself into my still sucking mouth. I taste his salty, warm semen in the back of my throat, and I have to swallow twice to get it all down. I keep my mouth on him until the last kick of his orgasm fades away. Pretty soon he's pulling me off of him.

"Please stop. I can't take any more of your mouth. Are you trying to kill me?"

"No, just trying to make you feel as good as you make me feel."

"If that's how I make you feel, then I'm amazing. And by the way, that was way better than what I fantasized about the first time I saw you with your hair down." I crawl back up and snuggle myself into the crook of his arm. He squeezes me tight.

"Happy to hear I didn't disappoint you. And by the way, you're great, a little slow, but great." I'm totally joking, but when I look up at Julian, he has a serious look on his face.

"I need to savor every second I'm with you, in case I don't get another chance to touch you. I need to memorize you in case you don't stay."

Bam! And just like that, we've gone from the totally physical to the totally emotional. I squeeze him back while I try to decide if I want to go there with him. I decide to follow his lead. I take a deep breath and force the words out of my mouth.

"I want to stay." The words come out in a whisper, but they come out.

Julian leans over and kisses me softly. I can taste myself on him, and I know he can do the same. It's erotic and personal, and at this moment all I want is to feel him inside of me.

"I want you inside of me, Julian." I speak softly, and my words seem to touch him in an unexpected way. He pulls back and looks at me tenderly. My heart immediately starts to race.

"Say that again, baby. Please." His voice is pleading, and I'm a bit confused. He can't be surprised I want him to be inside of me.

"I want you inside of me, Julian." I repeat myself, not understanding why he wants me to. He notices the question in my eyes and tells me why.

"That was the first time you called me by my name when we're being intimate." His smile is shy, and his eyes are bright. This is a huge deal to him. And I get it. He always uses my name when we're intimate, and it means so much to me. It makes me feel connected to him. It makes me feel he really knows who he's touching. It means he knows it's me and not just some random woman who luckily ended up in his bed. Right now I feel sad and disappointed in myself. I had no clue I hadn't used his name like this before, and I certainly didn't know he noticed, or cared for that matter.

"I'm sor—" Julian shushes me by putting his mouth on mine.

"I didn't tell you to make you feel bad. I don't need or want you to apologize. I just want you to keep saying it."

"I need you inside of me ... Julian ... now." My heart swells with more emotion than I know what to do with, and I need him inside of me, distracting me with his body, before I end up saying something more personal than his name.

He reaches over and grabs a condom off of the nightstand. He quickly tears the wrapper open and rolls the condom down his hard shaft. He wastes no time positioning himself between my legs. The size of his body forces me to spread my legs wide, and he's able to enter me with one hard thrust. He immediately settles into a steady rhythm. I lift my hips and grab his ass as he rolls into me. We fit so well together, our bodies molding together with each movement. I run my hands up and down his back and over his ass, pulling him into me as deep as I can. This is exactly what I wanted. This feeling of his body on mine is so stimulating and soothing at the same time. It really makes no sense. It just feels right.

Julian takes one of my hands and then the other and puts them over my head. He threads his fingers through mine and holds them down tightly. Every now and then, I sense Julian needs to feel dominant over me. I would never in a million years think that type of restraint would do anything other than cause me to panic, but it doesn't affect me negatively at all when Julian takes control like this. Whether I'm ready to admit it aloud or not, it's obvious to me my body trusts his. And I still don't know for sure, but my heart may not be far behind.

Julian arches his back and continues to roll his hips into me. I have the best view of his body, and I appreciate looking at every inch of it while he gets lost in me. His moves are fluid and rhythmical, and he looks beautiful moving back and forth into me. He catches my gaze and it's as if a thousand words pass silently between us. I know without a doubt that no matter what happens after tonight, I'm never going to be able to deny the incredible connection we share. He has seen my true feelings, and I don't think I'm going to be able to hide from him or them much longer.

Because he just came, I'm not surprised Julian is lasting as long as he is. It's obvious he's enjoying this, and he seems in no hurry to come again. I'm not so patient.

"I want to be on top. I haven't had you in me like that yet." He shows his approval of my idea by wrapping his arms around me and flipping me so that I end up on top. He's still inside of me. Impressive. He pulls himself up into a sitting position and leans back against my headboard. He looks at me sensually from under hooded lids. My knees are on each side of his legs, and I'm basically sitting in his lap. He places his hands on my waist and guides me as I begin to ride him. Our faces are inches apart, and I place my mouth on his. We don't kiss though. Our lips are just pressed gently together, and they slide softly back and forth over each other as they follow the rhythm of our bodies.

One of the reasons I'm anxious to get on top is because historically it's been the only way for me to have an orgasm through penetration without my clit being touched. Something about the position allows me to come pretty easily. I squeeze my thighs tight against Julian's legs and clench the whole bottom half of my body as I rub my clit up and down against Julian's dick. My hands are splayed across his chest, and he has moved his so they're cupping my ass from behind. He feels me tighten up, and I see he recognizes I'm trying to make myself come.

"I can help with that." I knew he would only be too happy to touch my very wet sex. He reaches around with one hand and puts his thumb directly on my clit.

I yank his hand away and shake my head. "You *are* helping. Stay hard, and stay still. I've got this." A look of actual surprise registers on Julian's face, and for the very first time I think I may have shocked him with my directness. But he does as I ask and stays still. I only have to rock my hips into him a few more times before I feel the orgasm I'm chasing roll through my whole entire body. Each orgasm I've had tonight has been as strong or stronger than the previous one, and I find myself wilting into Julian's chest as the last of my energy dissipates. Julian's eyes go black as he watches me take my pleasure from him and then feels me fall into him. He's so aroused that I swear I feel him grow harder. He flips me over again so I'm under him and starts rolling his hips into me. The look I just saw in his eyes as I came made me think he would be rough and fast as he chased his own orgasm. I'm wrong. He's still taking his time, each thrust deliberate and calculated as he savors the delicious feel of our bodies working together. He continues for just a little while longer before he calls my name and explodes into me. He lays his sweat-soaked body half on and half off of me and closes his eyes as he absorbs the last remnants of his orgasm.

There isn't a doubt in my mind, or his, I'm sure. We made love.

I just want to lie there in Julian's arms and bask in the afterglow of our lovemaking. I feel like some sappy Hallmark card writer when those exact thoughts pop up in my mind, but it's really the best way to describe how I'm feeling. For the first time in longer than I care to recount, I feel 100 percent sated, relaxed, and whole. I wish I could bottle this feeling and share it with everyone. The world would be a much happier place.

Unfortunately, the red light of my alarm clock catches my eyes, and I see it's already close to midnight. "Wow, times flies when you're having fun."

Julian opens his eyes and looks at the clock to check the time. "And that certainly was fun." He's talking softly, and I can tell he's tired. I'm exhausted, so I can only imagine how he's feeling.

"Not that you have actually even invited me to stay, but I can't. I have a really early meeting downtown in the morning, and I need to stop by the hotel first." I'm crestfallen. I hadn't asked him to stay, but I was hoping he would. This is probably how he felt when I bolted out of his bed last week. I almost can't believe how much things have already changed between us. The thought of staying with him last week almost gave me a panic attack, and now the thought of him leaving makes me want to cry. He looks up at me, and I know I don't need to tell him I'm disappointed. He can see it on my face. He reaches up and strokes my cheek gently with his fingers.

"Por favor, no me mires asi, Alexa. I can't stand it. I'll stay if you want me to."

I want to be selfish. I want him next to me. I haven't had nearly enough of him. But I realize I'm being really unfair. It's already late, and if he does stay, it will only be for a few more hours.

I take a deep breath and say what I need to say, not what I want to say.

"It's okay. I understand why you can't stay." Julian exhales, and I'm guessing if I had asked him to stay, he would have. We lie in silence for another five minutes before he rolls off the bed and heads to the bathroom. I'm dressed and sitting on my bed when he walks back in the room. He's still naked, and I can't help but stare at him. I can't imagine ever getting tired of looking at him.

"You didn't need to get out of bed." I don't want to admit I'm not ready for him to leave, and I want to spend every second I can with him. That means walking with him to his car.

I try to mask my sadness by being funny. "Now what kind of date would I be if I didn't at least walk you to your car after all of that?" I point and twirl my finger at my rumpled sheets.

He laughs as he puts his clothes back on. "A tired date. I guess you didn't get enough of a workout. Maybe we should go again."

"Hmm ... I assure you I was worked out good. But if you think you can go again, I'm in." I'm only half kidding.

He walks over to me, pulls me to a standing position, and holds me close. His eyes are blazing, and I can feel him hardening against me. "I can go all night, baby. You should think about that before you challenge me."

"I'm going to require some proof of that, maybe not tonight, but soon."

"I'll be happy to give you all the proof you need. As a matter of fact, I'm looking forward to it. But right now, I'm going to walk out of here before I end up back in your bed."

Julian holds my hand tightly as we walk outside to his car. He gets inside and rolls the window down. He reaches out and pulls my face to him so he can kiss me again. I feel his tongue in my mouth, and I only let it last for a minute before I pull away.

"I'm going to drag you back to my bed and make you stay if you keep kissing me like that." He groans but lets me pull away.

"Please don't take this the wrong way, but you did great tonight." I know exactly what he means, and if I'm being honest, it makes me feel good to hear him say it. I did do well. I didn't freak out once.

I smile and answer him. "I did, didn't I? Yeah me!" After one night of emotional honesty, I'm finding myself able to joke, out loud, about my limitations. It's kind of overwhelming, and I feel a rush of tears spring to my eyes. Julian notices and flashes me a reassuring smile. He turns the car on and fastens his seatbelt. I exhale sharply. He really is going to leave now. My heart swells, and I realize I already miss him. I'm falling for this man, hard and fast.

Before he rolls up his window, Julian motions for me to lean in. I think he's going to try to kiss me again, so I don't get too close. He doesn't try to kiss me though. "You know now that this is really going to happen, right, Alexa?" He points to himself and then to me. "And it's going to be amazing."

"Not just amazing, Julian. It's going to be epic."

Julian's eyes turn soft when I say those words, and he responds by placing his hand over his heart, indicating my words have touched him. He gives me a little wave and starts to back his car out of my driveway. He idles in the street, and I know he's waiting for me to get back inside. I walk through the door and turn around one last time. He blows me a kiss, rolls up his window, and drives off.

I float back to my room on cloud freaking nine. This may have been one of the best nights I've ever had.

CHAPTER 17

I'm rudely awakened in the morning by Marissa shaking me, telling me I need to get my ass up. I look at the clock. Shit! It's already seven forty-five, and I'm supposed to be at work by eight-thirty. It's only ten minutes away, but I need to take a shower and get dressed. I pop out of bed and head to the bathroom.

I call to Marissa over my shoulder. "Thank you! I forgot to set my alarm last night."

"Did all the great sex scramble your brain? You never forget to set your alarm." She's joking with me, and I'm in a great mood despite the fact I'm running so late.

"Maybe." I hear her chuckle as she walks away.

I look in the mirror and am greeted by the image of a satisfied woman. Talk about bed head. My lips feel swollen, and my body is deliciously sore. I quickly brush my teeth and put my hair on top of my head. There is no way I'm going to be able to wash and dry it, and I see a ponytail in my future. I turn the water on but don't wait long enough for it to warm up. The lukewarm water helps wake me up. As my brain "unscrambles", I start to think about Julian and last night. As I wash between my legs, I really feel the after-effects of my hot night with him. My thoughts, coupled with the innocent movement of my hands, cause a burst of heat to rush through my body, and I really wish I had the time to masturbate in the shower, using Julian as a muse. Unfortunately, I'm in a hurry. I wash the rest of my body quickly and hop out. I dry myself off and walk naked to my closet. I usually take the time to pick out my outfits, but I don't have that luxury today. I grab a pair of panties and matching bra from my lingerie drawer, pull on a kelly-green pair of cropped, cotton pants and a sleeveless, structured black top. I'm so tired this morning that the idea of teetering around all day on high heels isn't too appealing. I dig a pair of Sam Edelman leopard-print ballet flats out of their box and slip them on. My feet are already thanking me. I head back to the bathroom, run a brush through my hair, and pull it into a tight pony. I brush a little powder on my face, swipe the mascara wand over my lashes, and dab a little lip gloss on. I'm so glad I can get by without wearing much makeup. As a quick afterthought, I grab my makeup bag just in case I want to put some more on once I get into work. I slip some plain gold hoops on along with my watch and a big, clunky, black flower ring. I look at the time—eight-twenty. I take a final look in the mirror and decide I did a great job with the time I had. I hurry into the kitchen and pop a Vanilla K-cup into the machine. I pour some creamer in a travel mug and put the lid on when it finishes brewing. I check to see that my keys and phone are in my purse, and I head out the door. Marissa has already left for work, so I lock up and haul ass to work.

I'm lucky and don't hit any traffic on the way in. It's only eight forty-five when I pull into my spot, and I know that even if someone notices I'm late, nobody will care. The elevator arrives quickly, and I get in and head up to the sales office on the third floor. I make my way to my little office and plop myself down in my seat. I take a deep breath to calm down a bit. As I assumed, nobody is around to see I'm a few minutes late.

I realize I haven't checked my phone since I texted Julian yesterday. I've been so bad about answering it lately. I enter my code and notice I have an unread text message. It's from Luke.

Luke: *Nice fucking new Jag, Lex.*

Shit! Shit! Shit! He must have driven by and seen Julian's car. I didn't see this coming.

I was in such a great mood this morning, and this totally sucks. If things were okay with Luke, then everything would be perfect. I decide we will be fixing this today, no matter what. I respond to Luke's text. I figure he's sleeping, and I don't expect to hear from him for a few hours.

Alexa: *I prefer BMWs, you know that.*

Apparently he's up. He responds right away.

Luke: *WTF Alexa?*
Alexa: *Let's discuss WTF over lunch. Today. JUST us.*
Luke: *U came to Callahan's?*
Alexa: *Yes.*
Luke: *Ok.*

Alexa: *Sun Cafe @ 12.*
Luke: *Ok.*

We will be working through this today. I hope he knows that.

I open my computer and grab another cup of coffee from the kitchen while I wait for it to load. I run into Lauren in the kitchen, and she starts chatting me up about the seminar they went to yesterday. If she knows anything about what's going on between Luke and me, she doesn't let on. We talk about some clients, and she asks if I want to grab lunch. I tell her I have other plans, and she lets the subject go without asking with whom. There's definitely a different vibe between us. I decide that after I patch things up with Luke, I'll talk to her. We've gotten close, and I don't want that to change.

I get back to my desk and open my e-mail. I really only use this e-mail address for work; I need to give Julian my personal account info. I haven't heard from him yet, and I'm a little disappointed. He did say he had meetings all morning, but I still wish he would've sent me something to let me know he was thinking about me. I'm about to send him an e-mail with my other contact info when I get a call patched through to me from the front desk. I stop what I'm doing and spend the next fifteen minutes talking to my prospective buyer from yesterday. It looks like they're going to come in and sign if we can work out a few minor details. What a great start to my day. As the conversation is coming to a close, I reopen my e-mail browser and see a new e-mail from Julian. I look at the subject line and wonder if he's referencing the song Brighter than the Sun by Colbie Callait. I hope so.

To: Alexa Reed—AReed@W&Minvestmentgroup.com
From: Julian Bauer—JPB@BWproperties.com
Subj: Brighter than the Sun

Stop me on the corner (or in the stairwell)
I swear you hit me like a vision
I, I, I wasn't expecting
But who am I to tell fate where it's supposed to go

Heard this in the elevator this morning. Reminded me of you ... us. Fate?

JULIAN

He *was* referencing that song. Does this really happen in real life? I feel like I'm the lead character in an awesome chick flick. I reread the lyrics. I can't believe he just sent me that. I'm not sure what I started with this song and lyric stuff, but he seems to have taken to it. I want to hear his voice, so I find his number in my phone and call him. I'm disappointed when it goes right to voicemail. I'm about to leave a message when I hear the sound of an incoming text. I look down at my phone and see it's from Julian.

Julian: *In boring board meetings until after lunch. Can't talk but can e-mail.*

I open my personal e-mail and respond.

To: Julian Bauer—JPB@BWproperties.com
From: Alexa Reed—arrluvsshoes@hotmail.com
Subj: 100% Perfect—Again

Please note new email address. Don't like to mix business with pleasure. Which, by the way, was given to me by the truckload last night! If I didn't sufficiently thank you, I'll make it up to you.

Crashing into you in the stairwell may have been the best return on my shoe investment yet.

BTW, you're pretty good at the song lyric thing.

ALEXA

He must be waiting for my e-mail because he responds quickly.

To: Alexa Reed—arrluvsshoes@hotmail.com
From: Julian Bauer—JPB@BWproperties.com
Subj: Making your pleasure my business—100% in the plan

You thanked me multiple times if I remember correctly, but my mind is a little fuzzy from getting *blown* last night. Pun intended.

Love the e-mail address. What are you wearing today? Please stay out of the stairwell if there is a chance you may crash into another unsuspecting victim. It's not fair.

BTW, I'm good at most things. I'll prove it tonight?

JULIAN

If it's possible, I'm equally turned on by Julian's wit as I am his body. He's smart, confident, funny, and totally keeping me on my toes.

To: Julian Bauer—JPB@BWproperties.com
From: Alexa Reed—arrluvsshoes@hotmail.com
Subj: Great Business Plan

I approve of your plans. You may absolutely begin implementing them tonight. You say where and when. You will be pleased to know I'm wearing flats today so nobody is in danger. I was a bit wobbly this morning after my intense workout yesterday. I need to go sell some condos so I can buy more shoes. Let me know about tonight.

ALEXA

To: Alexa Reed—arrluvsshoes@hotmail.com
From: Julian Bauer—JPB@BWproperties.com
Subj: Implementation schedule

I'll call you after lunch to discuss. I need to pay attention so I don't agree to anything I'll regret later. I'd rather be distracted by you though. Speaking of workouts, I was able to skip mine this morning because of the one I got last night. My personal trainer is already jealous of you.

JULIAN

Okay. So this day is getting better and better by the minute. I can't keep the smile off of my face. I'm going to see Julian again tonight, and I can't wait to hear what he has in mind. I hope it includes more "working out".

The rest of the morning goes by quickly. I set some appointments and get the answers I need for my clients. It looks like the sale will happen and we'll be able to close in a few weeks. This is a bigger, more expensive unit with a lot of options, and my commission will be great. I finish up some paperwork and get myself ready to go meet Luke for lunch.

I have to admit, I'm nervous. I haven't been nervous to spend time with Luke since the night we hooked up. He's always made me feel comfortable around him. It's why we became such good friends. There has always been an ease in our relationship. That is until a few weeks ago. I know he has an issue with me seeing Julian, but he's going to have to get over it because it's happening. I find a space near the restaurant and go inside to get a table. Luke gets there a few minutes after me and starts to walk over to where I'm sitting. He flashes me a real smile and winks one of his baby blues at me. He's in blue, plaid cargo shorts, a plain, white T-shirt, and flip-flops. He looks great as usual, and I can't help but notice all the women in the restaurant check him out as he walks by. He pulls off the "I just rolled out of bed, and I'm still this hot" look very well. When he gets to me, he pulls me out of my chair and gives me a bear hug. I hug him back as hard as I can. My heart is instantly happy. I've missed him.

We place our order at the counter. I get a large Greek salad, and Luke orders a gyro and fries. I'm starved, and I realize I totally skipped breakfast this morning. We find a table near the windows.

He starts the conversation. "I'm tired of being mad at you."

I sigh. "Good, cuz I'm tired of being mad at you too."

He dips a fry in ketchup, takes a bite, and shrugs his shoulders. "So let's agree not to be mad anymore." He makes it all sound so simple, as if we just had a small misunderstanding. I wish it were that easy.

"I'd love that, but I think we need to talk about why we both are … were, mad." I know we need to talk this through or it will keep happening. Julian is currently in my life, and I hope he will be for a long time.

"Okay. Right now I'm mad because you've lied to me twice in a week. I'm not used to that from you." He's referring to me not telling him about hooking up with Julian and about me being busy last night.

"I know, and I feel bad, but you kind of forced me into it."

He shakes his head and chuckles. "I made you lie to me? How do you figure that?" Okay, so he isn't planning on taking any responsibility here.

"Well, I'm assuming you're referring to the lie I supposedly told by not telling you anything happened between Julian and me?" I realize we still haven't talked about "what" happened between Julian and me, and I'm starting to wonder if he really knows something or if he was just speculating. I don't offer up any details.

He looks down when I say Julian's name. "For starters."

"I didn't lie to you. I just didn't tell you." I know that sounds lame, and I've never liked that logic used on me, but it works here.

"It feels the same to me." He plays the sin of omission card.

"I understand, and I'm sorry. But you've been acting crazy since the first time you saw Julian paying attention to me. Why?" I hope he plans on being honest right now or we won't fix anything.

"I've told you. He isn't good for you. He's always with a different woman. Seriously. I've seen it. I don't want to see you get hurt again. That's the truth, Alexa." I know Luke isn't lying to me about the women. I've seen it myself. I try to hide my insecurity.

"And you honestly don't think he could be interested in me? I mean really interested?" I brace myself and wait for his answer. I know he'll be honest.

"Lex, any man who isn't interested in you is an asshole. So, no, I have no doubt he's *interested* in you. Interested in *what* is the question."

His response warms my heart and loosens me up. "Well, he clearly isn't after my money because he has tons of that himself. And I hope he isn't interested in my virtue because I lost that when I was seventeen."

Luke starts laughing and shakes his head at me. I know we're close to being okay. His next question just cuts through all the beating around the bush, and I'm glad he asks. "Are you seeing him?"

"Yes." I breathe the word out, and a weight lifts off my shoulders. I don't want to hide this from Luke. I can tell by the look on his face he really didn't want yes to be my answer, but he doesn't ask any other questions.

"And you and Lauren?" We still need to address that issue too.

"We've hung out a few times." In Lukespeak, that means had sex a few times.

He didn't push the issue about Julian, so I don't push about Lauren. However, I do need to say something about yesterday at Callahan's. "Next time we plan to meet alone, can you please let me know ahead of time if things change?"

He shrugs his shoulders. "I told her I was meeting you there after work, and she just showed up. I didn't invite her, and I didn't know how to tell her to leave." I know Luke, and I know he's telling me the truth. I'm so happy to hear he didn't invite her just to piss me off. I nod, letting him know I believe him.

We both finish our meals. He gets out of his seat and tells me he needs to use the bathroom before he leaves. He starts to walk away and then turns back to face me. He looks a little nervous. "Are we okay?"

I smile brightly at him so he knows I mean it when I say, "We're great."

I pull out my phone when Luke goes to the bathroom and see I got a text from Julian about ten minutes earlier.

Julian: *Hola, Corazón. What's your sexy ass doing?*

All this talk about honesty obviously has me not thinking clearly, and I tell Julian what my stupid sexy ass is doing.

Alexa: *Having lunch with Luke. Call you soon.*

I wait a minute and get no response. Crap. He always responds so quickly to my e-mails and texts. Dumb move, Alexa.

Alexa: *Julian?*
Julian: *Yes Alexa?*

Shit. Now I know what he meant about hearing a tone through texting. He's pissed.

Alexa: *I'll call you soon.*
Julian: *You said that already.*
Alexa: *You didn't respond.*
Julian: *Nothing to say about what you're doing.*
Julian: *Nothing you want to hear at least.*

I have no idea what he's talking about but know I need to finish lunch before I get into it with him. My suspicion that something happened between Luke and Julian grows, and I make a mental note to ask Julian about it later.

Luke comes back from the bathroom, and I get up and follow him outside. He wraps his arms around me and picks me up in another bear hug. We usually kiss each other hello and goodbye on the lips, but in light of our recent disclosures, it doesn't seem appropriate.

"Later, Hooka." He walks off down the street to his car, and I do the same.

I get into my car and head back to work. I put my phone on Bluetooth and call Julian. He doesn't answer, and I immediately assume he doesn't want to talk to me. He was just texting me a few minutes ago, so I know he has his phone with him. I leave him a message asking him to call me back. Damn. Why did I say I was with Luke? Okay, why wouldn't I say I was with Luke? I really need to get to the bottom of this. For about five seconds, I was happy. Julian and I were great. Luke and I were almost great. Now Julian is pissed. I can't win.

I pull up to a light and check my e-mail on my phone to see if I have any messages from Julian. Nothing. I check again to see if he has texted me back. Nothing. I call again, and this time it goes straight to voicemail. I try to convince myself he's not ignoring me, but in my gut I know I've upset him. A switch flips on in my brain, and I start to feel consumed with my need to talk to him right now. But with me there's only a window of time where I feel this way, and today it lasts for the drive back to work. Then the switch flips the other way, and if I can't talk to him now, then I won't talk to him at all. I swear I feel like I can't control it. I start getting all worked up, and I feel the panic setting in. Damn it! It's the same thing over and over. I'm not sure why this is happening now, but it is, and I can't stop it.

By the time I pull into my parking spot, I'm a mess and heading right into a full-blown anxiety attack. My heart is racing, and my palms are sweaty. I'm shaking, and my whole body is tensing up. There is tightness in my chest, and I'm having a hard time catching my breath. I feel like I want to crawl out of my skin. I know the impending sense of doom I feel is irrational right now, and I try really, really hard to calm myself. I know this will pass. I haven't had a panic attack in over two months, and they usually only last about ten minutes. I focus on the clock in my car and start to count slowly. Gradually my pulse slows down, and my breathing evens out. I sit in my car for another ten minutes to make sure this attack was flying solo today. I take a big drink of water from the bottle I carried out of the restaurant, turn my phone off, and head into the building. The same words keep running through my mind over and over. *Fuck this!* I'm so not doing this again.

When I get back into the office, I'm greeted by some customers in the lobby. Everyone else is out, and the receptionist tells me they have been waiting for about ten minutes. The last thing I want to do is show properties, but I have no choice. I tell them to hang on a second and go throw my stuff into my desk. I don't check my phone or e-mail. I end up showing units for about an hour and a half, and it turns out it was just what I needed. The customers are an older couple from New York who want to snowbird in Miami. They're friendly, funny, and keep telling me stories about their grandkids. It totally takes my mind off of Julian, and by the time I say goodbye to them, I feel much better.

It's already three-thirty. I haven't looked at my phone or personal e-mail since around one-thirty, and I'm not going to. If anyone is trying to contact me for work, I know they can reach me through the main number. I also know I'm going to get shit for this too. I used to have my phone on me 24-7. Now I have it off or on silent more often than not. Sometimes I retreat into my own world, and to be honest, I just don't want to talk to anyone unless I have to. That's where I am right now. My parents, sisters, Marissa, Shannon, and Luke are constantly on my case about it, but I haven't changed. It's become a coping mechanism and one I use often. It is never a good idea and always ends up making someone mad at me. You'd think I'd learn.

CHAPTER 18

I'm off this weekend and happy about it. I've pretty much worked at least one day every weekend for the last eight months. Most weekends, it has been both days. Now that there are only a few units to sell, the traffic is light. Ramon likes to work the weekends, and I take advantage of it. I sit at my desk for about an hour doing some paperwork and then decide to leave early. I make sure the floor is covered, and head home. It's a relatively nice day today, and going for a run sounds like a great idea. I'm really emotionally and physically tired and decide I'll only do a few miles. I started running a few months ago. I never understood the fascination until I found it was the one thing I could do that would help make the bad fade away. I change into running shorts and a tank, put my sneakers and headphones on, and go. I hit my stride easily, and pretty soon I'm totally absorbed in my music and the feel of my muscles working. I have a normal route through my neighborhood and cover three miles in great time. I'm rounding the corner onto my street in a slow jog when I notice the black Jaguar in my driveway. Holy hell, it's Julian. I'm tempted to run the other way, but he spots me before I can flee. He's at my house? Really? I'm not sure I even want to see him and certainly not looking and smelling like this.

He's leaning against his car when I get to the driveway. He isn't smiling and doesn't say anything.

I catch my breath for a minute before I say anything. Obviously he's waiting for me to talk. I skip the pleasantries. "What are you doing here, Julian?"

"Well hello, Alexa. How are you?"

"Hot and thirsty. I need some water." I turn to walk into the house. I look back at him, shrug, and lift my hands up as if to ask if he's coming in. I unlock the door, and he follows me into the kitchen. I'm very aware I'm acting bitchy, but I can't help it. I remind myself of the panic attack I had today before I turn and face him. He's leaning up against the island in the kitchen with his beautiful, long legs crossed, and he looks so damn good I almost cave. He looks like he just stepped off the cover of a magazine. He's wearing white, cotton pants, a plain, light-brown T-shirt that shows off all of his muscles, and canvas loafer sneakers. He didn't shave today, and I decide right then I prefer when he doesn't. Damn. It's not fair. I stare at him, and I swear I forget why I'm even mad at him. Unfortunately, looking at me all sweaty in my workout clothes doesn't have the same effect on him. He clearly remembers he's mad at me.

"Is something wrong with your phone? Because I've been calling it for the last four and a half fucking hours, and you haven't answered once."

Oh, he's really pissed. This is the first time I've heard him cuss outside of the proverbial bedroom. I shrug and reply. "It must be off." Lame, I know. But I have a feeling nothing I say is going to make this okay.

He's about to respond when Marissa walks in the door. I've never been so happy to see her. That lasts about a minute. She walks into the kitchen, sees the look on Julian's face, and then totally sells me out. "You need to keep your damn phone on, Lexie, or I'm going to charge you for being your secretary." I shoot poison darts at her head with my eyes. "Your mom, dad, and Jill have all called looking for you this afternoon. I'm sure Julian would have too if he knew my number, right?"

She looks at Julian, and he nods his head in agreement. Fuck, now they're forming an alliance.

"I finally called your work, and they said you went home early. I was so glad to hear you were alive."

Julian chimes in, "Me too." I think he's enjoying Marissa yelling at me. It saves him the trouble.

I take a big drink of water. "Dramatic much?"

"Seriously, Lex. I'm over this thing with you going dark. It fucking worries me because—"

I cut her off before she says anything else. I don't need her to start talking about how I sometimes used to go days without talking to anyone or answering my phone. I walk over and give her a hug and whisper I'm sorry in her ear. She pushes my sweaty arms away, gives me a little smile, and walks away to her room.

"Looks like I'm not the only one who's pissed at you." Julian is smirking and enjoying this a little too much.

I turn and face him. "You have no reason to be pissed at me. I called you back. You didn't answer. I went back to work, turned my phone off, and forgot about it. I was busy."

"Can we talk about this in your room?" I'm not sure being in my room with him is a good idea if I plan on staying mad, but I agree Marissa doesn't need to hear what I'm sure is going to be a not so nice discussion about my behavior. I walk to my room, and he follows. He shuts the door behind me and sits on my bed. I'm still sweaty and really don't want to touch anything.

"Can I at least take a shower before you yell at me?" I don't wait for a response and head into the bathroom. I take a quick shower, wash my hair, and hop out. I run a brush through my hair and quickly realize I haven't brought any clothes with me into the bathroom. Thank God I have a robe in here. It's short, lacy, and leopard print, but it covers my body. I'm not trying to throw any kind of sex vibe off. I'm still trying to be mad. It's getting harder and harder though because I'm not sure I really ever was mad. I just freaked, had a panic attack, and decided it was all Julian's fault. Oh geez.

When I open the door, Julian is laying back on my bed with his arms crossed over his face. His feet are on the floor, and his shirt is riding up so I can see a hint of his muscular, flat stomach. Did I mention it's almost impossible to stay mad at someone who is this hot? I walk over to my dresser and grab a pair of panties, a bra, jean shorts, and a tank and head back to the bathroom to change.

"I've seen you naked already," Julian says from under his arms.

My back is to him, so he can't see the smile on my face. I love that he feels so comfortable here already and that he thinks us changing in front of each other is where we're at. Unfortunately, I'm still feeling the need to have my emotional suit of armor on, never mind my clothes. I dress quickly and come back out. Julian is sitting up now, and I sit next to him on the bed. He looks straight ahead as if he's trying to focus.

"I'm just going to cut right to the chase so we can get on with the night. I started this day thinking about all the things I wanted to do with you and to you tonight, and arguing didn't make the list. So the sooner we talk about whatever we need to, the sooner I can start putting my hands and mouth on you." My stomach flutters, and my sex clenches when he talks about things he wants to do to me.

"I was pissed when you texted me you were having lunch with Luke. I don't understand your relationship with him, but that's a conversation I don't think we should have tonight. I reacted badly, and I'm sorry for that. I was working out when you called me back, and I couldn't answer. I called you when I finished and kept calling until like four-thirty. I finally called your office, and your receptionist said you had just left for the day. Like Marissa, I was happy to hear you were okay and that you really had been at work." He says the last part quietly and finally looks at me. He isn't mad anymore.

At first I don't understand why he would question me being at work, and then I get it. Oh crap! He thought I was with Luke, and that's why I didn't answer my phone.

"We just had lunch, Julian. We had plans last night, and I cancelled them to be with you instead. Did you think I was with him all afternoon?"

"I don't want to talk about Luke anymore, Alexa. I was serious about that. What's with the phone though? Have you even looked at it all day?"

Okay. I'll run with that. I really don't want to talk about Luke either. "No, I haven't." And I should have, seeing as Marissa told me my family was looking for me. I tell Julian to hang on a minute as I get my phone from my purse. I turn it on and stay in the living room for a minute while it powers on. Wow. Twenty-two missed calls. I look at the texts. They all basically say the same thing. *Where the hell are you, answer your phone*, etc. I read the messages as I walk back into my room. The last one is from Luke.

Luke: *You looked beautiful today. Glad we talked. Luv u*

I read it and immediately delete it before Julian or anyone else sees it. That even sounds like a boyfriend text to me.

Julian is now propped up against my pillows, with his shoes off.

"Make yourself comfortable." I offer up a teasing tone in hopes we can just erase the drama of the last few hours and go back to the good feelings we had this morning when we were planning a great night.

"Thanks." He smiles, and I know he isn't really mad anymore. "Your bed is pretty comfortable, but something is missing." He pats the empty space next to him. I climb into my bed and snuggle up next to him. He puts his arm around me and lets me lean into his chest. I inhale and breathe him in. My heart starts to race, and I get butterflies in my stomach. I wonder if I'll always get this feeling when we're close like this. I hope so.

I still have my phone in my hand and ask him to give me a minute. I send a quick group text out to everyone who was trying to get in touch with me today. I'm glad my parents actually text. It saves me a call.

Alexa: *Hi everyone. I'm fine. Just super busy at work today.*
Alexa: *Getting ready to go out for night. Call you all tomorrow. Love you xoxox*

Julian is looking down and reading my text as I write it. "Work was busy?"

I'm not sure why I decide to lie, but I do. "Very." I turn the phone on silent and put it on my dresser.

"Your receptionist told me you left early because it was slow. She shouldn't have given me that information, but I charmed it out of her." I look to see if he's joking, but he's being totally serious. Okay, I'm busted again.

"What do you want me to say? I didn't want to talk to anyone, so I turned it off. I do that sometimes. It's really not that big of a deal."

"Why?"

"Why do I turn it off or why don't I want to talk to people sometimes?" I ask for clarification although I don't really need it. I know what he's asking me.

"Marissa said you go dark sometimes, which I'm assuming means you check out from your life. Why?"

Note to self. Kick Marissa's ass. He's even using my Bourne Identity code word. My roommates and I were watching the movie one day not long after Brady died. I mentioned I wanted to pull a Jason Bourne and go off the grid or go dark so that the world would just leave me alone. I wasn't in a good place at the time I said it. We looked it up on urbandictionary.com.

Going Dark: Slang term in the intelligence world which means you go silent. You don't speak or communicate with anyone for a given period of time. It's a way of protecting yourself from someone who would do you harm.

It's clearly a little dramatic, and I'm no CIA operative, but it kind of stuck in everyone's minds. Now they call it that whenever I'm avoiding the world.

"Honestly, I get overwhelmed by things sometimes, and I just need to shut it all out. It's how I deal. It's probably not the best way to handle things, but it's how I handle things."

I fully expect Julian to give me a lecture about communicating. Everyone else does. He was just an unwilling participant in one of my going-dark episodes, and he wasn't happy about it. It was a little one too. I've gone for days not talking to anyone.

He leans over and kisses me gently on the lips. "Do I overwhelm you, Alexa?"

I can always count on Julian to hear what I'm not actually saying. "Yes." I really want this. I want him, and he's trying really hard to be patient with me. I keep acting crazy, and he keeps coming back for more. Either he's the crazy one or he's feeling the same as I am.

"Can you tell me why? I hate that you feel you need to 'go dark' from me." He sounds sincere and also a little sad. I'm quickly learning Julian has many sides to him. From everything I've personally seen and read, his public persona is powerful, confident, and guarded. But I've also had the privilege, and it is a privilege, of seeing the side of him that is tender, compassionate, and vulnerable. I know in my gut he doesn't show this side to many people, and I feel like I'm wasting a gift if I choose not to open up to him. I know there are still many, many things I'm not ready to share with him, but how I'm feeling right now, in his arms, isn't one of them. I do something really brave and move so that I'm sitting in front of him. I look into his eyes and try to explain why I'm acting like I am.

"Julian, with you, everything is … amplified. My emotions, my desires, they're stronger than they should be. All of my senses are heightened when you're around. We've only known each other for a few weeks, and yet it feels like so much longer, to me at least. Everything about this thing between us is overwhelming for me. I've avoided any emotional involvement for a long time now, and I wasn't looking for this. I feel like I keep going deeper into water I may not be able to swim in, and when you got mad, or annoyed, or whatever with me and didn't answer my call, I just didn't want to deal. So I went dark." I look down when I finish and notice my hands are shaking. That was such a big deal for me to say all that. He might not understand why, but I do.

I feel Julian's hand underneath my chin as he brings my face up to look at him. Before he says anything, I know he understands.

"I told you last night that all of this was overwhelming for me too. I understand how you're feeling, baby, I really do. I understand because it's the same for me. I'm dealing with a whole lot of feelings that make me uncomfortable. I'm a pro at avoiding emotional involvement, so I totally get it." He takes a deep breath. "Do you know the last time I went to a woman's house to find her? How about never. I'm over here acting like a crazy, jealous boyfriend. And I don't do crazy and jealous."

Wow! There's a lot for me to process in that admission. I run it through my head very quickly. One, he understands. Not surprised. Two, he feels the same. Freaking awesome. Three, he thinks he's the one acting crazy. Couples therapy maybe? And four, did he just say boyfriend?

I'm laughing in my head at my stream of consciousness. He made the mood lighter with that last bit about being crazy.

"So basically I'm the first woman you've ever stalked? I'm totally flattered. And kind of turned on now."

Julian comes forward, lays me down backward on the bed, and is on top of me before I can grasp what he's up to. "You *just* got turned on? I've been turned on since the minute I saw you all sweaty in those little running shorts and tank top. I must be losing my edge."

I feel Julian's erection pressing into me, and there is no doubt he's turned on. "No te preocupes. You still have your hard edge. I can feel it pressing into my stomach."

I'm not sure if it's me speaking to him in Spanish, that he's on top of me, or that I just acknowledged his massive erection, but Julian suddenly becomes a man possessed. He starts kissing me with the hunger of a starving man. His mouth is hot and wet on mine, and he forces my lips open with his tongue. He sweeps it around my mouth possessively and skillfully. I absolutely love kissing this man. Right now there is nothing gentle or tender about the way Julian is kissing me. He's staking a claim and telling me I'm his with his mouth. He pulls back far enough to be able to caress my breasts and run his fingers over my taut nipples.

Within a few minutes, I'm so turned on I can't think straight. All I want is to feel this man against me and in me. His touch sends me into a lust-filled frenzy. I wrap my legs around the back of his and pull him into me as hard as I can. Any space between us is too much. He moans deeply as his dick rubs against my sex. I grind myself into him, trying to find release.

"That's so sexy, Alexa, you rubbing your throbbing pussy against me. God, you make me so hard. You aren't just a little turned on now, are you, baby? You want this, don't you?" He thrusts his hips into me, and I hold on for dear life as the beginning of an orgasm starts rolling up my body. I pull his face to mine and thrust my tongue in his mouth as the shudders ripple through me. As I come back down to earth, I bury my face in his chest, close my eyes, and completely savor every second. When I open them, Julian is staring at me with an amused look on his face. I push him off of me and scoot over a little.

"What's so funny?" I'm panting and have actually broken a sweat. Talk about getting worked up.

"Nothing." Nothing my ass. He's gloating.

"You're proud of yourself, huh?"

"Little bit. That was the quickest I've gotten you off. And you were just a *little* turned on when we started."

"Oh, so we're timing things now, are we? I don't mean to burst your bubble or anything, but I've been turned on since you were posing all sexy in my kitchen with your tight pants and tight shirt emphasizing all of your assets."

He just lies there and laughs. All the drama and tension of the day is gone. The calm, relaxed vibe we had going last night is back. I roll over to him and put my hand on his crotch. That stops his laughing, and he groans and rolls his hips up into my hand. I love that my touch does the same thing to him as his does to me. I start to unzip his pants, but my plans are thwarted when he removes my hand.

"Uh uh, Corazón. The sex part of the program is taking an intermission right now."

Oh no, I don't think so. I'm not interested in an intermission. "Intermissions don't come after the first act. We need to get at least four or five acts in before we take a break." I put my hand back on his crotch and start rubbing it firmly over his hard shaft. He literally jumps out of the bed. What the hell?

"If you touch me again, we're never going to leave this room, and I'm going to end up fucking you all night long, like I promised. And as much as I want to do that, I'd prefer to start a little later. So we're going to have an intermission, go on a date, and eat dinner."

I stick my lower lip out in my best pout. "Why do you get to call all the shots? Maybe *I* want to stay here and fuck all night."

"Dios mío. You're seriously unlike any woman I've ever met. And I want you so bad right now. But I think we need to be a little less overwhelmed for a while."

As much as I want to lock myself in this room with Julian and never leave, he's right. We need to take things down a notch. "Okay, Julian. We can push pause here. But you'll need to feed me though, because I'm starving."

"Are you okay with going to Ursa's? You said you haven't been there, and it seriously is really good."

"I'm fine going there, but are you sure you want to go to work? Doesn't seem like much of a night off."

"I'll call Dario and tell him we're coming in. We can sneak in and eat in the kitchen. I do it all the time." He sees the look on my face when he says he does it all the time, and he knows I think he means with other women.

"*I* do it all the time. I eat there a lot, and I don't always want my staff to know I'm there. I've never done it with a date." That's awesome if it's true.

"Well okay then. Let's do it." I look at the clock and notice it's already eight o'clock. Time really does fly when we're together. "I need about twenty-five minutes to get ready," I tell Julian as I head to my closet to find something to wear.

"Do you have to work tomorrow?"

"No," I call to him from inside my closet. "I'm off all weekend."

"Good. Then while you're in there, you need to pack clothes for the weekend. You're spending the night at my place tonight, and we're going to the beach tomorrow. And pack something to go out in tomorrow night too." He starts rattling off plans like a cruise director. I poke my head outside of my closet.

"And if I have other plans?" Like it matters. I'd change them in a heartbeat to spend the weekend with Julian.

"Do you?"

"No, not really." I quickly wonder to myself if I should be playing a little harder to get.

"Then get packing, mujer."

"You know you're really bossy tonight, right?"

"I'm always bossy. Get used to it."

I head back into my closet with the biggest smile on my face. The idea of spending the whole weekend with Julian thrills me. At least it does at the moment. Each time we're together, I feel more at ease, but I was being serious when I told him all of this emotional stuff is overwhelming. I think the part that really excites me is that we're going to be going out and doing things like a normal couple. Up until this point, we have kept everything pretty much on the DL. I don't think Julian has been hiding me away, but other than a quick introduction to his brother, I haven't had any interactions with anybody in his world. I think it would help me believe in the realness of this whole thing if I met some of his friends.

I grab an overnight bag and start packing stuff into it for the weekend. I'm totally an overpacker, so this isn't easy. After careful thought, I come up with a few outfits and put the pieces in the bag. Of course I put several pairs of shoes in there as well. I can't leave home without them. For tonight, I change into a tank-style, white-and-orange, tie-dyed, gauzy maxi dress and slip into some Juicy nude, cork wedge platform sandals. Julian gives me the once over and whistles at me when I walk out of the closet. I don't think I'll ever get tired of him making me feel sexy and desirable. I walk to my dresser and dig out a bikini and a few sets of bras and panties.

"Why don't you 'forget' to pack panties? I'd love easier access." He says it so casually, as if he's telling me to pick up milk at the store. My whole body clenches at the thought of him just reaching over and putting his hands on me, in the car, in a restaurant, in his bed. I'm starting to feel hot and needy again, and he's just lying there looking relaxed and unnerved. I try to hide what he can do to me with just a few words and purposely let him see me add another pair of panties to my bag.

"Hmph. We don't all go commando. You don't just get to 'touch me' whenever you feel like it either." I say it as seriously as I can, but I'm not sure I pull it off. The fact of the matter is I wish he would never stop touching me. Julian responds to my declaration by getting off the bed, wrapping his arms around me, pulling my dress up around my waist, and pinning me up against the wall. Before I can say a word, his finger is underneath my panties and rubbing gently back and forth over my clit. He's staring at me intently, waiting for me to argue with the method he's using to prove me wrong. As if I would, or could, do anything to stop this. Within moments, I'm very wet and very turned on, and it seems I'm not the only one. Julian is hard against my leg, and we both moan as he slowly dips his finger in and out of me. I grab his face in my hands and bring it to mine. We continue to look into each other's eyes as I trace his beautiful full lips with my tongue. I slip it in just a little, and he meets it with his. He starts working my lips, my tongue, and my mouth with the same skillfulness he's using on my sex.

"You get this wet just thinking about me touching you, don't you?" There is no point denying it, so I just moan a yes into his mouth.

"Es lo mismo para mí, baby. I've been hard since the night I met you. You drive me crazy."

It is such a turn on to know I have the same effect on him.

Julian kisses my neck and then my collarbone and slides down my body until he's on his knees in front of me. He runs his hand up my calf and puts my leg over his shoulder. He's holding up my dress with one hand and pulling my panties to the side with the other. I moan loudly and grab his hair when he puts his hot mouth on me. Holy hell! I'm going to have to remember to challenge him more often. He runs his tongue up and down my cleft and over my clit with the perfect amount of pressure, and I'm amazed he already knows exactly the way I need to be touched in order to orgasm. I arch my back and push myself into him. It doesn't take long for him to have me coming apart in his mouth. My legs start to shake, and I grab my dresser to hold myself up. Julian keeps licking me until the last shudder of my orgasm leaves my body. I have to bring my leg to the floor before I fall. Julian removes his mouth from me but doesn't say a word. He straightens my panties and stands up in front of me. He kisses me softly on the lips and then leans to whisper in my ear.

"Panties or no panties, I'll touch you whenever I can. I can't help myself. And your body responds so beautifully that I know you're okay with it."

"So much for the intermission." And so much for me not being overwhelmed. My legs are not the only thing shaking. I feel a sensation in my chest, as if my heart is expanding. I would love to believe I'm responding this way to him because I haven't had regular sex in so long. I tell myself I'm making up for lost time. I tell myself I like sex, and Julian is a great lover so, all of these feelings are just par for the course. I tell myself these powerful orgasms he keeps giving me are messing with my emotions and muddying my thoughts. But deep down, in my soul, I know it's much more. I feel a craving for him and a need to have him near me. The way my body responds to his touch is unlike anything I've felt before, and it scares me almost as much as it turns me on. I shouldn't be so comfortable with his control over me sexually. But I am. I am because I'm already falling in love with Julian Bauer.

"Are you complaining?" He teases me with a smile on his face. Unfortunately, I'm not feeling witty anymore. The magnitude of what I feel for this beautiful man standing in front of me hits me like a ton of bricks, and I feel tears spring to my eyes as my heart opens to him.

He notices the change in my expression and looks worried.

"What's wrong, Alexa?" I hear the genuine concern in his voice.

I dig deep and find a smile for him. I whisper, "Nothing," and reach out to pull him to me. He wraps his arms around me tightly and holds me close. He doesn't let go of me until I pull slightly away. He kisses me on the forehead as we separate.

"Let me go finish getting ready. You keep distracting me, and I'm really starving now."

"You're the one who keeps distracting me. Pulling underwear out of a drawer, challenging me, walking around here looking all sexy in your high heels." Good. Light again. I'm so thankful he doesn't ask why I just got all emotional.

One look in the mirror changes my good mood. I look like a hot mess. I'm not the type of girl who wears tons of makeup or needs to always look perfect, but being around the hotness that is Julian makes a girl want to look her best, and I certainly don't at the moment. I got so caught up in the drama, and the sex, and the sex again that I forgot I didn't do a thing to my hair after my shower. My hair is thick and wavy, and when I don't help it out a little, it gets a bit wild. I can't start again or we'll never get out of here. I pull it back and work it into a loose side braid. It actually turns out pretty good and goes with the laid-back style of the dress I have on. I apply a bit of makeup and throw whatever other toiletries I think I'll need in my bag. I hear Julian talking in the other room. I peek out and see he's on the phone with someone. He's lying down on my bed, and I have to force myself not to go over and attack him. Even after two orgasms, I'm still craving him. He catches me staring at him and flashes me a big grin. He hangs up the phone and walks toward me.

"Can I borrow your toothbrush?" Um. We're at the borrowing toothbrush stage? The irony, that I actually wonder that, it not lost on me. Julian has had his mouth all over me, and I'm weirding out because he wants to use my toothbrush?

"I actually have an extra one you can have." I bought a double pack last time, and it's coming in handy now. I pull it out of a drawer and hand it over along with my toothpaste. I leave him to his toothbrushing and finish getting my stuff together. When he comes out, I'm ready to go.

"You look beautiful, Lexie." Lexie. Not Alexa. I like it.

"Flattery will get you everywhere, Julian." I wrap my arms around him and tilt my head up for a kiss.

He gives me the softest little peck on the lips. "I'm seriously hanging on by a thread here. So no more touching me for a while, okay?"

I shake my head. "Yeah. No. I'm not agreeing to those rules. I'm more than happy to take care of you right now."

He quickly pulls away from me before he has a chance to consider my offer. "You can take care of me later. I called Dario, and he's waiting for us."

I'm actually glad he pulled away. I haven't eaten a thing since lunch. I ran, and I had two orgasms. I'm starving. "Okay, your choice. I'll keep my hands and my mouth to myself."

He groans as he grabs my bag and walks out the door.

We find Marissa, Cory, and Shannon sitting in the living room drinking wine and watching a movie. Shannon looks down at my bag in Julian's hand and smiles.

I introduce Julian to Cory and tell them I'm spending the night at his place. I try to say it like it's the hundredth time I've said it. I don't want to sound giddy, but that's how I'm feeling.

"Don't let the size of the bag fool you; Alexa is only spending the weekend with me."

I make a face at him and laugh. "You're so funny."

"I'm going to keep an eye on her so she doesn't go missing again." Julian is only half joking when he says this, and Marissa and Shannon both flash him knowing smiles. Seriously, are they ganging up on me already?

"Yeah, I found him at hotbabysitters.com. What do you think?" They all laugh, and Julian swats me in the ass. I take a deep breath and acknowledge the normal.

We say our goodbyes and finally get out the door. It's almost nine-thirty. Julian puts my bag in the trunk. He opens the door for me and shuts it behind me. I knew he was a gentleman. What a difference from the last time I was in this car. This time I feel like I belong.

CHAPTER 19

The car ride to the hotel goes quickly. We chat about work, the weather, and sports. The conversation is light and a welcome change from all the heavy stuff. Julian isn't kidding me about not touching him. When I try to hold his hand, he squeezes mine and pulls his away. He smiles at me and shakes his head. I know what his touch does to me, so I try not to take it personally.

We pull into the hotel parking garage at ten o'clock, and Julian parks in his designated spot. He walks around and opens my door for me. He takes my hand, and I follow him quickly through the hotel until we end up in the kitchen at Ursa's.

Julian leads me to a spot in the back of the kitchen where a small, round table is set up. There is a single rose lying on the table, and a lit candle flickers softly. We're only there for a few minutes when a man, who I assume to be Dario, comes up and sweeps me into his arms for a hug and kisses me on both cheeks. He does the same to Julian. He starts speaking in

Spanish really fast, and I have a hard time understanding his accent. He finally stops talking, claps his hands, and walks away.

"Well, okay then." What a ball of energy he is.

"That was Dario. He's very excited I brought someone with me. I usually eat back here alone." Julian did mention that earlier, and I find it hard to believe. Why wouldn't he bring dates here? I'll ask that question some other time.

"Where's he from? I couldn't really understand his accent."

"He's originally from Barcelona, but he married a woman from Portugal and lived in Italy for fifteen years. I think he made up his own language. It took me a while to understand him, but I think I do for the most part. Sometimes we end up speaking in English if I can't understand his 'Spanish.'"

A waiter comes over and asks us what we would like to drink. I order water.

"Water? You can have anything you'd like." I'm sure if I ordered an expensive bottle of wine, it would be totally okay. But I know Julian really doesn't drink, and I'm feeling a little dehydrated after my run today. I'm also not really in a drinking mood. I'm calm and relaxed already.

"I didn't drink enough water after running today, so I'm going to stick with water for a bit."

Julian orders water as well. When the waitress brings it to us, he holds his glass up and starts to make a toast. I raise my glass too. He has a huge smile on his face as he says his toast. "To our first official date." My heart melts, and I repeat the words.

We are interrupted by Dario who comes up behind me. He's loud, and I think Julian is right about his made-up language. I wonder if anyone really understands him. He places a few small plates on the table, quickly tells us what's on them, and hurries off. The rest of the night follows suit, and each time we finish a dish, it's replaced by another. By the time we're done, I think I've tried at least half of the items on the menu, and I'm stuffed. I pass on dessert and order a café con leche.

We've been so busy eating that we really haven't talked much. I'm fine with that too. I'm just enjoying his company. It's really easy just to stare at him. I sip my café and find I can't seem to take my eyes off of his lips. I'm clearly not being subtle about it either because when he notices he actually licks his lips slowly and bites down seductively on his bottom lip. He's totally challenging me. And totally turning me on.

We are in public and I know Julian isn't a fan of PDA. Plus, one date outside in the real world doesn't mean he wants people to know what's going on between us. I want to respond to his challenge by getting up and biting his lip myself but don't feel comfortable doing that in this setting. So, I do the only thing I know that might work to turn him on. I put my finger just on the inside of my lips and run my tongue over the tip. Then I pull it in and gently suck on it. My sex clenches when I hear Julian's sharp intake of breath. He isn't the only one who can play this game.

He motions for me to lean in, and he does the same. His voice is a soft, sexy whisper. "Uh huh. That's exactly what I want you to do to my dick later tonight."

Okay. Check please!

I'm trying to come up with a witty response when a woman I haven't seen before walks hurriedly up to us. Of course she is tall, blonde, and beautiful. She also looks very serious. She apologizes to Julian for interrupting, tells him someone by the name of Rodrigo told her Julian was here, and tells him there's some major issue with a reservation that he needs to take care of right away. I bet this Rodrigo person told her Julian was here with a date. She never once looks at me, which I find incredibly rude but not surprising. Julian lets her finish and turns to me.

"Candace, this is Alexa. Alexa, Candace is one of our managers."

Candace is less than thrilled to acknowledge me but really has no choice at this point. She looks at me long enough for me to see she isn't happy to actually find Julian with a woman. Her smile is faker than her DD boobs, and as she sizes me up, I get the distinct feeling she's wondering why Julian is with me instead of her. She mumbles a "nice to meet you" and turns back to Julian before I even respond. His body language is formal with her, and I suspect they haven't slept together. Her body language confirms she definitely wants to though.

Julian tells Candace how to handle this "crisis" and basically sends her on her way. She gives me one last dirty look before she huffs off.

"I'm sorry she was so rude. She isn't usually like that. She must be having a bad night."

I can't help but laugh. He can't be that clueless. I call him out on it.

"Seriously? Her bad mood materialized when she found you here with me. Candace wants you. I'm going to go out on a limb and guess you haven't slept with her. She can't understand why you're here with me. And before you disagree with me, don't. Women know these things."

He doesn't deny her attraction to him but confirms my suspicions. "You're right, we haven't slept together. And I'm sorry we were interrupted."

I shrug my shoulders. "No big deal." It really doesn't bother me, and the petty, jealous side of me is glad I got to ruin bitchy Candace's night.

I hear a laugh coming from behind me, and Julian's face lights up in a smile. I turn around and see his brother, Danny, and another guy walking up to us. So much for being alone tonight. Julian stands up and shakes the other man's hand and pulls him in for a quick bro hug.

"Alexa, you remember my brother, Danny. And this is Rafael, my cousin, who didn't tell me he was in town."

Danny looks at me and flashes me the patented Bauer smile. "Nice to see you again, Alexa." He looks at Julian, and I see him nod slightly at him. I don't want to read anything into it, but it seemed like a tacit sign of approval.

Rafael reaches out to shake my hand and also tells me it's nice to meet me. Julian looks at me as if to ask if it's okay that they join us. I smile and nod my head.

"Why don't you two grab some chairs and join us."

Rafael answers. "We can't stay. I have someone waiting for me in Stellar. I just wanted to come and say hi. Danny said you'd be here."

Julian looks disappointed, and I sense they're close. "How long are you in town, Rafi?"

"Just until Monday." Julian quickly explains to me that Rafi is playing on a Triple A baseball team for the Orioles. Ah, another Bauer baseball player.

Rafi asks what Julian is doing tomorrow. "Alexa and I are heading up to Lauderdale to go to the beach." We are? That's news to me. Julian looks at me for approval again. I smile and nod.

"Come with us. Danny, bring Gabby and ask Marco too. And bring whoever you're meeting up with, Rafi." Julian starts making all kinds of plans, and within ten minutes it sounds like we'll be having a party at the beach tomorrow. I'm excited at the idea of spending time with all of these people in Julian's world. They work out all the details and get ready to head out to the club.

Danny looks at me and gives me the warmest smile. He's trying to tell me something with it, but I'm not sure what it is. "I'm looking forward to hanging out with you tomorrow, Alexa."

"Me too, Danny." And I mean it. What better way to get to know someone than by spending time with their close friends and family. Rafi also gives me a huge smile as they leave.

"I hope you really don't mind that I just invited all those people to spend the day with us. I haven't seen Rafi in months."

"It's great. I have no problems sharing you." Of course I'm referring to spending time with his family. But, in true Julian fashion, he takes the opportunity to use my words to clarify something about our relationship. He's smiling but serious when he responds.

"Is that so? That might be something we need to talk about then because I have a huge problem sharing you." I know what he means, and I would like nothing more than to establish the fact that he wants to be exclusive.

"Let me clarify then. I have no problem sharing you with your family, your friends, or your work."

"Hmm … yeah, my list might not be as inclusive as yours, but we can talk about that later." An image of Luke pops into my brain when Julian says this. I know in my gut Julian has issues with our friendship and would most likely prefer to keep him off of the approved sharing list. We've been having such a great night, and I want to steer clear of any topics that might change that. When Danny and Rafi stopped by, I thought about suggesting we all go up to Orion for a drink so I could say hi to Luke. It feels wrong for me to be here and not see him. But I decided it was probably not a good idea. Julian's last comment confirms it was better to keep that idea to myself.

I must look like I'm deep in thought because Julian asks what I'm thinking about. "Luke" would not be a good answer, so I lie. "I'm thinking it's almost midnight and it's way past time for this 'intermission' to be over."

That makes him smile. "I couldn't agree more. Let's get out of here."

We get up, and I follow Julian through the kitchen as he looks for Dario. We find him standing in a corner, waving his hands, and having a "passionate" conversation with another cook. His food is great, but I'm not sure I'd like to work for him. He's clearly very temperamental. He notices Julian and me and comes over to us. We thank him for the awesome meal. I speak to him in Spanish, and he responds in his Dario language. He gives me a kiss on each cheek and goes back to yelling.

Julian takes my hand and tries to lead me quickly through the hotel to the parking garage. Unfortunately, we don't make our exit unnoticed. First we're approached by a ginormous man who can only be hotel security. Julian listens to the story and tells him to make sure to discuss it with Ruben. Julian explains that Ruben is his second in charge and works nights. We continue through the lobby, and I think we're home free when I hear an annoyingly sweet, high-pitched voice behind us calling out to Julian. As he turns around, Julian lets go of my hand. Two women are walking quickly toward us. Great, more models. I try not to feel insecure, but all of these women who approach Julian look like SI swimsuit models, and I'm finding it harder and harder to stay confident. The one who called out to Julian is absolutely stunning. She has long, jet-black hair and light blue eyes. She's at least 5'11" and wearing a very short, very tight dress that shows off her long legs and exquisite figure. The other woman is Latina and equally as pretty with thick, wavy, brown hair and huge, brown eyes. She is also barely dressed. I thought I looked good when we left my house, but compared to these two I feel like I'm dressed in a housecoat and slippers with my hair in rollers.

These women are not shy and come right up and hug Julian. The one with the black hair even kisses him on the lips, and I can tell by both of their body languages they absolutely have slept together before. I focus on the other woman to see if I get the same vibe, and I'm glad I don't. I don't think Julian has slept with her but not because she doesn't want to. She's preening like a peacock and posing so her beautiful body is on display. I'm amazed at how some of these women act around Julian and pray I didn't do anything that resembled this behavior when we met.

Julian doesn't introduce me, and I get the very distinct impression he wishes I were not there. His back is straight and stiff, and he sort of positions himself in between them and me. The women have to see me but don't acknowledge me either. What the fuck? Is he really trying to hide me? I'm hurt, and I'm *pissed*.

I stand there for a few minutes and listen to black-hair tell him all about some issues they're having with the set up for a photo shoot they're supposed to be doing tomorrow. Yep. They're models. They mention something about the pool and the cabanas. Blah, blah, blah. It all sounds like bullshit to me. I'm not in the business, but I'm pretty sure managers and agents take care of stuff like this. These women are just looking for a reason to talk to him, and if it's so obvious to me, I wonder how Julian doesn't see it. It was the same when bitchy Candace came into the kitchen. Everyone is always clamoring for his attention. Everyone except me, that is. I personally just want to get the hell away from here.

Julian tells them they need to talk to someone else and that he's sure it will all get taken care of in the morning, but they're insistent about showing him what they're talking about. They both keep touching him—on the arm, on the hand. The brown-haired one even leans into him and lays her head on his shoulder. He doesn't reciprocate any touching, but he doesn't move away from it either. I'm starting to freak out inside, and I know if I don't walk away I'll do or say something stupid.

"Julian." I say his name quietly.

He turns around and finally acknowledges me for the first time since these two walked up. I'm not sure what I read in his eyes, but it's clear he's really uncomfortable. He starts to explain this is a work thing, but I cut him off before he finishes his sentence. I do so by silently turning around and walking the other way. I don't even look back as I head anywhere but here. Did he really expect me to just stand there and wait? If so, he doesn't know me at all. The worst part is he just lets me go and doesn't call out to me.

If I had a car, I would be out of here so fast. But I don't, and all my stuff is in his car anyway. Tears spring to my eyes, and I'm kicking myself that I'm in this situation. I wanted to go public. I wanted to be part of his world. I was so stupid. It's much easier to be with Julian in private. I definitely don't like sharing.

I go to the only place where I know I'll feel better. I go find Luke. I know Luke won't ignore me and make me feel invisible. And if I'm being honest, I know it will piss Julian off when he finds me there. I stop in the ladies' room before I head up to Orion. I need to compose myself before Luke sees me, or he'll know something is wrong.

Luke notices me a few minutes after I get to the bar. "What's wrong, Lex? You're either about to cry or kill someone. I can't tell." Well that took all of about two seconds. Luke knows me so well, and of course he can read my expression. So much for composing myself.

"I don't want to talk about it. Please just get me a shot of Patrón."

Luke looks at me quizzically. He knows I'm not really a shot girl.

"Seriously, Luke. Get me a shot please. Actually make it two."

"If you tell me what happened." He's just standing there staring at me.

I'm not in the mood to play games. "I'll go somewhere else. Just get me a shot."

He sees I'm serious, so he pours two shots and puts them in front of me. I down them quickly and feel the warmth course through my body.

"Jesus, Lexie, what the hell is wrong? You're freaking me out."

I really don't want to tell him what just happened. I know he doesn't want to hear about Julian to begin with, and I know he doesn't want to hear about Julian and other women. Or maybe he does. He does like to be right.

"I'm fine. Julian had to take care of some business, and I came up to say hi."

"You're a horrible liar, Lex. Did he do something to hurt you?"

Ugh. "No, but he pissed me off. Please just let it go."

"I told you ..."

Luke stops mid-sentence as Julian comes up and stands next to me at the bar. My body betrays me, and I have to summon all of my mental strength not to turn and address him. Thirty minutes ago, I was in his arms, and now I want to run away.

"I thought I would find you here." I hear the sarcasm in his voice, and I know he's pissed I ran to Luke. Good, serves him right. I keep staring forward and refuse to acknowledge him like he refused to acknowledge me.

"Uh huh. I came to see a friendly face."

Luke is looking back and forth between Julian and me, and I know he thinks it's awesome we're fighting. It doesn't surprise me Julian decides not to respond negatively. He won't get into this in front of Luke.

"Are you ready to go?" Julian sounds hostile and impatient. Seriously? He's the one who felt the need to run off.

"After I have another shot. Luke, please get me another." Luke looks at me like I'm nuts and shakes his head.

"I don't think so, Lex. The third is never a good idea for you."

Julian grabs my hand and tugs on it, physically asking me to look at him. I meet his glare with one of my own.

"Third? You've only been up here for twenty minutes."

"And?" I look back at Luke. "Another shot please." My voice is dripping with sarcasm.

Luke shakes his head and pours me another shot. I hold it up and toast to both Luke and Julian.

"Here's to you two men thinking you know what's best for me."

I down the shot quickly and turn to face Julian. "I'm ready to go now."

He's staring at me with fire in his eyes, and I know I've crossed a line. I've embarrassed him in front of Luke. I glance at Luke, and his expression matches Julian's.

"Are you okay to go, Lex?" Luke uses the opportunity to come to my rescue even though I can tell he isn't happy with me.

"She's good, Luke. Alexa, let's go."

I hear Luke become my white knight. "You don't need to speak for her, Julian."

Uh-oh. They're staring at each other, and it's anyone's guess which man will back down first this time. This is getting way too intense. Luke needs to remember Julian is his boss. I would hate for anything to happen to his job because of me, especially when he really is just looking out for me.

I lean across the bar and give him a quick peck on the lips. I know that is going to piss Julian off even more, but I really don't care.

"I'm good. I'll call you later."

Luke shakes his head at me and reluctantly walks away. I get off my stool and turn to walk toward the stairs. Julian follows behind me, and when we're out of earshot of the bar, he grabs my hand and turns me around.

"What did he mean by he told you? What were you two talking about when I walked up?"

I yank my hand away. "Nothing."

"I'm not playing, tell me what he meant? What did he tell you?"

I can't help myself. I'm pissed, hurt, and now a little buzzed. "He told me to stay the fuck away from you."

Julian's eyes blaze, and the laugh that comes out of his mouth isn't one of amusement. "And what was his reason for that?"

"Does it matter?"

"Oh yeah. I'd love to hear why Luke thinks you should stay away from me." Julian's posture is rigid, and I can tell he's trying to stay calm.

"Um, maybe because he doesn't want me to be part of your 'girl of the night' club." Sarcastic Alexa is fully out and not holding back now.

"Would that be *my* girl of the night club or *his*? Because I'm sure he'd be okay with you being part of his."

I shake my head. "What are you talking about?"

"Gimme a break. Luke goes home with a different girl almost every night. And he's worried about me?" Now I'm frustrated. This isn't about Luke. This is about how Julian treated me earlier.

"No, Julian, he's worried about *me*, and after how you just treated me, he appears to have good reason."

Julian's expression softens as he formulates his response. I'm anxious to hear how he's going to defend himself.

"I'm sorry I treated you the way I did, but it was the better of two evils. Victoria and Elyse are not nice women. Victoria, the one with the black hair, and I have been together a few times. She wanted more, I didn't. Had I put you in her line of fire, she would have gone after you. I've seen her do it. She doesn't understand why I don't want her, and she would question why I want you."

"Why? Because I'm not a model?"

He doesn't miss a beat. "Yes."

"And I'm sure it would've been really hard for you to explain it, right? I mean why you were with me." My heart is breaking as I realize this is how it's probably always going to be. People will always question what he sees in me.

"Were? No, Alexa. Are. I *am* with you, and I don't have a problem telling anyone why. But those two are mean and nasty. I didn't want them to even talk to you."

"Well thanks for protecting me. It sure seems like you surround yourself with some quality women. Present company excluded."

"I'm sorry. I really am." He tries to pull me to him, but I put my hand up to stop him. I'm not feeling okay with this yet.

Julian shakes his head. "Please don't do this."

"Do what?" My hands are on my hips, and my posture is defensive. I'm very stubborn when I'm hurt.

His answer isn't more than a whisper. "Pull away."

"Pull? Let's be clear here. You pushed, Julian. You pushed." The last part also comes out in a whisper, and I realize I don't want to fight with him about this. It's exhausting.

"Maybe. And you ran right to Luke, didn't you?"

"Julian, I'm not going to keep having this conversation about Luke. He's my friend, a good friend who's only looking out for my best interests."

Julian takes a deep breath and exhales. He's over this too. "Okay. I don't want to keep fighting with you about Luke, or anything really. I can't tell you how sorry I am we even came here tonight, but I really need you to do something for me."

"What?"

"Please just think about whose interests Luke is really looking out for."

Before I have a chance to reply, Julian pulls me in close to him. This time I let him. He kisses me on the forehead and holds me in his arms for a few minutes. He takes my hand, and I know he isn't going to let it go no matter what. As we walk through the hotel toward the parking garage, several other people try to approach him. He puts his hand up to each one and tells them to go find Ruben. He doesn't even stop.

Julian finally lets go of my hand when we get to his car. He opens the door, and I get in. I glance over at him as we exit the garage, and see he's pensive and tense. He's very quiet, and when I catch his eyes, he gives me a thin smile. My insecurities kick in, and I wonder if he's as worn out by this drama as I am. He has to be. We have been arguing or fooling around for the last twenty-four hours. This relationship, or whatever we're doing, is wearing me out big time. I feel like everything is different now, and in true Alexa fashion, I really just want to go home. I can't help but think about all the women Julian has brought to his place. I'm sure the girl from the bar has been in Julian's bed, and I can't get that image out of my head. I begin to feel anxious, and nothing good ever happens when I start feeling like this.

Before I can stop myself, I open my mouth. "Julian, you're not going to like what I have to say, but I think it would be a better idea if I went home tonight. I'd rather not get to your house and go through that drama again."

I watch Julian grip the steering wheel with both hands. Even though we're only a few blocks from his house, he pulls over. He takes a deep breath in and then exhales. He turns and looks at me, and I can see he wants off the roller coaster too.

"Alexa, it's one o'clock in the morning, and I'm exhausted from this day, which feels like it's lasted forever. We've been all over the map emotionally and physically, and all I want to do is get into my bed, wrap my body around you, and go to sleep. We seriously can do that. Just go to sleep. But if you really don't want to be with me, I'll take you home. But I won't stay."

Julian is calling my bluff. He's telling me he wants to wrap his beautiful body around mine, and I'm questioning his feelings? What is wrong with me? We started out this night with such great plans for the weekend. Damn it. Why am I letting everyone ruin this for me? I'm here with him, and he wants me. And despite every crazy emotion I've experienced today, I want him too. I need him.

I take a deep breath. "Never mind. Take me home with you. I'll stay."

He nods as he reaches over and squeezes my hand, and we make the rest of the trip from the hotel to his condo in silence. Even the elevator ride is quiet. The last time we were in the elevator, Julian had his hands and mouth all over me. I can't help but be a little turned on by the memory. However, I don't see a repeat of that night happening now. Aside from holding my hand and a hug or two, Julian hasn't really touched me since we left my house earlier. I think maybe that's some of the problem. I'm craving the contact. It helps ground me and lets me know without any doubt he wants me.

We enter his unit, and once again I'm amazed by how beautiful it looks with the moon and stars shining through the windows and across the floor.

"This view is so beautiful. I can only imagine what the sunrises and sunsets look like."

I know the way to his bedroom, but I haven't really seen the rest of the condo. I walk through the foyer and into the living space. The white slate floor continues throughout the whole area, and the whole back wall of the condo consists of floor-to-ceiling windows. The view is breathtaking. I look around and take in the rest of the place. The kitchen, dining, and living room are open concept and join together for a large living space. There is a huge, leather sectional sofa in a chocolate brown and a flat screen TV that covers almost one whole wall in the living room area. The other furniture pieces are a mix of white, grays, and browns. It's decorated very tastefully with muted, nondescript artwork, but in my opinion, the style is very impersonal. There are no pictures anywhere, and I don't know if I see Julian anywhere in this style. The hotel seems so much more warm and vibrant, like him. I wonder if someone decorated his condo for him. It's definitely expensive looking, but I find it cold. I would love to get my hands on this place and add some color and personal touches. My home is nowhere near as nice, and I definitely don't have these views, but it feels like a home, and we have pictures everywhere.

He's still not saying anything, and now his silence is making me uncomfortable.

I turn and face Julian, who is standing in the middle of the living room staring at me. "Are you not talking to me anymore?"

He has a resigned look on his face, and the tone of his voice matches. "I'm glad you're here. I just don't want to say anything that will make you want to leave."

Wow. He's scared of me leaving. I guess that shouldn't surprise me. I did leave the last time I was here. I also went MIA for a few hours today, and I just attempted to bail on him tonight. And each time I run, he has told me how much he wants me to stay. Rationally, I know I'm not being fair here, but emotionally, I'm having a hard time believing all this.

I turn to him and attempt a smile. "Let's just go to bed."

He carries my stuff into his room and sets my bag near a door I assume leads to his closet. I've been in the bedroom before, but I didn't pay much attention to what it looked like. I was too mesmerized by the view and by Julian. As I look around, I'm more convinced than ever that some overpriced decorator got ahold of Julian and convinced him that his style needed to fall into the category of cold and impersonal. First of all, his bedroom is spotless. I mean there is nothing out of place. It doesn't even look like anyone lives here. The massive king-size bed is set on a dark, wood platform, and his linens are various shades of browns mixed with white. There's no color in here and no personal touches. Not even a picture. There are two dressers and a few plants. That's it. Julian is warm and vivacious, and this place is so not him.

I'm lost in my redecorating ideas when Julian responds, "I'm going to take a quick shower. Do you want to go in before me?"

No, I want to go in with you, I think to myself. I shake my head no and tell him he can go first.

"You can use the other bathroom if you want. I'll show you where it is." I grab my toiletries bag and follow him down the hall. He grabs me a towel from a closet we walk past and leaves me to get ready for bed. This bathroom looks like the rest of the house. Good thing whoever designed this place didn't touch the hotel.

I shut the door and exhale. We have been intimate several times now, but we haven't stayed a whole night together, and I need the privacy. I use the bathroom, brush my teeth, and wash my face. Julian saw me today when I was a sweaty mess after running, so I'm not feeling shy about going makeup-less. That ship has already sailed. I finish up and walk back into Julian's room. I can hear the water running through the cracked door. I'm taking that as an invitation. Without allowing any time to question my decision, I take my clothes off and head into the bathroom.

Julian's bathroom is huge and is decorated like the rest of his condo, masculine and contemporary with clean lines. No surprise here. The double vanities are made out of the same dark wood that's in the kitchen, and the countertops are white stone. The floors and walls are covered with a mixed gray-and-white marble tile, and there's a huge, jetted white tub in the corner. The shower is massive and looks like something you'd find in a luxury spa. The walls and curb-less shower floor are made out of slate-gray and dark brown stone tiles. There's a white stone, floating bench, and the glass enclosure is frameless, which gives the appearance of the shower being totally open. I'm impressed with the shower but more impressed with the man in the shower. I stand there for a minute and stare at Julian. He has his eyes closed and his head tilted back with the water running over his face. He's so beautiful. My body comes alive, and I'm taken aback by my need to touch him. He opens his eyes, looks toward the door, and sees me standing there. A slow, inviting smile breaks across his face, and I can tell he's happy to see me.

I walk over to the shower and open the door. He immediately pulls me into his arms, and as the warm water washes over me, I feel the tension leave my body and disappear down the drain.

Julian is pressed up against me, and it feels incredible. I run my hands over his body, and within minutes I'm aching for him to be inside of me. His shower is state-of-the-art, and there's water coming out of jets in all directions. I close my eyes and get lost in the sensation of the warm water, the feel of Julian's rock-hard upper body beneath my hands, and the exquisite feeling of him running his hands all over me. I feel his erection against me as well. I knew when I got in the shower what my intentions were, but because Julian mentioned he was tired and just wanted to go to sleep, I decide to let him chart the course and set the tempo.

He sets a slow and sensual pace, and although I'm already completely turned on, I relax and savor the delicious feeling of him slowly running his wet, soapy hands all over my body. He doesn't miss a spot. He's caressing me and teasing me and torturing me in the most delicious way. His hands are on my breasts, on my ass, and between my legs. I'm quivering from his touch. I honestly think I could stand here and let him touch me like this forever, but I need to feel him too. I want to pleasure him and take care of him like he keeps doing for me. He gave me two orgasms earlier tonight, and although I don't think he's keeping score, it's his turn to be satisfied. I lather my hands and run them over his body. He begins to moan and shuts his eyes. I know by the sounds he's making and by the way he leans into my touch that he needs the physical connection as much as I do. His erection grows even larger as I stroke him steadily with one of my soapy hands. I reach around behind him and run my other hand over his ass. I pull him into me, and he groans loudly as I eliminate any space between us. He grabs hold of a bar in the shower to keep his balance, and I see that he's completely lost in my touch. I kiss his chest and run my tongue over his nipples. I bite down softly on one, and he thrusts his hips into me. I keep my hand on him, stroking his long, hard shaft as I sit down on the floating bench. I turn my head so the water isn't hitting me in the face, and I take him in my mouth. He finally speaks.

"Sí, baby. Sí. I've wanted to feel your mouth on me all night." There's no bigger turn on than to watch Julian let go and give himself to me. I feel powerful and in control, and I like it.

I take him as deep as I can and gently knead his balls with one hand. I run my tongue up and down and around his shaft and across the soft, wide head. Julian's hands are in my hair now, and he's gripping my head as he loses himself in the rhythm of me sucking him off. His whole body is moving into me, and I struggle not to gag as he thrusts himself deeper into my mouth. I look up at him and see he's watching me pleasure him. I feel a burst of warmth spread from between my legs and throughout my body. I pull back so my mouth is just covering the head of Julian's dick, suck harder, and taste the saltiness of his arousal. A loud groan comes out of his mouth, and I see his legs begin to shake. He's close. I keep my eyes on him and watch his expression as I slow things down and start gently running just the tip of my tongue delicately around the head of his pulsating dick. He's struggling not to break the connection with our eyes, but I can tell he's barely hanging on as his eyes flicker open and shut. And just when I think there's no way I can be any more turned on, Julian opens his mouth.

"Dios mío, you're driving me fucking crazy. Te quiero mucho, baby. I want to come inside of your beautiful mouth, and then I want to come inside of your beautiful body."

Yes please; I want that too. I stop teasing him and take him in as deep as I can. I grasp him firmly and stroke him hard and fast. He has one hand on my head and the other on the bar as he thrusts his hips wildly. I hear his breathing speed up, and his grip tightens on my hair. I feel his whole body stiffen as he calls my name and explodes into my mouth.

I keep my mouth on him while the last of his orgasm races through his body. When he's done, I stand up and face him. He reaches behind him and turns the water off. He takes my face in his hands and brings it close to him.

"You are so, so beautiful, Alexa. Thank you for that."

When his lips finally touch mine, they're soft and sweet. The kiss that follows is the same, and as waves of emotion course through my body, I know I need to stop worrying that I'm going to fall in love with this man. It's already happening, and there's nothing I can do to stop it.

Julian quickly dries himself off and wraps a towel around his waist. He grabs a second one and envelops me in it. I dry myself off and hang my towel on a hook on the back of the door. I'm usually a little more modest, but the way Julian is looking at my naked body makes me feel beautiful and confident. I walk back into the bedroom and take panties and a tank top out of my bag.

"You won't be needing those."

I turn around and see a naked Julian climbing into his big, comfy bed. Mmm ... I doubt I'll ever get tired of looking at that view.

I shrug my shoulders and put my clothes back in my bag. I run a comb through my hair, fix it into a braid so I don't look like a wild woman in the morning, and climb into bed. I'm barely in when Julian wraps his arms around me and pulls me tightly to him. After a little shifting, I find a comfortable position, take a deep breath, and exhale. It took a ton of work, but I'm finally where I want to be—in his bed and in his arms. Julian starts running his fingers across my stomach, and I have zero doubts he feels like he needs to satisfy me before we go to sleep. I had already decided before I got in bed that I just needed him to hold me. I wiggle out of his embrace and roll over so I'm facing him. He looks tired but peaceful. I place my lips softly on his and whisper, "Goodnight, Julian."

I know he understands when he replies, "Are you sure, Lexie?"

I nod my head, lay it against his chest, and fall asleep in his arms.

CHAPTER 20

The feel of Julian's very hard penis pressing against my ass isn't a bad way to wake up. Julian shut the blinds in his room last night, so it's still dark in here. The clock on his bedside table says 9:00 a.m., and I can't believe it's already so late. I don't remember the last time I slept so soundly or woke up this turned on. But now that I'm awake, I'd like to finish what we started last night. I wiggle my ass and push it against Julian. I'm not sure if he was awake before, but he is now. His penis twitches against me.

"Hmm ... good morning to you too."

He reaches around and puts his hand on my breast and starts caressing it. He rolls my nipple between his fingers, and I instantly feel a rush of wetness between my thighs. I moan and push back into him harder. He grips my hip and holds me to him. He's making slow circles with his hips while pushing his rock-hard dick against me. I take the hand that's on my hip and place it on my throbbing wet sex.

Julian whispers sexily in my ear. "Mmm ... is that what you want, baby? Do you want me to touch you here? Dime lo que quieres."

"I just want you to touch me, Julian. Wherever. However. I need your hands on me."

He groans as he slides his finger across my clit and into me. I rock my ass and hips back into him and fall into the rhythm of his touch. He kisses my neck, my shoulders, and my back. His tongue is hot on my skin. I feel a second finger enter me as Julian speeds up the tempo, and I can't help but moan in ecstasy. As good as this feels, I want the real deal. I want him inside me. I try to pull away so I can turn around to face him, but he stops me and whispers in my ear.

"No, Corazón, let's try something different this morning."

He gently rolls me over on my stomach, and I understand he wants to enter me from behind. I lie flat for a minute as Julian reaches over and grabs a condom from his nightstand. I hear him rip the packet, and I turn my head and see him rolling it on. I get up on my knees, and Julian positions himself behind me. He pulls me up so that my back is against his front and we're both on our knees. Julian reaches around with both hands and massages my swollen breasts. His hands find my nipples, and he tugs at them and rolls them between his fingers. His lips are hot on my neck, and I shudder as he dips his tongue in my ear. I arch back into his hands and make an undulating motion with my body. He reaches down with one hand and rubs his fingertips across my clit. I'm so turned on and so close to climaxing now.

Julian senses this. "Are you close, baby? You're so wet. I can't wait to be inside of you, but I want you to come for me first. C'mon, come for me."

Every muscle in my body tightens as Julian brings me to an amazing climax with his fingers and his words. He pulls his hands away when he's sure my orgasm is finished and leans into me in silent direction for me to get into a kneeling position. I do, and I feel his hard shaft slide easily into me. I can't help but gasp as he grips my hips and sinks all the way in. He's long and hard, and in this position I feel him so deep inside of me.

"Are you okay?"

I'm better than okay. "You feel amazing."

"*You* are amazing, baby. The way your body responds to me is such a turn on."

Julian's slow rhythm starts to pick up speed, and his heavy balls slap against my sex. He's so deep it almost hurts—but not quite. We're so fused together it's hard to tell where he stops and where I start, and I realize that not only do I want to be his, but I need to be his. And I want him to totally be mine. I make a vow right then, as he's pumping in and out of me, that I'm going to make every effort I can to make sure nobody else gets in the middle of what's happening between us. Julian must be feeling the same emotions because the next words out of his mouth are, "Eres mía, Lexie. Solo mía."

It isn't a question. He's telling me I'm his and only his. My heart swells at his declaration, and I want him to know that yes, I'm his and only his.

"Yes, I'm yours. Solamente tuya."

Julian slows down, and I feel him start to slowly pull out of me. I let him turn me over so I'm beneath him. He spreads my legs and sinks back into me. The few seconds without him in me were too long. I wrap my legs around him and grab his ass so I can pull him as close to me as possible.

Julian's face is right next to mine. I think he's going to kiss me, but he whispers into my mouth instead. "Say that again, please. I want to look at you when you tell me you're mine." His eyes are blazing with desire.

"I'm yours, *Julian.* I'm yours."

His lips find mine, and his tongue slips into my mouth. I touch my tongue to his, and they begin a slow, seductive dance that imitates the way his body is dancing with mine. We move so well together. We move like one. I feel Julian's muscles tighten, and I know he's close to coming. He pulls back, and I see his chest heaving and hear his breathing become more rapid. He's moaning softly and starts to thrust faster and faster until he releases all his desire into me.

He lies on top of me for a few moments, and I savor the feeling of his sweaty, shaking body against mine. He presses up into a pushup position over me and leans his forehead against mine. His eyes are closed, and he stays like that for a minute. When he opens his eyes and looks at me, I see everything he's feeling. He starts to say something and then stops. He kisses me deeply instead and lets his emotions pour into me through his touch.

Julian's mouth is on mine. Then it's on my neck, then my breasts, my stomach, and finally my sex. He spreads me with his fingers and flicks his tongue over my swollen clit. I'm still wet and very sensitive from his dick rubbing against me, and his touch causes me to squirm.

"Want me to stop?" Julian teases. His long, smooth tongue is gently moving up and down my cleft. It feels so amazing, and I feel the stirrings of another orgasm beginning.

"No, please, don't stop. I never want you to stop touching me. I want to come."

I've never really had a problem asking for what I want in bed, and I've had some vocal lovers in the past, but Julian makes me feel so comfortable that I'm able to tell him exactly what I want and need. Ironically, I really don't need to say anything to him because he already knows exactly how to take care of me.

"I told you, I won't stop until you come for me. I could stay in this bed and make you come all day."

The thought of Julian spending that much time between my legs coupled with the reality of his tongue licking me brings me to an explosive orgasm. I lie there trembling as Julian kisses the inside of my thighs and lays his head on my stomach. We're both silent as we savor the delicious moments we've shared this morning. All of the craziness from last night has disappeared, but I know there are some things we really need to talk about. As fantastic as the sex is, I don't want to get in the habit of using our bodies to say things our mouths can't or won't.

Julian gives me a quick kiss and tells me he's going to use the bathroom first. He shuts the door, and I hear the shower turn on. I don't join him this time. He's out quickly and walks into his closet naked. It's hard not to stare. He comes back out in turquoise board shorts that hang sexily off his hips and look great against his tan skin. He isn't wearing a shirt, and his abs are on full display. I'm not sure I'm going to be able to keep my hands off of him if he's dressed, or not dressed, like this all day. He sees me ogling him and flashes me a big, warm smile.

"I'm going to go make some coffee and breakfast. Omelets okay?"

I nod my head. "Wow, I'm a lucky girl. Great sex and now breakfast? You know how to treat a lady right."

I'm still lying naked in his bed. He walks toward me, bends over, and places a soft kiss on my lips. "This is just the beginning, Alexa."

My heart swells, and I smile brightly at him. For the hundredth time, I mentally pinch myself to prove this is real.

When Julian leaves the bedroom, I grab my bag and head into the bathroom. I take a quick shower, brush my teeth, and keep telling myself I deserve to feel this good. I wind my hair up into a messy bun and put on a touch of makeup. I fish my teal bikini out and put it on. It's halter style with neon-green ties and piping. I think it looks good on me and hope Julian agrees. I throw a matching three-quartered-sleeve mini cover-up over it, put some gold hoops on, and slip my feet into gold, Tory Burch thong sandals. I check myself out in the full-length mirror behind the door and give myself a mental thumbs-up.

I smell coffee and breakfast as I make my way into the kitchen. It's a beautiful kitchen with dark cabinetry, white countertops, and state-of-the-art stainless steel appliances. There's also a huge island in the middle. Julian's back is to me as I enter, and I see he's on the phone and cooking at the same time. It sounds like work, so I stay quiet. He has set a mug, creamer, and sugar out for me, and motions to the coffee pot when he notices me. I make a cup and walk over to the door leading to the terrace. Julian nods that it's okay to go out, so I open the door and step out. It's already hot and humid, but the terrace is covered by an awning and is somewhat shaded. This space looks similar to the private one at the hotel, and for the first time I see Julian's design stamp. I sit on the white couch, tuck my feet under me, and enjoy the gorgeous views of the ocean, intercoastal, and downtown. No wonder people pay so much to live here. I would spend all my time outside if I did.

I hear the door open behind me, and Julian tells me breakfast is ready. He has made veggie omelets that look and smell delicious. A carafe of orange juice and cut strawberries sit on the table as well. A perfect, healthy breakfast served to me by a hot man in a swimsuit. I quietly wonder to myself what chick flick or fairytale I woke up into this morning. Julian is still on the phone and motions for me to start eating. I wait and drink my coffee. After a few minutes, he gets off.

"Sorry about that. I usually go in every morning, and my staff aren't accustomed to not seeing me first thing."

"Do you need to go in? Because—"

"No, they'll be fine." He cuts me off, and I let him. I'd rather he not go in.

I take a bite of my omelet. It's delicious. My man can cook too.

"Thanks for breakfast. This is yummy."

"You're welcome. It's my way of saying thank you for rocking my world last night and this morning."

"Well, in that case, I need to cook for you the rest of the week because you keep rocking mine."

Julian smiles brightly. "I talked to Danny. We're going to stay here instead of heading to Lauderdale. It's late already. Do you mind?"

"No. It doesn't matter to me. I'm not sure why we were going to leave and go someplace else anyway."

"Neither Danny or I really like to hang out here. People know who we are and think they can bother us with work-related stuff. You saw what happened at the hotel last night. I'd love to hang out there, or here, but it turns into work most of the time."

Julian's answer makes a lot of sense, and I tell him so. What I don't say aloud is that as long as I'm with him I'm okay and I'd be happy anywhere as long as we were together. We finish eating, and I help him clean up. It's normal couple stuff, and it feels awesome. His phone rings again, and he gets back on with work. His being on the phone makes me think about my phone. I walk back to the bedroom, sit on the bed, and grab my phone out of my purse. I turn it on and notice I have a few texts from Luke. Two are from last night, and one from just twenty minutes ago.

Luke: *Lex...?*
Luke: *Ok, it's morning. Call plz*

I text him back instead of calling.

Alexa: *It's all good. Thanks for checking on me. Off 2 beach. Call you later.*

I know I won't be talking to him the rest of the weekend if I'm with Julian, and I hope he gets the hint. It's not that I don't want to talk to him, but Julian and I finally seem to have found our groove, and I don't want to jeopardize it by talking to Luke. Julian is still on the phone, so I check my e-mails and send a few texts to my roommates and parents so they all know I'm okay. I look at the rumpled sheets on the bed and decide to make it. I pick up Julian's pillow and inhale. It smells like him, and I hold it close to me and breathe him in. I love that after we have sex I can smell him on me as well. Julian walks in the room, sees me hugging his pillow, and breaks out in a huge smile.

He opens his arms. "That pillow doesn't hug back."

I walk into his arms, and he hugs me tightly. He gives the best, most sincere hugs, and being in his arms has become one of my happy places. After a few moments, I reluctantly pull away and begin making the bed. Julian joins me. He has a smile plastered on his face, and he keeps glancing over at me.

"And what are you thinking about?" I ask seductively.

I can only imagine. I'm staring at his half-naked body and thinking about what I want to do to it later. I assume his response will mirror my X-rated thoughts.

"I'm thinking about how good it felt to fall asleep with you in my arms and to wake up next to you."

Okay. Not what I expected. Better than I expected. I walk around the bed to where he's standing and put my arms around his neck, stand on my toes, and kiss him softly on the lips.

"How do you always know the perfect thing to say?"

"Was that the perfect thing to say, Alexa? It wouldn't have been better for me to tell you I was thinking about your naked body and all the things I want to do to it?"

As he says these words to me, he's rubbing his hand up and down my back and over my ass as he holds me tightly to him. A throbbing begins between my legs, and a slow heat starts to spread throughout my body. My body is saying yes, but my mind doesn't care for his response. He answered my first question emotionally, and when I responded in kind, he went the sex route. I know I've been avoiding the emotional stuff, but if he starts avoiding it too, we'll never move forward. I quickly wonder if he crafted his answer so I'd be comfortable with it. I'm feeling very close to him right now, so I answer truthfully.

"Julian, I can't describe in words how incredible your desire for me makes me feel, and I'm more than willing to climb back into this bed and let you do whatever you want to my body. But your first answer was the right one. I know I have a hard time with the emotional stuff, but I don't want this to only be about the physical stuff. I hope you know that."

Julian hugs me tightly and doesn't let go for a few minutes. I can feel his heart beating against mine, and I know I've touched him with my response. When he pulls back and looks at me, his eyes are soft and tender.

"*That* was the perfect thing to say. And in answer to your question, no, I'm not always sure what you want. Sometimes I don't know if you want me to fuck you or make love to you. I don't know if you want me to only tell you how amazing you make me feel physically or if it's okay to tell you how I'm feeling emotionally. I'm not sure you know either. And right now that's okay. I'm enjoying your body so much that I'm willing to make sex the focal point because you seem more comfortable with that level of intimacy. But whether you want to admit it or not, this thing between us has not been *just* physical from the second you ran into me in the stairwell."

I'm not really sure how to respond because everything he said is very true. Except the part where he thinks I don't know what I want or how I feel. I do. I'm just not ready to tell him my feelings because I'm scared to death of them. I'm also scared of how he may be feeling for me. It's all so quick and so intense. Emotions start to bubble up inside of me as I find myself overwhelmed by his ability to just lay it all out there.

His arms are still around me, and he's looking down at me, waiting for my reply. In this moment I want to tell him everything. I want him to know about Brady, about why it's so hard to trust how I feel, and why it's even harder to trust how he feels. I want to tell him my heart feels happy and light for the first time in so long. I want to tell him what's happening between us feels magical, and that I want to fall asleep and wake up next to him every day for the rest of my life. But the very fact I'm thinking about forever with Julian is enough to make me start flipping out. We have been together for just a few weeks. This incredible man is asking me what I want from him, and I can't make any of those thoughts become words. I'm determined not to let this special moment pass, so I say the only thing I can.

"I just want you. That's all I'm sure of. I just want you."

When Julian's mouth finds mine, it's no longer soft and sweet. It's hungry and greedy. I've obviously given him enough with my few words. He backs me up and lays me on the bed. His hands are on me, impatiently tugging at my cover-up. I feel his erection on my leg, pushing into me with its hardness. I'm untying his shorts when I hear voices in the hallway. It startles me, and I push Julian off. He seems more frustrated than concerned.

"Were you expecting visitors?"

"It's Danny and Rafi."

"Oh, I thought they were meeting us at the beach. I didn't know they were coming here first."

"Danny lives in the building too, on the third floor. He has a key. I need to remind him to knock first."

Julian gets off of me and adjusts his shorts, his erection still very visible. I shrug my shoulders and smile. I get off the bed and do some adjusting of my own. Julian calls down the hallway and tells them we'll be right out. He walks back over to me and takes me in his arms again. He leans down and whispers in my ear. "I'm all yours, Alexa Reed. I'm not sure how this happened, but I'm all yours."

I squeeze tighter and try to hold back the tears that spring to my eyes. Oh my God. All mine. I hope he doesn't mind telling me that until I actually believe it.

Julian throws on a T-shirt, and we walk out of the bedroom hand in hand and find Danny and Rafi waiting for us in the living room. They both hug and kiss me on the cheek and act as if we're old friends. They tell us they're all set up down at the beach. Julian asks Danny why they even came up.

"Just wanted to make sure you were coming down, bro. I didn't want you to get stuck in the house all day."

They both turn and look at me, and I'm sure I'm blushing. Did they think we wouldn't be able to get out of bed long enough to get down to the beach? They really aren't that far off. They did just interrupt the beginning of another promising encounter.

Julian and I grab the rest of our stuff, and he throws his phone and keys into my beach bag as we head down. The conversation is light and casual, and I just listen as Julian catches up with Rafi. It's great to see him interacting with his family. I want to know all of him, and this is a perfect way to make that happen.

CHAPTER 21

They weren't kidding when they said they were set up. Umbrellas, chairs, and coolers are out, and Danny points to some chairs that are set up for us. I'm not sure who did all this, but I could get used to it. A pretty, petite brunette walks up, and Danny introduces me to Gabby, who I assume is his girlfriend. There are six people in this little beach encampment, and one by one they all come up and introduce themselves to me and say hi to Julian. They're all super friendly, but I get the distinct feeling that either they're surprised to see Julian with someone period, or they're surprised to see him with someone like me.

Julian takes off his shirt, sits down on his chair, and I follow. I take my cover-up off and put it in my bag. I catch Julian's stare as I turn back around. His gaze is hot and full of desire.

"Uh-oh. Tenemous un problemo?" I know he isn't serious, so I don't panic.

"What problem do we have?" My tone is teasing, and I can't wait to hear what he has to say.

"Well for starters, your tits look amazing in that top. Actually your whole body looks amazing in that bikini. I can barely keep my hands off you as it is with your clothes on, and here you are half naked. I'm hard and horny again, hence the problem."

"Phew. I thought you meant a real problem." I chuckle a little and flash him a smile. "I can handle hard and horny problems. As a matter of fact, that's my favorite problem of yours to handle. And by the way, I've been wet since the minute you walked out of the closet in those shorts."

I'm staring right at him when I say this, and I watch him grip the arms of his beach chair tightly. He needs to remember I'm pretty good at the sexual banter too.

He leans as close to me as he can get while still sitting and whispers in my ear. "Stay that way all day, baby, because I plan on fucking you all night long."

Um okay. I feel his words between my legs, and I have to cross and uncross them and shift in my chair to try to calm myself down. My toes are actually curling. To make matters worse, Julian offers to rub sunscreen on my back, and I let him. The feeling of his hands on my back and shoulders is intense and delicious and intensifies my desire. I grab the sunscreen and make him turn around so I can do the same thing to him. Rubbing my hands all over his body does as much for me as it does for him, and I'm not sure how I'm going to last all day without having him in me. It's official. I'm addicted.

I'm lost in my fantasies of Julian on top of me when two of his friends, Marco and Steve, walk up. They sit in the sand in front of us and chat for about fifteen minutes. When they leave, I sit back in my chair and look around. These people are eating, drinking, listening to music, and just hanging out, but I keep catching their glances as every single one of them checks me out. Nothing is overt, but I feel like I'm on display, and it's making me feel anxious. I need to get a grip of this if I ever plan to be out in public with Julian without freaking out.

Julian must be watching me closely because he grabs my hand and squeezes it tightly.

"Just grab my hand when you start feeling overwhelmed."

"Is it that obvious?"

"To me, yes. I'm getting pretty good at reading you. These people are family and friends and all good people. You don't need to feel uncomfortable."

"Everyone seems really nice, but I kind of feel like an animal on display at the zoo. They keep giving me the once over like they're trying to decide if I belong here with you."

Julian laughs at my description. "Alexa, there's something you should know. It might make you feel a little better. They are looking at you, but not because they don't think you should be here with me, which, by the way, is just a stupid thing to say anyway. They're looking at you because I never—and when I say never, I mean never—show up to these gatherings with my close friends and family with a woman. I really don't date like that. I haven't in years, and nobody here is used to seeing me with someone like this. So yes, you're a novelty of sorts."

Hmm ... his words make my heart happy, but I'm reminded that he obviously has some serious commitment issues. We haven't had any conversations about old lovers, and although I'm dying to know why Julian is still single, I know opening that Pandora's Box will mean I have to discuss my past. I must have a pensive look on my face because Julian continues before I respond.

"You look like you don't know what to say to that. I'm guessing you want details but are worried I'll want them too. Right?"

I shake my head. "If the hotel owner thing doesn't work out for you, I see a mind-reading career in your future."

Julian chuckles and squeezes my hand again. "It's not complicated. I'm pretty confident that you want to know me, and I want to know everything about you. And I will, someday soon. I'm not a patient man by nature, but I'm trying really hard not to push things with you. I don't want you disappearing on me."

"I'd be an idiot to go anywhere." I sweep my hand out like I'm surveying my kingdom. "Beautiful scenery, great set-up here, and the hottest guy at the beach sitting next to me. Life is good."

I think my compliment is going to earn me a kiss, but we're joined by Rafi, Danny, Gabby, and Sonia, the girl Rafi is with. They pull up chairs, and we all sit and chat about this and that. They ask me questions about my background—my job, where I grew up, where I went to school. They don't ask anything too personal and nothing that makes me uncomfortable. I can tell they're genuinely interested in knowing more about me. Julian sits back and does a lot of listening. I can't help but think he's observing how I fit into his personal life. He might also be hoping to glean some new information about me. If so, he will be disappointed. I'm not much of a sharer. Julian eventually gets up and heads to a cooler. He opens it up and checks to see what's inside. He turns and offers me a drink.

"Beer, water, soda, or a Mike's?"

It's hot outside, and I had those shots last night and not a ton of sleep. If I start drinking now, I'll be asleep by five o'clock. "Just water please."

He comes back with two waters and hands one to me. I notice nobody is really partying, and I can't help but compare this group to the people Brady and I hung out with. When you live in South Florida, you spend a lot of time at the beach. At least we did, and whenever a group of us would go, there would be several coolers of beers brought with us. I've never been a big fan of drinking at the beach. The sun and the alcohol wear me out quickly. But I usually ended up drinking way more than I ever wanted to, because everyone else was doing it. We'd start early, and by four o'clock, everyone would be hammered. Nobody would stop until all the alcohol was gone. Sometimes people would throw up or pass out or both. Looking back, I'm so embarrassed by our behavior. We'd have to stay until someone was sober enough to drive home. It was usually me, or Luke when he was with us. More than once I had to help get Brady out of the car and into bed because he had passed out. I'm not sure how I ever thought any of that was okay.

Julian leans in and whispers in my ear. "Where did you just go?"

I turn my head, and his face is right in front of mine. I know he really isn't into PDA, and we aren't alone, but I need to touch him right now and bring myself back to the present. I put my lips on his and kiss him softly. He doesn't pull away and kisses me back.

"Somewhere I'm glad I'm not anymore."

Julian kisses me again and takes my hand. He squeezes it tightly as if he thinks I'll fade away. I know he doesn't understand why I check out like this, and he's so incredibly patient with me. I wish I were able to explain it all, but in doing so, I know I'm not going to be painted in such a good light. I was a willing participant in almost all the bad stuff that happened, and I don't want him to see me as that girl because that isn't who I am anymore.

"Want to go in the water?" Julian gives me an out, and I'm grateful.

I nod, and we get up and start walking toward the shore. Halfway there, he pulls me to him and wraps his arms around me. I'm sure everyone is watching too. He doesn't say anything. He just hugs me tightly. As always, I feel safe and protected in his arms.

I pull back and look at him. "Thank you. I know you did that for me."

"Nope, that one was for me. I have no idea what memories I'm competing with here. I just needed to remind you to stay with me here in the present."

As we walk into the water, I wonder how the hell we got here already. Both of us are nervous and vulnerable and unsure of what to do with all the feelings we're experiencing. I know what my issues are but have no clue what's making Julian act the way he does. We wade in up to where the water is waist high on me. Julian wraps his arms around me, and I reciprocate by wrapping my legs around him.

"Hmm … this might not be such a good idea if you're going to be wrapping yourself around me like that. I can't be held accountable for my actions with your body pressed up against me."

I can feel his growing erection pressing into me. I giggle. "My bad." I start unwrapping my legs from around him, but he grabs them and stops me. His dick is pressing right between my legs, and I can't help but rub against him.

"You are so bad. I can't slide into you right now because I don't have a damn condom, which by the way is an issue we need to address. I want you all the time, and because we're exclusively sleeping together, we should be okay on that front, right?"

I'm not sure how thrilled I am to be having the "safe sex" conversation in the ocean, but we do need to address it.

"I'm not sleeping with anyone else if that's what you're asking."

"Neither am I." His gaze is intense. "I haven't had sex without a condom in seven years, and I've been tested."

This is a great opportunity to share something meaningful with Julian, so I take a deep breath and push the words out. I look over his shoulder and out to sea as I tell him my story. "Well, I've had unprotected sex. And the person I was with wasn't as exclusive as I was led to believe. It was a year ago, and I've been tested twice. I'm fine, and I want to stay that way."

"Look at me, Alexa." I look Julian in the eyes. "Someone cheated on you?"

I nod.

"Is that why you're so reluctant to let me in? Why you hold back so much?"

Uh-oh. What have I started here?

"Yes. And that was very hard for me to share with you, so please don't ask any more questions right now."

If he only knew the cheating was just the tip of the iceberg.

"I'm sorry someone hurt you like that." Julian is looking at me with so much compassion in his eyes that it suddenly becomes perfectly clear that he was hurt the same way.

"Thank you. I'm sorry someone hurt you that way too."

He tilts his head to the side and starts to say something. I put my fingers on his lips to stop him.

"You aren't the only one who's good at reading signs, Julian. I see what you choose to show me. Actually, I probably see more than you want me to see." Julian kisses my fingers and doesn't attempt to contradict my statement. I guess we'll dig into his past at some other time, and I'm perfectly happy with that plan.

Once again, things have taken a turn for the serious. I'm starting to believe we won't be able to stay away from the deep stuff for very long. We really didn't finish the condom conversation, and I'd like to, so we don't have to discuss it again.

"So back to the condom discussion. You're healthy, and I'm healthy, and that's a beautiful thing. But as much as I don't enjoy using condoms, I'm not ready for you not to use them. So, until further notice, I'd like to just continue to proceed with caution." I try to make light of an uncomfortable conversation. We're floating in the ocean on a beautiful day after all.

Julian looks disappointed. "Okay. I'd never force you to do anything that made you uncomfortable, but can you at least tell me what it's going to take to not have to 'proceed with caution,' as you put it?"

It is a fair question, and I wish I had an answer that wouldn't be insulting. It's really hard for me to look at him and tell him I really don't trust him, or that I don't trust me or these feelings I'm having. He keeps telling me I'm the only one he wants, and I want to believe him so badly. But I can't. I've thought I was the only one more than once, and after the scare I had when I found out Brady had cheated on me with multiple women, I vowed that not only would I always protect my heart, but that I would protect my body as well.

I'm still wrapped around him, but I look out to sea again. I'm honest but succinct. "I need to believe."

He either doesn't get what I'm saying or he isn't letting me off the hook so easy. "Believe what?"

"Believe in this. Believe in you and me. It's pretty simple."

He brings his hand out of the water and turns my face so I'm looking at him. "You don't trust me?" He's challenging me with his eyes, and I can't help but see the hurt he's trying to hide.

"No. I don't trust you, Julian. I don't trust you, and I certainly don't trust myself."

The moment the words leave my mouth, I know they've caused some serious damage to the foundation we've been building. Julian's hold on me becomes almost non-existent, and I swear I can see walls rising up around him. I hate that I had to say what I did, but I don't know how else I can explain why I keep taking one step forward and two steps back. I unwrap my legs from around his waist and wiggle out of his weak hold on me. He isn't even looking at me now.

"I'm going to get out and get something to eat. Are you hungry?"

Oh wow. His tone is cold and flat. I'm not sure what I expected, but it wasn't this. Actually that's a lie. I wanted him to tell me I can trust him and that he would never do anything to hurt me. I wanted him to hold me closer and whisper I'm the only one and that he'll do anything to make sure I know it. But he didn't say any of that. He couldn't say those words any more than I could tell him that I trusted him. A wave of sadness rushes through my body, and my normal feelings of anxiety start creeping in. As usual, I want to run away. I'm at the beach surrounded by his family and friends, and I have no car. I don't see an easy way out of this. Damn.

Julian walks out of the water just a little bit ahead of me, and I follow him. He doesn't take my hand and I don't reach out for him either. It's probably not obvious to everyone we're not in a good place at the moment, but I still feel like there's a neon sign over my head with one of those pointing fingers. The sign is flashing: "Stay away ... damaged ... broken ... not worth the trouble."

Julian walks to where the coolers are. He looks back over his shoulder and asks again if I want anything. I ask him to bring me a bottle of water. My stomach is in knots now, and there's no way I'm going to eat anything. I dry myself off with my towel and sit down in my chair. I notice Julian is taking his time coming back to me. I feel very alone. I fish my phone out of my bag and send a text to Marissa.

Alexa: *What are you doing?*

Thankfully, she responds right away.

Marissa: *At my parents, why?*

Awesome. They live in Surfside, so she isn't that far away.

Alexa: *bc I want out of here and hoping you would come get me.*
Marissa: *Y?*
Alexa: *I just can't deal with all this shit.*
Marissa: *What shit? Are you ok? What happened?*
Alexa: *Emotional shit. I hurt Julian's feelings and now he's ignoring me. Whatever.*
Marissa: *What did you say to him?*
Alexa: *That I didn't trust him.*

Marissa: *Really Lex? Ouch. Not nice.*

Alexa: *Honest.*

Marissa: *Stay. It'll be ok. You'll never trust him if you keep bailing.*

Damn it. I should have known she was going to side with him on this. I think she's seeing the good in this and wants to help me not screw it up. I'll probably be thanking her later.

Alexa: *Fine. But keep your phone on.*

Marissa: *Good girl.*

I'm so into my texting and so into my escape planning that I don't notice Julian has walked up and is handing me a bottle of water. He says my name, and I look up. I take the bottle out of his hand and thank him. It's all very formal. He sits down next to me, and I see he's eating some kind of sandwich and drinking a beer. Hmm. A beer. Not such a bad idea anymore. I get up and walk to the cooler I saw him get the drinks out of earlier. I had put my phone on my chair when I got up to get the beer, and I see that the texts from Marissa and me are right there on display. All Julian would have had to do is glance down. I put my phone away and pray he didn't see anything.

"Let me finish eating, and I'll take you home." Shit! Shit! Shit! No such luck.

He won't even look at me. I have no idea what to say. This is a critical moment, and I know it. He stands up and reaches for my hand. I think we're leaving, so I grab my bag.

"Leave it. I have something to say to you, and I don't want anyone to hear me. Just walk over here with me for a minute. Then we can go if you still want to."

My heart is pounding. I take a drink of my beer and set it down. I don't take his hand but get up and follow him to a little courtyard that's close to the condo and away from the others.

He leans up against a planter filled with hibiscus, and I can't help but think how hot he looks. I feel a lecture coming on, and I still want him. Talk about conflicting emotions.

His voice is filled with resignation. "I'm not sure where to even start, so I'll just say it all. I'd appreciate it if you let me finish before you respond. First of all, you don't need to have anyone rescue you from me. If you want to go home, I'll take you home. You're not my prisoner. I'd appreciate you not making me look like an asshole in front of your friends when I haven't done anything to deserve it. You did it last night with Luke and then again with Marissa just now."

He takes a breath and continues. He's on a roll here. "You're right. You did hurt my feelings, and I can't remember the last time a woman was able to do that. I'm not sure what I did to deserve it either. I haven't done anything at all to make you doubt my intentions, and I've been completely honest with you since the day I met you. I get that you have some serious trust issues, and I'm trying to be patient and understanding, but you're not the only one that has a fucking hard time trusting people."

Julian is trying to stay calm, but I can tell he's mad, hurt, and frustrated. "Do you want to know how many people I really trust, I mean really trust?" It's a rhetorical question, so I don't answer. I just stand there and listen to him get this all out. "Three. My mom, Danny, and Rafi. That's it. I know a shitload of people, and only three really know me. I was beginning to believe I would be able to add you to that list, but now I'm not so sure."

I was okay until that last part. Now my heart is sinking.

"You accused me last night of pushing you away. You're doing the same to me, and I'm not threatening you, but if you don't stop I'll walk away. I don't want to, but I will. I can't or *won't* stay in a relationship without trust."

He stops, and I wait to see if he's going to continue. It seems he's finished. He stands there with his arms crossed staring at me, waiting to hear what I have to say for myself. All I know right now is that my heart would break if he walked away from this. I want to wrap my arms around him and give him the biggest hug, but I can't tell if he would be receptive, so I stay where I am.

"I'm sorry what I said hurt you. It wasn't my intention. I was just trying to be honest. I want you to understand why I'm struggling with all of this. I run when I feel scared and vulnerable. I'm aware it isn't the best way to handle things, and I'm trying hard to not do that, but it's been my go-to way of self-preservation for a while now, and it's going to take some time to change. I shouldn't have said anything to Marissa, or Luke, and I won't do it again. My list of people I really trust, people that really know me, isn't much bigger than yours, so I get that completely. I'm honored you want me on that list, but that level of emotion also scares me to death. We just met a few weeks ago."

Julian is still just staring at me, letting me finish like I did for him. "It would break my heart if you walked away, but I can't tell you there won't be more times like this." I stop, and he waits to see if I continue before he responds. When he sees I'm done, he asks me a simple question.

"Do you want this to happen? I mean really happen?"

I swear he's holding his breath, and in this moment I know he wants this as much as I do. I walk to him and wrap my arms around him. He does the same, and it feels right. I look at him directly in the eyes so nothing is hidden.

"Yes. I really want this. More than anything I've wanted in so long. It's going to be epic, remember?"

He smiles as he remembers the conversation we had a few days ago in my driveway. Geez, was that only a few days ago? It seems like forever ago.

"If you keep telling me that, I'll do the same, and maybe someday really soon we'll both believe it."

He takes my hand and starts to walk back to the beach. I tug on his hand, indicating I want him to stop. He does and turns to face me. There's something else I need to tell him. I stand as close to him as I can and reach up and touch his face.

"I need you to promise me something."

"What?" His voice is quiet and a little timid, as if he's scared of what I'm about to ask him.

"Please don't let me ruin this."

His response is a sweet kiss and a whisper. "Okay."

The mood is definitely lighter when we join the others back at the beach. I'm not sure if anybody noticed our absence. Honestly, this whole scene is a little odd. Julian and I are here with these people, but they're all giving us space. When I hang out with my friends at the beach, we all bunch together. I wonder to myself if Julian wanted it this way. I make a note to ask him later.

We sit back down, and Julian asks me to get his phone out of my bag. I watch his expression as he checks his messages, and when he turns to look at me, I know he's about to tell me bad news.

"I need to make some calls. There are some issues at work. I'm sorry. I really was hoping not to work much today."

"It's okay. I understand you don't have a nine-to-five job."

He's already on a call before I finish. I pull an *InStyle* magazine out of my bag and start flipping through it. I can't help but listen to Julian's conversation, and I deduce they're having some issues with their reservation system. I enjoy listening to Julian work. He's calm and respectful to whoever is on the other end. He's trying to problem-solve, but it quickly becomes obvious he's going to have to go in. We've only been here for a little while, and now that we're okay again, I really don't want to leave.

"I'm really sorry, but I have to go in. This is something I need to deal with personally. You can come with me or stay here."

I'm not sure I like either option. "I can call Marissa and ask her to come get me. She's in Surfside, so it's no big deal."

Julian leans over to me and whispers in my ear. "That wasn't a choice, baby. You aren't leaving. I might not get you back today." He stands up and motions to Danny to come over.

What is he doing? "I have to go in for a little bit. Computer issues, and Robert, my IT guy, is MIA. Alexa is going to hang with you guys until I get back."

Seriously? He just asked his brother, who I hardly know, to babysit me. "It's okay, I'm a big girl. Danny doesn't need to babysit me."

Julian can tell I'm annoyed, so he jokes back. "But Alexa, I hired him from hotbabysitters.com." I can't help but laugh. He stole my line.

Danny looks back and forth between us and smiles. "I'd like to hang out with you, Alexa. Julian has kept you all to himself today. Go ahead, bro, we're good here."

I'm standing there listening to this conversation that's about me, and it's surreal because I apparently have no say in what's going on. Julian is giving me a "don't question this plan" look, and I'm not in the mood to argue with him anymore, so I stay quiet. I do give him a fake smile though.

He takes me in his arms, in front of all these people, and gives me a very passionate kiss. He's talking to Danny when he says it, but he's looking into my eyes. "Take care of my girl, Danny." Julian tells me he will be back as soon as he can and heads off the beach. I watch him go, take a deep breath, and turn to face Danny. He has a huge smile on his face. He picks up my chair and brings it over to where the rest of the group is sitting. He places it next to him, and I sit down. He continues to stare at me, and I finally have to say something.

"Is there something you want to say, Danny? You keep staring at me."

"There are a ton of things I want to say to you, but I'm not sure my big brother would approve. So I'm just going to say thank you."

I'm confused. "Thank me for what, Danny?"

Danny is still smiling. "For bringing my brother back."

That is a loaded statement, and I decide to leave it be. If I were sneaky and devious, this would be the perfect opportunity to dig for info about Julian, but I don't want to know anything that Julian doesn't want me to, so I don't ask any questions. Instead, I just sit there, drink another beer, and quietly enjoy the rest of the afternoon in the company of Julian's family and friends.

I finally get a call from Julian around three-thirty. He apologizes profusely but tells me he's still going to be there for at least another hour. We were getting ready to leave the beach, and now I'm not sure what to do. He tells me to have Danny let me in his condo. I agree to stay if he brings food, and he promises to bring my favorites from Ursa's. I haven't eaten since this morning, and I'm really hungry.

Danny walks me up to Julian's and lets me in. He invites me to come and hang out at his place with the others, but I'm ready to be alone, so I politely decline. He gives me a huge bear hug and tells me where he is in case I change my mind. I like Danny. He's sweet and very open. I wonder if Julian was ever like that.

It feels weird to be here alone. I haven't spent enough time here to feel at home, and I'm not sure what to do with myself. Again, if I was sneaky, I would snoop around his place, but I don't need to go looking for trouble. I decide a shower is probably a good and safe idea. I love Julian's shower with all its fancy jets, and I stay in there until my skin starts to prune. When I get out, I change into cut-off jean shorts and a white tank top. I also blow-dry my hair. I feel so much better. The sun and the couple beers I had have made me sleepy, so I get my magazine and lie down on Julian's bed and start reading.

CHAPTER 22

I feel something warm on my stomach, and I slowly open my eyes to find Julian placing soft kisses on my belly. I look at the clock and see it's six in the evening. I must have fallen asleep. I stretch my arms up, and Julian seizes the opportunity to pull my tank over my head. I'm not wearing a bra, and I can see the approval in his eyes.

"I'm sorry I'm so late. I've been calling you for an hour, but you didn't answer. I thought you might have left, so I sent Danny up here to check. He told me you were sound asleep in my bed. I loved how that sounded, and I couldn't wait to get back to join you."

"You thought I left?"

He nods, and I shake my head at him. "I told you I was staying."

Julian is in jeans and a black V-neck T-shirt. I reach up and pull the shirt over his head and then pull him down to me so I can feel his skin against mine. Our mouths find each other, and the kisses that follow are slow and lazy and so deliciously arousing. Julian is taking his time with me, savoring finding me in such a relaxed state. A warm, smoldering heat is spreading slowly throughout my body, and I feel my desire for his touch growing with each moment. I reach down to unzip his jeans at the same time he reaches down to unzip my shorts. We're lying on our sides facing each other. Our mouths are leisurely sliding over each other, and when I slide my hand into Julian's jeans, I'm happy to find him bare, hard, and hot. I grasp his dick in my hand and stroke him at a rhythmic pace. He moans into my mouth and slides his hand into my shorts. He also finds me bare, wet, and hot for him.

"Mmm ... it looks someone forgot to put her panties on."

Julian teases me with his words as he teases my wet sex with his fingers. He slowly pushes two fingers in and out of me while he drags his thumb up and down my clit. I haven't let go of his hard shaft, and I continue to stroke him firmly. He pushes his hips into my hand, letting me know what pace feels the best to him. We continue to kiss while looking each other in the eyes. His touch feels so good that I don't want to come yet. After a little while, he asks, "Does this feel good for you? You're so wet. I want you come for me."

I lessen my grip for a moment and gently massage his balls. This causes him to moan and bite down gently on my bottom lip. We're both breathing rapidly, and I can feel his heart beating against my chest. I don't want to take my mouth off of his for one second, so I whisper into it, "It feels so good that I don't want it to end."

"Are you close? Because I am, and I want to get off with you, baby."

I whisper, "Yes," into his mouth, and his fingers start working faster on my swollen clit. I grasp his shaft harder and also quicken my pace. I don't let go even as I feel my own climax shooting throughout my body. I'm simultaneously rewarded with Julian's hot cum on my hand. His body shudders as his orgasm reaches a peak, and we lie there, our mouths still on each other, until the very last drop of pleasure subsides in our bodies.

I move my hand so it's resting in his jeans and on his hip. He does the same, neither one of us wanting to break the connection. As we lie there and stare into each other's eyes, I question why either one of us doubts the realness of what is going on between us. I can only speak for myself, but that was one of the most passionate sexual encounters I've ever had.

"That was incredibly hot. Feel free to wake me up that way whenever the mood strikes you."

"I agree. It was hard waking you up though. You looked so peaceful."

"How long were you here?" Great, he was watching me sleep. I hope I wasn't drooling.

"Honestly?"

"Always."

He squeezes my hip. "I lay here next to you for about a half an hour before I started touching you. The minute I did, you started waking up. I love how your body responds to my touch. It's so sexy."

"Well that must have been exciting," I say sarcastically. I'm really uncomfortable with the thought of him just lying there watching me sleep.

"I know you're being sarcastic, but it *was* a turn on. You're a very beautiful woman, and I loved coming home and finding you asleep in my bed. You obviously felt comfortable, and that's huge. Don't turn it into something bad or weird."

He definitely knows how to turn things around. "Nope, nothing bad or weird tonight. Only good stuff."

I get his big, happy smile, and my hearts melts.

"Are you still hungry, or did you eat?" Julian asks as he gets off the bed and heads into the bathroom. He comes back out naked a few minutes later and grabs a pair of black cargo shorts from a dresser drawer. Every time I see him naked like this, I get turned on. I'd forgo eating if he comes back to bed. I present my best and final offer.

"I haven't eaten anything since this morning, and I'm starving. But I can forgo eating if you want to get back in bed." I'm still lying on the bed, topless with my shorts unbuttoned. I strike what I believe to be a seductive pose.

Julian chuckles and backs away from the bed. "That's the best offer I've had all day, but I told you earlier I plan on fucking you all night. In order to do that, I need some strength, and I'm starving too. So get your sexy ass out of bed and join me in the kitchen."

I get that now familiar feeling of warmth and longing between my legs as I watch Julian's own sexy ass disappear down the hallway. We might not have the emotional thing down yet, but we are definitely scoring all A's in the sex department. I put my shirt back on, use the bathroom, and join him in the kitchen. Julian must have thought the whole beach group was joining us for dinner because there's enough food for ten people. Dario has outdone himself and sent over all of his best dishes.

"There's a ton of food here. You should call Danny, Rafi, and the others and have them join us."

"Are you sure? That was the plan, but I don't want you to have to spend any more time with them if you don't want to."

"Your family and friends are great. I ended up having a nice afternoon."

Julian calls Danny and invites him up. Danny, Gabby, Rafi, Sonia, Marco, and Steve are all still hanging at Danny's, and they say they'll be up shortly. Julian asks me if I want to invite any of my friends over for dinner. I'm not sure they'll want to come down to the beach if we're not going to be here long.

"Are we going out tonight?" Yesterday Julian had mentioned something about going out dancing. I'll go if he wants to, but I really would rather stay in.

"Do you want to?"

"Do you?" We're both trying to please each other.

"Actually, I'd rather turn music on here, eat, have some cocktails, and relax."

"That sounds perfect. I'll call Marissa and Shannon and invite them. However, I would appreciate you putting some clothes on. You look way too good half naked."

My comment draws a laugh from him. "Well maybe you should put some more clothes on too. You know, like a bra."

Oops. I forgot I didn't have one on. I follow him into the bedroom and pull out a bra and a brown, black, white, and dark-purple tie-dye camisole with thin, crisscrossed back straps and layered, raw-edge ruffles at the hem. I keep my jean shorts on and slip back into my Tory Burch flats. I feel like we're having a little party now, so I duck into the bathroom and apply a little makeup and touch up my hair. I have a great glow from the sun today, and I think I look pretty. I go around getting ready like I'm at home, and when I finally look at Julian, he's sitting on the bed staring at me. He has on black cargo shorts and a gray resin, washed, fitted Henley T-shirt that really fits his upper body. Damn.

"See something you like, Julian?" I feel playful and flirtatious.

"Sí. I like seeing you here, in my room, getting ready and feeling so comfortable."

"I'm not sure how any woman stands a chance against your charms. You sure have a way with words, among other things."

He smiles warmly at me. "Just calling it like I see it."

I walk over to the bed, and he pulls me onto his lap. He slides his hand underneath my tank and caresses my breast. "You always look beautiful. I can't take my eyes off of you."

This time I'm the one who stands up. We'll never leave this room if he keeps touching me like that. "Let's go before we end up back in bed … or against the wall … or in the shower."

Julian groans and follows me from the room. While he gets the food out, I call Marissa. She and Jenna are hanging out at my house and want to come join us. Shannon is out with Cory. I put Julian on the phone, and he gives them directions, tells them how to get into the garage, and where to park. After I get off the phone, I start helping Julian get ready for this impromptu gathering. He shows me where everything is in the kitchen, and we end up setting up a pretty serious spread. Julian pulls out a few bottles of wine from the wine refrigerator in the kitchen and sets them on the table. He asks me if I want something to drink.

"Are you having anything?"

"I'm going to have a Vodka Tonic. But I can make you whatever you want. Or you can have wine or beer." He leads me out of the kitchen into an area nearby that serves as a butler's pantry. I have him make me a Vodka Cranberry and walk back into the living room as Danny and the others come walking in. Within minutes, everyone is eating and drinking. Julian turns on music, and just like that we're having a party. I grab a plate and head out to the terrace. Gabby follows me and asks if it's okay if she joins me.

"Of course." I sit on one couch, and she sits opposite me.

"I'm sorry we didn't get to talk much today. It was kind of a strange day, and I hope you didn't feel uncomfortable."

I have no idea what she is referring to, but I hope nobody sensed Julian and I were on the outs.

"I had a nice time. It sucked that Julian had to leave to go to work, but everyone was very friendly."

"It was a shock he was there at all. I've been with Danny on and off for a year, and I've only seen Julian at the beach one other time. And that was just for an hour or so. He's always working. That must bother you."

I'm not sure if she's making innocent conversation or if she's on a recon mission. "I understand he has to work a lot. We haven't been together long enough for it to bother me yet. Maybe at some point it will, but I'm not upset about today." I already had the impression Julian was a bit of a workaholic, and this just adds more credibility to my thoughts.

"Do you mind if I ask how long you've been seeing each other?"

Yes, I do mind. I think this but don't say it aloud. I'm not sure where this is heading. "We just met a few weeks ago."

"Seriously?"

"Seriously. Why?" Now I want to know where she's going with this. My heart is starting to race, and I prepare to hear something I don't want to.

"I just assumed you'd been seeing each other for a while, that's all."

"And why is that, Gabby?" She's actually starting to get on my nerves with her evasiveness.

"Honestly?"

Geez, what's with these people having to ask if they should be honest? Didn't anyone ever teach them lying is bad?

"Yes, honestly. If you have something to say, I'd appreciate you just spitting it out."

"Alexa, nobody has seen Julian bring a date to any family or friend function. I've been to many of them over the last year, and I've never seen him with someone, not even once. He even came to a wedding alone. But honestly, that's not even really it. Julian looks at you like he's totally in love with you, and you look at him the same way. I just assumed you've been together for a while."

Oh whoa. I actually choke a little on my drink. Luckily I'm not forced to respond because just then Julian walks outside with Marissa and Jenna. Thank you, girls! I introduce them to Gabby and excuse myself to go back inside with them. I didn't want to say anything to Gabby because I'm sure she'll share whatever I say with Danny, and he would probably share it with Julian. I just dodged a bullet, but I can't get her words out of my mind. I do know what she was seeing though. I've seen the flashes of love in his eyes. I have since the first night we were together. It's what freaked me out so badly.

I don't want to get all bogged down in emotional stuff while we're having a party. I show the girls where the food and drinks are and introduce them to the others. I'm not surprised they fit right in. I stand back a little and watch all these people orbiting around each other, and I can't help but be amazed at how seamless my and Julian's worlds have become. The only thing that's missing for me is Luke. In any other circumstance, I would have invited him too.

Julian comes to me and takes my free hand in his. "What are you standing here thinking about?"

I turn and kiss him softly on the lips. "Only good things. I promise."

"Do you want to dance with me, sexy girl?" Oh hell, yes. The first time we danced was hot, and I would love to see him move again.

"I'd love to dance with you."

"Can you salsa?"

"Sí. Vamos a bailar."

Julian flashes me his flirtatious smile, clicks the remote on his sound system, and the sounds of Juan Magan fill the room. He takes my drink out of my hand, sets it down, takes me in his arms, and starts moving with me to the music. I've seen how well Julian can move his hips, but his dancing is even sexier. I let him lead me, and I quickly get lost in the music and the delicious feeling of his body pressed against mine. The others see us dancing and start moving some of the furniture. Pretty soon the living room is a dance floor, and everyone is joining in. Julian makes sure the music keeps playing. I'm not sure what playlist he has on, but he must have gotten it from his DJ at Stellar, because it sounds like we're in the club. Marissa and Jenna look like they're having a blast, and I'm so happy they're here. We dance song after song for hours. Julian is loose and relaxed, and I love seeing this side of him. He always seems a bit reserved in public, and tonight I'm getting to see a different side of him. He's fun and flirty and has his hands are all over me. There isn't a single place I'd rather be.

I eventually notice the time and it's close to midnight. The night has flown by, and although I'm having an amazing night with all of our friends, I'm ready for them to leave so I can be alone with Julian. The dancing, flirting, and drinking have left me wanting him desperately.

I whisper seductively in his ear. "It's time to kick all these people out. You told me you were going to fuck me all night, and that needs to start now."

He groans, pulls me close to him, and kisses me passionately. He whispers back, "I did promise you that, didn't I? I never break my promises. I hope you're ready for me, baby, because I've been hard for you all night."

I show him I'm ready by slipping my tongue into his mouth and grinding my hips against him. I've made my point. Julian turns the music down, and the others seem to immediately get the message the party is over. Everyone offers to help clean up, but Julian assures them it's not necessary. I'd rather them leave now too, even if it means I'll be cleaning up later. Julian says goodbye to my friends, and I walk them out to the elevators.

Jenna gives me a hug. "That was so much fun. Thanks for inviting us over. You look so happy."

"I'm glad you guys came. It was a fun night."

The elevator doors open, and they get in. Marissa looks at me before the doors shut and says, "You're crazy if you have any concerns about how Julian feels about you, Lex. I watched him watching you all night. He couldn't take his eyes off of you. He's so into you. Try not to screw it up."

I give her a big smile. "I'm trying, Mari. I'm trying."

I walk back in and find Julian in the kitchen cleaning up. He has changed the music on his system, and slower music is playing softly in the background. He hears me come back and turns and looks at me.

He sounds apologetic. "I won't be long. I can't leave this all out. It'll drive me crazy."

I smile at him and start helping. "I figured you weren't the type of guy to go to sleep with a big mess like this. Your condo is spotless." I look around at the aftereffects of the party. "Or was."

He smiles back at me. We make small talk and get busy. Before too long, we have all the food put away, the trash picked up, and the furniture back in place. It doesn't even look like anyone was here. Julian dims the lights in the living room, and the moon and stars are illuminating the room beautifully. Julian walks by me, and I pull him close. He wraps his arms around me and holds me tightly. We are both tired, and I'm a little buzzed. I'm also very relaxed and sense he is as well. I stare out into the night and savor the feelings of completeness I'm experiencing. We stay like that for a while, neither one of us wanting to break the mood by saying anything or moving. As we stand there in each other's arms, I hear the intro music to a song come on. A song that says so many of the things I can't say to Julian but want to. A song that fits our situation better than any other we've shared. It's the song Stay by Rihanna and Mickey Ekko. I ask him to turn the volume up a little. I don't need to say anything else. As the lyrics play, we look deeply into each other's eyes and mentally sing the words to each other.

Julian sings the last verse to me out loud as he stares into my soul.

Not really sure how to feel about it, something in the way you move,

makes me feel like I can't live without you.

It takes me all the way.

I want you to stay, stay. I want you to stay.

The emotions racing through my body are the rawest I've ever felt. I'm stripped down and exposed, and I know Julian can see and feel everything I've been holding back. I want this man to desire me, need me, and most of all, love me. I want him to feel like he can't live without me because that's how I'm feeling in this moment. I have no idea what the morning light will bring, and I'm sure before long I'll be back on the rollercoaster of emotions I've been on since I met him. Deep down I know I'm not quite ready to let him totally in yet, but I know now with absolute certainty I want to.

Julian's mouth finds mine, and everything he's feeling pours into me through his kiss. It's deep, searching, and laden with desire. I melt into his embrace and get lost in the sensation of his lips and tongue on my face, my neck, and my hungry mouth. We've spent the last few weeks in a tug of war, fighting for control of what's happening between us. Until tonight I've held my ground. Right now I just want to be his, so I let go of the rope. No games, no sarcasm, no holding back. I press my lips to his ear and whisper, "I'm yours Julian. I want to stay, and if you want me, I'm yours."

Julian doesn't answer me. Instead, he picks me up and carries me to his bedroom. He does break a promise to me tonight, but it's okay. Julian doesn't fuck me all night long. He makes love to me slowly, passionately, and with nothing held back. We spend the next few hours completely lost in each other's bodies and hearts, and as I fall asleep in his arms, I know, deep in my core, whether or not I'm willing to tell him, Julian Bauer owns my heart. I just hope he doesn't break it.

CHAPTER 23

The sun shining through the top of the window shades wakes me up. Morning has come way too soon. I immediately feel the absence of Julian next to me, and as I open my eyes and roll over, I get confirmation I'm in the bed alone. We didn't get much sleep last night, and my head is pounding. I glance at the clock and see it's only nine-thirty. Ugh. Why am I up so early on a Sunday? And where the hell is Julian? I pull on my shorts and tank top, brush my teeth, use the bathroom, and head out to find him. He's standing outside on the terrace, and I see he either went for a run or to the gym downstairs. He's dressed in white athletic shorts, tennis shoes, and nothing else. I hope he wasn't running through the streets of South Beach looking this hot without my supervision. He's dripping with sweat and looks sexy as hell. I admire him for a minute or two before I slide the door open and join him.

"You should have woken me up." I stand next to him and take in the gorgeous views.

He turns and flashes me a smile. "You were sound asleep, and I didn't have the heart to wake you. I wanted to get a workout in before I went into work."

My heart sinks a little. I'm not sure why it didn't occur to me he would be working today, but it didn't, and I'm disappointed.

Julian grabs a towel and dries himself off a little bit. "Are you hungry, or do you want some coffee?"

"Just coffee, please." I follow him inside and sit on a stool at the massive island. Julian makes me a cup of coffee, and I notice he must have been paying attention when I made it yesterday. He makes it perfectly with one sweetener and a splash of cream.

"Thank you." Julian hands me the cup, kisses me on the forehead, and begins to make himself a protein shake. When he's done, he turns and leans against the island. He looks like he's about to say something he knows I won't like. His tone is apologetic, and I feel myself tensing up immediately.

"I want to let you know now that the next two weeks are going to be super busy for me. We're implementing a new reservation system starting tomorrow, which may or not may not be a good idea as far as timing goes. I'm hoping it fixes all the problems we've been having, but I could end up with more problems than I started with. I'm also going on a business trip to Naples and Sanibel to check out some properties we're thinking of buying. Danny, my dad, and I are heading out Wednesday morning, and I'm not sure what time we'll be back on Sunday."

I take it all in. He's basically telling me he won't have any time for me over the next week. I guess that's why he wanted to spend this weekend together. I look at him stoically, but a sinking feeling is growing in my belly. The reality of his life is colliding with the reality of my insecurities. I remain silent, and he continues.

"And next week is going to be crazy too. You've lived here all your life; you know how busy Memorial Day weekend is. We're totally sold out, and we have a bunch of events on the calendar. We have several live acts playing, starting Wednesday night. I need to be around as much as possible in case anything goes wrong."

Okay. Make that two weeks. All the warm fuzzies I was feeling this morning dissipate as I realize the little bubble Julian and I have been in this weekend has popped. I process all the information that he just gave me but get stuck on his mention of Memorial Day weekend and his choice of words. I mean, what could possibly go wrong over Memorial weekend, I think snidely to myself. I've been trying as hard as I can to push away any thoughts of it because I know it will be full of painful memories for me. I'm still not sure how I'll be able to get through it all without freaking out. Maybe it's a good thing Julian's going to be busy the next two weeks. If he's focusing on work, he won't be focusing on me. I start to feel anxious thinking about it, and apparently Julian sees or senses it.

He takes my hand and squeezes it. "I'll make time for you, and we will see each other. I just wanted you to know what was going on so you don't think I'm blowing you off."

Uh-oh. I begin to feel the anxiety start pulsing through me. I yank my hand away before he feels how sweaty it is and how it's beginning to shake. He looks hurt by my rejection. Damn it, this is coming on quickly. I stand up and walk toward the bedroom. There's no chance I'm going to let Julian see this play out.

I call back over my shoulder. "It's totally fine. I'm not worried about it. I know you're a busy man. I really don't expect you to spend all of your time with me. I have a life too."

I'm rattling away trying to mask the fact I'm headed toward a mini meltdown. I grab my bag and hurry into the bathroom. I lock the door behind me so Julian can't follow me. I turn the water on and step in before it's even warm. The cool water is oddly soothing and helps calm me a bit. I sit down on the floating bench and bring my knees up to my chest. I take deep breaths and let the water beat down on me until my heartbeat is steady again. It doesn't take very long, and I'm thankful the duration of these recent panic attacks has been shorter. When I'm sure I'm okay, I stand up and finish taking a shower. I dry myself off and get dressed. I put on the last of the clothes I brought for the weekend, a white cotton miniskirt and a navy and white, striped tank top. I pull my wet hair back into a ponytail. I'm assuming I'm heading home soon, so there's no need for me to get ready to go anywhere, but I'm hoping my outward appearance masks my inner turmoil. I put a little powder, mascara, and lip gloss on. I slide into white-and-blue, Onex cork, wedge sandals. When I walk out of the bathroom twenty minutes later, I'm surprised I don't find Julian waiting for me in the bedroom. I pick up the rest of my stuff, throw it in my bag, and head out with it to the living room. He's not there either. I notice the sliding glass door is cracked open and correctly assume he's back out on the terrace. Julian is sitting on one of the chaise lounges with his eyes shut. He hasn't changed his clothes. I sit on the chair to his right. He turns his head so he's looking at me and I see confusion, frustration, and a little sadness staring back at me. After the incredible night we had last night, I don't blame him for being upset with me. I'm upset with me.

"What was that about?" His question is direct, and I know he isn't going to let me talk my way around this. I try anyway.

"Nothing, Julian. Everything is good. But I was thinking, it's probably a good idea for me to drive myself here next time I come over, so you don't have to take me home. It's totally inconvenient when you need to go to work."

He shakes his head, sits up, and turns so he's directly in front of me. "You asked me not to let you screw this up, so I'm going to ignore that comment, and you're going to tell me why, after the amazing night of love making we shared, you're recoiling from my touch. I must have missed something here, because last night I couldn't touch you enough."

Yeah okay. I'm not getting out of this unless I want to start a big fight. Maybe if I acknowledge it and apologize, he'll let it go. I reach over and grab his hand. "I'm sorry. Of course I want you to touch me."

Julian's eyes turn dark, and he pulls his hand away. "Damn it, Alexa, are you going to tell me why you just had a panic attack, or let me assume something about being with me freaks you out so badly you need to run away? And don't bother denying it. I felt your hand and saw the panicked look in your eyes."

Damn it! Note to self: add annoyingly perceptive to my list of Julian's strengths. I'm embarrassed and feel like an idiot, so of course my response is sarcastic and defensive.

"Fine. I have panic attacks. If you want to take credit for that last one, go ahead, but in reality they just come and go as they please."

"Really? Is that how it works for you? Because when I used to get them, it usually happened because of a trigger."

He doesn't sound sarcastic, but I know he's being facetious. Why am I not surprised we have something else in common?

"Okay, Julian, you win. I'm not surprised you figured it all out. I don't seem to be able to get anything past you." I try to lighten the mood by changing my tone. It obviously doesn't work because when Julian responds, he's still totally serious and looks a little hurt.

"Why do you feel the need to get anything past me? I thought we decided we were trying to make this happen."

Geez. This is way too heavy of a conversation for me this morning, but he isn't letting it go. I continue to deflect and try to make my tone sound flirty. "A girl has to have her secrets."

Uh-oh. My deflection is an epic fail, and now Julian's empathetic look has been replaced by a pissed one. "Is that how you really feel? That secrets are okay? Because if you do, this relationship stops right here, right now."

He's glaring at me, and I know he's serious. Apparently Julian has some non-negotiables as far as relationships go. I need to carefully word my response, because while I agree with him that secrets aren't a healthy part of a relationship, I know I'm hiding a whole lot of stuff from him, and if I totally agree with him here, I'm going to be a big hypocrite.

"Julian, we've known each other for like five minutes, and I've been very upfront about my trust and intimacy issues. There are a lot of things you don't know about me yet, good and bad. I'm sure that's the case with you too. I want you to know me, but I'd prefer it be the good stuff first. The panic attacks are not the good stuff. I'm embarrassed you saw any of it, and I needed to get away before you saw all of it. But in answer to your question, your touch isn't a trigger. I mean it triggers my body in all kinds of delicious ways but not in any bad ones."

Julian just sits there for a minute with his head down. He finally looks back up and takes my hands in his. "Alexa, do you think you and I are at a place where we should be sharing serious things, you know, important things about our pasts? This isn't a trick question with a right or wrong answer, but I would appreciate you at least telling me the truth about that."

I wonder what he thinks I'm lying to him about, but I decide not to ask. I'm still in defensive and protective mode, and I need to be very smart with my answers.

"Before I answer that, can you tell me why you're even asking me the question?"

Julian looks at me with a sincerity that melts my heart. "I'm not saying this to hurt or offend you, but you seem to not really know where you want our relationship to go. One minute you're pulling me close, and the next you're pushing me away. I can *see* how you feel when I look in your eyes, and I can *feel* you care when I touch you, but you don't *tell* me anything about yourself. And because you don't tell me anything, I'm not sure what it is you want to hear from me."

"Well, I guess you're just better at this relationship stuff than I am." I'm half joking, half serious with a heaping dose of sarcastic thrown in. I'm feeling a little bit backed into a corner, and I don't like it. He hasn't shared much either, so I'm not sure why I'm on the hot seat here.

He snorts. "Better at it? I bet if we ever did have that talk— you know, the one where we 'share' relationship histories—we'd find out you'd be the one with more relationship experience."

He's totally trying to make a point about my inability or unwillingness to share information about my past. What Julian doesn't understand is *why* I don't ask him a lot of questions. Yes, I'm scared to hear the answers because of my insecurities and trust issues. But it's more than that. I don't ask because then I feel obligated to reciprocate and share something about me. I'm not good with the quid pro quo method.

"Me? I'm sure you'd have me beat hands down." I quickly run through a mental checklist of my past relationships: Tony in junior high, Adam in high school, Ryan and Scott each for a few months in college, and Brady. It all totals up to about five years' worth of "committed" relationship time in my twenty-five years of life. I'm hardly an expert.

"Not that you're asking, but since the age of eighteen, I've been in one relationship. One. Until now."

The last part of that sentence makes my heart skip a beat. I can't help but smile, but my walls are still up, and my sarcasm is still flowing. "One? Seriously? I doubt you've spent more than a few weeks tops alone, ever."

"Seriously?" Okay, I'm not the only one feeling defensive. "I haven't spent much time by myself, but that doesn't mean I haven't been alone. I know you know the difference, right?"

Unfortunately, I do.

"I'm great at dating, and I think I'm pretty good at fucking. I can show a girl a great time. I know where to take her, what to buy her, how to make her come. And I'm not gonna lie. I've done a lot of that. But relationships? I haven't been in one for eight years."

I just sit there looking at him. Of course I want to know why he's been single so long. I've wanted to know since the day I met him, because I've never understood why he wasn't already married. But I never asked because I'm sure it will ruin me when he tells me about the one girl that broke his heart and got away. I don't want to hear that he has never quite gotten over her. I'm feeling so many emotions for the first time with Julian, and I don't want to know he's already experienced this kind of connection with another woman before. Nope, staying quiet here. After a few minutes of my silence, he sighs and asks again.

"Do you know what you want from me? Last night I was sure you did, but right now I'm convinced you have no idea."

Well that makes two of us, I think to myself. Half of the time I want him to take me in his arms and tell me he'll love me forever, and the other half of the time I cringe when anything emotional comes out of his mouth. I'm a mess.

I choose my words very carefully. "I'm sorry you don't think I know what I want from you, because I do. I want to keep moving forward, and I want us to keep getting to know each other."

I know that Julian is really referring to the emotional part of our relationship, but I throw in a comment about our physical connection to change the course of the conversation a little bit. "And as far as our physical relationship goes, I think things have progressed rather quickly. You definitely know my body very well." I say these words with a lightness that I'm not really feeling.

Julian smiles at me, but it's a sad smile, and I know he knows I'm avoiding his question. He's still holding my hand and rubbing his thumb gently back and forth over it. He slowly shakes his head. "I do know your body, and I don't want to make that seem like it's unimportant. You're an amazing lover and you make me feel things I haven't felt in maybe forever. And when I'm inside of you, I feel so close to you. It's part of the reason I can't stop making love to you."

Wow. That was honest, and it makes me feel great. I bite the inside of my lip to keep myself from saying anything sarcastic about sex.

"I feel very close to you when we have sex too." For some reason, I'm having a hard time saying the words "make love". He keeps using them too. He either doesn't notice or chooses to ignore my word choice. When he does respond, his tone is desperate.

"Can you please tell me what you want to hear from me? Do you want to know me? I mean the real me. Because I can keep giving you the public me that almost everyone else gets. I'm very good at not letting people get close to me. They think they are, but they really aren't. I'm very good at being who everyone else needs and wants me to be, and to be honest, it's how I feel most comfortable. For some reason, I feel myself wanting to let you in though. But if you're not ready for that or don't want it, please be honest with me."

I'm pretty sure my mouth drops open as Julian is saying those words. Those are *my* words, as in I could say the exact same thing to him. I had no idea Julian was holding himself back from me on purpose, or at all. Holy shit, if this is Julian holding back, I'm in serious trouble when he really tells me how he feels about me. I better find my life preserver.

"Are you always going to be honest with me? Because it's very hard for me to open up to anyone I don't trust 100 percent."

"I'll always be honest with you, Alexa. It's the only way I do things. It can make a situation brutal. I can be brutal, but I promise you'll always get the truth from me. I told you earlier. No secrets and no lies."

How did he know those were exactly the words I needed to hear? I've been lied to so many times. If it wasn't someone lying to me directly, it was them lying to me about the nature of their feelings for me or about what they wanted in the way of a future. Brady lied to me about everything. I've always had some trust issues, but the events that happened with Brady took things to a whole new level. My faith in my own judgment and everything I knew about myself was shattered in the last few months of Brady's and my relationship, and deep in my core I have a hard time believing I'll ever be able to fully trust a man again. But, for the first time in a very long time, I want to, and Julian has helped me realize that.

"Then yes, I *really* want to know you." As I say the words, I know I mean them. The problem is that I don't know if I want Julian to really know me.

We've been sitting separately and across from each other this whole time. When I tell him I really want to know him, he reaches over and pulls me into his lap and holds me in a tight embrace. It's as if he's thanking me for making that decision. I rest my head against his chest and let myself feel okay with these new revelations. We sit like that for a while, and I wonder if we're done talking for now or if this is just a break. I'm kind of hoping for the former, and I don't ask another question even though I have a million. I'm dying to know about the whole "no girlfriend in eight years" thing, but I'm not feeling any desire to talk about my exes right now. So after all of that, I'm not sure we actually learned anything about each other except that we want to learn more about each other.

When he finally speaks, it's to tell me he needs to shower and get into work. Oh yeah. I'm being dismissed for the afternoon. He kisses me gently as we stand up, but there's definitely a different vibe between us. There's a distance that was not there before, and deep down I know Julian isn't okay with the way I handled this morning's discussions. When he heads to the bathroom, I text Marissa and Shannon right away.

Alexa: *Can either of you come and pick me up from Julian's? Like now?*

Shannon: *Yes. Are you ok?*

Alexa: *Yes. He has to go into work and it's easier if you get me.*

Shannon: *Leaving now. I'll be there ASAP.*

Marissa: *Does he know you asked for a ride?*

I told her what happened yesterday when I texted her for a ride and Julian found out and got pissed.

Alexa: *He will when he gets out of the shower.*

Marissa: *Lex* ☹

Alexa: *See you soon.*

I sit there thinking about the right way to tell Julian I'm getting picked up by Shannon. Marissa is right. He's going to get mad, and I know it, but it really is a better idea. He'll lose an hour if he drives me home. I convince myself I'm doing him a favor and walk into the bedroom to tell him. I find Julian sitting on his bed putting his shoes on. He's wearing a coral-colored, button-down linen shirt, jeans, and brown Mephisto loafers. I smile inside because, first, I know what brand he's wearing and, second, I see he really does like nice shoes like me. The difference is he really can afford them. He looks so handsome, and I can't help but smile at him. He returns my smile.

"I'm almost ready."

"Julian, please don't get mad, but Shannon is coming to pick me up. It's so out of your way to take me home when you need to get into work. I swear I'm just trying to save you time."

I skip the part where I want to avoid a big goodbye scene. I'm feeling a little raw this morning and sad that this weekend is over. The very, very, very last thing I want is for me to have another emotional breakdown. One or two in a day is my limit. This way we can have a quick goodbye.

He starts to argue but then stops. "Okay. But you're not an inconvenience to me."

He walks over and takes me in his arms. He holds me for a minute, and I feel his heart beating rapidly against my chest. I find it odd. He seems a little nervous, and I feel the distance growing even though I'm in his arms. I pull back and look up at him.

"Are we okay?"

"You tell me, Alexa. Are we?"

Damn. We took a million steps forward this weekend, and I've managed to put us back near the start. I press my lips to his, trying to bridge the gap that developed since my freak-out. His lips feel warm and soft on mine, and what was supposed to be a peck turns into more. I can't help but slip my tongue into his mouth to deepen the kiss. Julian is hesitant at first, but our bodies take control, and in moments we're kissing passionately. I feel the distance ebb a little. I whisper into his mouth.

"We're all good. Thank you for an incredible weekend. I had such a great time with you."

"That sounds like a goodbye." He sounds sad, and I know I'm not imagining it.

"It is a goodbye. Goodbye for right now. I'm going home, and you're going to work." How did we go from me feeling all insecure to him feeling that way too? Shit. What a mess.

I hear a beep on my phone, and I figure it's Shannon texting me she's here. I'm right, and I text back that I'm on my way down. Julian insists on walking down with me. Shannon is waiting in front of the building, and Julian greets her and thanks her for coming to get me. We stand outside the car to say our goodbyes. He takes me in his arms and squeezes me tightly. Tears spring to my eyes and I don't want to look at him, but he forces me to by tilting my head up.

"I'll call you later." No mention of when we'll be seeing each other again, but at least he's going to call. How in the world did we get here where I'm even questioning that?

I kiss him softly on the lips. "Okay. I'll talk to you later then." I slip out of his arms and into Shannon's car. I tell her to go, and I don't look back. If I did, I would have seen Julian watching me drive away.

Shannon sees the look on my face and knows something is up. "How was your weekend? Mari said last night was a blast."

I turn up the radio a little. I'd rather not talk, but I don't want to be rude because she did just come and get me. "Good. Kind of crazy. Emotionally draining."

"Not physically?" Her face is dead serious, but I know she's teasing me. I can't help but smile.

"That too. Have you seen Julian?"

She laughs. "Yes, I've seen Julian. That's why I asked."

She asks me if I'm hungry, and I remember I didn't eat yet and it's already lunchtime. We stop at a little cafe near our house, and I get a Cuban sandwich. We chitchat about her weekend and about Cory. Things are going great, and she actually thinks he'll be proposing soon. I'm so happy for her, and it feels great not to be focusing on me. As I listen, I realize I've been so caught up in my own drama lately that I haven't been a very good friend. I make a promise to myself not to be so self-absorbed.

I walk through my front door exhausted. I unpack my bag, make myself an iced tea, and park myself on the couch with the remote. My plan is to veg out for the rest of the day and night. I need to process everything that's happened. We have gone from zero to sixty and back again in the blink of an eye, and I have mixed feelings about all of it.

I've been good about checking my phone all weekend and have responded to all of my calls, e-mails, and texts from everyone. Everyone except Luke, that is. Now that I'm away from

Julian, I can let myself think about Luke. I miss him, and I hate that I'm being made to choose between him and Julian. I'm not sure what's caused all this bad blood between them, but if I need to keep them separate in order to have them both in my life, then I will. I text Luke to check in and ask if he's going to come over tonight to watch True Blood with me.

Alexa: *Hey. Checking in. Are you coming over?*

Luke responds in minutes.

Luke: *Am I allowed?*
Alexa: *Seriously? Don't start. Miss you. Plz come.*
Luke: *Just us?*
Alexa: *Nope. Sookie, Bill and Eric will be here too.*
Luke: *Order pizza*
Alexa: *k. see you later* ☺

It's only two o'clock, and I'm bored. I can't stop thinking about Julian. There's no way I'm going to be able to sit here and do nothing. I decide my laundry isn't going to get done by itself, so I throw a load in and do a little cleaning around the house. Marissa walks in while I'm emptying the dishwasher an hour later.

We catch up for a little bit, and she tells me she's going to go for a run. I decide to join her. I haven't been exercising much lately, unless you count all the sex I've been having as exercise. The run turns out to be exactly what I need. It's a little on the hot side, so we decide to only run three miles. We find a steady but slowish pace, and I tell her about the parts of my weekend she wasn't there for.

"I saw it with my own eyes, Lex. He's totally into you. You should just tell him about Brady already. There isn't anything you need to be hiding from him. You didn't do anything wrong."

I nod my head and agree with her even though I really don't agree at all. She's saying all the same things I've heard from everyone for a year—that I have nothing to feel bad about and that nothing was my fault. The problem is that they aren't entirely right. I just can't get anyone to understand that the very fact I stayed with him says a lot about me. That's a part of my past I'm hiding from Julian. Once I tell him about Brady, he's going to wonder what kind of girl would stay in that kind of relationship.

"Mari, I agree with you. He was totally into me this weekend, and it was freaking awesome. But now he's apparently going to be too busy to really see me for the next few weeks. So how do I know he's not planning on being totally into someone else?"

"You don't know, but you trust him and believe him when he says you guys are exclusive."

"You haven't seen how women act around him. They fling themselves at him every five minutes. They're all over the hotel and all over him. And I'm talking about gorgeous women."

She shakes her head in frustration. "Just try and trust him, Lex. I know it's hard, but try. If everything you told me is true, he isn't going anywhere anytime soon. But I still think you need to tell him about Brady."

"I know I should, but I can't. Honestly, I'm kind of glad he's going to be so busy the next few weeks. I've been having a hard time dealing with all the memories that are coming up right now, and it's hard to hide them."

I tell her about my panic attack, which is huge, because I only really discuss them with Ellen. I can tell she's worried about me, which is exactly why I don't tell her how frequently it's happened lately.

"Lexie, what happens if you totally freak out about something when you're with Julian? This is going to be a rough couple weeks for you. If you tell him now, it won't be a big deal then."

"I'm not going to freak out again. I'm good." We're rounding the corner for home, and Marissa reluctantly lets it go.

I take a long, relaxing shower and blow out my hair. When I finish doing my laundry, it's still only six o'clock. This day is dragging. I told myself earlier I wasn't going to keep checking my phone, but I can't help it. There are no missed calls or texts. Nothing. I can't help but be disappointed. I haven't stopped thinking about Julian for five consecutive minutes since I left his house, and it appears he isn't thinking about me at all. I want him to call me first.

Luke isn't coming over for a few more hours, so I need to occupy my time. Planning my outfits for work ahead of time saves me time in the mornings, so I start doing that. While I'm in my closet, I try to organize my shoes into a better system. The only thing I dislike about this house is my closet because it's too small. When I give up trying to figure out what to do with all my shoes, I straighten up the rest of my room. As I move around it, I think about how much better I like it than Julian's. He has the view, which is magnificent, but the rest of his room is boring and impersonal. Mine is covered with photos, colorful artwork, and candles. My comforter is white with a huge, orange poppy on it, and I have tons of fun accent pillows. My bed looks comfortable and welcoming. I find myself thinking about what I would do to Julian's place if I had the chance but force myself to stop. The future isn't a place I need to be spending any time in right now. I'm having a hard enough time dealing with the present and the past.

I start to change my sheets, but when I smell Julian's scent on them, I stop. Instead I lie in my bed and surround myself with the memories of him being here. When that makes me feel worse, not better, I get up and strip the bed. How in the world can I miss him this much already? I hate the feelings I'm having. This is exactly why I didn't want to get emotionally attached to anyone.

After I make my bed, I head back into the living room with my laptop. I'm going to shop for shoes because that always makes me feel better. An hour later, I've bought a pair of sexy, black Charles David pumps with wide straps that crisscross at the top and a pair of bone-colored Ralph Lauren espadrilles that tie around the ankle and have raffia on the heel. I'm three hundred dollars poorer but a bit happier.

When Luke walks in the door at seven forty-five, he picks me up and gives me a huge bear hug. It feels so different than when I'm in Julian's arms, but the familiarity and warmth are comforting and welcome.

He puts me back down on the couch and sits next to me. "Have you ordered food yet? I'm starving."

I admit I haven't and grab my phone to make the call. There are still no messages from Julian, and although it's bumming me out, I'm determined not to let it ruin my night. I order our usual large, half-pepperoni, half-mushroom pizza and large

Caesar salad. Marissa is in her room, and Shannon went to Cory's, so we're alone.

"So how are you, Hooka?" Luke is smiling, and I can tell he's in a good mood. Hopefully he stays that way. Luke generally is one of the most easy-going people I know, but lately he's been moody and impatient. The last thing I need is any drama, so I steer clear of anything Julian related.

"I'm good. How about you? What's new?"

"Nothing's new. I went to see my parents today. That's always fun." I hear the sarcasm in his voice.

"Really? That surprises me. You're in a good mood." I'm referring to the fact that he usually isn't after he sees his parents. He goes through the same routine as I do with my parents. The difference is he's an only child, so they're always on his case about something.

"Oh yes. Cecile and Clark were their usual pushy, condescending selves, but I'm here with you now, so even though my day was torture, at least it will end on a good note."

I lean over and kiss him on the cheek when he says this. I'm happy he wants to be around me. We haven't been close lately, and it makes me sad. I've missed him. We keep the conversation light, and Luke tells me stories about people at Orion. He's a great storyteller, and pretty soon I'm laughing so hard I have tears in my eyes. I needed this so bad. The food shows up, and Luke pays even though it's my turn. I let him because I just spent three hundred dollars I didn't really have on shoes. We bring the food into the living room and sit on the floor around the coffee table. True Blood will be on in about thirty minutes, and we talk about last week's episode. After a few minutes, Luke finally brings up Julian.

"So how was your weekend? Were you with Julian the whole time?"

I finish my bite before I answer him. "Do you really want to talk about this? I don't want to fight with you."

He nods. "I wouldn't have asked. I've been worried about you since Friday night, but I didn't want to interrupt anything."

"I had a nice weekend, and yes, I was with Julian for most of it. Please don't worry about me. I'm happy."

He shrugs his shoulders and looks unconvinced. "Really? Because you didn't look happy on Friday. What happened?"

I get up to get us something to drink and reply over my shoulder, "I still don't want to talk about it."

He waits for me to walk back in the room before he answers. "You know you can tell me anything, Lex. Did it have anything to do with two other women?"

Seriously? Now what does he know? "Why do you ask that?"

He looks me dead in the eyes. "I'll take that as a yes. I ask because two women came looking for Julian right after you two left. They stayed by my bar for a while, and I listened to their conversation. One of them, the one with black hair, was talking about, um, her "relations" with Julian and how she'd like to resume them. She couldn't seem to understand why he wasn't into her anymore, and she told her friend she was going to change his mind this week. They were talking about some photo shoot and some other event that was going on at the hotel Memorial Day weekend."

I feel sick to my stomach and put my pizza down. This was the last thing I needed to hear tonight. I don't have the strength to deny that this was exactly what upset me on Friday.

"Yes, I had the pleasure of seeing those two with their hands all over Julian. I didn't like it, and I didn't like the way he handled it. We talked about it, and everything is okay now."

My voice is shaking a little, and Luke recognizes this was a big deal to me.

"Lex, I didn't tell you to hurt you. I really am trying to stop you from getting hurt. I'm not saying Julian did anything to encourage them, but when I tell you I watch women throw themselves at him all the time, I'm not exaggerating. I just don't know how you're going to be able to deal with that."

I don't want Luke to see how much his words have hit home, so I lie. "I can handle it because we've decided we aren't going to see anyone else, and I trust him."

Luke actually snorts when I say the last part. "C'mon, Lexie. It's me you're talking to. You don't trust anyone. Are you telling me that after a few weeks you think someone with his history is just going to become a one-woman kind of guy? I mean, I hope for your sake it's true, but I think you're being pretty naïve." Hello, obnoxious Luke is back.

"Thanks for the ego boost. Apparently you don't think I'm good enough for someone to want to just be with me." I'm hurt by his comments and insinuations, and I'm pissed that what was a great night is now taking a turn for the worse.

"Lex, you know how I feel about you. You're awesome, and I never said you weren't girlfriend material. It's not really about you. I don't think Julian is boyfriend material. I've heard he hasn't been in a relationship for like ten years."

"It's been eight years, not ten, and I'm not sure what criteria you're using to judge because you haven't had any serious girlfriends since I've known you either." I'm trying really hard not to sound pissed, but he's throwing salt on a wound right now.

"Exactly, and I'm not great boyfriend material either. I will be when the time is right though."

I look at Luke and say the words softly, hoping he will agree with me. "Maybe the time is right for Julian." It isn't really a statement but more a question. He senses he's crossed a line and pulls back.

"Maybe, Lex. If that's what you really want, then I hope he has changed."

Luke squeezes my hand and looks toward the TV. The conversation is over, which is fine by me. True Blood is coming on, and the room is filled with the Bad Things theme song. It's fitting, as my mood just turned bad. I can't help but hear Julian's voice in my head asking me to question Luke's motives. Luke doesn't really know Julian but is acting like he does. And while I believe Luke is concerned about me getting hurt, he's really acting a little over the top.

We don't talk about anything other than the show while it's on, and when it's over, I tell Luke I'm tired and that I want to go to sleep early tonight. He looks disappointed but doesn't question me and gets up to leave. It's true, I'm exhausted but I also don't want to talk about Julian anymore. Unfortunately, Luke isn't done with the sensitive topics yet.

"Have you made plans for Memorial Day weekend, Lex? I'm sure Julian is going to be slammed at the hotel, and I'm not sure if you want to be alone or not." Luke sounds genuinely concerned. He was with me for most of that weekend last year and knows this is a rough time for me.

"My plan is to cross that bridge when I come to it." I say it with a matter-of-fact tone that lets him know I have no desire to continue talking about it.

He's standing outside on my porch now. "Okay, but I'm here for you if you need me. I'm on to work the whole weekend, but I can change my schedule if you need me to."

"Thanks, I'll be fine." That's actually the biggest lie I've told yet. Judging by my panic attack this morning, I'm not fine, and I'm sure it will get worse before it gets better.

Luke gives me a small smile and leans in to hug me. I hug him back, and as we're pulling apart, he kisses me on the lips. It's soft and tender and not just "friendly". What the hell? Why did he just do that? I don't ask because I don't want to know.

"Night, Luke."

He looks like he wants to say something more, but he doesn't. He just tells me goodnight and walks to his car as I shut the door. This is *so* not good.

I throw the dinner trash away and get ready for bed. I'm so done with this day. I feel like an emotional wreck, and my stomach is in knots from all the stuff Luke said, as well as from the kiss he just gave me. I really want to hear Julian's voice. I need to hear it. I pick up my phone and dial his number. It goes straight to voicemail. I'm not sure where he is or what he's doing on a Sunday at ten o'clock, but I know he isn't with me. I don't leave a message and opt for a text instead.

Alexa: *Just wanted to say goodnight.*

I'm about to turn my phone off when it rings. I see Julian's name on the caller ID, and my heart begins to beat faster.

"Hey, Julian." My voice comes out in a whisper as I try to hide my excitement.

"Well hello, Alexa. It's about time you called me." His tone is teasing, but I hear the seriousness underneath.

I can tease too. "Is there something wrong with *your* phone, Julian?"

"No, Corazón, it works fine. I was just letting you miss me. It took too long. I was about to cave and call you."

My smile couldn't be any bigger. He was waiting for me to call him.

"Well if I would have known that, I would've called you from your condo before I left today because that was when I started missing you."

There's silence on the other end, and I'm not sure how Julian feels about what I just said. He doesn't tell me either, which unnerves me a little. He asks about my day and what I did tonight.

"It was certainly not as entertaining as the rest of my weekend, for sure. I cleaned a little, did laundry, changed my sheets, went for a run, and bought some new shoes. But not in that order." I omit the whole Luke part of my day.

I hear him laugh softly. "I'm hurt you changed your sheets. I didn't. Mine smell like you."

Seriously? Are we really so alike? "I had to change them. I lay down in them, and it made me sad. It made me miss you more."

I know the tone of my voice changed when I said those words. I do miss him, and I was sad. I don't feel like playing games and hiding behind snarky comments.

"I miss you too, Corazón. I thought about you all day today, and the only thing that made me feel better was when I got into bed a little while ago, and I could smell you on my sheets. It didn't make me sad though. It made me hard."

I laugh at his comment, but it comes out sounding as phony as it is. I'm not in that kind of mood at all. I stay quiet. I don't know what I need to hear him say to make me feel better, but he isn't saying it.

"Are you okay?" Julian's voice is soft and gentle.

I lie. "Yes, just exhausted. It was a long weekend. I just need to go to sleep." Oh damn it! Tears spring to my eyes, and my voice cracks.

He responds quietly. "Okay. I'll let you go then. Sweet dreams."

All I hear are three words: *Let. You. Go.* That's the problem. I don't want him to let me go.

"Goodnight, Julian."

As I hang up the phone, I don't allow myself to consider his reaction to my coldness. I turn my phone off, pull the covers up, and let some of the tears come. I'm crying because I have no idea how to handle all of these feelings that are running amok through my body, heart, and mind. I've been numb for almost a year, and as Julian breaks down the walls around my heart with his perfect words and loving touch, I'm being brought back to life. It's absolutely wonderful and absolutely terrifying.

CHAPTER 24

I wake up the next morning feeling better. I needed to sleep, and despite all the drama of the weekend, I slept well. I already blew my hair out yesterday and picked my clothes out too, so getting ready for work takes no time at all. I'm wearing a fit and flare dress with a colorful and fun, multicolor-blocked and striped print. I put a skinny, brown belt around my waist and put on a pair of patent leather, nude Via Spiga Mary Jane pumps.

I grab a banana and some coffee and am at work by eight-thirty. I'm the first one in, so it's quiet. I turn my computer on and check through some new messages. As I'm scrolling down, I see the last one Julian sent me with the lyrics from Brighter than the Sun. I bet he doesn't feel that way this morning. I was like a big, dark storm cloud last night when we talked. I should call him and apologize, but I'm not feeling brave enough for that this morning. I decide to send him lyrics from one of my favorite songs, Breathe In Breathe Out by Mat Kearney.

To: Julian Bauer—JPB@BWproperties.com
From: Alexa Reed—arrluvsshoes@hotmail.com
Subj: Deep Breaths

We push and pull
And I fall down sometimes
I'm not letting go
You hold the other line

I'm sorry about how rudely I got off the phone last night. I was tired, and I was sad. I missed you terribly yesterday. I hope you have a great day.

ALEXA

I hit send and get back to work. I actually have a busy morning and end up showing a couple of units. Andrea also called, and she's coming in to see me before lunch. She wants to talk about my promotion and what will be happening in the next few weeks. Lauren and I plan to go to lunch after. I'm doing everything I can to take my mind off of Julian.

My meeting with Andrea goes great. It looks like I'll be moving down to South Beach in a few weeks. I'm very excited at the opportunities this move will provide. The commute will be different, but I can't help but think it means I'll be closer to Julian. When we're finished, Andrea calls Lauren in for a meeting. I leave the room and head back to my desk. I check my personal mail for the first time since this morning and smile when I see an e-mail from Julian. It came in shortly after I sent one to him earlier.

From: Julian Bauer—JPB@BWproperties.com
To: Alexa Reed—arrluvsshoes@hotmail.com
Subj: No Doubts

I don't know this song, but I like the lyrics. I'll listen to it later. I missed you yesterday too. I still missed you this morning. I prefer waking up with you in my bed. I hate that anything about being with me is making you sad.
My day is better now.

JULIAN

I feel much better that he has reciprocated and said that he misses me too. I wish he would've written more, but he probably doesn't have time to spend making me feel better and more secure.

To: Julian Bauer—JPB@BWproperties.com
From: Alexa Reed—arrluvsshoes@hotmail.com
Subj: My bed was too big too

Nothing about being with you makes me sad. It's being *without* you that I have a problem with. I got a little spoiled this weekend. A few days away from you, and I'll be back to being my less needy self.

ALEXA

I want to write in my e-mail that we could avoid the whole missing each other thing by seeing each other, but I don't want to seem desperate. I assume, in most normal relationships, people slowly get to know each other, and as they do, the amount of time they spend together grows. Brady and I started spending all of our time together right from the start, and that ended horribly. Julian and I just spent most of the weekend together, and as great as it was, it was also exhausting. I was fine being alone just a few weeks ago, and I'm going to be fine now. At least that's what I keep telling myself.

I just finish sending my e-mail when Andrea and Lauren walk into my office. Lauren has a big smile on her face. "Looks like you're stuck with me." She's beaming, and I guess correctly that she's making the move to The Promenade with me. I'm genuinely happy for her. We work well together and have both been successful here. I get up and give her a hug.

"Congratulations! I'm so happy for you. And for me."

Andrea tells us a few more specifics and leaves for another appointment. Lauren and I grab our things and head out to lunch. We ride the elevator down and talk about how great it's going to be that we're moving together. We grab lunch at a great Thai place in Cocowalk.

"We haven't really talked since we went out that night a few weeks ago. I figured you've been mad at me because I hooked up with Luke." Lauren brings up the conversation, so I decide to tell her how I really feel about her and Luke being together.

"I was never mad at you. I just didn't, or don't, think Luke is a good person to try to be in a relationship with. I thought that was what you wanted, so I tried to steer you in a different direction. It really isn't any of my business, so I'm sorry for getting involved."

"No, I understand where you're coming from. I'm sure Luke has told you we really aren't seeing each other anymore."

I feel bad for her because she looks upset by this, but I'm not at all surprised.

"I have no idea what's going on with you two. Luke hasn't said a word to me. We've been avoiding relationship topics."

She seems disappointed I don't know anything. I'm thinking she was hoping to get some information from me. "Really? I thought you two talked about everything."

"We used to. Ever since I met Julian, things have changed. He isn't a fan and doesn't want to hear anything about what I'm doing."

"It's just because he's jealous."

"Jealous? Luke isn't jealous of Julian, or anyone for that matter. You know him, he thinks highly of himself." I'm only half kidding. Luke doesn't think many men are competition for him.

"I don't think he's jealous of Julian like that. I just think he's jealous that Julian is spending time with you, time you used to spend with him."

"Did he say that to you?" I'm very curious what Luke has said about Julian and me to other people.

"Not in so many words. I just sensed he misses hanging out with you."

I ponder what Lauren said for a moment. Maybe Luke is just jealous that I'm not spending so much time with him. I'd rather think that's why he has been acting so crazy than think it's because he has romantic feelings for me.

"I miss hanging out with him too, but things were bound to change when one of us got into a relationship."

Lauren shrugs her shoulders. "Well he might be having issues with you for a while because he definitely isn't interested in being in a relationship."

She tells me a little bit about what happened between them, and I just listen. It was exactly what I thought would happen. She wants more, and he won't commit. Typical Luke. She asks about Julian, and I tell her a little. She doesn't push for information, and I'm glad because I'm not in much of a sharing mood as far as that subject goes. We pay the bill, and she goes to use the bathroom. I have a minute, so I check my phone. I have a missed call and a text from Julian. They both came in about a half an hour ago.

Julian: *Going dark?*

Uh-oh. I thought I was being good about this. I sent him two e-mails this morning, but I remember I didn't check to see if he ever responded. I would call, but I don't like being on the phone when I'm around other people.

Alexa: *No Julian. I'm here. Why?*

He responds right away.

Julian: *Where is here?*

Hmm ... is he checking up on me?

Alexa: *Here is at lunch in the grove with my coworker Lauren. Heading back to office now.*
Julian: *Ok. I'll wait.*
Alexa: *Wait for what?*
Julian: *You.*
Alexa: *I'm confused.*
Julian: *Check your email*

I open my e-mail and see one from Julian from an hour ago.

From: Julian Bauer—<u>JPB@BWproperties.com</u>
To: Alexa Reed—<u>arrluvsshoes@hotmail.com</u>
Subj: Needs

I would prefer you don't stop needing me. I also got spoiled this weekend. It was a major change for me, and I liked it. I also like to see you happy, so I'm coming to you. See you around 2.

JULIAN

I glance at my watch and see it's two-thirty. He's waiting for me? I could not be more excited to see him. I text him back.

Alexa: *Be there in 20.*

I tell Lauren we need to hurry back and explain that Julian is waiting for me. She sees how happy I am and offers to cover for me if I want to sneak out for a little while. I text Julian back and let him know to meet me at a little park in the community.

I find Julian sitting on a bench under a tree in the shade. His back is toward me. I come up from behind him and wrap my arms around his neck and kiss him on the cheek. He grabs my hand and pulls me around him and onto his lap. He flashes me a warm smile and kisses me softly on the lips.

"Hey, you," Julian says to me as he pulls his lips away from mine.

"Hey, you."

I can't stop smiling. I'm so happy to see him. It has only been a little more than twenty-four hours since I saw him last, but it really feels like so long ago.

"You look beautiful as usual." Julian is running his hand up and down my back, and I feel the energy between us start to buzz. He's wearing black slacks and a white, linen shirt that he has rolled up at the sleeves. His outfit is plain and basic, and he makes it looks hot.

"You do too. And by the way, flattery will get you everywhere."

I lean in to kiss him again, and he meets me halfway. He wraps his hand around the back of my neck and holds me close as he slips his tongue into my mouth and deepens the kiss. I feel it *everywhere*. We're in a public place with people around, so this can't go any further. I pull away before I start ripping his clothes off.

He moans softly and removes his hand. I stand up and sit down next to him instead of on him. I can't help but notice I was not the only one turned on by that kiss. Julian notices me staring at his erection and chuckles but doesn't say anything snarky. He seems a little reserved, and I wonder if something is wrong.

"Thank you for coming to see me. I'm so sorry I kept you waiting. You know I suck at checking my phone and e-mail."

He's looking at me with tenderness in his eyes. "I've been waiting for you for a very, very long time. I'm just glad you're finally here."

Oh my God. Really? I must be back in the fairytale with the prince because this stuff doesn't happen in real life. I'm speechless so I just grab his hand and thread my fingers through his.

"Did you really come down here just to see me?"

"Yes. Is that okay?"

"It's awesome. Now I don't have to miss you for a little while."

"That was the plan. You sounded sad last night, and I haven't been able to get your voice out of my head."

Great. I didn't want him to come here because he feels sorry for me. It makes me feel a little pathetic.

"I was okay. I *am* okay. I just enjoyed being able to spend so much time with you."

He thinks about what I said for a minute before he replies. "So did I, Alexa. But I'm not sure I'm so okay. I pretty much have been living my life the same way for the last eight years. I work a lot. I spend some time with my family and friends, and I haven't been a monk, but I'm not used to being around anyone as much as I was with you this weekend."

He had been looking straight ahead, and when he turns and looks at me, he sees the panic in my eyes. "What's wrong?"

"Nothing. I'm just bracing myself for the big *but* that sounded like it was coming at the end of that last sentence."

He shakes his head as if he can't believe I'm questioning his feelings. "I came here because I couldn't stay away. I'm not sure I'm okay because every feeling I'm having is totally new to me. Every single thing that happened with you this weekend doesn't happen in my world, by my choice. The part that's messing with my head is that it all felt so right and so natural. I just can't wrap my head around the fact I've only known you for a few weeks, and I can't go a day without missing you."

I start to speak, and he interrupts me. "And if you say something sarcastic right now, it will not go over well."

I was going to say something along the lines of it must be all the great sex we're having, but I take heed of his warning and answer honestly instead. "I feel the same way."

Judging by his smile, my answer is well received. We sit quietly for a few minutes.

"What are you doing tonight? Do you want to come over?" I don't want to push it, but I'd love to spend more time with him.

"I'd love to, but I'm having dinner with my mom at seven. I'm not sure when I'll be done, but it'll probably be on the late side. I haven't spent any time with her lately."

Well, I guess I can't be upset by that. He doesn't say much about his family, and this seems a good time to ask a question or two.

"Are you and your parents close?"

"I'm very close to my mom. My dad and I are not close." He says it matter of factly, and I get the distinct impression he doesn't want me to dig any deeper.

"What about you? Are you close to your parents?"

"Yes and no. They're good parents, and they love me, but they have a different vision for my life than I do, and it strains our relationship."

Julian looks curious. "What's their vision for you?" It's a fair question, so I respond honestly.

"They want me to be married, or at least be getting close to getting married. My two sisters were married by this age, and my parents have been married since their early twenties. Their idea of what makes people happy is also different than mine."

"In what way?" He's looking at me intently, and I realize we're having a real "getting to know you" conversation.

"They place a lot of emphasis on the importance of money, and I don't. I like nice things, and I work hard for what I have, but nothing could convince me that money makes people truly happy."

"So let me get this straight. They want you to marry a rich man, and soon?"

This conversation just took a weird turn. A beautiful, single, rich man is sitting next to me holding my hand. "Pretty much."

"And you're against marrying a man with money?" He says it playfully with a twinkle in his eye.

"Nope, just haven't been asked by one yet. You wouldn't happen to know any that are in the market, would you? Frank and Claire, my parents, would be so grateful for any help you could give me in that area."

One day he will learn I can keep up with his sarcastic teasing. Julian looks directly at me when he replies, and his tone isn't playful. It's serious. "I just might know the perfect man for the job. Let me get back to you on that one."

Holy hell! Are we really having a conversation about marriage? I mean a conversation about marriage and us? Yeah, I'm so not ready to go there. I change the subject back to his parents.

"Where are you going for dinner?"

Julian lets me change the subject. Maybe he realized it was heading some place a little crazy.

"Just to their house. My mom, Marisol, is an amazing cook, and her food is better than most restaurants. She wants to cook for me."

"Sounds nice. Where do they live?"

"Miami Beach. On North Bay Road."

Wow. That area is beautiful and expensive. "Do they live in one of your properties?"

"No, they live in the same house I grew up in. My mom doesn't like condo living and didn't want to raise kids that way." I can't help but notice how Julian's face lights up when he talks about his mom.

"Well, your mom and I agree on that. I would prefer to live in a house when I have kids."

As soon as I say that, I hope Julian doesn't think I want to talk about having kids. The marriage and kids conversations are a little heavy and definitely premature. He doesn't say anything about kids though.

"I think you and my mom would agree about a lot of things. She would like you."

"That's sweet. I'd like to meet your mom someday." Not soon, but someday.

"It would be hard for her not to like you. You'll remind her of Isabelle."

Oh. This is the first time Julian has brought up his sister since the first night when I asked him about his tattoo. That's quite a statement he just threw out there. I'm not sure I want to remind anyone of a dead family member, but I'm curious why he thinks that, so I ask.

"Do I remind you of your sister?" I can't decide if it's creepy or not.

"Yes, in certain ways. Isabelle was feisty like you. She had a very quick wit and was great with the snarky comebacks. She was beautiful, smart, loyal, and complicated. I think if she had lived, she would be the kind of woman you are."

Tears actually fill my eyes. That was so not creepy. It actually might have been the nicest compliment anyone has ever given me. I'm at a loss for the right words, so I just lean in, hug him, and whisper, "Thank you," in his ear. I look down at my watch and realize we've been sitting here talking for over an hour. I'm technically still working, so I reluctantly pull away and tell Julian I need to get back to work. We stand up, and he takes me in his arms and holds me tightly. I look up at him, and he's staring down at me. We both smile. All is right in Julian and Alexa world at the moment.

"I think we're onto something here."

"Hmm ... what are we onto?"

"In case you didn't notice, we just had a great get-to-know-you session where nobody freaked out, and by nobody, I mean me. And we were able to really talk because nobody's clothes were removed."

He laughs at my description of our mini date. "You're right. Nobody freaked out, and that's definitely a good thing, but I'm not going on record agreeing with the 'no clothes being removed' as a good thing. I'm a big fan of removing your clothes." Julian the flirt is back.

"You misunderstood me, Julian. I'm also a big fan of you removing my clothes. I just think it's good for us to spend time getting to know each other outside of the bedroom. On some levels I feel like I know you so well, and on others I feel like a stranger."

I know it sounded like I was joking when I said we were onto something, but I really wasn't. Time like this is precious to me, and I feel closer to Julian because of it.

"I know what you meant, baby, and I agree. Now let's get you back to work." He takes my hand, and we walk toward my building. We stop in front, and Julian tilts my face up so I'm looking into his beautiful eyes. They're mesmerizing. He says what I want to hear.

"Can I see you tomorrow night?"

"Yes, please."

Julian kisses me tenderly on the lips and turns to walk away. I'm opening the door to my building when he calls my name. I turn to look at him and see him place his hand over his heart. It's the same gesture he made before he pulled away in his car that first night at my house. I interpret it to mean I've touched his heart. He definitely has touched mine today. I respond with the same motion and walk into the building on a cloud of air. I send him a text before I get in the elevator.

Alexa: *I already miss you*

He replies immediately.

Julian: *Yo también, Corazón. Yo también.*

Lauren is sitting at my desk when I walk in. Apparently a customer I had been working with is coming back in today, and she was looking for information on their previous visit. I thank her for covering for me and tell her I'll deal with these clients.

"Good, because the woman seems like a real pain the in the ass."

I laugh because she's right. "You're so right, and they won't be buying anything, so don't feel left out."

I'm right. These clients are just wasting my time. It's their third time in, and they're no closer to making an offer. They do help the afternoon pass quicker though, and I'm thankful for that. All the talk about parents has made me think about mine, so I call my mom on the way home from work. We actually have a nice conversation, and she doesn't bring up marriage once.

I'm lying in bed at eleven watching a taped episode of Dancing with the Stars. I love watching Latin ballroom dancing. Tonight I can't help but think about Julian and the way he danced with me the other night. The thought of him dancing with me actually makes me hot and bothered. I call him, and he answers right away. He sounds relaxed, and I wonder if I'm waking him up.

"Hey, you. I was just about to call. I just got home about twenty minutes ago."

"Hey, yourself. Did you have a nice night with your mom?"

"I did. I told her about you."

Hmm ... that's kind of huge. I didn't expect the conversation to lead off with that.

"Really? What exactly did you tell her?"

"She asked me what had put such a big smile on my face. I told her I met a girl."

I'm sure right now my smile is bigger than his.

"And she let you off the hook with that answer? No asking for details?"

"No. I think she was too busy picking her mouth up off the floor to ask details. That will come later."

I steer the subject back to more neutral territory because the whole parent thing makes me uncomfortable. "What time are you coming over tomorrow?"

"Probably around seven. I want to run tomorrow, and I'm not sure if I'll be up for it in the morning. I'm pretty tired."

"Come here, and we can run together. I want to get a workout in too."

"That sounds like a good plan, Alexa. I love the idea of watching you get all hot and sweaty."

"Well if that's the case, let's skip the run and work out some other way."

"We can get hot and sweaty, then clean, then hot and sweaty all over again. I promise you'll get a good workout."

"Promises, promises."

"Have I broke one yet?" He's referring to his promises of hot sex, but when I answer, I'm not just talking about sex.

"No, Julian, you haven't." I say it softly.

"And I won't, baby. I won't."

CHAPTER 25

Tuesday ends up being a super busy day at work. My clients who wrote an offer a few weeks ago are back in to finalize details and make their final selections. It's just me today, because Lauren took the day off, and Ramon is sick. I'm with clients almost the entire day, and before I know it, it's six-thirty. Julian and I had exchanged texts earlier in the morning confirming he was going to be over at seven and that we would get dinner after our run. He told me he was going to be busy and in meetings all day, so I didn't expect to really hear from him. I find I'm okay with not talking to him because I know I'll be seeing him tonight.

I end up leaving work a little late and pull into my driveway just a few minutes before Julian does. He gets out of his car and grabs an overnight bag from the backseat. I take this to mean he's spending the night, and I couldn't be happier. He's already dressed to run in orange running shorts and a loose, black tank top. Yum. Yes, that's what I think. He's yummy. He walks to where I'm waiting for him and leans in for a kiss. Double yum.

"Nice shoes."

Julian is staring at my feet and smiling. I love that he appreciates my love affair with shoes. I'm wearing a pair of Dianne Von Furstenberg rose-and-black, snake print, strappy stiletto sandals. They're a little bold, so I'm wearing them with a simple, black shirtdress.

"Thank you. Sorry I'm running late. Work was busy today."

We talk about our days a little as we walk through the house to my room. It feels good to be able to talk to Julian about what I do for a living. I know he gets it because he's in the business, and it's great common ground for us. He sets his stuff in the corner of my room and sits down on the bed. We're still talking about work, but a vivid image of his naked body in my bed flashes through my mind, and I have to turn and walk into the closet before I end up on, or in, the bed with him. I hang my dress up, put my shoes away, and walk out in my bra and panties. My workout clothes are in a drawer across the room, and I have to walk by Julian to get there. As soon as I'm close enough, he grabs me and pulls me into his arms. He's sitting on the bed, and I'm standing between his legs. His face is at the same level as my breasts. I can feel his hot breath on my skin, and I start to feel flush. Okay, walking out half naked was a bad idea. Or, a good idea. I can't decide.

"Mmm … are you teasing me?" He's kissing my stomach and that spot just between my breasts with soft gentle kisses.

"Who's teasing who here?" Julian laughs as I pull away and keep walking to my dresser. My heart is racing, and I need to get some clothes on quickly if we're planning on leaving my room. I put on a neon orange and gray, striped tank and gray running shorts. I grab a pair of socks and get my shoes out of my closet. Julian follows me into my closet, and I bump into him when I turn around.

"Hello. Did you need to borrow something to wear?" I ask jokingly.

"Nope, just wanted to see where all of your shoes live." He looks around at the shoe boxes that take up more than half of my closet. "Looks like you're going to need to build an addition here soon."

I feel like I've been caught with my hand in the cookie jar.

I walk around him and out of the closet. I don't make jokes about my shoes because I know I'm a little excessive about it.

"It works for now, but I'll make sure their next home is bigger."

"Next home? Are you planning on moving?" He has a concerned look on his face.

"Eventually. Probably before the end of the year."

"Why?"

"Well, I'm not sure if I mentioned it, but Marissa is engaged, and her fiancé, Kevin, is stationed overseas. He'll be back in November, and they most likely will either move out of state or move in together. And Shannon practically lives with Cory as it is. I see them making it official around that time too. This is her uncle's place, and as soon as she goes, I'm sure we all will."

None of this is new news, but for some reason saying it all out loud like that just totally bummed me out. Julian's next question doesn't help either. "Where will you live then?"

"No clue." This really isn't a good subject. Julian senses it and changes the topic.

"You ready to go?"

"Yep." We walk outside and stretch for a few minutes before we take off. I pull my hair back into a ponytail and ask Julian how far he wants to run. We agree on seven miles. I have a couple of different routes I run, and he lets me lead the way. I've been thinking about running with Julian ever since we talked about it last night. I've been wondering how fast he runs, if he likes to talk, does he listen to music? I have no idea what his routine is, so I just do my thing and hope for the best. After about five minutes, I realize Julian is going to let me dictate the pace. I run at a decent speed, and he clearly has no issues keeping up. We don't talk at all, which is actually okay with me. I usually use this time to think. I really started running after Brady died. I found that the rhythmic pounding of my feet on the pavement would block out the demons I was fighting. Pretty soon I grew to enjoy it. It's a different type of therapy for me and something I need to do at least a few times a week.

The only thing I can think about today though is this gorgeous man running next to me. Julian left his T-shirt at my house, and out of the corner of my eyes I keep catching glimpses of the muscles in his legs, stomach, and arms flexing. I can't look directly at him because I know it will be too distracting. His body really is stunning, and I smile on the inside knowing I'll be enjoying it later tonight. Julian catches me sneaking a peek and winks at me. I know he knows I was checking him out. I can't help but notice how in sync our bodies move as we run next to each other. Physically, we're undoubtedly compatible. I pray we can stay on the same page emotionally as well. When we get back to my house, we go inside and grab a few water bottles. We sit in the kitchen as we cool down.

"That was a good run." I look at Julian, and he's smiling, sweaty, and sexy as hell.

"That was a great run. Great scenery." I know he's referring to me, and my heart swells. He makes me feel so confident and beautiful.

Eventually, we head to my bedroom. I think about the shower we took together at Julian's, and hope for a repeat. However, it seems Julian has other ideas. He closes and locks the door behind us and takes his shoes off. I do the same. He pulls me to him and presses his sweaty body to mine. He does the same with his eager mouth. We haven't really touched each other since Saturday night, and all of the desire we have been holding in comes pouring out of both of us. There are times when no words are needed, and this is one of those times. I can feel how much Julian wants me. There's a quiet desperation in his touch, and I get it. I crave his touch as well, and tonight I'm not interested in him being tender or gentle with me. He pulls away from me for a moment and reaches down to get a condom from his bag. While his back is to me, I quickly finish undressing. His eyes blaze with lust when he turns and finds me naked. A soft groan escapes from his throat. He doesn't say a word. He just pulls me up into his arms. I wrap my legs around him and let him carry me to the bed. I'm feeling a little self-conscious because we did just get back from a run, but Julian seems totally okay with not taking a shower first.

Julian sits me down near the edge of the bed so my legs still touch the floor. He positions himself over me, between my legs, and presses his erection into me. I lift my legs and wrap them around his waist and pull him closer. He rocks into me several more times, and each time I feel the heat of his hard penis pressing against my bare sex through his shorts. I'm dying to feel his skin against mine, so I reach up and pull both his running and compression shorts down. I wrap my hand around his hard shaft and stroke him firmly. He allows me to pleasure him this way for a few minutes, and I'm so turned on by the look of lust in his eyes that I can't help but move my hips in a small circular motion. He finally stands straight up, and I'm forced to let go of him. His eyes stay on me as he rolls the condom on. He strokes himself a few times, and I feel the heat that has been building between my legs start emanating throughout my body. He's biting his lower lip in an incredibly erotic way, and I want his lips back on mine. I no longer feel shy or self-conscious. I feel hot, horny, and needy.

"Kiss me." The words sound like the command they are.

Julian bends down and places his lips on mine. He pushes his tongue into my mouth at the same time he pushes his finger into my swollen sex. I don't wait for him to ask me if I'm ready or if I want him. I'm beyond ready, and I tell him so.

"Yes. I'm ready for you. All of you. Please, I want you inside of me. Please."

No sooner are the words out of my mouth than I feel Julian's hardness slide into me. It feels incredible, and I instantly feel connected to him in a way I haven't for a few days. He starts out in a slow rhythm, making sure I'm comfortable with him inside of me. I savor the feeling of his gentle strokes but quickly realize I want more. I wrap my hand around the back of his neck and pull him down so my lips are on his ear. I suck on his earlobe and dip my tongue in his ear. I can taste the sweat on him, and it makes me wetter. I whisper what I want from him.

"Fuck me, Julian."

Julian's whole body tenses, and he pauses. I imagine he's thinking he heard me wrong. He pulls back so he's looking at me.

"Otra vez, Alexa."

I was right. He wants me to say it again.

"I want you to fuck me, Julian."

Oh wow. Now I know what happens when Julian is given that green light. He wraps one arm under my ass and scoots me further up the bed without pulling out. He lifts my left leg in the air and rests it on his shoulder. My right leg is bent at the knee, and he pushes it out gently with the palm of his hand. Then Julian does exactly what I asked him to. He fucks me, hard, and with each thrust I feel my body open for him. This is exactly what I needed and wanted. I close my eyes and let myself get lost in the steady rhythm. I feel a delicious touch on my sex, and I open my eyes to see Julian working me with his fingers. I'm swollen and sensitive, and the pressure of Julian's hard dick against my clit has left me very aroused. I arch my back and raise my hips in the air. Julian slows down his thrusting and focuses on getting me off. It doesn't take long for me to orgasm, and when he feels the rush start in me, he resumes his driving rhythm. I look up at him, and we lock eyes. His own release quickly follows, and I don't look away until the very last shudder of Julian's orgasm subsides.

He slowly pulls out of me, and we lie next to each other as we catch our breath and come down from that incredible high. I turn on my side and look at him. He's staring at the ceiling and looks deep in thought. Julian has been pretty quiet all night, and it's starting to make me question if something is going on with him. He's acting normal, but not talking.

"You're very quiet tonight. You haven't said more than a hundred words since you got here."

He gives me a little smile but still doesn't say anything.

"Okay. You stay here and keep being quiet. I'm going to go shower, and then we can eat." I'm only half joking. What's up with him?

I start to get off the bed, and he grabs me and pulls me back down so I'm under him. He's propped up on one elbow and rests his other hand on my belly.

"There are a million things I want to say to you. I'm quiet because if I open my mouth and start talking, I'm not sure what's going to come out. You're not ready for all this, and I don't want you to run."

His words scare me. Ready for what? What is he hiding from me that would cause me to run? Oh crap. He also has some big secret he's keeping. I don't want to know, but I have to know.

"You said no secrets. What the hell are you hiding from me?" My voice is shaky when it comes out, and it's evident I'm scared by whatever it is I think he's going to say.

He looks perplexed. "No secrets. I'll tell you anything you want to know about me. All you have to do is ask. I want you to know everything. I told you that the other night."

"Then what are you talking about. Why would I run?" I really am confused.

"Are you ready for me to tell you how I'm feeling about you? About us? About what I want and what I need from you? If you say yes, and you really mean yes, then I won't hold back. I don't want to hold back. No creo que estas lista. Am I right?"

Oh no. This is Julian holding back? The last few weeks have been incredibly intense in every way. We just met each other, and I have opened up to him more than I even thought was possible for me. He knows how much I care about him. Doesn't he? I know he cares too. I know he wants me. He's asking if I'm ready to know more. I do. I want to know everything. But then he'll want to know everything too. It's how he is. And I'm not ready for him to know everything about me.

I nod my head indicating that yes, he's right, I'm not ready. He looks crestfallen, and it breaks my heart. I'm second-guessing my decision when Julian gets out of the bed and heads toward my bathroom. His posture is rigid, and I know he's really disappointed. I want to follow him, but I don't. I hear the shower turn on. I'm a little mad right now. Why can't he just let things be? I feel like he's always mad or disappointed in me.

We were having a good night. We had a good run and then great sex. Why can't that be enough?

Julian isn't in the shower long. He comes out with a towel wrapped around his waist and walks over to the bed. He leans down and kisses me on the forehead. "I'm sorry. I don't want to argue or fight with you tonight. Forget I said anything."

I'm glad he apologized. I really don't want to fight either. I smile at him. "Forget what?"

He smiles back and gets his clothes out of his bag. He puts on a pair of black shorts and a white T-shirt.

"I'm going to order dinner. Chinese? Italian? What do you want?"

"Chinese is good. There are menus in the drawer next to the stove."

Julian leaves the room to order the food, and I hop in the shower. I finish quickly, towel dry my hair, and put on a pair of gray, fleece shorts and a pink, off-the-shoulder tunic. I find Julian in the living room talking with Shannon and Marissa. He tells me he ordered dinner for all of us. I love that he included my friends. The food comes, and we all sit and talk. Julian tells us about what's going on at the hotel in the next few weeks and encourages all of us to come and hang out Memorial Day weekend. Marissa and Shannon both give me sideways glances, and I try my best to ignore them. I think Julian picks up on it, but he doesn't say anything. After we finish eating, Marissa and Shannon excuse themselves. I begin to clean up, and Julian asks if it's okay for him to make a few work calls. I find the question odd. I just nod at him and walk into the kitchen. I hear him talking first to Candace and then to Ruben. He isn't on long and wraps up his conversation as I sit down next to him on the couch.

"Sorry about that."

I'm not sure why he thinks he needs my permission to work or why he feels he needs to apologize. "Julian, if you need to work, I'm cool with it."

He shrugs and smirks. "You are now."

I must look perplexed, because he clarifies what he meant. "Alexa, I'm a workaholic and a bit of a control freak when it comes to the hotel. I have a hard time not being there every night. I want to be here with you, which is a major change for all of my staff, and me as well. I'm trying to make sure to focus on us, but it's hard for me to let go."

I'm moved by his honesty and consideration. I know all about not being able to let go of things and needing to be in control. This is another thing we have in common.

"Julian, I appreciate your honesty. I wouldn't expect you to put me first. I'm happy you're here with me tonight."

Julian pulls me onto his lap and wraps his arms around me. He looks me directly in the eyes. "Alexa Reed, I'm glad you're happy I'm here because there isn't any place I'd rather be. But you have this all wrong. You should come first, and I want to put you first. You don't deserve to come second."

I really wasn't playing the martyr role, and his response touches me. So much so that I feel tears spring to my eyes. He sees them right away and kisses each of my eyes. He doesn't ask me why I'm suddenly so emotional, and although I appreciate him not questioning me, I feel a need to tell him why his words mean so much to me.

"Thank you. It means more to me than you know to hear you say that. I've come in second more times than I care to remember. Sometimes it was third or fourth." A small tear threatens to escape, and Julian kisses it away. "I've stopped expecting things from people, because if I have no expectations

I can't get disappointed. I don't want people to expect things from me either. That way nobody gets disappointed."

Julian starts to say something, but I cut him off.

"I feel like I always disappoint you. I'm trying to meet your expectations, but I always feel like I fail, at least emotionally. Tonight is a perfect example. You wanted something from me, and I let you down."

Whew. That wasn't easy. Julian's expression is unreadable at the moment, so I'm not sure my little speech was a good idea. He stands up, takes my hand, and walks toward my bedroom. I guess he wants privacy? We're alone in the living room, but Marissa or Shannon could walk out any minute. When we're in my room, he shuts and locks my door and sits down in the chair at my desk. I sit on my bed and face him. His arms are crossed over his chest, and to be honest he looks a little mad. I brace myself for his response as he takes a deep breath and exhales.

"You haven't told me much about your past, so I really have no idea who or what hurt you so badly that you feel you can't expect good things. If I knew who it was that did this to you, I'd go kick his ass right now. But I have a feeling you aren't going to share that information with me."

I nod my head and Julian continues. "I'm so sorry I make you feel like you always disappoint me, because you don't. But as far as tonight goes, you're right. I was a little disappointed. I'm sorry I made you feel bad about anything. I think you and I are in different places emotionally, and that's a little hard for me to accept. I've been waiting to feel this way for years, and now that I do, I want to share it all with you. I don't know what's too much and what isn't enough."

With tears in my eyes again, I whisper, "I don't know either."

Julian walks over and sits down next to me on the bed. I'm having a hard time looking at him because I really don't want to start crying. "I understand more than you think I do. I've spent years trying to figure out what I wanted. It all became perfectly clear to me the minute you ran into me in the stairwell." Julian puts his hand under my chin and turns my face so I'm forced to look at him. "Te quiero. I want you. You can count on me. Whether you know that or not, it's true, baby. Please try."

The compassion and sincerity shining through his eyes is overwhelming. I want so badly to tell him he's wrong. We're not in different places emotionally. I know what I want. I just can't believe he feels the same way. I don't believe he'll stay when he learns about my past and finds out I'm not exactly the person he thinks I am. I can't believe he won't find someone better. I just don't believe. But because he's asking me to, I make a vow to try.

I lean into Julian and place a gentle kiss on his soft lips. He responds by pulling me down onto the bed, taking me into his arms, and just holding me tight. There's no place I'd rather be.

We lie like that for quite a while. I sense he won't make the first move to pull away because he knows I need this. I also need to make sure he knows I'm on the same page as him as far as what I want and what I feel for him.

My voice comes out in a whisper. "I'm scared this is all a really good dream and that I'm going to wake up and find out I imagined you."

He presses his lips to my ear and whispers back. "This is very real, and I'm here, baby. I'm not going anywhere."

His lips start on my ear, then move to my neck, and find their way to my shoulder. They're leaving a trail of warmth and desire on my skin. I move my arm down from Julian's waist and wrap it around his ass and pull him into me as close as I can. A small groan comes out of my mouth as he does the same to me. The tenderness gives way to passion, and we quickly help each other remove our clothes. He's looking at me and asking me what I need with his eyes. I gently push his shoulder back, indicating I want him on his back. His eyes are blazing with desire as I climb on top of him and kiss him with every bit of lust and love I'm feeling. Our mouths and tongues are hot, wet, and hungry, and he kisses me back with a matched intensity. He's raising his hips and pressing his massive erection against my sex. I know if I move a tiny bit he will slide in. I'm so ready for him, and I'm also so tempted to forgo the condom. At the last second I decide against it and move so I'm kneeling next to him. He groans his disapproval.

"Please. I want to feel you, baby. All of you."

His plea is desperate, and I almost cave. I don't want to argue this point with him right now, so I try to distract him with my mouth. I run my tongue over each of his nipples and suck them gently. Julian grabs my head and weaves his fingers into my hair. I make my way down his stomach, making sure to kiss every inch of his flat, muscled torso. I glide my tongue over his hip bone and down his thigh and eventually position myself so I'm kneeling between his legs. I take his shaft into my hand and begin to stroke him in the rhythm I've learned pleases him most. He's moaning softly and whispering his approval.

"Sí, sí. Se siente tan bien. No pare."

"I'm not going to stop. Not until I taste you and feel you come apart in my mouth."

The groan that comes out of Julian is primal, and as I lean over and take him in my mouth, I revel in the heady feeling that comes over me.

I take all of him deep in my mouth and stroke his shaft simultaneously. I massage his heavy balls with my other hand and run my nails up and down the inside of his thighs. Julian's hands are in my hair, and he's rocking his hips up and down as he thrusts himself into my mouth. When I pull out and run my tongue around the soft head, I taste him, and it turns me on even more. I run my tongue down the underside of his shaft, take his balls into my mouth, and suck with just enough pressure to drive Julian crazy.

"Oh my God, Alexa. Yes, suck me, baby. I'm going to come for you."

I do as he asks and take him back in my mouth. I hear him call my name as I taste the warmth and saltiness of his desire fill up my mouth. I swallow twice and then continue to suck until I'm sure he's completely spent.

"Thank you. That was incredible."

As Julian praises my blow job skills, he flips me onto my back and begins to return the favor. His hot mouth finds me very ready. Julian spreads me open with his fingers and launches the most delicious assault on my wet sex. I squirm underneath him as he runs his tongue slowly up and down my cleft. Julian alternates between gently sucking, blowing on, and flicking his tongue over my engorged clit. He's taking his time with me, and although I want to savor each minute, I find I can't hold back.

"Make me come, Julian, please." I'm desperate for the sensation that's building in me to peak. I need it.

"Mmm ... hold on. You taste so sweet. I could spend the rest of the night between your legs."

My whole body feels that comment and clenches in response. "I can't wait. You make me feel so good. It's so good, baby."

STAY

I'm breathless, desperate, and quivering beneath him. His touch sets my body alight, and the slow burn he has ignited spreads and reaches every inch of my body. The climax I was chasing finds me. It's powerful and leaves me spent and sated. I lie still and catch my breath as Julian gets off the bed to get a condom from his bag.

"Good God. Are you trying to kill me?"

He laughs as he rolls the condom on. "Death by orgasm? Not a bad way to go."

He climbs back on the bed, and I ask him to lie on his back. I want to be on top. "You can have me anyway you want me. I'm all yours."

Of course he's referring to the sexual position we're in, but I like the sound of him being all mine. "I like the sound of that."

I climb on top of him and take his penis in my hand. He's hard again and ready to go. I guide him into me and slowly slide down until I'm filled with all of him. The feeling of him deep inside of me makes my body tingle with desire. Julian is looking at me, his eyes burning with lust. I feel empowered and in control as I slide my wet sex slowly up and down his hot shaft. Julian's hands are on my hips, and he helps me keep my balance and my rhythm. His moans of pleasure spur me on.

"Tell me what I need to do to help make you come again, baby." He's remembering the first time I was on top, when I asked him to stay still. I take his hands from my hips and put them on my swollen breasts. Julian doesn't need any other direction from me. His large hands alternate between massaging them firmly and rolling my nipples between his fingers. It feels amazing, and I arch my back into his hands, savoring his touch. I want his mouth on me, so I lean forward. The feeling of his tongue on my sensitive nipples is too good. He's taking turns licking and sucking and biting and caressing my breasts. I begin to feel another orgasm brewing in my core, and when I clench my whole lower body, the sensation starts to spread. I pull back from Julian's mouth and begin to ride him quickly as the warmth of my climax spreads through my body. Julian never takes his eyes off of me, and when he senses I'm done, he wraps his arm around my waist and flips me over onto my back. He thrusts into me hard and fast as he chases his own orgasm. I marvel in the beauty of his body and the images of his muscles flexing and pulsating with desire. I wrap my legs and arms around his ass and hold him close to me as his orgasm racks his body. We stay this way for longer than necessary, our bodies and hearts fused together.

Julian eventually gets up and heads to the bathroom. When he returns, I do the same. As I climb back into bed with him and snuggle up to his hot, naked body, I wonder how I was ever able to sleep without him next to me. It just feels so right. I glance up and find him smiling down at me. He looks so relaxed and so happy. I hope I'm mirroring the same emotions because that's how I'm feeling.

"What are you smiling about?" I want him to tell me I just rocked his world.

"You called me, baby." He says it shyly, and I'm touched. I didn't realize I said it. It must have slipped out.

I hug him tightly and press my face to his chest. I kiss the skin over his heart, and he squeezes me back.

"What time do you get up for work?"

Damn. I'm snapped back to reality. "Around seven. What about you?"

"I'm going to hang out with you until you leave. We're planning on leaving around one o'clock."

I try not to get emotional when I think about Julian being away from me for five days. It sounds so long. I remind myself I managed to live for twenty-five years without him. Julian notices my mood change. "What are you thinking about?"

"I'm going to miss you."

He kisses me softly on the lips. "I'm going to miss you too."

I'm exhausted and need to sleep, but I don't want this night to end. Despite my best efforts to remain awake, I can't. Julian's warm body pressed against mine along with the soothing feel of his fingers running slowly up and down my back lull me into a peaceful deep sleep.

I sleep so well that I don't even hear my alarm until it's been going off for thirty minutes. I hit the off button and roll over. Julian isn't in my bed, and my heart sinks when I think he must have already left. I throw a robe on, quickly brush my teeth, and head out to see if I'm right. I find him in my living room with his laptop on the coffee table in front of him. He's dressed, and it looks like he has showered. Damn. I guess this means no sex this morning. I'm greeted by a huge smile.

"Good morning, Corazón."

"How long have you been up?"

"Since six. I hope I didn't wake you?"

I rub my eyes. "No, and I wish you would have. I'm already running late, and I can't even blame it on sex."

Julian reaches for me and pulls me onto his lap. "I'm sorry, baby. You looked so peaceful. I told you I have a hard time waking you up."

I lean over, nip his earlobe, and whisper, "For the record, I love being woken up with something hard."

Julian moans, and I feel him harden. "Sit tight." I hurry back to my room and grab a condom from the dresser. On the way back to the kitchen, I hear Marissa's shower turn on, and I know I have at least twenty minutes before she'll come out of her room. Shannon went to Cory's last night, so I'm not worried about her catching us either. I walk back into the living room, put the condom on the table, straddle Julian, and begin unzipping his shorts like a woman on a mission. I find him hot and semi-hard.

"Have I told you lately how much I appreciate the fact you don't wear underwear?" I slide his shaft out and stroke it gently. Semi-hard turns into very hard quickly.

For the first time since we met, I think I've shocked Julian. He's speechless for a minute. He looks around, unsure we should be doing this here.

"We have about twenty minutes for you to put that condom on and fuck me. I know we don't have a lot of time this morning, so I'm keeping you out of my bedroom, but if you think you're leaving without coming again you're very wrong. And by the way, I'm already wet and ready for you."

An actual growl comes out of his mouth before it meets mine. Julian slides his hot tongue into my mouth and kisses me passionately. "Dios mío. That's so fucking hot. I don't like to be rushed with you, but I'll take what I can get."

I let go of him and watch as he takes the condom out of the wrapper and rolls it on. Julian slides his hand under my robe and runs his fingers over my sex. He feels that I was not lying about being wet and moans again. I shift in his lap, position myself over him, and slide down. The feeling of him so deep inside of me coupled with the thought of possibly getting caught excites me, and I can't believe how wet and turned on I am. Julian reaches into my robe and exposes my breasts. He massages one with one of his hands and finds my clit with the other. I ride him and grind my hips into him and lose myself in the exhilarating sensation of his touch. Our movements are hard, fast, and raw. I've been moaning quietly but as I get close to coming, I become a little louder.

"Are you close, baby? I am. Let's do this together, okay. Come for me."

His voice, his fingers on my swollen sex, and his hard dick inside me make that an easy request to fulfill. I clench down as the first waves of my orgasm start pulsing through me and hang on to Julian tightly as he thrusts into me and finds his own release.

I want to sit and savor the moment, but I hear Marissa's door opening. I stand up quickly and adjust my robe. Julian gets up and rushes to the hall bathroom. I pass Marissa on the way down the hall and try to hide my guilty little smile.

"You're going to be late, Lex. It's already after eight."

"I know. Getting in the shower now."

I take a quick shower and fix my hair into a ponytail. I really haven't left myself much time to get ready. It was totally worth it though. That was hot. I apply a little makeup and walk out of the bathroom naked. Julian is lying on the bed.

"Hmm ... you should get dressed right now, or you're going to be really late for work."

I giggle as I walk into my closet. I put on a simple, navy, tank sheath dress with a black, skinny belt. I slide my feet into the black, Charles David pumps I recently bought. I come back out, and find Julian in the same position.

"You should stop lying on my bed looking so hot if you don't want me to be really, really late to work."

Julian chuckles. I'm glad he thinks I'm funny, but I'm only half kidding. My desire for him doesn't seem to wane at all. I crave his touch. He sits up, gets off the bed, and comes to me. He puts his hand on my chin and tips my face to look up at him. He places a soft kiss on my lips.

"Thank you for a rather unexpected and incredibly satisfying morning, Corazón. You're making it harder for me to leave you know."

I kiss him back and push away the sadness I'm feeling about him leaving. I will not ruin this morning. "Well hurry and go already so you can come back."

We walk out together and say our goodbyes, and I sense he's hesitant to go as well. After many kisses and hugs, he finally gets in his car and pulls out of the driveway. As I watch him drive down my street, I wonder how it's possible for me to miss him this much already.

CHAPTER 26

"In all the time I've seen you, you've never been so emotionally open. I'm happy to see it. It's good for you."

My session with Ellen started with me close to tears. She asked how things were going with Julian, and when I told her he would be away for a few days, I got choked up. If it were anybody but Ellen witnessing this, I would be mortified. She has been with me through some pretty emotional moments, but there haven't been many, and they all happened right after Brady died. I've been able to keep it together for months now, and I was hoping I'd be able to stay that way. It isn't looking good for me.

"I'm glad you see it that way, Ellen. I am emotional, and I hate it. I'm all over the place. Julian just left this morning, and I'm already missing him. I feel needy, desperate, and anxious— all the things I swore I'd never feel again. Add that to the fact I'm dealing with all the Brady memories, and I'm a mess. I think I'd rather be numb."

"Well that's honest, and I can understand why you feel it's easier, but it's no way to live, Lexie, and you know that. It's normal to feel all these emotions. I would encourage you to talk to Julian and tell him how you feel. Tell him what's going on with you."

"One of the biggest changes in me since Brady is my inability or unwillingness to talk about my feelings. I used to be able to share so easily. My heart was open, and I let everyone in. I could trust. I miss that so much. The problem now is I'm still an open book as far as my body language goes, but verbally I'm a vault. The words I want to say just run rampant through my head but then don't come out of my mouth. I know Julian needs to know what's going on with me. I need to tell him about Brady, especially now that the memories are so powerful. I know I'm not hiding anything from him, but at the same time I'm hiding everything, if that makes sense."

"It makes total sense. You keep telling me how well Julian reads you. I understand because I feel the same way about you. You don't hide your emotions well, but it's hard to know what they are. I imagine it confuses him."

"Ugh. It does, and he wants to talk about how I'm feeling all the time. I'd actually prefer to keep it more on the physical level, but it just doesn't seem possible."

"Why is that?"

"Why do I want it just physical or why isn't it just physical?"

"I'd like to hear both answers."

"Well, I'm comfortable with the physical stuff. The sex is amazing, and I feel powerful and confident when we're together. He shares control with me, and I like it. The physical is easier than the emotional because I trust my body more than I trust my heart."

Saying those words out loud actually feels good.

"That also makes perfect sense, but you can trust yourself with both." I shrug my shoulders in response. I don't agree.

Ellen continues. "Why do you think things can't just be physical between you two?"

"Because they're not. We do have an emotional connection, a strong one, and we both feel it. He seems so ready to dive into this thing, and I just don't think we should move so fast."

"You definitely need to go at a pace that's comfortable for you, and there's nothing wrong with being a little cautious. But based on everything you've told me, I'd bet Julian is as invested in this relationship as you are."

"That may be true, Ellen, but that's not a bet I'm ready to make."

CHAPTER 27

The rest of my week basically sucks. I hear from Julian via text a few times Wednesday and Thursday, but everything is quick and impersonal and in response to me texting him. I try to call him late Thursday night, but it just goes to voicemail, and I begin to get frustrated. Before he left, Julian told me what his schedule was going to be like, so I knew he'd be busy. Their plan was to look at five different properties on the West Coast, and Julian said they had several meetings and dinners with the sellers and other investors. I figured he'd be with people all day, so I didn't expect much from him then, but I did think I'd hear from him at night when he got back to his hotel room. By Friday night, I'm really anxious and need to hear his voice. It's midnight when I call, and when he answers, I hear people and music in the background. Julian's voice is quiet and impersonal, and he gets me off the phone quickly.

"Hello. I'm still out with some business associates. I think we'll be wrapping things up soon. I'll call you later."

"Okay. Sorry to interrupt. Talk to you later."

I hang up feeling like a total idiot. I'm at home doing nothing, and he's still out doing who knows what with who knows whom. It occurs to me I really don't know much about what Julian's life is like outside of what he does with me.

I hang up and think about how, throughout our short relationship, he really hasn't initiated the communication between us. I'm the one who usually calls, texts, or e-mails him. Ironically, I'm the one who's bad at that, so we're really in trouble if it's all left up to me. My train of thought takes a turn, and I start to think about how we spend time together too, and realize it's usually on his schedule as well. Before long, I manage to get myself worked up about not being a priority for him, and instead of waiting to talk to him tonight, I turn my phone off and try to go to sleep. It ends up being a rough night, full of tossing and turning, and when I wake up in the morning, I'm still in a foul mood.

I literally feel the darkness settling on me as I take a shower and get ready for work. I'm not in a good place at all, and I know it. Unfortunately, once I start shutting down like this, I have a hard time stopping. I wanted to talk to Julian so badly last night, and this morning I don't care if I hear from him at all. So much for him not putting me in last place in his world. I leave for work before anyone else is up, grab Starbucks, and head in. Thankfully, my day at work is pretty busy, and I have something other than Julian to focus on. Lauren is working with me today and tries her best to pull me out of my funk. She doesn't ask what's going on with me, and I'm thankful. I really just want to be left alone.

I finally turn my phone back on around two in the afternoon on Saturday. As I expected, I have several missed calls and texts from Julian. I also have a few from Luke. Luke wants to know if I'm coming to Stellar tonight and also tells me he can't come over Sunday for our regular True Blood date.

Alexa: *Hey there. Just got these. Busy at work. No and why? Tired and staying in tonight.*

Luke: *Ok. Figured. I got asked to work Sunday anyway. But you probably know that.*

Alexa: *Figured why? I don't discuss your work schedule with Julian.*

Luke: *Lunch next week for sure. Miss you*

Alexa: *Miss you too. For sure.*

I don't try to analyze Luke's texts and move on to the messages from Julian. The first one is from one-thirty last night. There are three others from today. I delete the voicemails without even listening to them. Hearing his voice will only soften my resolve. I do read the texts though.

Julian: *Hey baby. Called last night. Sorry it was so late. Have time this morning.* (8:00 a.m.)

Julian: *Call me.* (8:45 a.m.)

Julian: *Alexa. Call me please.* (10:42 a.m.)

Julian: *Seriously? Hope you're ok.* (12:17 p.m.)

I'm not going to lie. It feels good to have him on the other end, wanting to talk to me. I know I'm being childish and petty. I know he's busy, but I don't care. I just don't want to feel like this. As much as I want to ignore him, I also respect that he's working and doesn't need to be dealing with my disappearing act. So I respond.

Alexa: *Why wouldn't I be ok?*

Julian calls back immediately, and I send the call to voicemail. His text follows.

Julian: *Answer your phone Alexa. You're obviously on it. I don't have time for this.*

Now I'm annoyed and totally prefer that emotion over sad. Doesn't he know me at all? Like I'm going to do what he asks now. I really should ignore the text, but I can't.

Alexa: *Clearly. I don't have time for this either. Or the inclination.*

Julian: *Inclination for what? To talk to me? Please answer your phone.*

Julian: *I want to hear your voice baby. Even if it's mad.*

Alexa: *I don't want to hear your voice right now Julian.*

Alexa: *I did when I called you on Thursday & again when I called last night but I'm over it now.*

Julian: *Did you listen to any of my messages? I'm guessing not.*

I laugh a little. He does know me.

Alexa: *No. Like I just said. Didn't want to hear your voice.*

Julian: *Figured. You would have heard my voice telling you I really miss you.*

Julian: *And that I'm sorry I haven't been able to talk.*

Julian: *Never alone. Being with my father for this many days is rough and he needs all my attention. My voice also told you I had the most awesome dream about you last night. I wanted to share the details. I have meetings all day today and it looks like we may end up with two properties. I'll call later. Hopefully you'll be inclined to talk then.*

His patience with me throws me for a loop. I'm acting like a brat, and he's backing off. I feel a little bad because I really have only thought about how this time apart affects me. I don't know much about his dad, but Julian has told me they're not close, and I didn't think twice that Julian may be dealing with his own stuff. The reality that I've avoided getting to really know him is blatantly obvious too. It's hard to stay mad at him.

Alexa: *My curiosity about your dream wins. Call me later. I'll probably answer.*

After work, I have my car washed, go to the grocery store, and go for a quick run. I'm trying to keep my mind off of him, but it's not working. Ten o'clock comes and goes, and still no word from Julian. The good feelings that surfaced this afternoon are gone now. I hung on to them as long as I could, and now I'm done. I'm a twenty-five-year-old who's sitting at home on a Saturday night waiting for a man to call me. It's pathetic, and I'm mad at myself. I wish I was still one of those girls who would just say fuck it and go out to prove I didn't need a man. But I'm not. I have no desire to prove anything to anybody. I turn off my phone and get into bed. Ironically, it's Brady I think about, not Julian.

From the minute I gave Brady my phone number, he called me or texted me. For the first six months of our relationship, we were either together or on the phone. I can't remember ever going hours without hearing from him, never mind days. We were pretty inseparable, and the only time we were apart was when we were working or when he was studying to retake his bar exam. I never wondered if he was thinking about me, and even when I look back now, I'd say we were genuinely happy in the beginning.

Things started to change after the holidays that year. Brady started partying more, and we started spending less time together. Work was busy for me, and making the trip up to Broward County where he lived became a hassle. We still saw each other a few times a week, but it was different, and if I didn't make the effort, it wouldn't happen. But he still called and texted me constantly. It was during this time I first thought of ending the relationship. His partying was coming between us, and I was sick of dealing with him when he was drunk or high. I tried to break up with him for the first time in late February. He begged and pleaded with me to give him another chance. He had all kinds of reasons and excuses, and I bought them all. We fell into a terrible pattern of breaking up and making up after that, and it became harder and harder for me to get out. Each time I would agree to stay together, I would lose a little piece of myself because I knew how toxic our relationship was. The same scene started to play out over and over again. Brady would promise to slow down the partying, and he would for a week or so. When he did, I would get the Brady back that I fell in love with, and I would hang on to that with everything I had. But it never lasted long. One of the hardest parts was nobody else was acting like Brady had a problem, so I was the bad guy when I made a big deal about the partying. Looking back now, I see that Luke started distancing himself from the situation toward the end. He knew it was bad, but he got tired of telling me to break up with Brady, because I wouldn't listen. Luke watched me get sucked in deeper and deeper and felt powerless to stop me. I know

STAY

that's why he acts the way he does in regards to Julian. He really doesn't want me to get hurt.

I fall asleep with these thoughts in my head, so it's no surprise my sleep is wrought with my recurring nightmares. I get very little sleep, and when I get out of bed Sunday morning, my whole outlook is different.

CHAPTER 28

I wake up in a horrible mood again Sunday morning, and when I say horrible, I mean really bad. I've convinced myself the feelings of insecurity, confusion, and jealously that have plagued me since I met Julian are not signs of a healthy relationship or a healthy me and that I want nothing to do with them. I've also convinced myself I want to be alone. I shove all of the good memories of the last few weeks with Julian into the corners of my mind and heart. I'm not in a place where I can separate the feelings I'm having about Julian with the feelings I'm having about Brady, and they all begin to mesh together into a big ball of hurt.

Julian going away for five days was the worst thing that could have happened to our budding relationship. His physical presence is what has kept me grounded during this whole rollercoaster ride, and without his touch and arms around me, I've drifted back toward the place where I'm more comfortable being alone. I feel the depression seeping back in, and it sucks. I was sure I was past this, but I was wrong.

When I let Julian in and decided to feel again, all of the emotions I had been repressing for a year took it as an invitation to reappear. I'm completely and totally overwhelmed. The fact I haven't slept well in two days isn't helping either. To add insult to injury, I also realize my period should be here this week and that PMS is making all of this even worse. Holy hell! The conditions are totally ripe for the perfect emotional storm.

I don't feel the need to bring anybody into this drama, so I get out of the house before I see my roommates. They have both been busy and in and out this weekend, so they really don't know what's going on with me, but they think I'm fine, and that's good. I don't check my phone, and I don't check my personal e-mails the entire day. I know Julian is coming back sometime today, but I don't want to see him. Too bad he has other plans.

I get home from work around five o'clock to find Julian waiting in my driveway. Shit. My heart starts racing, and I know this is going to be ugly. He gets out and walks around his car toward mine. He barely gives me enough room to open the door and get out. As I do, he pulls me into his arms and holds me tightly. My body betrays me and melts into his touch. My heart and mind are not as weak though, and I'm able to pull away. Well, I'm able to *try* to pull away. His hold on me tightens, and he ups the ante by kissing me firmly on the lips.

"I thought that might be the best way to start the conversation we're about to have, Alexa." I assume he's referring to the kiss. It's obvious by the tone of his voice and his posture he isn't happy. I shrug my shoulders and pull away. This time he lets me. I make no move to go into the house, so we stay in the driveway. I decide going on the offensive is my best plan of action. I know Julian, and I'll lose the upper hand here if I don't come out swinging.

"I'm not in the mood for a lecture, Julian, so if you planned on giving me one, you may want to reconsider."

Yep. Bitchy and rude and right on target. The look on Julian's face is one of confusion and hurt. I try not to let it get to me. I made a decision this weekend to end this, and I have to be strong here.

"What the hell does that mean? I don't lecture you all the time."

"Yes, you do lecture me. I'm always doing or not doing or saying or not saying something wrong. Right now I'm not in the mood to hear whatever you think it is I did wrong this time."

"Can we go inside?" Julian's voice is no more than a whisper. I know he won't let me just stand in the driveway and fight with him, so I nod and go inside. Julian walks straight to my bedroom, and I feel like I have no choice but to follow. I really didn't think this through. I wouldn't have chosen to do this here. I actually should have done it over the phone, but it's too late for that now. I walk in, and he shuts the door behind me. He starts pacing back and forth. I move away from him but stay standing.

"What's going on? And please don't play games here, because I'm really confused."

I take a moment to gather the words that have been in my mind the last few days and try to push them out of my mouth. They don't want to come out. Julian's physical presence is throwing me off. I'm finally able to get them out, and they taste horrible because they're all lies.

"I don't want you here right now. Actually, I don't want you here at all. This time apart was good for me. It showed me how crazy this whole thing between us is. It really is like a rollercoaster ride, and I enjoyed being off of it. I want off."

Julian is looking at me like I'm nuts. He also looks pissed. His voice is no longer calm. "What the hell happened while I was gone, because I have no idea why you're acting this way? Are you trying to break up with me, because that's what it sounds like?"

My heart is racing, and I'm trembling a little. It's so hard to be around him and not touch him. I need to stay strong though. "Nothing happened. I just told you, I had time to think. I can't do that when you're around because my judgment is clouded by the great sex. I've had a very peaceful couple days, and I just don't think you and I are good together. Our relationship isn't healthy."

Julian finally sits down on the bed and runs his hands through his hair. He's staring at me but not saying anything. It's unnerving, and I want him to respond. He doesn't, and the silence is deafening, so I continue. I'm starting to feel badly, so I try and take total ownership of this situation.

"Do you remember the first song I sent you? The one about not wanting to hurt again? I meant it. I can't do this. I need out before this thing between us wrecks me. This isn't really about you—"

Julian cuts me off. His voice is impatient. "It's me, not you? Is that where you're going with this? Because if so, you can just stop. The only thing crazy is how you're acting right now."

He takes a deep breath and exhales. "I have no idea where to start here because you just fucking blindsided me, and I make it a point to never let that happen."

Julian gets off the bed quickly and takes me in his arms before I have a chance to respond or move away. He's holding me tightly, and my arms are pinned to my side. He presses his lips to my ear and whispers, "First of all, you're not breaking up with me, so let's take that off the table and move on to whatever is really going on."

His tone is calm, and his touch non-threatening, but I don't process it that way. With no warning, my past and present collide in a major way, and an image of Brady holding me in a similar way and telling me he wasn't letting me leave bursts into my mind in the most vivid way. For a split second, I'm there, in his room, and Julian is Brady. I'm overwhelmed with a feeling of utter panic, and when I look up at Julian, he's noticeably shocked by what he sees in my eyes. He lets me go before the words even come out. He sees my fear and takes a step back. There's venom in my voice when I speak, and I don't even sound like myself.

"Let me fucking go, and don't ever tell me what I'm going to do or not do! Who the fuck do you think you are coming in here and telling me I have to be with you. Maybe you didn't hear me the first time! I was trying to be nice, but I'll skip that this time. I don't want to be with you anymore. I wish you didn't come here tonight. I wish you never came into my life at all. Just leave, Julian. Please."

The words come out in a torrent of pain and with them come the tears. Julian looks shell-shocked, and it makes me feel worse. He has no idea what's going on. He has no idea that Brady's and my last night played out something like this. I wanted out, and Brady wouldn't accept it, so I stayed. I stayed the night, and it changed my whole life. Julian has no idea I felt dead before I met him and that being away from him for five days was so hard for me. He has no idea I already need him that much. He has no idea I need to push him away so I never feel that kind of hurt and betrayal again.

Julian backs up and sits down at my desk. He's as far away from me as he can be in my room, but he still feels too close. He shakes his head slowly.

"I'm staying because I said I would and because you have asked me to over and over again. I'm staying because you're not okay right now, and I have no idea what's happening or what happened while I was gone. You're scaring me a little here, and I don't want to go. But if you tell me the truth, and I see you're okay, I'll leave. Okay? And please be honest with me. We promised each other we would always be honest."

His voice is gentle, and his eyes are filled with compassion, and my need to pull him close edges out my desire to push him away. Through my tears, I try to give him the truth he does deserve.

I sit down on my bed and try to find the words. "I was doing fine until you came along. Now everything I've worked so hard for is gone."

"What's gone? What have you been working for? I'm not trying to be a jerk, baby, but I don't understand any of this. I know we didn't get to talk for a few days, but I'm having a hard time believing this is all because of that."

It becomes so obvious to me that my refusal to tell him anything about my past has really left him in the dark. "I don't want to be this girl. I didn't used to be this girl. I *hate* this girl." He still looks confused, so I continue.

"The girl who can't go a few days without talking to her boyfriend, or whatever you are to me, without freaking out or getting all insecure and jealous. The girl who waits by the phone on a Friday and Saturday night hoping he'll call her. The girl who, after only a month, missed him so badly it actually hurt her heart. That's the girl I don't want to be."

Julian stands up and takes a step toward me. I shake my head no. I'm calming down, and if he touches me, I'll lose it.

"Can I sit by you? I won't touch you." His voice is pleading, and I see his own pain. I may not have completely opened up to him emotionally, but I have physically. This man has touched almost every inch of my body, and now I won't let him near me. I don't blame him for being upset by that.

I nod yes, and he comes and sits on the edge of the bed near me. He doesn't try to touch me. He just stares into my eyes and speaks in a whisper.

"I'm so glad you're that girl, Alexa, because that girl belongs with the guy who couldn't stay focused on work because all he wanted to do was get back to Miami. She belongs with the guy who freaked out when his girlfriend refused to speak to him and tried to find a way to cut his very important business trip short. That girl belongs with the guy who missed her so much it actually hurt his heart too. That girl needs to stay with the guy who, despite his best efforts to not feel this way, can't imagine her not being in his life."

My tears have stopped, and I'm feeling a tiny bit better. His words are soothing.

"You can't say things like that to me and then disappear. I can't stay in this relationship if you can't even make time to call me."

"I'm so sorry, baby. I fucked up here, and I see that. I don't want to make any excuses, but I was extremely busy and never alone. I even shared a room with Danny on three of the nights. These trips are like that. We were being wined and dined, and it was non-stop. I tried to come home Saturday after you refused to talk to me, but I couldn't leave my dad and Danny there without me. One day soon I'll tell you about my dad, but now isn't the time. Please just know I never stopped thinking about you for a minute."

I sit and process what he said. I'm really curious about what's going on with his dad, but he made it clear he doesn't want to talk about it now, and we have our own issues to deal with.

"Why do you want to do this? I clearly am a mess. You don't need this drama. You don't deserve it."

Julian gives me a small smile. It's the first one tonight. "You definitely keep me on my toes. You're passionate, and I love that about you."

I can't help but smile back at him. "That's a nice spin on my crazy. Passionate has a better ring to it."

I reach over and thread my fingers through his and squeeze. He squeezes back.

"You do know I would never ever force you to do anything, right?"

Great. He isn't letting that go, and I'm not surprised. My reaction to his touch a little while ago was extreme.

"Yes, I know that. I just overreacted. I was mad at you, I'm tired, and I have PMS." I try to say it convincingly, but Julian isn't buying it.

"Do you also know you can tell me anything, baby? I mean it. Anything."

Oh yes. He's on to me. This is the second time I've reacted badly when he touched me. The first time ended with me having a panic attack, and this time with me freaking out and bursting into tears. He knows something is going on with me, but there's no chance we're having this conversation right now, so I do what I think will distract him. I scoot over on the bed where he's sitting, wrap my arms around him, put my lips on his, and slide my tongue inside his mouth. He kisses me back and holds me for a minute but then pulls away. He shakes his head.

"I can't make you talk to me, but I'm not going to let you try and avoid dealing with what happened tonight by distracting me with sex. I've never wanted you or needed to touch you and feel you more than I do right now, but I don't think that's really what you want."

"You're wrong. It *is* what I want. It's what I need from you too. I'm fine." I try to kiss him again, and he turns his head.

"You were scared of me, baby. I saw the fear, and now I'm scared to touch you."

I'm not sure how much longer I'm going to be able to hide my past from him. I try to offer enough information so we can move past this.

"I'm not scared of you. It's not about you, and I'm so sorry I made you feel that way. Your touch makes me feel only good things." I take the hand I'm still holding and place it over my heart. "Please touch me, Julian."

Julian leans in and gives me the softest kiss. He pulls me into his arms and holds me. He's touching me, but it isn't the same. My reassurances didn't work. I'm not sure what to do to make this better.

"Please lie here and hold me. Don't pull away. I'm sorry." I'm begging, and I know it.

I get what I want, and Julian and I lie down on my bed face to face. He has his arm around me and is gently stroking my back. When I look into his beautiful eyes, all I see is compassion, concern, and love. Yes, love. I'm crazy. I'm crazy for not holding on to him as tightly as I can.

"Tell me about your trip. It was successful?"

I hope the change in topic will help even things out, and it does. Julian tells me about the properties they looked at. He comes alive when he tells me he thinks Bywater will be acquiring a small hotel in Sanibel that's similar to Hotel del Marco. They will also be taking over the construction for a condo complex in Naples where the builders ran into financial problems and need to sell. He gives me details and specifics, and I'm totally interested and thrilled he's sharing it all with me. He hardly mentions his dad, and I find it odd seeing as his dad is the CEO of Bywater and was with him on the trip. It sounds like he was the one who was brokering all the deals, and I can see he really was busy. We talk about it for an hour, and when I look at the clock, I'm shocked to see it's already nine-thirty.

"Are you staying here tonight?" I try not to sound desperate, but I need him to.

"Do you want me to?" His question is honest, and I can tell he's still on edge.

"Yes. I want you to stay. My earlier 'passionate' request for you to leave has been rescinded."

That makes him smile. "Then I'll stay. But we need to eat, because I'm starving."

We head to the kitchen where we find Marissa cleaning up. She tells me her mom sent her home with lasagna tonight and that there's plenty if we want it. She sits with us while we eat, and Julian tells her about his trip as well. If I didn't just live through it, I would never believe that a few hours ago I was trying to end this relationship.

After we eat, Julian goes out to the car and gets his bag. He obviously came straight here when he got back into town. "Is it cool if I take a quick shower?" He's already headed to my bathroom and doesn't extend an invitation for me to join him.

"Yes, if you promise to hurry back."

Julian turns, looks over his shoulder, and winks. "Hang tight, baby, I'll be back before you miss me."

I take my clothes off, dim the lights, and get into bed. I'm lying there with my eyes closed when I feel Julian slip in next to me. I open my eyes and gaze into his. They're soft, and his voice is quiet. "Tell me what you need from me, Alexa."

Right now I know exactly what I need. "Make love to me. I need you to make love to me."

Julian pulls me tightly to him and buries his face in my neck. I can feel his heartbeat pounding in his chest. I know why he's having this reaction. I asked him to make love to me. I chose my words carefully. I know what I said, and I know what it means.

He reaches into my nightstand, takes out a condom, and puts in on. He doesn't take his eyes off of me for a second. When he's done, he positions himself on top of me and enters me slowly. He feels incredible inside of me, and once again I'm amazed at how my body responds to his. We fit together perfectly; like two pieces of a puzzle. My mouth finds his, and I slide my tongue in and kiss him like it's the last time I'm going to have a chance to. I pour all of the hurt, anger, sadness, and desperation I've been feeling into this kiss. I want to pour myself into him. I need him to feel how I feel about him. He has to know how much I want and need him. I know he gets it when he pulls away for a minute and whispers in my ear, "Let it all go, baby. I've got you. You can hold on to me. I'm here. I'm here."

As Julian slides slowly in and out of me, he continues to whisper beautiful things to me, and every last bit of doubt and tension I've been feeling for days fades away. I'm not sure what I did to deserve him, but Julian is here with me, and despite my best attempts to chase him away, he has stayed. As a result, I'm healing, and I'm so grateful. I hold him tightly until his climax subsides, and I savor the feel of his hard body on top of mine. After a few minutes, he gets up and goes to the bathroom to throw the condom away. He quickly gets back in bed and pulls me close to him.

"It's not a good idea for me to go that many days without you. I need this. Not necessarily the sex, but the physical connection. Your touch. I need it." I'm opening up to him in hopes he really understands it wasn't just the lack of talking that got me all crazy. It was the lack of his presence period. His strength and energy help center me.

"I get it. I feel off when you're not around, and I'm glad you're bringing it up now, so we can talk about how not to let this happen again. I have a crazy week coming up, and I think you should come and stay with me at my place. I would come here, but I need to stay close to the hotel."

Wow. He's asking me to stay with him for the week. This week of all weeks is the one week I shouldn't spend so much time with him, but after the crazy behavior I just displayed, I'm not sure how I can say no. I don't want to say no, I just have a bad feeling I'm not going to be able to keep it together all week. Julian takes my silence as a no and tries to convince me.

"Don't freak out. I'm not asking you to move in with me. It's temporary. I'll be working a lot of hours, and I just want to be able to come home and find you in my bed. You can just come over late if that works better for you."

He sounds so nervous, and I find it endearing. "Julian, I'm just trying to think about what I need to pack. You saw how much stuff I brought for two nights didn't you? I don't travel light."

I get a real laugh out of him this time. "So you'll come?"

"Don't I always?"

"Hmm … yes, you do always come. It's another thing I love about you."

I take a deep breath and exhale. We're okay. The banter feels like us. I snuggle into him and close my eyes. I quickly begin to drift off to sleep. This day has kicked my ass big time. I'm just about asleep when Julian whispers in my ear. I don't know if he thinks I'm awake or not. "Let me be here for you, Alexa. I need this too. Let me help you heal, baby."

My heart swells with his words, and I take a minute to absorb them before I respond. The old Lexie would turn around and tell him she was fine and that there wasn't anything to heal. The old Lexie would be mad and hurt that he felt the need to fix her. But thank God the new Lexie found some strength tonight and is willing to admit she needs and wants that from him. I know Julian knows something traumatic happened to me, and I bet he even might know what it is. But he isn't going to make me tell him until I'm ready. That means more to me than anything right now.

I don't turn and face him, but I make sure my words are loud enough for him to hear. "You are, Julian, you are."

CHAPTER 29

Something is shaking me, and I can't tell what or who it is because it's so dark. At first the shaking is soft, but it becomes stronger as the moments pass. I want to yell and ask what's going on, but the words won't come out of my mouth.

"Alexa, wake up, baby, you're okay!" I hear Julian's voice in the distance. He seems so far away.

"Please, Alexa, you're having a nightmare. Wake up!"

The last part of his sentence along with the shaking jolts me awake, and I sit straight up. I'm not disorientated because I've been through this before. But I'm scared because I have no idea what I was saying or doing. Julian has turned the light on and is sitting next to me on the bed. It's four in the morning. He looks a little freaked out. Oh crap. My dream starts coming back to me, and I can feel the tears on my cheeks. It was the dream where I find Brady dead. Julian takes me in his arms and holds me close. I wait for him to say something first because I don't want to share any more than is necessary.

"My God. Are you okay?"

I nod my head yes.

"Do you remember your dream? Do you want to talk about it?"

"Not really." I'm totally lying. I remember it all.

"You're crying. You kept saying the words 'I forgive you,' over and over again. Who do you need to forgive? Who hurt you, baby? Please talk to me." His voice is pleading and desperate.

I wipe the tears from my face and look into the eyes of the man I'm falling in love with. The man who is begging me to let him in. It breaks my heart when the words come out of my mouth, but I can't tell him about this. Not yet.

"I don't remember the dream. I have no idea why I was saying any of that."

He just shakes his head at me and looks down for a minute. When he looks up, I see the sadness he isn't afraid to show me in his eyes. His voice is little more than a whisper when he responds.

"You and I both know you're not being honest. I'm not going to push you because I have a feeling that would be worse. But you're going to need to talk to me, or someone, about whatever's going on with you. It's going to tear you apart, and it's going to tear us apart. Secrets do that. They always do."

I'm not going to argue with him or try to prove he's wrong. There's no point.

"You asked me earlier what I needed from you. Well right now I just need you to hold me. Is that okay, Julian? Can you please just hold me?"

He turns the light off, lies back down, and pulls me to him. I close my eyes and try to absorb the warmth that's radiating from his body. He never lets me go, and I fall back into a fitful sleep.

I'm woken up again before my alarm. This time it's by the horrible cramps that usually accompany my period. I wiggle out of Julian's arms and head to the bathroom. Yep. My period is here. I put a tampon in, take three Advil, and head back to bed. I feel completely hung-over, and I didn't drink a thing last night. My head hurts, my stomach hurts, and my heart hurts. The fact that I haven't slept well in four days just makes everything worse. It's almost seven. I make the decision right then that if I go into work at all today, it isn't going to be until later.

Julian is sound asleep, and I take the opportunity to watch him. I'm hurting right now, and until the pain meds kick in, I won't be falling back to sleep. The morning sun is peeking through my blinds and landing on Julian's face. He looks so young, so peaceful, and so beautiful. The stress of last night isn't showing on his face, and I'm happy to see he was able to fall back asleep. I'm hoping he's as calm when he actually wakes up. I stay there looking at him for another thirty minutes and try to memorize his face. I run my finger over the scar above his eye and make a mental note to ask him where he got it. My touch makes him stir, and his eyes slowly open. He reaches for me and pulls me close. I flip around so we're spooning.

He whispers in my ear, his voice heavily coated with the remnants of sleep, "Good morning, beautiful."

"Good morning, handsome."

"Have you been awake long?"

"Not long." I lie because I don't want him to know I've been staring at him.

"Don't you need to get up?" He looks at the clock. It's now seven forty-five.

"I'm calling in sick today, so no, I don't need to get up."

"Are you okay? Or just tired?" He sounds concerned, and I know the memories of my nightmare are not far away.

"I got my period this morning, and I have horrible cramps. My head is killing me, and I'm exhausted. So no, I'm not really okay."

He rubs my stomach. "Can I get you anything?"

He's extremely nurturing. It's an odd quality in a man who supposedly doesn't get close to people.

"Thanks, but I already took a few Advil. They should be kicking in pretty soon."

He continues to rub my stomach and even massages my lower back a little. I have to ask.

"Julian, don't take this the wrong way, but who taught you to be so nurturing and such a good caretaker? You say you don't get close to people, but it's so hard to believe."

"I spent a lot of time with Isabelle when she was sick. I also pretty much took care of Danny in the end, when Isabelle was dying. My parents were a mess and didn't have much to give to him. I guess that's where it comes from."

He says it like taking care of his dying sister and his little brother was no big deal. I'm in awe of his modesty.

"They both were so lucky to have you. You have such a soothing energy. I can only imagine how safe and loved you must have made them feel."

"I hope so. I hope that's what she felt at the end. I think she did." He sounds far away, and I'm sure he's lost in a distant memory.

I flip over so I'm facing him. "I'm sorry if bringing it up upset you."

He looks me in the eyes and without skipping a beat responds. "It's okay. I have no problem talking about my past with you. I want you to know me. I keep telling you that. You couldn't really know me if you didn't know about Isabelle. About her dying."

Well okay. We both know what that comment really means, but I'm not biting. I don't want to fight, so I change the subject.

"When do you need to leave?"

Julian narrows his eyes and gives me a look that says he knows I'm deflecting. "I need to be at the hotel by ten. We have a staff meeting every Monday at that time."

"What time do you usually get home? I'll make you dinner, if that's okay with you."

"Dinner? Absolutely! I'll make sure to be home by seven. I'll leave a key for you at the desk. Ask the doorman to bring your stuff up and park in spot 532. That one is mine too."

We talk for a few more minutes before Julian gets out of bed. He uses the bathroom and tells me he'll let himself out. He suggests I get some sleep, seeing as I had such a rough night, and I agree. I pull the covers up and burrow in. Julian kisses me on the forehead and tells me he'll see me later.

I text both Lauren and Ramon to let them know I won't be in today because I'm not feeling well. I also send an e-mail to Andrea and our receptionist, Molly. After that, I fall back asleep and don't wake up until after noon. I'm a little groggy when I wake up, but my headache is gone, and my cramps are tolerable. After I shower and blow out my hair, I head into my closet to figure out what I want to bring to Julian's. I decide I'll just pack for Tuesday and Wednesday. I have my appointment with Ellen on Wednesday, so I can swing by home after and pick up more clothes. It's two o'clock by the time I've gotten my things and myself ready. I open my laptop and check my e-mails. I answer a few time-sensitive ones and close it back down. I'm officially off today anyway. I still need to go to the grocery store, but I have hours to kill before I need to get dinner started at Julian's. I can't stop thinking about him, and I want him to know it.

Alexa: *Missing you. Counting the hours. 5 more*

He responds right away.

Julian: *Hope you slept and are feeling better. See you at 7*

I haven't seen my parents in a few weeks, and we really haven't talked either, so I call my mom to catch up. She's in a great mood. She can't stop talking about the new house Tracy is thinking of buying and about Jill trying to get pregnant. She tells me stories about my nieces from her recent visit to Atlanta. She's distracted with my sisters, so there's no pressure on me at the moment. I'm okay with the fact she really doesn't ask anything about me. She's not like Julian's mom. She would never let the story end with, "I met a guy." I haven't told anybody in my family about Julian. Not even my sisters. I'm not ready to introduce even the idea of him until I'm 100 percent sure he'll be sticking around. We talk for about forty-five minutes. I tell her to give my love to my dad and promise I'll come for dinner soon.

When Julian walks into his kitchen at 6:52 p.m., I greet him, in a patterned pink sundress and J. Renee beaded, thong sandals, in the kitchen. The smell of my Thai-inspired shrimp stir-fry and jasmine rice fills the air. I've made it a few times and know it's yummy. He walks in, picks me up in a bear hug, and kisses me passionately.

"Well how was your day, dear?" I'm trying to be cute. This scene is very domesticated.

"Better now. It smells awesome in here. I'm starving. Is it almost ready?"

"It is ready. Just waiting for you."

Julian looks at his watch. "And I'm on time. Early, even." He's in a playful, relaxed mood. I love this Julian.

I figured we'd eat at the island, and I have it all set up. He sits down, and I bring the food over. I picked out a bottle of Riesling to go with dinner but ask Julian if he'd prefer something different.

"This is perfect. My mom and Dario are the only people who ever cook for me, and never here, so this is a treat."

"Great. No pressure. You told me your mom is a great cook, and Dario is an award-winning chef. Not sure my cooking skills can compare."

"Well, if they're as good as all of your other skills, this is going to taste amazing." Julian winks at me and takes a bite. "This tastes great! What *aren't* you good at?"

Um. Communicating my feelings? Letting people in? I'm not good at all kinds of emotional stuff, and he knows it, but if he wants to focus on my culinary and bedroom skills, I'm cool with it.

I answer playfully. "Well, I'm not going to tell you that, Julian. I'll just keep trying to dazzle you with my many talents."

"If I was any more dazzled by you, I'd be blind. You're a very beautiful woman, Alexa Rose, inside and out."

I smile at him; he does know how to make me feel good about myself. Even when I have cramps and am feeling bloated and gross, he finds me beautiful. "You do know you can call me Lexie, right?"

He shrugs his shoulders. "I do call you Lexie."

I shake my head at him. "No, you really don't. You have a few times when we were having sex, but it's Alexa 99 percent of the time."

He thinks about it for a minute. "I guess you're right. You made that comment about nicknames a few weeks ago, and I guess it stuck with me. You're Alexa to me now. Does it bother you?"

Damn. I knew I never should have said that. I was right when I thought it bothered him at the time. "A little. The people closest to me call me Lexie."

"Am I one of those people now?"

I look him directly in the eyes. "I hope so." And I mean it.

My response makes him smile, and on the way back from bringing his plate to the sink, he stops where I'm still sitting and hugs me. "Thank you for dinner, Lexie. It was delicious."

We spend the rest of the night being normal. We talk about our days and snuggle together on the couch watching TV. He rubs my back and gets me ice cream when I mention that I totally crave sweets when I have my period. We get ready for bed together, in his bathroom, and I can't help but think how far we've come in such a short time. I silently give him all the credit. I asked him to not let me ruin this, and he has kept his end of the bargain. As I fall asleep in his arms, I actually give myself permission to relax and be happy.

Tuesday morning is a continuation of Monday night. We both slept well, and I'm in a great mood. I'm trying as hard as I can to focus on what's right in front of me, and I even convince myself that this weekend will pass with no major issues.

Julian lets me shower first, and while I'm in here, I think about when *we* were in here, and it gets me a little hot and bothered. This is the first time I've had my period since we started seeing each other, and the whole topic is uncomfortable when you don't know how the other person feels about being intimate during that time. One guy I saw for a few months in college treated me like I had the plague when I had my period. He was an idiot and didn't last long, but it stuck with me. I don't want to have intercourse right now anyway, but I'm not sure I can keep my hands off of Julian all week. It's especially difficult when he sleeps naked and walks around his room the same way. He's naked when I come out of the bathroom, and I can't take my eyes off of him. He catches me staring.

"Stop looking at me like that, Lexie, or I can't be held accountable for my actions."

"Then stop walking around here naked. I'm out of commission here, and it's killing me."

"Oh, we can fix that really quickly, Corazón. There are all kinds of things I can do to help you out." Julian walks over to me, and before I can say another word he has removed my bra and pinned me to the bed with his beautiful, naked body. His mouth feels hot and wet on my breasts, and as he caresses, licks, and gently bites at my swollen nipples, he presses his erection into my panty-covered sex. I grind my hips into his and am coming in record time.

As I catch my breath, I give him the praise he deserves. "Good God, you make that look so easy. I think I just went from zero to sixty in less than five minutes. Your mouth is dangerous."

He rolls off of me and laughs as he heads to the shower. "It takes two people. I told you before; your body was made for mine."

"Hey, you're not out of commission. Come back here and let me return the favor."

Julian calls back over his shoulder, "You can return the favor as often as you want tonight, baby. I'll be looking forward to it all day."

I finish getting dressed and think about all the ways I can pleasure Julian tonight. He's always so considerate of my needs, and I want to make him feel as good as he makes me feel.

I brought a couple outfits and decide on a black-and-white, tank, sheath dress with touches of light yellow in the print. I wear it with a pair of yellow, open-toed Marc Jacobs pumps and my favorite silver hoops. I know I look good when Julian comes out and whistles at me.

"Have I told you I love the way you dress? You have a great sense of style."

"Thanks. If you don't stop complimenting me, I'm really going to get a big head."

"Just calling it like I see it."

He smiles at me and heads into his own closet to get ready. I follow him in. I've never gone in before, and when I do, I fall in love. Talk about a dream closet. It's huge, and it's filled to the brim with clothes and shoes. I can't help but laugh.

"Seriously, Julian. You're never allowed to comment on my shoe addiction again. It looks like a department store in here."

"I told you I liked shoes too. It wasn't a secret. Why do you think I felt sorry for your closet?" He's laughing as he gets dressed in a pair of tan slacks, a chocolate-brown, button-down shirt, and pair of brown leather Prada loafers I know cost at least six hundred dollars. I swear I'm jealous of my boyfriend's shoes. As I watch him finish getting ready, I think about how nice it would be to have a closet like this, and I allow myself to think about my stuff in here. I allow just a little hope in.

We both head off to work after grabbing a cup of coffee, and Julian tells me to meet him at the hotel for dinner tonight. I can't wait.

CHAPTER 30

I don't usually come down to the beach during any kind of work hour traffic, so I don't plan my time well. I don't get to the hotel until seven-thirty. I text Julian to let him know I'm running late but never hear back from him. I really don't even know where to look for him, so I just go to the front desk and ask for him. The woman at the desk gets a little possessive and wants to know who I am and asks if Julian is expecting me. When I answer yes, she looks skeptical but calls him anyway. I stand in the lobby waiting for about five minutes before I see him coming through the lobby. He sees me and breaks out in a huge smile. I walk toward him, and when I'm close enough, he wraps his arms around me and gives me a sweet kiss on the lips. So much for no PDA. When I look around, it's obvious by everyone's expressions they're surprised at our interaction.

I whisper into Julian's ear, "You have just totally shocked your staff."

He whispers back, "Because I kissed you? Just imagine what they'd think if I greeted you the way I wanted to and started ripping your clothes off."

I pull back, and he's smiling his sexy smile at me. "Want to find out?" I'm kidding, but my response elicits a groan from him.

He takes my hand, walks me over to the front desk, and starts introducing me to the staff as his girlfriend. Holy shit. I was not expecting this. I haven't even told my family about him, and he's telling all these people who work for him who I am to him. We have kind of danced around the topic, but I was just trying to break up with him forty-eight hours ago. Who knows what I'll do next, and I'd hate for it to embarrass him. I kinda feel sick to my stomach now.

I'm not the only one a little shocked by Julian's declaration. These people all look totally shocked too. Everyone, that is, except Candace, who has joined us in the middle of introductions. She looks disgusted and is shooting venom eye darts my way. What a bitch.

I put the fakest smile I have on my face and turn and face her directly. I even extend my hand, which she takes reluctantly. "Hi, Candace. It's great to see you again."

Her smile is equally as phony, and I know we're on the same page. She doesn't like me, and the feeling is mutual. "It's great to see you again too, Alison."

"It's Alexa."

"Oh yeah, sure. Um, Julian, are you getting ready to leave because we really need to go over some details for the shoot and your interview on Saturday."

Another photo shoot? And an interview? Julian hasn't mentioned either.

"We can talk about it tomorrow, Candace. Lexie and I are leaving." He wraps his arm around me possessively, and I appreciate it.

Candace scowls at me and turns to walk away. As we head toward Ursa's, Julian once again tries to defend her behavior.

"She really is a nice person."

"Ha. Maybe. But she'll never be nice to me. She wants you, and now that you announced I was your girlfriend, it will only be worse." Something in my voice clues Julian in to the fact that maybe I wasn't totally on board with that information going public.

He stops and turns me to face him. He looks hurt, and Candace is no longer the topic. "You're upset I told my staff you're my girlfriend?"

Crap. This isn't the way I wanted this night to start. "Kind of, but not for any reason you might think of."

"Seriously? Please explain why me telling people we're together is an issue." He sounds frustrated.

"It makes me feel awesome that you want to tell people we're together, but I kind of prefer keeping things private. I was a crazy chick two days ago trying to break up with you. I don't want to do anything to embarrass you, and if people know, it'll just be worse."

Julian tries to absorb my ramblings before he responds. "Last week you were upset I didn't introduce you to Elyse and Victoria. Now you're upset that I did introduce you to people here." He shakes his head and continues. "You aren't an embarrassment to me, and I don't see you becoming one either. Yes, you were acting crazy trying to break up with me two days ago, but that isn't going to happen again, so we can just move past it."

I could try to explain that it's completely different, but I don't bother. He hid me from those girls and didn't even acknowledge me. That was a different issue, but I'm going to let it go. I don't want to argue or put a damper on the night. I reach up and wrap my arms around his neck. He wraps his around my waist.

"I'm sorry. Thank you for wanting people to know who I am to you." Julian smiles and kisses me. I made him happy, but the uncomfortable feeling I have lingers. I have no doubt I'll do something to screw this up.

When we get into the kitchen, Dario has our table all set up. The food is awesome, and the rest of dinner passes without any more drama. We don't get back to Julian's house until almost ten. We both go into the bathroom to brush our teeth, and I walk out first, so I can change. I'm still not feeling great and am ready to get into bed. I know Julian is probably expecting a little action, but for the first time since we met, I'm not up for it. I'm bloated, cranky, and I ate too much. Ick. We both have been sleeping naked, and when I put on a pair of purple-and-white-striped sleep shorts and a white tank top, I hope Julian gets the hint. He does and puts a pair of black, cotton pajama bottoms on.

He doesn't seem upset though. "If you're trying to not look sexy, it's not working."

I shrug my shoulders, smile, and get under the covers. "You can still sleep naked."

He climbs into bed and snuggles me close to him. "Too tempting."

"I hope it's okay that I'm just not feeling it tonight. I do owe you."

He shakes his head and looks offended. "Lexie, I'm not keeping score. You can say no whenever you need or want to." I may be hypersensitive but I think I hear a double meaning in his comment, and I quickly change the subject.

"I think I might spend the night at home tomorrow night. I have plans, and I wouldn't get back here till late." My plans are with Ellen, and I could be back by eight-thirty, but I've been feeling a little on edge since the whole girlfriend thing happened, and a little space is probably a good idea. Julian doesn't see it that way.

"Plans? Are you going out?" He sounds a little annoyed and a little jealous. I did originally agree to stay here all week. I pause for a minute and then decide to tell him about Ellen. I put a caveat on my admission first. "I'll tell you what my plans are, but I would prefer you don't ask me a lot of questions after. I'm trying to be open with you, but it's still hard for me." I exhale and wait to see if he agrees.

"Okay. No questions. I promise." Good.

"I see a therapist every Wednesday night. I have for almost a year. Her name is Ellen."

Oh wow. I can almost see the wheels turning in Julian's head, and I know he's regretting he made that promise. I feel bad for him. "Okay, one question, but seriously, just one."

He looks at me pensively for a minute, and I think he's trying to decide what to ask. I'm wrong. He doesn't ask a question. He makes a statement. "I'm glad you have someone to talk to. Someone you trust. Maybe one day I can be that kind of person to you." There isn't a hint of any other emotion but sincerity, and it melts my heart. He really is a good guy.

I can't find the right words, so I just hug him tightly. After a few minutes, Julian reaches over and turns off the light. I flip over so we're spooning. Things just got a little emotional, and I can't take the edge off with anything physical. I feel a little raw because I believe Julian is only going to put up with my issues for so long. He keeps putting himself out there, and I just can't meet him halfway on a consistent basis. It makes me feel inadequate.

"Goodnight, Alexa." My heart sinks. It's Alexa again.

In my dream, I'm running through Stellar screaming Brady's name. I think I keep getting glimpses of him, but then he disappears each time I get close. I find Luke behind the bar, and I ask him to help me find Brady, but he won't. I beg, and he just tells me he won't help me because I refuse to take his advice. I keep yelling at him that it's going to be too late. I'm desperate and crying when I hear Julian's voice coming through my dream.

"Wake up, Alexa. You're dreaming again. It's just a dream."

I feel the tears on my face as I slowly open my eyes. Julian is looking down at me. I turn my head to look at the clock. It's two forty-three. I roll over and pull the covers up to me. I don't want to talk about it.

"I'm sorry I woke you up again. I'm okay. Let's go back to sleep."

"Look at me, baby."

I shake my head no. I'll start crying harder if I look at him. God, this is so fucked up. I'm not going to be able to spend the night with him if this keeps happening.

His voice is soft and pleading. "Please, Lexie. Mírame."

I relent and turn over. He brushes his fingers over my face and wipes away my tears. "I know I promised I wouldn't ask questions, but this person you see, Ellen, is she helping you with your nightmares?"

"She's trying." I whisper the words.

"You kept saying it was going to be too late. I know you remember the dream. Talk to me. Please."

Yeah. Not happening. "Maybe I should go home or sleep in the guest room or on the couch. I feel awful I keep waking you up."

Julian shakes his head slowly. "Damn it, Lexie. Why do you keep doing that? You keep pushing me away. I'm begging you to let me in. I understand more than you think I do. I had horrible nightmares after Isabelle died. It helps to talk about it."

I try to offer a small smile. "I'm glad talking helped you heal. I do talk about it, and to be honest, it hasn't helped much. Let's just go back to bed, okay?"

He isn't going to just let this go. "Maybe you need to talk to someone else if you aren't getting any better."

Hmm ... getting any better? His words are interesting. He's implying something needs to be fixed. This is why I don't tell him anything. I don't want him to think he needs to fix me.

"And you're volunteering for the job?"

He doesn't hesitate. "Yes."

"I can't talk to you. Especially you. I don't want this to be how you see me. I didn't want you to know about the nightmares. I told you, I don't want to be that girl. Why can't you understand? I hate it that you keep seeing me like this. I just want to run." The tears come again and roll slowly down my cheeks.

"I'm not going to let you run, baby. I need you to stay with me. You just need to stay."

I flip back over and let him pull me close. I don't close my eyes though. After a while, I hear Julian's breathing turn deep, and I know he's asleep. I wiggle out of his arms and get out of bed. I quietly make my way out of the bedroom and head toward the terrace. I grab a throw off of his couch and go outside. It's almost three-thirty in the morning. It's actually warm outside, and the breeze feels nice. My thoughts are so jumbled, and once again I feel my past, present, and future all colliding. I'm tired, emotionally and physically. I just don't know how long I can keep doing this.

I fall asleep for a few hours but wake up again at six-thirty when I feel the sun shining on my face. I open my eyes and find Julian sitting next to me, watching me. He doesn't look upset. He smiles at me. "I've always thought about sleeping out here."

I'm so glad he doesn't seem upset. I really can't handle it. "It's pretty comfortable."

"You must be exhausted. Let me go get you some coffee." He heads to the kitchen to get me some coffee, and once again I'm amazed at his willingness to deal with my drama. He comes back, hands me my coffee, and sits down next to me on the couch. He rubs my feet but doesn't say anything else for a few minutes.

I feel the need to try to explain my actions, again. "Julian–"

"You don't need to say anything. I'm not happy about it, but you've made it clear you aren't willing or ready to share whatever's haunting you right now. I won't keep begging you to talk to me. I'm willing to let this go for a while because I want you to stay, but for your own sake, you need to figure out how to work this out, whatever *it* is. We have only been together a month, and I can see how badly it's tearing you apart."

Everything he said is right. His use of the word haunting is spot-on too. I change the topic and remind him I'm going to spend the night at my house tonight. He's either okay with the plan or just not complaining because he knows it's a good idea. We get ready for work without talking very much. There's definitely tension between us, and I know I've put it there. We agree to talk later and go our separate ways. I have that sense of impending doom the whole way into work, and it follows me the whole day.

CHAPTER 31

I'm looking forward to my session with Ellen today. She gives me a big hug and smile when I walk into her office. I take off my shoes and settle into her comfy, brown couch. I know she can tell by my energy I really need to talk.

"How are you?"

"Shitty, Ellen, but you already know that." She smiles, and I love that I can be honest with her.

"I know this is a rough time of year for you." I started seeing Ellen at the end of the summer last year, a few months after Brady died.

"Yeah. And I'm not dealing very well with all the memories I'm having."

"Are you having nightmares? Or flashbacks?"

"I've had a few nightmares lately." Or every other night this week, I think, but I don't offer that up. I refuse to acknowledge my memories as flashbacks. I don't have PTSD or anything like that. Ellen knows my feelings about this and doesn't push.

"What are the nightmares about?" I'm not sure why she asks. We've gone over this before.

"Same as usual." Most of my current nightmares are a variation of me trying to tell Brady I forgive him for that night. I beg him to listen and tell him that it's very important that he knows I forgive him. I keep telling him everything is going to be okay and that we're going to be fine. In most of the dreams, he's lying down with his back to me, and I keep shaking him trying to get his attention. He never responds. When I first started having these dreams, I would wake up screaming in frustration. Now I just wake up crying or in a cold sweat. I guess that's progress.

I know exactly what these dreams mean, and I don't think it takes a PhD to figure it out.

"Obviously you're still feeling guilty about not forgiving Brady before he died. Lexie, we have gone over and over this. Brady overdosed. He was an addict and an alcoholic, and that was not your fault. It was also not your fault he chose to swallow a deadly amount of pills and wash it all down with a bottle of whiskey. You didn't make him do anything else he did that night or any other night during your relationship."

Anything else he did that night? Ellen is looking right at me and challenging me with her eyes and words. We have become very close over the last eight months, and I know when she doesn't believe me. She has always suspected there's more to this story than I've shared with her. She never forces me to talk about things I don't want to, but she does push my comfort boundaries on a regular basis. She has a good bullshit detector, and it's going off right now. I'll give her a little bit of what she wants to hear from me so we can stop the fishing expedition.

"I know none of it's my fault. I didn't deserve for him to treat me like he did. And although I know I didn't help the situation by enabling and participating in a lot of the partying, I do know it was his choice. I feel guilty because he tried to talk to me and get me to forgive him, and I wouldn't. I wouldn't talk to him. I wouldn't listen. And now he's dead, and it all seems so pointless. I feel like so much bad shit was going on in his life and that I should have been the one good thing." I've said all of this to Ellen before. Almost verbatim. She's not buying it.

"All that bad shit that was happening in his life was because he was an addict. Do you think if you would have forgiven him, he would still be here today? That he would have stopped using? Because from everything you've told me, he was very much in denial about his addiction, and very deep into it. He wasn't going to change overnight because you forgave him. You didn't have that kind of power over him. I'm sorry to say it like that because I know you two loved each other, but his choices were *not* about your actions or reactions. He could have chosen to get clean and earn your forgiveness."

Ellen isn't usually so harsh when she talks about Brady. I guess after all this time the kid gloves are coming off. She's making me uncomfortable, but that's what usually happens when my skewed perceptions of things collide with reality. I've been looking down while she's talking to me. I'm trying to fend off the hurt, sadness, anger, and acceptance that are racing through me. I want to look up and tell her she just doesn't understand how I feel and that I *know* I could have changed him if I had more time—if he wouldn't have died. But deep down, I know it's bullshit. I've lived with my guilt over Brady's death for so long now it has become like an old, ratty sweatshirt. It's dirty and torn and doesn't fit right anymore, but it's familiar to my body, and it's comfortable.

"I guess I'll never know what my forgiveness would have meant to him." I look up at her with tears in my eyes and whisper the words. What I do know with absolute certainty is that it's the unknowing that has me stuck and unable to really let go of the guilt.

Ellen sees I'm processing everything she just said and decides to take the subject down a different path. "Have you shared any of this with Julian? You keep telling me he can read you so well. I'm curious if he's questioning your moods or your nightmares." Oh yeah, Julian. That's a whole other issue.

"No, I haven't told Julian anything about Brady, but I know I'm going to have to pretty soon. I've had two nightmares in front of him this week, and I won't tell him what's going on. He's losing patience with me. The only thing in my favor is that I've been a basket-case since day one, so he hasn't grown too accustomed to normal Lexie yet, whoever that is." I try to joke my way through this conversation, but if I know Ellen, she isn't going to let me take my secret hoarding so lightly.

"Do you see yourself having a lasting, meaningful relationship with Julian?"

"Do I see it, or do I want it? Those are too very different questions." She'll be getting frustrated with me very quickly if I keep this up. I'm feeling defensive and vulnerable, and when that happens, I become a master at deflection.

"They can be, but they don't have to be. Your negative view of your value in this relationship absolutely has the power to end things between you and Julian. It sounds like he's making a real effort to get to know you, and I'm sure you're not making it easy on him." Wow, she just hit the nail on the head. I guess that's why she sits in the chair, and I sit on the couch.

"Well, the way I look at it, it's pretty much a double-edged sword. I don't tell him anything about me and why I'm acting so crazy, and he gets frustrated and bails on the broken girl. Or I tell him all this crap, and he bails because he doesn't want to deal with all of the broken girl's crap."

"Why do you think you're broken?" Ellen looks at me with sadness in her eyes.

I answer honestly. "Because nothing has really felt right since Brady died. Maybe even a little earlier, when things were starting to spiral out of control. I feel like something's missing, in me, inside." I feel a tear escape and roll down my cheek. I don't even try to wipe it away. "And no matter how great my job is or how awesome my friends and family are, something in me feels like it was broken as a result of my relationship with Brady. All of you have tried to tape and glue me back together, but a piece of my soul is broken beyond repair, and although I'm trying so hard to change, I know I'll never be the same Alexa I was before."

After all these months, that may be the most honest I've been with Ellen and with myself. I've analyzed my and Brady's relationship with my inner circle over and over, and no matter what anybody says, I still feel this way. I made so many poor decisions and put myself in more than one really bad situation. I know this is why I question my judgment in regard to my relationship with Julian.

"Lexie, you're not broken. I know you don't believe me, but you really have all the tools you need to have a successful and happy relationship. You just need to be ready to accept that someone can love you because of, and despite, your past."

I'm crying a little harder now as our session comes to an end, but I feel a sense of relief that I've at least admitted one of my biggest fears. However, I still wish I had the strength to be 100 percent honest with Ellen, or with anyone else about my feelings. "Thank you, Ellen. I'm working on it. I have a way to go, but I'm getting there." I take a deep breath and exhale slowly. "I just wish I knew how I was going to get through the next few weeks."

Chapter 32

I call Julian on my way home from Ellen's. He's still at work, and it sounds like he's in the middle of something. He tries not to be rude, but I can tell he's busy. He promises to call later, and we get off quickly. I'm actually hoping my roommates are home when I get there, but they're both out too. Despite my better judgment, I decide to text Luke and see what he's up to.

Alexa: *What time do you have to be at work tonight?*
Luke: *Not working tonight. Y?*
Alexa: *Want to come over?*
Luke: *Sure. See you soon*

I know this isn't a good idea. Things between Luke and I have been weird for weeks, but I want to see him. I'm feeling like I need to talk to someone. He shows up thirty minutes later. I'm sitting in the living room drinking my second glass of wine when he comes in. He takes one look at my face and knows something is up.

"What's up, Lex. You look like hell."

"Hey. That's nice. Appreciate it."

"You look exhausted. And sad. What's wrong?"

"I'm tired and sad. This week is sucking for me in a big way."

He looks hesitant to ask but does anyway. "Julian ... or Brady?"

I knew he would get it. "Both. I'm being bombarded with memories of Brady, and I've had three nightmares in the last week. I can't stop thinking about him."

Luke comes and sits by me. "Me either, Lex. I've been thinking about him a lot too. I miss him."

I look at Luke, and for the first time in months, I think about him, not me, in regards to how this is all affecting him. They were friends their whole life.

"I want to remember good things, and I can't. There were good things though, right? I didn't make that up?" I think that if I can remember some of the good things, maybe I'll be able to push the bad memories out.

"No, Lex. There were good things. A lot of good things. But there was so much bad too. I know how hard this is for you, and I wish I could say something to make it better."

"Knowing you get it helps more than you know. I feel like you're the only one who really understands."

Luke hugs me, and I let him. "I'm here for you, Lex. I know things have been weird lately, but I'm here for you."

I pull back after a few moments and take a drink of my wine. "You want a glass?"

Luke gets up and goes to the kitchen. He comes back with a beer and the bottle I opened earlier. He refills my almost empty glass. "Want to talk about Julian?"

"Yes. But do you want listen?"

He laughs a sarcastic laugh. "Not really, but I will. I miss talking to you, Lex, and if I have to hear about Julian, I'll try to suck it up."

"Good, because I miss talking to you too. I hate that me being with him has caused problems between us, and I'm not really even sure why, but I'm glad you're willing to listen."

Luke sits back down next to me on the couch. "So what's up? How are things going?"

"It depends on the day or night really. Things could be really good if I'd let them."

"And why don't you let them?"

I'm starting to feel a little buzzed after my two and a half glasses of wine, and it's loosening me up.

"For all the reasons you can imagine. I don't know for sure if I can trust him. I'm scared to let him get close to me. I'm worried when he finds out about all the Brady stuff he may feel different about me."

Luke is clearly surprised by this. "You haven't told him about Brady? How have you managed to avoid that topic?"

I shrug. "I haven't really managed it at all. I've had two nightmares and a panic attack around him. He knows something's up. He just doesn't know what."

"He doesn't ask?"

"Every day. I just keep making excuses and changing the subject."

"And he lets you?" Luke looks even more surprised when I admit Julian hasn't been able to crack my emotional vault code yet.

"Let me? Luke, you know me. Nobody really lets me do anything. I kind of do what I want."

That makes him chuckle. "True, Lex, but I've spent enough time around Julian at work to know that he likes and expects things when he wants them and how he wants them. He isn't the type of guy who gives passes."

It's my turn to be surprised. Obviously I know they work together, but I guess I didn't think their paths crossed that much. "Well, he gives me passes all the time. He has been ridiculously patient with me. I'm totally over me, but he keeps hanging in there. I would've bailed by now."

"I'm happy to hear he's treating you good, Lex. I've been worried about that."

"He treats me better than I treat him." I haven't been fair to Julian, and I know it.

Luke gets up and walks to the kitchen to grab another beer. I guess we're done talking for now. I pour another glass of wine knowing that I'm going to be paying for it in the morning, and not caring. I'm operating on very little sleep too, but I feel relaxed right now, and I needed the wine.

Luke stays until about eleven o'clock, and we watch one of the Fast and Furious movies on HBO. When Luke sees I'm falling asleep, he gets up to leave. He bends over to give me a kiss goodbye and whispers in my ear, "You are totally worth waiting for, Lexie. Julian would be a fool to let you go without a fight." His words are sweet, and I can't help but feel they're also very personal.

I don't want to sleep on the couch, so I head unsteadily to my room. Wow. I'm buzzed.

I had left my phone in there charging and pick it up before I go to sleep. I have a missed call and voicemail from Julian.

"Hey, you. It's nine-thirty. I just got home. I'm missing you. Call me."

I call him back, and he answers right away. "Hey, baby."

"Hey back. How are you?"

"Lonely ... and a little horny. I wish you were here in my bed."

I giggle. "My bed is feeling kind of big too."

"How was your night, Corazón?" I know he wants to know about my session with Ellen, but I'm not interested in talking about that.

"Mellow. Just hung out here and had a few glasses of wine." I leave out the part where Luke joined me.

"Hmm ... so you're buzzed huh? Too bad I'm not there to enjoy that."

"You can come over." I extend the invitation but doubt he'll come. I'm right.

"I wish, baby. I have to get up really early tomorrow. Busy day at work, and I want to work out first."

"I can help you get a work out tonight so you can sleep in." I know I'm teasing him, and it's fun.

"You are a bad girl. That's not fair. I'm actually more than a little horny, and your teasing isn't helping."

"I'm not teasing. My offer is legit. But if you insist on staying home, I can offer some other services that may help you with your issues."

"Okay. I'm in."

I don't miss a beat. "Yes, Julian, you're in. You're deep in me, and I feel your hard dick all the way to my core. You feel so good, and I want you to fuck me hard until you come. Can you do that for me? Can you fuck me all night long?"

I hear his sharp intake of breath, and I know I've shocked him. "Oh my God, Lexie. You're something else, baby. Yes, I can fuck you all night long, and I'm going to keep my dick inside of you until you can't take it anymore. I want you screaming my name when you come for me." Wow. What did I just start?

The conversation that follows is totally X-rated and totally hot, and after about twenty minutes of us telling each other what we want to do to each other along with some self-stimulation, Julian and I have both come. Holy hell. I've never done that before, and I'm wondering why. I have no problem talking dirty, but it's usually in the moment and when I'm actually having sex.

We're both quiet for a moment as we catch our breath. Julian speaks first. "You're amazing. That was totally unexpected and totally hot."

I laugh. "I guess if the real estate thing doesn't work out, I can always become a sex line phone operator."

Julian laughs back. "Well you're certainly qualified, but I'd prefer if you don't talk to any other men that way. Save that all for me, Corazón."

"Right back at you, Julian."

"You're coming over after work tomorrow, right?"

"Uh huh. Should I meet you at home or the hotel?"

"Meet me at home. I'll be there by seven. Be naked. We're going to bring that little phone scene to the big screen tomorrow."

My body tingles at his words. "Your house, your rules."

That makes him chuckle. "Goodnight, baby. Dream about me."

"Goodnight, Julian."

CHAPTER 33

I wake up in the morning happy but a little hung-over. I wish I could call in sick, but I've already taken this upcoming weekend off, so I have to go in. I get a cute text from Julian around nine-thirty.

> Julian: *Workout ok. Yours are better. Can't wait to see you tonight.*
>
> Alexa: *I'll make sure you get sweaty. Have a great day.* ☺

Around four o'clock, I get a text from Luke that doesn't make me so happy.

> Luke: *Hey Hooka. You coming to hotel Saturday for photo shoot?*
>
> Alexa: *Huh?*
>
> Luke: *Julian's shoot this weekend?*

Um. I remember Candace mentioning a photo shoot, but why is Luke calling it Julian's?

Alexa: *Oh yeah. Not sure.*
Luke: *Ok. I'm working all day/night. Off Friday. Come see me if you're here.*
Alexa: *Will do.*

I sit there for a few minutes and try to decide if this is a conversation to have over text, over the phone, or in person. I choose text because I can hide how I'm feeling.

Alexa: *Heard you were having a photo shoot this weekend?*

He replies immediately.

Julian: *Yes. I told you about it.*
Alexa: *Nope. Wouldn't forget that.*
Julian: *Answer your phone. Calling now.*

He calls right away, and I answer. I guess we will be *talking* about this. "Hey, baby. I told you we were doing a photo shoot this weekend."

So he's sticking with his story. "Candace said something about an interview and a shoot, but I didn't get the impression you were involved in the actual shoot. Are you?"

He hesitates, and I know he knows he needs to come clean. "Yes. I thought I told you. The magazine, VIVA South Beach, is doing a spread on the hotel, and they want me to be in it. Who reminded you anyway?"

Okay. Now I'm annoyed. "Luke told me. He didn't remind me. You know you didn't tell me, and I'm wondering why. Who's in the shoot with you?"

The words come out bitterly, and I'm disappointed in myself. Here my totally hot boyfriend, who could be a model, is getting the opportunity to showcase his hotel, and all I can think about is who's going to be modeling with him. I assume it's Victoria or Elyse.

"Victoria. But I'm sure Luke already mentioned that part to you."

I assumed correctly, and it all becomes clear why he "forgot" to tell me. I'm instantly jealous and insecure. The conversation Luke overheard where Victoria mentioned hooking up with Julian plays back in my head.

"Don't make this about Luke. He assumed I knew and just asked if I was going to be there this weekend. He didn't say a word about what the hell you were doing or whom you were doing it with."

"What the hell is that supposed to mean, Alexa?" He's pissed. I probably shouldn't have said that.

"Why didn't you tell me about this? No secrets, remember?"

He pauses for a second. "Honestly?" It sounds like a challenge.

"That would be nice." I challenge back. Not a good idea on my part.

"Because we're barely hanging on here, and I really didn't feel like adding anything else to the list of things you're pissed at me about. This is great for the hotel, and if I thought you wouldn't freak out and get jealous, I would have told you. I was obviously going to tell you. I just wanted to do it right when it happened. I figured if you were here, it wouldn't be a big deal."

I feel like he just punched me in the gut, and I'm not sure what to process first. He just admitted we were barely hanging on, so at least we agree on that. I've been feeling that way all week. We're also obviously at the point where my freak-outs are impacting his ability to share his life with me. I'm so hurt, and all I want to do is hang up. I try to be a little more mature though. A little.

"You say you want to know me, right? Well here's a little tidbit you should know. I *hate* walking into situations that are more than likely going to be uncomfortable for me without some fucking warning. I'm surprised you even thought that would be an acceptable plan."

"Maybe it wasn't a good plan, but then again, nothing I've done lately has been acceptable, has it?" I haven't heard this tone from Julian before.

"You know what, Julian? You can turn this around and make it all my fault, but the fact that you didn't even mention something so important and exciting to me shows you aren't all that willing to share your life either. If there was nothing for me to freak out about, and for you to hide, you would've told me."

"That's almost funny. You hide stuff all the time. And I'm not just talking about your past."

"What are you talking about? What am I hiding?"

His voice is almost a hiss. "How was your night with Luke last night? Did you two have a good time getting drunk together? Or was it disappointing? You sounded so turned on when you talked about getting fucked I figure maybe he couldn't close the deal and left you horny."

Holy shit! This is bad. Really, really bad. Julian never talks to me this way. I have no idea what the best way to respond to this is, so I'm quiet for a moment. Julian takes my silence as confirmation he's right. "Oh. So I'm right, huh? Well at least I got off too."

"Oh my God, Julian. Stop! You're so wrong. Please tell me you really don't believe I was with Luke like that. Yes, he was over, and clearly I should have said something, but we're not together that way. I keep telling you that. I'm with you. Only you." My anger has turned to fear. I've never heard him like this. "How did you even find out?"

"Your *friend* Luke has a big mouth. He came to work today talking about his night off with you. He said it right in front of me. He wanted me to know he was with you when I wasn't. He was talking to Jordan about how you needed someone to talk to and about how he comforted you over drinks. He's lucky I didn't kick his fucking ass."

"Julian, nothing happened between us. I asked him to come over. I hardly see him at all since we've gotten together. He had a couple beers, and we talked. We talked about you." I think it might help that I was talking about him. Wrong again.

"If you want to talk to Luke about your shit, that's fine, but I'd appreciate it if you didn't talk about me. I'm his boss, I can't stand him, and he uses whatever you tell him as ammunition against me."

"I was telling him I was happy, and that you were treating me great. There's nothing bad to say."

"Whatever, Alexa. You know I'm a very private person. Luke Miller is the last person I want knowing about my personal business."

"Why don't you fire him if you have such a problem with him?"

"Because he's a good bartender, and the ladies love him. I've thought about it, but he's good for business. Oh, and he's also your 'best friend.' How would you feel if I fire him?"

"I'd feel bad I caused any of this. This is so stupid. I can't even believe we're talking about this."

"You are a very smart, very perceptive woman, and for the life of me I can't understand why you can't see what's right in front of you."

"All I can see is that you and I are in a really bad place, and right now that's more important to me than Victoria, a photo shoot, or Luke."

I hear him take a deep breath. "Damn it, Alexa. I'm sorry I didn't tell you about the shoot. I'm tired of fighting with you. I just want things to be okay between us, and I knew it would upset you that I would be spending time with Victoria. When I heard you saw Luke last night, I got so pissed. You won't tell me what's going on with you, and it really, really bothers me to know that Luke is the man you're turning to. I won't share you, Lexie. I told you that. It's just me and you, or this doesn't happen."

"It is just us. I'm sorry I didn't tell you about Luke. I guess I felt the same way you did. I didn't want to fight."

I look at my watch and realize we've been arguing for almost an hour now, and it's time for me to leave work. Not too professional on my part. I now have no idea if our plans are still on for tonight.

"Are you still coming over?"

"Do you want me to, Julian?" My heart races as I wait for his reply.

"I need you to. I need you to."

"Then I'll see you soon."

I had already planned on spending the night at Julian's, so I don't need to go home. As I head there, I think about what just happened. We never really resolved anything, so I know we'll continue talking about this. Ugh. I don't want to talk. I just want to be with him. My period is pretty much gone, and I need to feel him close. I call Marissa on the way down to South Beach. I tell her about what happened with Luke and ask her if she thinks he's trying to cause problems. She doesn't hesitate to tell me, yes, she thinks it probably was intentional. We also talk about the whole photo shoot thing. She convinces me I need to be supportive and excited for Julian and that I also need to appreciate the fact my boyfriend is so hot they want to put multiple pictures of him in a magazine. She tells me what's going on with her, and we catch up for the rest of the ride. I'm in a decent mood when I pull into the Bellavista, and I thank her for keeping me in line once again.

Before we got in a fight today, it was my intention to be naked in his bed when Julian came home. But after this afternoon, I'm not so sure it's the best way to start the night, so instead of being naked, I change out of my work clothes and into a cotton, sea-foam-green-and-gray, bandeau-style, halter maxi-dress. I can wear it if we go out to eat, and it's comfortable to hang out in as well. I take my hair out of the braid I had it in and leave it loose. I freshen up my makeup, pour myself a glass of wine, and wait for Julian outside on the terrace. It's six forty-five, so I'm expecting him soon.

I hear him come in and wait for him to find me. He walks out onto the terrace, sees me sitting there, and shakes his head. "Can't you stay out of trouble, Alexa?"

I have no clue what I've done now, and my stomach turns. He sees the look on my face and knows I'm trying to figure out what I've done wrong.

"I told you to be naked when I got home. You're not. And although you look beautiful, I was expecting less."

Without saying a word, I stand, untie the strings from my halter top, and start pulling it slowly down over my body. I'm not wearing anything underneath, and I see the approval in Julian's eyes. We have never been together here on the terrace, and I wonder why. The air is cool from the breeze, and the views are magnificent. Julian's terrace is very private, so I don't worry about being seen, but something about being outside makes this even more erotic. He stares at me for a moment, taking me all in, and as usual I feel revered.

"Don't move, baby. I'll be right back." I know he's going to get a condom, and I want to tell him to stop, that he doesn't have to use one, but I don't. I don't move, and Julian finds me in the same place. He walks to me and takes me in his arms. His clothes feel rough against my skin, and I want them off. I unbutton his gray shirt and slide it off his shoulders. He's working on his belt at the same time, and when I finish with his shirt, I'm able to just push his pants down. He had taken his socks and shoes off when he came in the door, so after his pants drop, he's naked too. He presses himself to me, and I can feel his desire. He grabs my head and pulls my mouth to his. From the minute our lips touch, I know he's needy. There's something about his kiss that says he needs to claim me. I try to mirror his intensity because I'm needy as well. I want to eliminate any distance between us, and I know I can physically do that. Our tongues and lips are hot and desperate as they slide over our sensitive skin. I can't hold back a deep moan when Julian runs his soft, wet tongue down my neck, across my chest, and around my swollen nipples. I'm literally quivering with desire and want him in me. I grab his shaft and begin to stroke him steadily.

Julian groans with pleasure. "Sí, Lexie. Toqueme asi."

"I'll touch you any way you want me to as long as you keep touching me. I need it. I just want to feel you close."

Julian guides me back and lays me down on the chaise lounge. He positions himself between my legs, and when it appears like he's going to go down on me, I ask him to stop. My period just ended, and I'm not comfortable with that. I take his hand instead and place it between my legs. He moans softly when he feels how wet I already am.

"I want to watch you touch me. I want you to see what you do to me. You need to see how good you make me feel. Only you."

We don't take our eyes off of each other as he slowly slides his fingers in and out of me. I'm so wet that on one pass his finger slips out of my sex and gently touches a spot a little further down. I involuntarily moan, and Julian's eyes darken with lust. We have never talked about anal play nor has he attempted anything even close. It's something I have very little experience with too. I don't say yes, and I don't say no. I leave it up to him, and he chooses not to take it any farther. A little piece of me is disappointed. I want to share my body with him in every way possible. The thought of Julian and I experimenting with that turns me on even more, and I find that my race to orgasm has sped up. I feel the rush starting in my toes as Julian's fingers find my clit and work their magic. As the energy of my orgasm pulses throughout my body, I call out his name and totally let go.

I would love to return the favor and pleasure Julian with my hands or my mouth, but he moves to get inside of me so fast I don't have a chance. I was so lost in the aftereffects of my orgasm that I hardly noticed him rolling a condom on. He spreads my legs with his knees and with one thrust he's deep inside of me. Our eyes have not left each other, and we're able to say so much without speaking. Our soft moans of pleasure, the sounds of our bodies fusing, and the sultry sounds of a summer night all join together and make the most beautiful music.

It isn't long before Julian orgasms and explodes into me. I grip his hips tightly and hold him close. He's breathing rapidly, and I can feel his heart beating against mine. When his orgasm fades, he rolls halfway off and keeps his leg across mine. I put my hand over his heart and flatten my palm. He places his hand over mine and squeezes it. There's nothing else that needs to be said now. He has my heart, and I have his.

Julian gets up and throws the condom away and comes back with the blanket I slept with the other night. He arranges us on the lounger so I'm in his arms and pulls the blanket over our naked bodies. We watch the stars come out, and it makes me think of being at the hotel that first night we were really together. Thinking about the hotel makes me think about the damn photo shoot and about the fight we got into today. We need to talk about it.

"I'm really sorry about today. About not being honest with you."

He squeezes me tighter. "Me too, Corazón. Me too."

"Tell me about what you're doing with the magazine."

Julian smiles at me, and I can tell he does want to share. "They want to do a three- or four-page spread on the hotel and feature all of the renovations and new venues. It's an awesome publicity opportunity, and the hotel will be on the cover. Making sure the hotel looks perfect has kept me busy this week."

"That's really exciting. You're going to be in it?"

He looks a little more reluctant to talk about this part, but he does. "Yes, they want me in it. I thought it would be just a little picture or something, but this has gotten all blown out of proportion, and now it has turned into a shoot with models. I'm not convinced this weekend is the best timing because we're booked solid, but they want to get it out for the July issue."

"And how did Victoria get picked to be in the shoot?"

"Not by me. The magazine chose her." I believe him but am amazed by his belief it was not something she helped orchestrate. "We haven't been together for a while, and it was never anything serious. You know that, right?"

"I believe you, but you need to stop being so naïve about all these women, Julian. They all want you. Candace, Victoria, Elyse, Caroline. I've seen how they all look at you. Luke overheard Elyse and Victoria the night we ran into them. He said they were talking about how Victoria was planning on rekindling your romance this weekend. It's kinda why I freaked out."

"Well, it doesn't matter what they want or think, baby. I'm with you. As far as Luke telling you things, you really need to ask me first before you jump to conclusions."

"I know you have issues with him, but Luke doesn't lie to me. He never has."

"Maybe he doesn't lie, but he does manipulate things to look different." I start to defend Luke, and Julian places his lips on mine to stop me. It works, and I'm distracted.

"I don't want to talk about Luke or Victoria or anybody else. I want to hold you and make love to you again. And eat. I want to eat too."

I can't help but laugh. "That was so romantic, 'til you got to the eating part."

Julian laughs and tells me he brought food home. I swear I could get very used to this life. He brings the food out to the terrace, and we sit and talk about the interview he'll be giving. He actually asks for my opinion on a few things, and I'm grateful he's trying to include me. After dinner, Julian carries me to his bedroom where he does make love to me again. Three times. It may be all the sex we had or the wine or just the fact we've stayed away from talking about my "issues", but I fall asleep easily and have one of the best night's sleep I've had in a month.

It looks like Julian needed the rest too. I forgot to set an alarm last night, and when I finally wake up, it's eight-thirty. Shit, I have to be at work at nine. There's no way that's going to happen. I shake Julian and wake him up. He opens his eyes and pulls me to him. I wiggle out of his arms.

"No time. It's already eight-thirty." I head to the bathroom to take a quick shower. I hear him call after me.

"Call in sick and get back here. I'm not done with you."

He can't see my smile, but it's big. Last night was great. And to be honest, not having time for sex is a good thing. I'm a little sore. I take a very quick shower and skip washing my hair. I put it in a bun and brush my teeth. I walk back out, and Julian is still lying in bed. He looks yummy.

"Must be good to be the boss, huh?"

"If you worked for me, I'd let you call in sick every time you wanted to stay in bed with me."

Work for him? He's joking, right? "As tempting as that is, I think I'll hang on to the job I have."

I slip into a scarf-print jersey dress in pinks, yellows, and oranges. It has a bateau neckline and capped sleeves. I dig in my bag and pull out a pair of straw-colored, Ralph Lauren peep-toed sandals with dark wood stacked heels and platform. The heels are super high and flirty. I root around for my makeup bag and make some frustrated sounds when I can't find the earrings I'm looking for.

"You can leave things here if you want." I stand up, look at Julian, and try not to freak out. First he tells me to come work for him and then to leave my stuff here. He needs to slow down.

"You have no room in your closet for my stuff. You have too much of your own." I say it jokingly as I walk into the bathroom and hope he doesn't notice the panicked look on my face. Julian follows me in and brushes his teeth as I apply my makeup. He kisses me when he's done and pats me on the butt.

"Stop freaking out. You travel heavy. Thought it might be easier to keep a few things here."

I raise my eyebrows at him and shrug my shoulders. He smirks at me and starts walking out. "I do know you a little." Well, I guess he does.

I put on a few more finishing touches, and when I come out into the kitchen, Julian hands me a cup of coffee in a travel mug. He kisses me passionately and tells me to go before he removes my clothes and convinces me to stay. Last night, we talked briefly about my plans tonight, and he asked me to come to the hotel with my friends. He pointed out I haven't been back to Stellar to dance for weeks. I don't tell him that my plan was to stay in all weekend and hide. He brings it up again as I'm walking out, and he looks so hopeful that I can't help but say yes. I hope my friends are on board.

CHAPTER 34

I call Marissa on my way in to work, and she agrees to go with me tonight. Shannon, Jenna, and Lauren do as well. I text Julian when I get to work and let him know I'll be there by ten o'clock. He tells me to let him know when I'm close, and he'll come out and meet me. I doubt I'll do that. I can just find him inside.

I don't hear from Julian again for the rest of the day. I'm getting used to the fact that when he's at work, he's pretty much out of contact. He does give me all his attention when we're together, so I try to deal with it. I figure they're prepping for the shoot tomorrow, so I stay out of his way.

Marissa and I go for a run after work, and when we get back, we get ready to go out. Everyone is meeting here at eight, and the plan is to eat first. I want to look especially good tonight. I'm no model, but I can look sexy, and I want Julian's focus to stay on me. I know he likes my boobs, so I look for something that accentuates them. I choose a form-fitting mini dress made of a black crochet pattern over a nude lining. The neckline is scooped in the front and back. It's simple and fits in all the right places. I choose a pair of Vince Camuto strappy, black stilettos. I leave my hair down and wavy. I line my eyes with kohl eyeliner for a dramatic effect but keep the rest of my makeup simple. I put on a pair of oversized, gold pavé fringed hooped earrings and several gold bangles. I'm ready to go by eight o'clock, and when the girls all get here, we pile into Shannon's car and head to the beach. We eat at a great Italian restaurant on Washington Avenue, and everyone but Shannon, who is driving, ends up drinking way too much wine. We get to the hotel just before ten, and Shannon valets. I have no desire for Julian to come outside to meet me, so I don't text. We jump the long line when Marty see us.

I feel good. It may be the wine or the company or the anticipation of seeing Julian. It doesn't matter. I feel like I'm going to roll right through this weekend. We do our normal pit stop in the bathroom, and when I come out, I find Julian standing by the door waiting. He gives me the once over with his eyes, grabs my hand, and walks me away from the others. We stop when we're alone, and he turns me to face him.

"First, you look way too sexy in that dress to be left alone tonight. I swear it looks like you're naked underneath. And second, why didn't you text me?"

I wrap my arms around his waist and kiss him firmly on the lips. "Hola, Julian. Thanks for the compliment. I was hoping you'd approve. Second, I don't need an escort. I was going to come find you."

"Um. Someone has been drinking red wine. You taste delicious." He kisses me again, and this time he lets his tongue slide in and wrestle with mine for a moment. I can't close my eyes because when I do I get a little dizzy. "I'm not sure I approve of your dress. Like I mentioned, you look naked underneath. And I know you don't need an escort; I was just anxious to see you. I missed you today."

"I missed you too. And I am naked under the dress. I've taken a page from your book and stopped wearing panties."

Julian groans, grabs my hand, and leads me down a hallway and into a big office. I'm assuming it's his. He locks the doors and turns to look at me. He shakes his head at me. "You are very bad. You're going to make me break a major rule I have."

"And what rule is that?"

"The one where I don't fuck in the hotel."

I'm totally turned on by this even though I don't believe it. "C'mon. It's a hotel. With beds. It's a great place to fuck." The alcohol is definitely making me loose.

He walks toward me, stalking me. I take a step back and bump against his desk. "I told you the first night I made you come. I don't mix business with pleasure. It's just you, Lexie. I won't be able to focus on anything else tonight if I don't feel you around me. I've been thinking about it all day, and either we leave now or we take care of business here."

"Well I just got here, so I guess if we need to 'take care of business,' we just have to do it here."

I reach over and run my hand over Julian's crotch. He's in jeans and a tight-fitting black T-shirt. He looks very casual and very hot. He moans and pushes his hardness into my hand.

"Is getting your dick sucked against the rules too, Julian? Because I don't want to get in any more trouble." I ask him the question as I slowly unzip his pants. His massive erection springs out.

"Dios mío," he moans as I get on my knees and take him in my mouth. "Yes, it's against the rules, but I'm willing to make an exception."

Julian looks down at me as I slide his shaft in and out of my mouth. Just as Julian's learned how I liked to be touched, I've learned how best to please him, and I pull out all the stops so he gets the most pleasure out of my blow job. His hands are in my hair, and he grips it tightly as he thrusts himself into me. It doesn't take long before he's exploding into my mouth. He finishes, pulls me up, and kisses me hard. He turns me around and has me bend over the desk. I feel his dick against me and push back into it. Julian pulls my dress up around my hips and groans when he finds me panty-less.

"I told you I wasn't wearing any panties."

He groans again. "Please tell me you have a condom in your purse."

I pull my dress down, stand up, and turn and face him. "No, I don't. Didn't think I'd need one here. You really don't have one?" I try to hide my disappointment.

"Like I said, I don't fuck at the hotel. It wasn't in my plans to do this here, but you came in looking like that, and I couldn't help it." He isn't hiding his disappointment.

"It's okay. You can make it up to me tonight at your house."

"You really won't be with me without a condom? Still? I want you now, baby."

I shake my head no. I know he doesn't get it, but I'm just not ready for that. He looks upset for a moment but then lets it go. He reaches down, pulls my dress up again, sits me on the desk, and spreads my legs. He drops to his knees this time.

"I'm going to fuck you later, but right now I'm going to taste you and make you come with my tongue."

I want to ask him if that's against the rules too but lose my ability to speak when Julian's tongue starts moving between my legs. I'm so turned on and so wet it doesn't take him long to make me orgasm. When he's certain I'm done, he stops and stands up. He wraps his arms around me and pulls me to him for a kiss.

He flashes me a big smile. "Thank you for that. I think I might be able to make it through the night now. Let's go find your friends."

I smile back. "Happy to help. Always happy to help."

I find my friends on the dance floor in Stellar. Julian dances with us for a song and then leaves to go do whatever he does. I give them details of my steamy little encounter, and we toast to great sex with a round of Patrón Silver shots. We dance some more and then toast to good friends with another shot. We dance a little more and toast to a bunch of other random things with two more shots. These shots mixed with the bottles of wine we all had earlier have hit me hard, and by the time Julian comes back a few hours later, I'm no longer buzzed. I'm drunk. So are Marissa, Lauren, and Jenna. Unfortunately, it becomes obvious when he starts talking to us. Julian doesn't look happy, and I feel a lecture coming on. I try to sidestep it by kissing him. It doesn't work.

"Are you okay to drive, Shannon, or should I get you a ride home?"

"Nope. I'm good, but thanks. I've only had two drinks all night."

He turns and looks at me. "I'll have someone take you to my house. I need to stay a little longer."

"Um. I didn't know I said I was ready to go."

"No, you didn't, but you should have. You're drunk and need to call it a night."

I'm a little mad and a lot embarrassed that this is going down in front of my friends. Two minutes ago, we were all having a great time, and now the mood is somber. It's like we're a bunch of teenagers who got caught by someone's dad. "Thanks, Dad, but I'm a big girl. I know when I need to stop."

Julian grabs my hand, and I pull away. "Seriously, I'm good, Julian." I'm so not good. I stumble in my five-inch heels, and he catches me. I'm starting to feel nauseous now too. This is going bad really fast.

He narrows his eyes, and his words come out in a hiss. "You need to go home. Stay here and I'll make arrangements for you to get a ride." He walks away, and when he does, I grab Shannon's hand and pull her toward the exit. The other girls follow.

"Let's go. You can take me home." I think she thinks she's taking me to Julian's house, but I plan on going to my house. He isn't the only one who's angry. I'm a grown woman, and I wasn't doing anything wrong. Shannon is surprised when I tell her to just go home, but she doesn't argue. Lauren starts going on about how I'm going to be in serious trouble when Julian comes back and finds me gone. Something about the way she says it sobers me up a little. He's already mad, and this will definitely make it worse. I should at least let him know I left. I pull my phone out to text him, and it rings. I see his face on the screen, and he's smiling at me. I know happy Julian isn't who is going to be on the other end of this call. I answer and brace myself.

"Where the fuck are you? I can't believe you fucking left!" Oh this is bad. Julian hardly ever cusses at me.

"I'm on my way home, to my house. You told me to leave, so I did. I didn't want to wait for you. I'm always waiting for you." I look up and see Marissa shaking her head at me. She's whispering for me to get off before I say something stupid.

I hear Julian call my name. Damn. We're waiting for the car, and I'm unable to make an escape before he finds me. I turn around and see him walking toward me. He looks seriously pissed. I walk toward him and away from my friends. They don't need to hear this.

"Julian, don't make a scene. You told me to go home, and I am."

He considers what I said before he responds. "I'm not going to debate which of us is really making a scene with my girlfriend who's too drunk to know that she had a guy rubbing his dick into her on my dance floor in my club while I watched."

Uh-oh. We were all dancing, and there were guys out on the floor, but I didn't think it was a big deal. I guess I was wrong. "Fine. You win. I'm drunk, and I'm leaving. You can lecture me about this tomorrow."

Surprisingly, he doesn't argue. "Please text me and let me know you got home okay. Can you at least do that?" He kisses me on the forehead and walks away before he hears me say yes.

Alexa: *I'm home safe.*
Julian: *Thanks.*

I don't continue the conversation because I'm too busy running into the bathroom to get sick. I spend most of the night on the cold tile and finally crawl into bed around six in the morning. Thank God I'm able to sleep.

Chapter 35

When I wake up at ten, I can hardly move my head. I'm hurting bad. I force myself to get out of bed and get some Advil and water. I crawl back under the covers and check my phone. There are no messages from Julian. I'm glad. Maybe he went home and went to sleep. He does have a photo shoot today. I had told him I was going to be there with him today, but now I'm not sure it's such a good idea. He got so pissed last night. I did have too much to drink, but I really wasn't doing anything wrong. I think his main problem is the drinking. I know he doesn't drink much, but neither do I. Usually. I'm not going to lie. I've been drinking more than usual lately. It seems to help keep the memories and nightmares at bay. I'm well aware of the fact it isn't a great way to deal with any issue, but it's working right now, so I'm running with it.

I fall back asleep and don't wake up until after two in the afternoon. I still feel like hell. I get up and head to the living room. Marissa is on one couch, and Jenna is on the other. They look as bad as I do.

"Whose idea was it to drink so much last night?" I joke as I plop down next to Marissa.

They both groan and Marissa sits up a little. "Have you heard from Julian? I don't remember much after the third shot, but I do remember him being really pissed."

"Not today. But I haven't looked at my phone recently. I'm in no mood for a lecture."

Jenna chimes in. "Yeah, what's up with that? Why was he so mad?"

"He said I was letting some guy grind against me. He also isn't a big fan of drinking, or me drinking, I guess. I really don't know what set him off."

We sit there and talk about the night for a little longer, at least what we remember. I need to go to the bathroom, and I grab my phone on the way. Nothing. Shit, he's still pissed. I go back to the living room and resume my position on the couch. We discuss eating, but nobody can think of anything that sounds good. At about three-thirty, I get a text from Luke.

Luke: *Hey Hooka. Did you and Julian get in a fight last night?*

Seriously? That place is gossip-freaking central.

Alexa: *Why?*
Luke: *bc that's what I heard from some people and bc Julian has been a dick to everyone all day*
Luke: *and bc you're a no show*
Alexa: *It's all good Luke. Ttyl*

Luke: *So yes, rumor true and you're hiding out. It's cool. you don't need to tell me.*

Alexa: *it's all good Luke. Go make a drink or something.*

I really, really don't want to text Julian, but I know I need to. I pretend like things really are all good.

Alexa: *Hey you. Hope things are going well today. Call when you're free.*

It's six-thirty before he responds. I've spent the afternoon stressing about it, and I'm almost scared to look.

Julian: *It's all good, Alexa. Isn't it? I'm busy. Not sure when I'll be free to deal with this.*

Wow. That was rude. Oh well, I tried. If Julian wants to stay mad, he can. I still don't even know why he's so mad. I'm curious about his choice of words though. "It's all good" is what I said to Luke when he asked what was going on. I text Luke.

Alexa: *Did you talk to Julian about me today?*
Luke: *No, why?*
Alexa: *Not at all?*
Luke: *We don't talk about you. Why, Lex?*

I don't answer. I'm not sure what happened, but something did. I swear this is so messed up. I turn my phone off. I don't want to deal with either of them. I make us some grilled cheese sandwiches, and I spend the rest of the evening watching episode after episode of House Hunters with my friends. I get in bed at ten-thirty. I napped on and off all day, so it's no surprise

I can't fall asleep. I think about Julian and Luke, and then I think about Brady. I'm not good with all this jealousy stuff. I didn't have to deal with it with Brady. Maybe because at the end I had no clue he was too busy using and cheating on me to pay much attention to what I was doing. I sleep fitfully, and when I do wake up in the morning, I'm anxious and panicky. It isn't a good way to start the day—especially this day. It's officially the one-year anniversary of the last night I spent with Brady.

I go for a five-mile run and try to calm my nerves. It doesn't help like it usually does, and all I can think about as my feet hit the pavement is that I don't want to feel anything. I get back at ten, take a shower, and turn my phone on. I still haven't heard from Julian. I decide to try one more time to smooth things over. Maybe if things are okay with him, I'll feel better. I call instead of text. He answers, and I hear people in the background. He isn't at home.

"Hey, Julian."

"Hey, Alexa." Not "Hey, you."

"What's up?"

"Just working." His voice is cold. I literally feel myself starting to shut down.

"Well then I'll let you go. Call me when you have time to deal with me," I say sarcastically.

His response is flat. "Will do."

Screw that, I think as I hang up and turn off my phone. What the hell? I won't be calling him again. I grab my keys and head to the mall for a mani/pedi, hoping it will help take my mind off all this drama. It doesn't, and even hours of shopping for shoes doesn't help. As the day goes by, I feel sadder and more anxious, and I keep watching the clock. I turn my phone on when I get back into my car and see Julian still hasn't called. It's already five o'clock. I was sure I would've heard from him by now. He's trying to hurt me, and I don't get it. I push back the tears and the feelings of panic that have been hiding in the shadows all day. I'm not going to be able to make it through this night alone, so I call the one person who will understand. I call Luke. He isn't working and tells me he can meet me at my house in an hour.

I feel better when I see Luke. I don't have to say anything. He knows what's going on with me and that I need him to comfort me. We sit on the couch, and I lay my head on his chest. I know what I'm doing is wrong. I should be with Julian. He should be the one comforting me. But he's not even talking to me. He's not here, and I need this. Luke understands me. He understands what I went through. We sit there for hours not talking. We're both lost in the memories of this night a year ago, and as Luke strokes my hair, I let the tears fall.

CHAPTER 36

When Julian walks in at nine, he finds me on the couch with my head on a pillow in Luke's lap. Shannon let him in, not thinking she needed to give me a warning. I haven't really told them about the feud that's been going on between Luke and Julian, so I can't be upset with her. I hear Julian come in, and I sit up and move away from Luke. He looks at my tearstained face and then at Luke. His body is pulsating with anger. Shannon stays in the room, and I'm glad. I may need backup.

Julian is so mad I can see the veins in his neck popping out. His voice is icy when he speaks. "If you don't mind getting out of Luke's lap, I'd like to talk to you."

Luke stands up and answers before I can. "Don't talk to her that way, Julian. She didn't do anything wrong."

Holy shit! This is bad. "It's okay, Luke. I need to talk to Julian. Please go before this gets worse. I'll call you later." I look at Luke and plead with my eyes. I get up and walk toward the door, hoping he'll follow. He shakes his head.

"Not this time, Lex. I'm not leaving you alone again."

I freeze and look at Julian. He looks confused. Thank God Shannon jumps in. "Just go, Luke. I'm here. Lexie will be fine."

He relents and comes toward me. I grab his hand and walk him to the door. I give him a huge hug and tell him I'll be okay and that I'll call him later. As he walks out the door, he shoots Julian a deadly look. I turn around and see Julian heading down the hall to my bedroom.

Shannon asks me if I'm okay, and I lie and tell her yes. I'm shaking. That was so intense. Before she goes to her room, she gives me a hug and tells me she's sorry for letting Julian in like that. I tell her this is so not her fault.

When I enter, Julian is pacing back and forth. My room isn't very big, and he looks like a caged animal. I shut the door behind me and stay standing up next to the door, waiting for him to calm down. I don't say a word because if I know anything right now, it's that nothing I can say is going to make this okay to him. I'm not scared of him at all, but I've never seen him act this way, and it's kind of freaking me out.

"Have you been sleeping with him?" Okay, so he's going to just get right to the point. "And I don't just mean tonight." His voice is like ice.

Oh my God. He really thinks Luke and I have been sleeping together? And tonight? This is worse than I thought. I try to keep my voice steady and calm.

"No, Julian, we haven't slept together, ever. How many times do I need to say we're just friends?"

"Have you kissed him? I mean really kissed. I'm being specific here because I've been lucky enough to see his lips touch yours more than once."

I can see the anger in his eyes, but I also see the hurt. He really believes Luke and I have been together recently. I've told him time and time again we haven't, and I don't know why he doesn't believe me. We need to put this to rest already.

"Yes. I've kissed Luke before. We hooked up when we were in college, *seven* years ago, but we didn't sleep together." I say this in a way I hope will calm Julian down and help him realize he has nothing to be upset about. Although I think he's overreacting, I do want him to know he's the only man in my life.

"Really? And why is that? Why didn't you sleep together, Alexa? From where I stand, it looks like Luke never misses the opportunity to get into a pretty girl's panties."

Well obviously I'm the only one who feels the need to play nice here. I'm not happy with where this conversation is headed, and I'm not going to listen to Julian attack Luke.

"That's ironic. Because Luke told me the same thing about you the night we met. He actually used those words too. He told me to stay away from you because you only wanted to get into my panties."

Julian snorts in disgust. "Well, he was right. I did want to get in your panties. At least I'm honest about what *my* intentions were."

"Were? Or *are*?"

He ignores my question and asks his again. "Tell me, why didn't you two sleep together? Were you not into one-night stands back then?" The minute Julian says those words, he crosses a line. I can't hide the hurt or anger I feel.

"Fuck you, Julian!" I hiss at him. "I didn't sleep with him because he didn't have a condom the first time we tried. I would have otherwise. And no, just like now, I have no problems with one-night stands. Actually, I've always preferred them. With a one-night stand, I can just get off and not have to deal with the bullshit I've had to deal with for the last month."

I'm really not the type of girl who has one-night stands, but I'm so hurt I want to say anything I can to either piss Julian off or hurt him back. By the look on his face, I'm doing a pretty good job. He looks positively livid. "You know what, Alexa, you can keep deflecting my original question by trying to piss me off, but you still haven't really answered it."

"Yes I did! Are you having a hard time following me? I just told you I didn't have a condom."

I'm not sure why, but Julian changes direction, and his tone softens just a little. Maybe he knows he's pushing this too far.

"Is he my competition? Is Luke the reason why you have such a hard time letting me get close to you?" Julian's tone has totally changed, and the way he asks me this question suggests this is something he's reluctant to ask. I take a deep breath.

"No, Luke isn't your competition. I know you're having a hard time believing that for some reason, but it's not like that between us. We don't feel that way about each other."

Julian walks slowly to my bed, sits down, and puts his head in his hands. He sits silently like that for a few minutes. I walk over to the bed and sit down beside him. This day has been awful, and this situation is reminiscent of that last night with Brady. I feel myself starting to get emotional, and I fight it. I've already cried a bucket of tears today, and I don't want to break down in front of Julian. Julian finally picks his head up and looks at me. His eyes, which were just so full of anger, are now soft and sad. I can't meet his gaze and look down at my hands.

"Do you really not see it?" His tone is no longer confrontational.

"Yes. I can see why it looks like we have feelings for each other. We're very close, but it's like a brother-sister thing."

I hear myself saying these words, and for the first time ever they don't sound believable, even to me. A small flicker of acknowledgement floats through my mind, but I'm not quite ready to go there. Julian shakes his head slowly and reaches up and puts his hand gently on my face. He turns my head so I'm looking directly at him. It's the first time he's touched me tonight, and even though we're not in a good place at the moment, my body responds like it always does. My heart starts to beat rapidly, and I feel butterflies in my stomach. I wonder briefly if it will always feel this way when Julian touches me. That thought is followed up by the thought this may be the last time he touches me if we don't get this all cleared up.

"Luke loves you, Alexa, and not in a brotherly or just-friends kind of way. You have to know that in your heart." Julian's voice is calm and matter of fact, as if he *knows* this information and isn't just speculating. He won't let me look away.

"I know what a man in love looks like. I know that I'm right. And so do you, even if you can't or don't want to admit it to me. Please at least admit it to yourself."

Right now, at this moment, I'm unable to keep defending my "friendship" with Luke. It's as if some dam has suddenly broke in my mind, and every questionable interaction between Luke and me is presenting itself as something different than I thought it was an hour ago. Holy hell. Have I really been this blind? Why now? Why did Julian have to make me see this?

I mouth the word "no" and shake my head.

"Yes, baby." Julian continues to look at me with tenderness in his eyes. It's breaking my heart, and I realize I'm so wrapped up in the idea of Luke actually being in love with me that I haven't even thought about whether or not Julian thinks I feel the same way toward Luke.

"Julian, I don't feel that way about him. No matter how he feels. I don't feel that way about him." I hear myself saying these words, and I know in my heart they're true. Whether or not I'm willing to say the words to Julian, he's the man I'm falling in love with.

"Please tell me you believe me," I plead.

Julian gently traces my lips with his fingers. "I want to, Lexie. God I want to."

I see so much vulnerability in his eyes, and it melts my heart. This man wants me to be his, only his. I am, and even if I can't say it to him, I need to show him how much he means to me. I lean over and gently place my lips on his and give him a soft, tender kiss. He responds as if I've just ignited a fuse of desire in him. He grabs my head from behind, pulls me closer, and deepens the kiss. It feels like he's drowning and needs my breath to survive. He has kissed me passionately before, but it's never felt as if he *had* to, as if he wouldn't survive without his lips on mine, his tongue in mouth. My whole body is completely stimulated, and I feel his need to my core. His tongue is rough and possessive, and as he licks and sucks and bites gently at my mouth, I start to melt into him.

I'm so entranced by what his mouth is doing I hardly realize he has scooted me up toward the head of my bed. While still kissing me, Julian pulls my shorts and panties down in one quick motion and tosses them on the floor next to my bed. He breaks our connection for a moment while he stands up and takes his pants off. He's rock hard, and as he crawls back onto the bed, I feel the heat of his erection on my leg. Julian always makes sure I'm wet and ready to take him all in comfortably before he enters me. He also usually makes sure I orgasm first as well, either with the help of his fingers or his magical tongue. But tonight he has no patience, and I see that the considerate lover I'm used to has been replaced by a man who is beyond his threshold of control. Julian spreads my legs with one hand and guides himself into me with the other. I gasp as he plunges deep into me with one thrust. In the back of my mind, it registers he isn't wearing a condom, and irresponsible as it is, I don't care and don't stop him. He needs this, and I need this. I want to be as close to this man as I possibly can be. I want him to touch every part of my soul, and with each thrust, I feel him staking his claim on me.

I look up at him and am surprised to find his eyes are closed. He usually makes love to me with his eyes open. I love that he does that because I feel like it deepens our connection. Right now though, he seems to be lost in his own world as he plunges his hard shaft into me in a punishing rhythm. He's trying to tell me something with his body. I wrap my legs around his waist, grab his ass with both of my hands, and try to take him as deep as I can. My sex opens up wider, and he growls as he presses even further.

Julian's breath is labored, and he's panting hard. He opens his eyes and finally looks at me. "Eres mia? Tell me you're mine, only mine." Julian asks me this in a pleading tone. He keeps thrusting into me as he waits for my response.

I lock my eyes on him and try to send everything I'm feeling in my heart through my stare.

"Yes, Julian. I. Am. Yours. Only yours." I want to tell him I love him, but I just can't.

As soon as the words leave my mouth, I feel Julian start pumping himself into me. He says my name repeatedly as his orgasm overtakes him. I feel him start to tremble as feelings of ecstasy rack his body. He's coming apart in front of me, and I feel my heart swell with love as I watch and feel this man literally pour himself into me. He doesn't stop or slow down until he has given me every last drop of him. Julian lowers himself onto me as the last embers of his orgasm fade away.

He's heavy, but I love the feel of his sweat-covered body pressing against every inch of mine.

After a few minutes, he rolls off of me. He pulls me into a sitting position and quickly takes my shirt and bra off. He removes his own, leaving us both naked. He lies back down on his side and pulls me to him so we're spooning. He wraps his arm tightly around me and holds me close. I feel his heart beating rapidly against my back. I thread my fingers through his and clasp his hand tight. We don't speak, and I'm okay with that. I think we've probably done enough talking for one night. Julian's breathing starts to slow, and I think he may be falling asleep. This has been an exhausting day for me and an exhausting night for both of us. I'm ready to leave it behind, and I'm glad to be in Julian's arms. Things definitely were headed in a different direction just a few hours ago. I take a deep breath in and slowly exhale, pushing all the tension I've been feeling out of my body. His presence is soothing. I find myself wondering if I should have just let Julian be there for me today. If I would've told him about Brady, I know he would have been. I know he would understand why I've been acting so crazy. He'd understand about Luke too. I know I'm going to have to tell him soon.

"I'm so sorry, baby." Julian isn't asleep.

"So am I." I squeeze his hand tighter.

"I didn't mean the one-night stand comment."

"I know." And I do know.

"And I'm sorry I didn't take care of you tonight. You should always come first. I just couldn't stop myself. I needed to be inside of you right then. And I'm sorry about not using a condom. I just wanted to feel all of you." Julian sounds like a little boy who has gotten in trouble for acting mischievous.

"Please stop apologizing. This is my fault."

"No, Lexie. This is our fault. We'll figure it out. We have to."

I roll over and face him. I kiss him softly. "Tell me you know you're the only man in my life, Julian. We need to deal with all of the other stuff that happened this weekend too, but we have to start there. You need to believe that."

Julian squeezes my hand and says he needs to tell me a few things about Luke. I'm hesitant and tell him so, but he thinks it will explain a lot, so I let him. I spend the next hour listening, in shock, to Julian telling me in detail how, for the past month, Luke has done everything he possibly could to make Julian believe I was seeing him as well and that we were way more than friends. Apparently, Luke has been telling people at the hotel we've been together for years but that we have an open relationship. Julian explains how Luke made sure he knew he was with me that other night, and tonight as well. Luke knows they all talk, and he started texting other staff members, knowing it would get back to Julian. It's so hard to believe, but I see Julian is telling me the truth.

"Why didn't you tell me this was going on?" I know the answer, but I ask anyway.

"I tried. Several times. You didn't want to hear it."

That's true. He did try to tell me. "It's so hard to believe he'd do that, but I know you wouldn't lie to me about this. I don't understand. None of what he said is true. I've been completely honest with you about our relationship. I swear."

"He's in love with you. It's simple. People do crazy things when they're in love."

CHAPTER 37

I'm off on Monday, but Julian has to go in. He wants me to hang out at the hotel so we can see each other, but I pass. I tell him I plan on talking to Luke today, and he tries to talk me out of it. I finally convince him I have to, and he makes me promise to call him afterward. We also make plans to spend the evening together. I'm hopeful we have turned a corner and can really move forward now.

All I can think about is Luke, and maybe that's a good thing. Brady is a distant second right now. Oddly, I can't get ahold of him all day. I text and call him and start to think he's avoiding me. Around five o'clock, I decide to just go to his house. I'm not sure if he's working or not, and I need to do this today. He answers the door with a beer in his hand, and it's obvious it's not his first. He doesn't seem surprised to see me and lets me in. I walk in and ask why he has been ignoring my calls and texts.

"Because I don't want to deal with your shitty life today, Alexa. It just causes me grief."

Wow. So that's how this is going to go down. I get right to the point. "So when did you decide to try and start ruining my shitty life?" I know I sound dramatic, but I'm so hurt by what Julian told me last night. I don't share details though. I wait to see how this plays out. I want him to admit what he's been doing.

"I'm ruining your life? That's rich. This guy is totally going to break your heart, and you have your head so far in the clouds you can't even see it. You aren't living in a fairytale where this is going to have a happy ending, Lex. Not with this guy."

"Well right now, you're the one who's breaking my heart, Luke. *You.* I've never seen you act like this before. I don't even know who you are lately."

"I'm me. I'm the same guy who has been taking care of you and protecting you from getting hurt. I'm the same guy who comforted you last night when Julian was too busy for you. As a matter of fact, it feels like that's *all* I've been doing for the last fucking year."

"Well I didn't realize it was so much of a fucking chore for you to be my friend. You deserve a medal for taking care of the broken girl. Feel free to take off the knight in shining armor costume now, because I. Am. Fine!"

"My God, Lexie. You don't get it, do you?"

"I guess not, Luke. Why don't you explain it to me, seeing as you think you have all the answers?"

We're talking in circles and alternating between being calm and being on the offensive. It's a strange little dance we're doing, and because this is totally new territory, neither of us is on solid footing.

"It tore me up to watch what you went through with Brady and after Brady. It seriously broke my heart." I hear the anguish in Luke's voice when he brings up Brady. It's such a painful topic for both of us.

"I know. I understand it was really hard for you too, and you've been such a great friend to me. But Julian isn't Brady, and you can't keep trying to sabotage my relationship with him. I'm happy, and you're trying to ruin it."

He shakes his head. "Do you really not know why I'm acting like this? Why I'm having such a hard time seeing you with him?"

I do know, and I can't believe this is finally about to come out into the open after all these years. I really don't want to hear it because I know in my heart there will be no going back from here. But I know this has to happen now because if things keep going the way they have been lately, I'll end up hating Luke, and I would do anything to prevent that from happening.

Before I can answer his question, Luke continues. "He's not the one for you, Lex."

"Why, Luke? Why isn't Julian the one for me?" I know the answer, but I ask anyway.

"Because *I'm* the one for you. Me. I'm the one you're supposed to end up with. I'm your happily ever after." There's so much conviction in his voice that I'm 100 percent sure Luke believes everything he's saying to me.

Before I can even get a word out, Luke walks over to me, pulls me tightly into his arms, and kisses me with the stored-up passion of seven years. The familiarity I feel with Luke works against me, and I find myself wrapping my arms around his waist and falling into his kiss. His tongue is soft and gentle, and I really can feel the love he has for me coming through. I feel completely conflicted, and for a moment my body operates without my mind or heart's permission. I know I need to stop. I need to stop doing this because I know deep in my heart I've found my soul mate in Julian and if I continue kissing Luke like this, all I'm going to accomplish is to hurt both of them. I push him away and take two steps back.

"Stop, Luke. This is wrong." I shake my head and put my hands up as he steps back toward me. He looks surprised but stops.

"Wrong? Did that feel wrong to you? Because nothing in my life has felt as right as kissing you does. The first time it was right, and it was right now too. You know it. You felt it. Don't you dare deny it!"

The truth is it did feel good to kiss Luke. There's passion and chemistry and even love between us, and maybe before I had met Julian it would have been enough. It may have even been great. But Julian is able to reach my soul with his touch, and I know in my heart I'll never feel that way about Luke.

"Luke, I'm with Julian. You know that. You know how I feel about him."

"Well, let me be honest here. I don't give a shit about Julian. *I love you*, Lexie Reed. I'm in love with you, and after that kiss, there's no doubt in my mind you have feelings for me too."

"Luke, I do love you. You're right about that, but I'm not in love with you. I don't think you're in love with me either." I'm not sure who I'm trying to convince, him or me.

"I think you've mistaken friendship, loyalty, and attraction for romantic love. I don't think it's real. What you think you feel for me, it's not real." I say these things in a last-ditch attempt to save our friendship.

He's insulted. "Are you seriously going to stand there and tell me how I feel about you? How dare you just blow this off like I'm some guy with a *crush* on you." He's really yelling at me now. "I fucking *know* you, Lexie. I know you, and I know how I feel about you." He tries to keep going, but I interrupt him.

"And I really know you too. You don't have the market covered on insight into this relationship. I've been watching you fuck your way around Florida for years now. I've been standing right in front of you the whole time, and now, when I'm finally in a good relationship, you decide to dump this all on me and tell me you're in love with me. It's bullshit. You just don't want me to need another man. It might ruin your hero reputation."

"Really? Have you already forgotten about all the 'relationships' I've watched you jump in and out of over the years now? Have you already forgotten Brady? I was nothing but supportive of that fucking train wreck of a relationship."

Okay. Here we go.

"Yeah, and maybe you were so supportive because you introduced me to the conductor of that 'fucking train wreck.' Don't mistake guilt for support. I did for a while, but I figured out a long time ago that most of what you feel for me is based on guilt. Your need to 'protect' me now comes from your guilt over not protecting me then. I've told you a million times, none of what went down was your fault."

"I tell you I'm in love with you, and you tell me I just feel guilty about what Brady did?" I hear a double meaning in that question but decide not to probe further. Luke switches his line of questioning when I fail to respond.

"Do you question Julian's feelings? Because I know he doesn't really know you well enough to care about you like I do. You guys have been together for like what, five minutes, and if I know anything about you, it's that you're not a big sharer when it comes to your past. You still haven't told him about

Brady, have you? Does he know your nightmares are really flashbacks? Does he know you see a shrink every week, and have for a year?" Luke is taking this conversation somewhere it really shouldn't go, and I need to stop him.

"Now you're just being ugly. Does it make you feel better to point out all of my flaws?" I try to hide the hurt in my voice because this person in front of me, this Luke that I don't even know, seems ready, willing, and able, to exploit my vulnerability.

He answers me with a snide tone. "*I* have no problem with any of your flaws, Alexa. That's exactly what I'm trying to make you understand. I love you, flaws and all. Can you say that about Julian? How serious can he be about you when he doesn't even know you? Your refusal to answer my earlier question was answer enough. You haven't told him *shit*."

Luke's words are like a dagger through my heart. He's right. I haven't told Julian anything substantial about Brady. I'm scared he won't feel the same way about me if he knows all the ugly stuff from my past. Luke knows that, and he's using it against me. I understand he's hurt by my rejection, but the backlash I'm getting is way more severe than I ever could've imagined. This man who says he loves me is breaking my heart.

"Julian *doesn't* know me like you do. Not yet. You and I have been best *friends* for seven years. We have a ton of history together. But we're getting to know each other, and I've been opening up to him. He's a good guy, Luke, and he does care about me. I'm sorry you can't see that and be happy for me."

"I'm not sure how I'm supposed to be supportive of the guy who is with the girl *I* want. *I* want to be the one holding you, touching you, and making you happy." My Luke is back for a second and says those words tenderly. I really don't want to hurt him, but I can't let him think there's any chance of us being together. It's not fair to him.

"You do make me happy. You're a fantastic friend, and I don't want things to change between us." My words sound like a plea, and as I'm saying them, I know I'm wasting my breath. Everything has already changed, and I know there will be no going back.

"Well, I guess I had it all wrong. I must not really know you at all." Luke's tone is ice-cold again. "You really are going to choose someone you just met over me?"

I nod my head slowly in response. I've chosen Julian, and I really am growing tired of Luke making me feel bad about it. He has had seven years to tell me how he feels.

Luke continues his tirade. "I've done *everything* for you. I fucking waited all this time for you to be ready! I waited to share my feelings because I wanted to make sure I could be the guy you deserve. I wasn't that guy in college, and I've been working on becoming that guy every day since the first night we hooked up. I know it doesn't seem like it, but I've been trying to get all my shit straight so we could have a future. What a fucking waste of my time you've been."

I seriously can't believe he just said the last seven years have been a waste of his time. Our friendship has been so precious to me, and I can't believe he's ending it like this. His words are like a slap in the face, and I feel the sting in my heart. The tears I've been holding back this whole time start to run down my cheeks. He ignores my hurt and continues his verbal assault.

His next words drip with venom. "Oh stop fucking crying, Alexa! You don't even really feel bad. Maybe you're the one who feels guilty. You've been stringing me along for years, and now you're acting like the victim. But hey, you do play that role nicely."

"Please stop! You don't mean any of this. You're just hurt and drunk." The tears just keep coming harder.

"Oh, I've meant *everything* I've said. I just poured my heart out to you, and you fucking broke it. If that makes you feel bad, tough shit! You did this. You can own it."

I've heard enough, and I need to get out of here. I stand up and head toward the door. I'm speechless. Luke is using everything he knows about me against me. It's as if he's decided that if we can't love each other, we'll hate each other instead. And just when I think there's nothing worse Luke could say to me, he unleashes the worst type of hurt imaginable.

"Before you leave, know this. When Julian finds out who you really are deep down and learns about how damaged you really are both emotionally and *physically*, don't come running back to me looking for a shoulder to cry on. I won't be here."

His emphasis on the word physically stops me cold in my tracks. Oh. My. God. He knows.

I turn and face him and whisper, "You know?" Even after a year, I still can't say the word out loud. Luke, on the other hand, has no problem with the word.

"What, that Brady raped you?" He shrugs his shoulders. His eyes are hard and dark. "Yes, I know. I've always known." His tone implies we're talking about something as casual as the weather.

"How?" I want to know if he guessed or if Brady actually admitted it to him.

"Brady told me. How else would I know? You sure as shit didn't tell me anything. You're supposed to be my best friend, and you didn't share with me. No, you just let me believe that he was begging for forgiveness for hitting you that night and for cheating on you. He fucking needed your forgiveness, Alexa, and you denied him." Luke is literally snarling at me, and I swear

I'm looking at a stranger. I have no idea who this person in front of me is. "I've known the whole time, and I've waited for you to tell me. It's been a whole year, and you still can't talk about it. You can't even say the word *rape*, can you? You're still all fucked up. You're just the only one who doesn't see it. But give Julian some time. He's a smart guy. He'll get sick of your drama really soon. And you'll be alone again."

Luke might as well have just punched me in the stomach. I literally can't breathe. I don't even try to hide the hurt in my eyes when I look at him. I want him to see what he just did to me. He can own the fact that he just torpedoed a seven-year relationship and ripped my heart out in the process.

"So you want to bring up Brady, huh? Well, let me finish this conversation the same way I finished my last one with him. I'll *never ever* forgive you for this."

CHAPTER 38

I grab my purse and run out of the house. Thank goodness I left my door unlocked and am able to quickly get inside my car. I'm having a hard time finding my keys in my purse and end up dumping it all over my front seat looking for them. I really shouldn't be driving. I can hardly see through my tears, but I need to get away from his house even if I just go around the corner. I pull over at a park a few blocks away. I turn the car off, put my head on the steering wheel, and let the sobs I've been holding back just consume my body. I'm not sure how long I stay there like that, but it must be for a while because when I finally look up it's dusk. I glance at the clock on the dashboard. Holy shit. It's almost seven-thirty. I got to Luke's at around five-thirty and was there for about an hour. I find it odd I haven't heard my phone ring once. A moment of panic races through me as I realize I've either left my phone at Luke's or I've had it on silent. I promised everyone I wouldn't do that anymore. I dig through all the crap I dumped out of my purse, and I'm relieved to see my phone sitting on the seat. I'm scared to look at it, but I enter my security code anyway.

Oh no. Fifteen missed calls and texts. Julian, Marissa, and Shannon have all been trying to get a hold of me for the past two hours. I turn my car on and start heading home. I set the phone to Bluetooth and call Marissa first. Most of the calls were from her.

She answers on the first ring. "Where the hell are you? I've been trying to get hold of you for over an hour. Luke texted me and said you and him got into a huge fight and that you ran out of his house crying." She sounds so worried, and I feel even worse, if that's possible.

"I'm on my way home. I'll be there in twenty minutes, and I'll tell you everything. Can you let Shannon know? She called and texted a few times too."

"Okay, but are you all right? You sound awful." The concern is so evident in her voice, and I love her for it.

"No, not really." I try to cut the phone call short because I need to call Julian. There were several calls and texts from him as well, and I don't need to read them to know he's freaking out too. Marissa confirms my suspicions.

"Lex, you really need to call Julian. He called me after he couldn't get a response from you. He said he texted you a few times and that you and him were supposed to meet up. He's even been here looking for you. He told me you were planning on seeing Luke today. I tried to get hold of Luke, and he didn't answer his phone either. I didn't know anything until he called." The words just keep pouring out of Marissa in a rush, and I feel horrible she's been so worried and has had to deal with Julian too. "I told Julian I had no idea where you were, and he's freaking out. I tried to reassure him you were fine, but

I wasn't very convincing because after Luke called, I was freaking out too."

"It's okay, Mari. Let me go so I can call him. I'll see you in a few minutes." Before I get a chance to dial Julian's number, I see his face pop up on my caller ID. I take a very deep breath and try to steady my voice. I know he's worried, and I don't want to make it worse.

"Hey, you." I say it softly and brace myself for what's headed my way.

"My God, Lexie. Are you okay? Where the hell are you? Nobody has been able to find you for hours." He sounds out of breath and panicked.

"I'm fine, and I'm almost home. I'm so sorry I worried you." I think my voice sounds steady, but apparently I'm not fooling anyone.

"That's okay, baby. I'm just glad you're all right." He hears me choke back a sob. "Are you okay? You sound like you're crying." I honestly didn't think I had anything left inside of me, but the concern in Julian's voice unlocks the floodgates again, and I start sobbing so hard I can't talk. "What the hell is going on?"

I pull into my driveway and open my mouth to answer him, but before the words come out, I see his car pull up behind mine. I hang up my phone. He must have been out looking for me. I really, really don't want him to see me like this, but there's no way out of this mess. I turn the car off, and before I can even unbuckle my seat belt, Julian is opening the door and taking me in his arms. He reaches down and unbuckles my belt for me. As he kneels beside the car, I wrap my arms around him, lay my head on his chest, and continue to sob. After a few minutes, he takes the keys from the ignition and pulls me gently from the car. He shuts and locks the door behind me and leans me up against it. He puts his hand under my chin and forces me to look at him. I can only imagine what I look like. I've been crying for over an hour, and I must have makeup running all down my cheeks. Concern and confusion are written all over his face. He looks me up and down as if to see if I'm physically harmed and takes a deep breath when he sees that I'm intact. Well, at least on the outside. Inside, my heart is shattered in a million little pieces. Julian kisses me softly on the lips, takes my hand, and leads me into my house. Marissa is standing by the door, and I know she was watching this all go down. She gives me a huge hug when I walk by her and whispers in my ear, "It's going to be okay." I shake my head no because I don't think it's going to be okay. I can't answer her through my sobs.

I tell myself I'm crying because of what happened between Luke and me, but if I'm going to be honest, I need to acknowledge that I'm crying because the fact, the truth, that I was raped by my now dead ex-boyfriend is out in the universe. Someone else knows, and I was just forced to admit it out loud. I've told myself for a year if I didn't tell anyone, then I could pretend it never happened. Luke officially ripped that Band-Aid off tonight, and the wound he revealed is a huge, gaping one. I'm terrified that now that it's exposed it will never stop bleeding.

Julian picks me up and carries me to my bedroom. He lays me down on the bed and lies behind me. He pulls me close to him and holds me tightly. I can't stop crying. I've talked about Brady and most of the bad stuff with my friends, with Ellen, and with my family. I've shed tears too, but I've always managed to keep my emotions under relative control and for the most part private. I thought I had done a good job working through all of it. I didn't realize, until this very moment, that no matter how hurt I thought I was, I had never really *felt* the pain of the rape and his death. Everyone kept telling me I was strong, and I took comfort in the fact that I kept it all together. The storm surge of feelings racking my body right now proves that I never really dealt with anything at all.

Adding to the horribleness of the situation is that Julian has a front-row seat to my breakdown. I'm horrified, and I want him to leave, but judging by how tightly he's holding me, he has no intention of going anywhere. He doesn't say anything; he just holds me and strokes my hair. It's exactly what I need even if I don't want it. My sobs finally give way to deep breaths, and I'm finally able to talk. "Thank you," I whisper as I squeeze his hand. I'm nervous to say anything at all because I'm not ready to tell him about what just happened with Luke, never mind what happened with Brady. I think he senses I'm not ready to talk because he just squeezes me back and kisses my head.

We lie like this until I eventually fall asleep. I drift in and out, and each time I wake up, I feel the tears on my cheeks. Julian has stayed and is still holding me. I'm so conflicted. I want him here, but then I don't. I know there's no way I'm getting out of talking to him now. This meltdown was a hundred times worse than anything he has seen, and he will not be giving me a pass now. I'm scared of what the morning light will bring.

CHAPTER 39

I get out of bed at six-thirty and try not to wake Julian. My reflection in the bathroom mirror is horrifying. I look like I've been crying for weeks, not hours. I splash cold water on my face, brush my teeth, and go to the kitchen. I grab a cucumber out of the refrigerator and cut two big slices. I sit down on the couch, put them over my eyes, and hope it helps. I'm not normally such a vain person, but I look awful. I'm only there for about thirty minutes when Julian comes and finds me. I hear him come in, and I take the cucumbers off my eyes. I try to make a joke. "If I'd known you'd look that bad too, I would have cut you some slices."

He does look bad: tired and worn out. I've done this to him. He doesn't think my joke is funny. "Come back to bed. I don't care how you look."

I follow him back into the bedroom and get into bed. He sits down next to me. "It's early, and I know we're both exhausted, but you have to tell me something."

I know better than to argue. "Okay."

"Did Luke hurt you last night? Because it took everything I had to not go find him and kick his ass." I see in his eyes he's serious.

I put my hand on his arm. "Not how you might be thinking. I confronted him, and we got in a huge, ugly fight. You were right. He was trying to break us up. He admitted he has feelings for me and wants me for himself. We won't be friends anymore, and it hurts."

I make the story a little easier to swallow, but I don't lie about any of it. Julian isn't really buying it yet though. "Are you sure that's all that happened?"

"I really don't want to go into specifics, but yes, that's what happened."

Julian crawls back in bed and pulls me close. "I'm sorry. I know how bad losing someone close to you hurts." I assume he's referring to his sister, and I don't ask for details. I'm not able to have that discussion this morning so I just squeeze his hand.

I look at the clock and groan. I have to work today. I was off all weekend, and I took a day off last week. I'm about to get a promotion, and I need to show I'm taking it seriously. I wiggle out of Julian's arms and sit up. He reaches for me to pull me back down, and I dodge him.

"I have to work, and I need to take a shower." I need a break too. I need to be alone. I want to cry in the shower, but I don't want Julian to see any more of my tears. He won't believe this is all about Luke if I don't pull it together.

Julian is up and dressed when I get out of the shower. "I can be here by seven tonight. I'll pick up dinner." Ugh. I don't want him to come back. I need some space. But I can't say the words, so I lie.

"That's sweet. Thanks." He kisses me and gives me a big hug. I can tell he wants to talk, but I think he knows it won't go the way he wants. I walk him to the door and tell him I'll see him later. I plan to get out of it somehow.

The minute he leaves, the tears start to fall again. I have no idea how I'm going to make it through this day. Marissa hears Julian leave and comes to check on me. She finds me lying on my bed crying.

"I'd ask if you're okay, but you clearly aren't. Can I do or say anything to help?"

I shake my head.

"What happened, Lex?"

Marissa is my best friend in the whole world, and I should tell her about the rape. But I worry she'll react like Luke did and be upset that I waited a year to tell her. I know she'll be really hurt, so I don't say anything. I tell her everything else though. Everything that Julian told me and everything that Luke confirmed. She listens, and when I'm finished, she hugs me and promises things will be okay. If she knew the whole story, she might not be feeling so positive.

I go to work looking like hell and try to hide behind makeup. Lauren and Ramon are not fooled. I tell them I don't want to talk about it, and I figure they think I got in a fight with Julian. I let them. Julian texts me about ten times today. He keeps checking on me, and each time his concern has the opposite effect. I really just want him to back off. I'm overwhelmed and raw, and if I didn't think he would come to my work looking for me, I'd turn my phone off. Both Marissa and Shannon keep texting me too. I appreciate the concern, but as the hours pass and the tears start to dry up, I feel myself sliding back behind my wall. I don't want to talk to anyone.

I get home at six-thirty and wait for Julian. He said he was going to be here by seven. I get a text from him a little after seven.

Julian: *Can't leave yet. Need to take care of something. Be there by 9:30.*
Alexa: *You don't have to come. I'm tired anyway.*
Julian: *I'll be there by 9:30.*

I tried. At least I have a few hours alone. I go for a run and try to clear my head. It doesn't work this time either. I shower when I get back, eat a baked potato, and pour myself a glass of wine. Marissa comes home and joins me. I'm on my third glass when Julian shows up at ten o'clock. Marissa gets up to let him in, and when I see his face, I instinctively know the thing he had to take care of was Luke. Marissa sees his face and leaves the room. Great. Not this again. I get up, take my glass with me, and walk into my room. He follows and shuts the door behind him. I sit on my bed.

"Tell me about Brady, Alexa."

I was right; he did talk to Luke. I wonder what the fuck Luke said. "Why, Julian? You obviously spoke to Luke tonight. I'm sure he told you about Brady."

"Not exactly. I confronted him about what happened yesterday, and all he kept telling me was to ask you about Brady. Who's Brady?"

"An old boyfriend. I've mentioned him." I'm trying to ascertain what Julian already knows.

"Why would Luke want me to ask you about him? Have you been seeing him?" Oh wow. Luke set me up. He's trying to force me to tell Julian. What a bastard.

"No, I haven't seen Brady." My stomach turns as the words come out. This is perverse.

"This is bullshit, and I don't appreciate being made to look like a fool. Tell me about Brady." His voice is raised, and I can see he's finally over it. Over me, over this. Well so am I. I see my opportunity, and I take it.

"You want to know about Brady, Julian? Fine. But don't blame me when you don't like what you hear. And I assure you that you won't." Julian is challenging me with his eyes. He wants this. He has been waiting for this. He nods.

"Brady loved me. He loved me and treated me great for about six months. He said all the right things, just like you, and put me first. He always called. He always made sure I was a priority, and we were inseparable." I take a deep breath and gauge Julian's reaction so far. He's calm and waiting for the rest. I'm not calm. My pulse is racing a mile a minute.

"Then he changed. He decided drugs were more important than me, than anything. He stopped putting me first, and I got all caught up in it. Our relationship became the poster child for dysfunction, and I stayed. I stayed when I should have run as far away as possible. I turned myself inside out to try and make it work." I stop, hoping it's enough. It's not.

"Keep going. What happened?"

"I'm telling you what happened. Do you need to hear the details of how we fought and broke up and made up with amazing sex? Do you want to know how much I was partying? How much I drank? You must love to hear that. I know how you feel about drinking." I'm trying everything I can to make him mad so he just leaves.

He's steely eyed and tense. "What happened, Lexie?"

I hate Julian's tone, and I hate that he won't leave this alone. I'm angry at him for making me do this. I'm devastated that Luke would do this to me. I'm angry, and I'm scared, and it's very apparent in the way the words come out.

"You just can't let this go, can you? Well I hope you get what you need by hearing that Brady loved me. He loved me, and then he cheated on me. He even got another girl pregnant. And when I found out and tried to end it, he hit me. And then he begged me to stay. And I fucking did."

I look up and see that Julian's expression has softened. I've finally given him enough, and I can stop right here. I could pull this off. But something inside of me can't stop. My body is trying to expel the poison I've been holding on to for so long. It needs to get out. I also feel the horrible need to make Julian feel as bad as I do right now. I want him to share this pain. It's so fucked up. He gets up and walks toward me and starts to say something. I put my hand up to stop him. My words are harsh, and my voice is eerily calm. I'm starting to feel like it isn't even me talking and that this happened to someone else.

"Was that enough for you, Julian? Did you hear enough to make you feel like you know what the fuck is wrong with me? Is there enough stuff here for you fix? Because there's more." It's all pouring out, and I'm powerless to stop it now. "After he hit me, and I *stayed*, he raped me. But you know that, right? You guessed that already. You just needed me to admit it, right? You thought it would be good for me to talk about it, right?"

The look on Julian's face tells me he didn't have all of these pieces put together. He looks shocked and once again starts to speak. I cut him off.

"Let me finish, because this horror story just keeps getting better. You said no secrets, so I need to tell you everything, right?" My voice is cold and dripping with sarcasm. I know he doesn't deserve any of this, but I can't stop.

"He felt bad. In case you're wondering. He felt so bad that he begged me to forgive him. He called me non-stop for two weeks trying to apologize. I had to hide out from him. I had to go totally dark to avoid him. But he wouldn't stop, so I finally agreed to see him. I went to his house to talk to him, and guess what happened?" I look at Julian and give him the opportunity to speak. His voice is calm despite the fact he looks like he could kill someone.

"Did he hurt you again?"

The voice that comes out of me this time is devoid of any emotion.

"Yes, Julian, he hurt me again. He swallowed a bunch of pills, drank a fifth of whiskey, and died. And I found him. I found him with a note next to his body that said *forgive me.* That's it. Forgive me. But I can't forgive him, because he's dead."

There. I did it. I've finally said it all out loud. Not to my family, or friends, or my therapist. I've said it all aloud to the one person who I'm not certain will be able to handle it. How fucked up is that? I never planned to tell anyone about the rape, so I never considered how I would feel afterward. I was shattered when Luke confronted me with it, but that might have been more because I was shocked that he knew and never said anything and because we were dealing with all kinds of other issues. Right now I feel nothing. I'm not freaking out and losing it. I'm not even crying.

I'm so busy thinking about how I'm feeling right now that I almost forget I've just dumped all of this on Julian. I look up and meet his stare. He has tears in his eyes and is gripping the chair so tightly his knuckles are white. If my goal was to share my pain with him, I'd say I was 100 percent successful. He gets up a third time and comes to me. I don't stop him this time. He wraps his arms around me and holds me so tightly that I can hardly breathe. I've loved being in his arms since the minute I met him. I've craved his touch and needed to have him close. Right now I feel nothing—not lust, not love, not anger or pain. I just feel empty. I'm numb.

"My God. I'm so sorry. I'm so sorry that happened to you, baby. I had no idea. I'm so sorry."

These are the right words for him to say to me. He's trying to comfort me. But all I hear in his voice is pity, and it makes me sick to my stomach. I never wanted him or anyone else to feel bad for me. My bad judgment put me in this situation, and nobody is ever going to be able to convince me I'm not partly responsible for Brady dying. It's almost a full year later, and I still don't believe I deserve to feel okay about any of this. Luke's words about me denying Brady my forgiveness are ringing in my ears. I did deny him that, and he died.

Julian is rubbing my back and whispering soothing words in my ear. He's doing everything right, yet it feels so wrong. It's all wrong. I don't feel like the new Lexie anymore. That girl has been hanging on by her fingertips for weeks now, and she can't do it anymore. She is gone again, and the Lexie who doesn't want to feel anything is back.

"Tell me what you need from me. I'll do anything for you. Anything. Just tell me how I can help you." I see a tear run down his cheek, and I still feel nothing.

I wiggle out of his arms and stand up. "Anything? Do you really mean that?"

"Yes. Of course I mean it."

"Do you promise you'll do whatever I need you to do?"

I see a hint of skepticism cross his face, but he still promises. "I promise. What is it, baby? What do you need from me?"

I walk toward the door and open it. "I need you to leave. I want you to leave and never contact me again."

CHAPTER 40

I look at Julian as I'm saying the words. I look right in his eyes so he knows I'm serious. He needs to know I'm not testing him or playing a game. I want him to leave. I *need* him to leave. The numbness that took root in my heart is slowly spreading throughout my body like venom, destroying every pure, warm, loving feeling I had. I can hardly breathe.

He doesn't move at all, and it looks like he's having a hard time breathing as well. I see the disbelief, sadness, and compassion he's feeling shining through his wet eyes. I'm not surprised by his reaction to what I've just shared with him. Since day one, Julian has been very sensitive to my feelings, and I do know he cares about me. I am, however, surprised by my reaction to what just happened. I truly am numb.

"Julian, please. You have to leave." My voice comes out cold and flat.

He still doesn't move. He looks like he's in shock. It's probably only been a few minutes, but it might as well be forever. The longer he sits there, the more chance there is we'll keep talking about this. I figure he knows this, and that's why he's not moving. I've threatened to end things between us before, and he stayed. I need to convince him this is different. Everything is totally different now.

He finally speaks, and when he does, his voice is shaky. I've never heard him like this. "I'm not leaving, Alexa. I can't. I don't believe you really want me to."

Apparently, I haven't been very convincing, so I say it more firmly. "I'm serious, Julian. You promised, and it's what I want."

"Let's talk about this, Lexie. Por favor. You can't tell me all that and expect me to just walk away. Please, let's talk about this."

"There's nothing else to say. You know everything now, and I don't want to talk about this anymore. I want you to leave, and I need you to respect that. If you ever cared about me, you will do as I ask. Just leave." The last few words come out in a whisper. My body is feeling the effects of this now. I'm shaking and starting to panic.

"If I ever cared about you? Seriously, how can you even say that to me? I care about you now, so much. That's why I'm staying."

I close the door because I hear Marissa coming out of her room, and I don't want her to know what's going on. Julian obviously has no intention of leaving any time soon. I feel a panic attack coming on, so I just slide down the door and sit on the floor. I put my head between my legs and try to calm my breathing. I hear the bed frame creak and know Julian is coming toward me. I put my hand up to tell him to stop. He sits down on the floor next to me but doesn't touch me. We silently sit there for at least ten minutes, and the only sounds in the room are those of us breathing. As soon as I feel more in control, I turn my head and rest it on my knees. I look at Julian and ask quietly, "Why won't you go? You're making me beg you. Why are you staying?"

I close my eyes and take a deep breath.

"Mírame, Lexie." I open my eyes and do as he asks. "You don't know why I'm staying, baby?"

I just shrug my shoulders.

"I'm staying because I wish someone would have stayed for me. I wish someone would have fought for me when I was spiraling out of control. I was left on my own and stayed that way until you fell into my life. You need someone to hold on to, and it can be me. It should be me."

I hear the words, and I truly can't understand why he wants to deal with any of this. We have only been together for a short time, and I've been a mess for most of it. I'm giving him such an easy out, and I don't understand why he won't take it. "Why? Why should it be you? Why do you even want it to be you?"

He makes sure I'm looking at him before he responds. When he does, I see the sincerity in his eyes. "Because I love you, Lexie. I'm *in* love with you, and I have been since the first night we were together. You know that. I know you do. You haven't believed it's real. But it is. It's so *fucking* real. None of what you told me changes that. That stuff makes me love you more. You're so strong, baby. You amaze me."

Julian's voice is soothing, and it helps me absorb a little of what he's saying. This incredible, beautiful, patient, loving man is sitting on the floor of my room and telling me that despite everything I just told him, he wants me.

The problem with all of this is that I don't believe he can actually feel this way because he doesn't really know me. I'm a lie.

"You don't even know me. This relationship isn't real because the Alexa you think you're in love with isn't real. I've been lying to myself and everyone else for so long that I'm not even sure what's true anymore." I sit up and lean against my bed. I'm physically creating more space between Julian and me in my attempt to push him away.

"I do know you. You've tried really hard not to let me in, but it hasn't worked. I understand now, baby, and I wish you would've told me all of this so I could've supported you. I feel like there are so many things I could've done differently. I came on so strong. I'm sorry for that, or if I pushed you too hard."

As Julian recounts all the things he thinks he has done wrong, something inside of me softens a tiny bit. I still want him to go, but I want him to leave knowing this isn't his fault. I owe him that.

"You didn't do anything wrong. You need to know that. You're a great man, and I was a willing participant in everything that happened between us. I'm just sorry I let it get as far as it has."

Julian's expression darkens. I guess he thought I was going to change my mind about breaking up with him. He processes my words and understands my intentions haven't changed at all.

His voice is laced with desperation and fear. "Far? We were going for epic, Lexie. Remember? This isn't over. I understand you may need some time to process all of this. I get that telling me was a big deal. I'm sure when you first shared this with your friends and family, it was hard to feel comfortable around them. But nothing has to change between us. It will only get better without all of this between us." He reaches over to take my hand, but I pull away. I can't let him touch me. I'm not sure what will happen if he does.

"Julian, as of right now, almost a year later, there's only one person who knows everything that happened."

Julian's expression registers his disbelief. "Me?"

"Yes. You. You're the only person I've told about the rape. Brady told Luke, but I didn't know that until the other night when he threw it in my face. I thought if I kept it to myself, I could pretend it didn't happen. I haven't told my family, my friends, or Ellen. And nobody knows about the note. Nobody knows his death was my fault."

All of this is pouring out of me despite my initial unwillingness to talk about it. I don't feel anything when I'm saying it, and that's the worst part. I should hurt, but I just don't. I look into Julian's eyes, and I see *he's* hurting. This is all so wrong.

"I'm not going to pour any of my stuff into this, but I do understand what guilt can do to you. I understand loss and death and keeping secrets, baby. I understand pain. The kind that consumes you and makes you just shut down." Julian reaches over and gently laces his fingers through mine. I don't pull away this time. I don't crack or fall apart. I just tell him the truth.

"I wish I felt the pain right now. It would be better than not feeling anything. I don't feel anything, and you have to accept that. I can't do this. I don't want to hurt you. You don't deserve this." I mean every word.

He scoots closer to me, looks me right in the eyes, and asks, "Can I hold you?"

Oh. There's an emotion. Guilt. I feel this. The look in Julian's eyes is making me feel guilty. Guilt is the last thing I want to feel right now, so I nod slowly. Julian doesn't hesitate and pulls me quickly into his arms. He arranges us so he's leaning against the bed, and I'm on his lap. He's holding on to me as if his life depends upon it, and I can feel him trembling. This has been hard on him too. He strokes my hair, and a flicker of warmth passes through me quickly. It's tiny, but it's something. I take a deep breath, exhale, and lean into his embrace. Everything I've experienced in the last few days—the drama, crying, drinking, panic attacks, lack of sleep, running, and emotional stress—has taken a tremendous physical toll on my body. It's almost one o'clock in the morning, and I'm drained. He isn't leaving, and I just can't find the strength to make him.

We sit there wrapped up in each other until our breaths become one. We don't speak. I let everything he's said to me tonight loop on repeat through my head. I try to steer his words out of my head and into my heart. He told me he loves me. I want to feel it. I want to believe it. I cling with desperate hope to the realization that I still *want* to feel. After a long while, Julian picks me up and lays me down on my bed. He lies behind me and pulls me toward him. He wraps himself around me as if to protect me. He doesn't understand the damage is already done and that he can't protect me from this. I'm grateful he wants to try though.

I'm so grateful that I force out the words he wants so desperately to hear "You can stay, Julian," I softly whisper.

His response is also a whisper and a plea. "I'm going to stay. I'm not going to leave you. You just need to hold on to me, baby. Please, just hold on."

I thread my fingers through his and grip as hard as I can. As if my life depends on it. I hold on, and I stay.

THANK YOU SO MUCH FOR READING!

Dear Readers,

I truly hope you enjoyed meeting Alexa, Julian and all of their friends in STAY: book 1 in the Alexa Reed series. I had an amazing time developing these characters and am so glad that I got to share them with you. There is so much more to Julian and Lexie's story and it continues in Hold On, which is the second book in the series. A yet untitled third book will follow as well!

One of the best parts of being an author is connecting with readers. I love getting emails, messages and reviews from people who have read the book. The feedback is always appreciated because it helps me grow as a writer and it lets me know what is working well with readers. To be honest, I also just love to talk about the characters. I've spent so much time with them that they sometimes feel like they are real ☺

I can be reached in a number of ways. My website is hilarywynne.com and that is always a good place to start. I am also on Facebook at Hilary Wynne and on Twitter @HilaryWynne. If you want to know how I visualize the characters and settings in the Alexa Reed series, please check out my Hilary Wynne boards on Pinterest too! I hope to connect with you soon.

Your support in purchasing and reading my work is so appreciated. If you are so inclined, and I hope you are, a review on Amazon, B&N or Goodreads would also be a huge help. Reviews truly are the best method of helping indie writers like me get the word out about our books.

Again, thank you so much for your support. I know there are a ton of books out there to choose from.

Sincerely,

Hilary Wynne

EXCERPT FROM HOLD ON,
BOOK #2 IN THE ALEXA REED SERIES

Julian's eyes snap open. "You need to stop. I want you, but not like this. I can't. This isn't who we are and I don't want you like this."

He immediately stops, rolls off of me, and sits on the edge of the bed with his back to me. He doesn't say a word and all I can hear is him trying to get his breathing under control. I just lie there, not sure what to say to him. I'm not sure if I should touch him. I'm not sure I can. The silence in the room is deafening and I fully expect Julian to get up and leave. There's a grand canyon of distance between us right now and I see, for the first time since we've been together, sex isn't going to help fix what's wrong. Actually, it just made it worse and I have no one to blame but myself for forcing the issue. He knew it was a bad idea and I didn't listen.

When he stands up and starts putting his pants back on, I feel compelled to say something. "Julian, I'm sorry. I should've listened to you. You didn't want this and I forced the issue. Please don't feel bad."

When he turns around, I'm taken aback by what I see.

ABOUT THE AUTHOR

Have you ever woken up one day and said, "Today's the day I'm going to do (insert thing here)?" Well, I did, and the result is my first novel, Stay. I always thought of myself as a decent writer, and then a trip down memory lane through my ninth grade book of poetry confirmed it. I realize that I have always had a romantic side and a way with words. With support from my husband and kids (and an unspoken agreement to leave me alone for a few hours every night), I embarked on this incredible writing journey.

I'm originally from sunny Southern California and spent my summers in South Florida. I attended college at FSU and received my Masters in New Mexico. I finally settled in the Washington, DC area. My happy place has always been anywhere near the water.

When I'm not writing, I help run a business with my husband, watch an inordinate amount of sports (my kids play something 365 days a year), indulge my competitive spirit on the tennis court, and spend time with my awesome family and friends.

I feel so blessed that my love of books inspired me to finally do something that I forgot I had always dreamed about doing.

My someday has arrived!

ACKNOWLEDGEMENTS

To all of the awesome people who have touched my life and may see some of themselves in my characters, thanks for helping make me who I am.

To Michele M., my BFF: Thanks for always being there and knowing me well enough to understand what I need to hear. Your friendship means the world to me. Marissa is the kind of friend to Alexa that you have been to me for twenty-five-plus years, and I hope I did her justice. Sorry for having them do tequila shots without a napkin safety net ... Kamikaze's seemed a little outdated. I'm so happy you got past page 13, and I appreciate the help with the Spanish and geography. I know you lived in S. Florida your whole life ... *Thank you very much*!

To Lisa H., my partner in crime who has loved and supported Julian and Alexa since day one: Thank you for listening to my stories and encouraging me to put them to paper. Thank goodness for long drives to tennis matches in Bailey's Crossroads. I may not have done this had you not wanted more and had your toes not curled! Your support through this entire journey has kept me going. The tequila shots are for you. Love you, Hooka!

To Heather H., my word-nerd friend who kept helping me find missing words: Your encouragement was so appreciated. You continued to believe when I wasn't sure and helped me back away from the ledge more than once. I would have been *crestfallen* if you didn't like it!

To Becca SS, my cousin: Thanks for all your suggestions and for sharing your love of books with me. Hopefully the cover (number 58 out of 275) helps sell the book!

To Hannah SS, my younger cousin: You were right. Alexa is better than Alexis. If this series sells, we will talk names for my next book!

To Rachelle E: Thanks for test-driving a few pages, Rach. Hope the window stayed open for a little while afterward!

To My Bookin It Group: Thank you for your shared love of books and your support and encouragement. You all rock!

To my family, my heart ...

To my boys, Jesse—Justin—Jake—Jared

To my mini-me Jared who changed my name on his phone contact info to say "the author" instead of Mom: You can't read this book, but your support meant the world. Thanks for letting Mom follow a dream.

To Jake: Thanks for just being interested in what I was doing. I know that it's not always easy for a thirteen-year-old boy to do that. Your constant questions and suggestions made me think. You have a heart of gold, and I love you so much. P.S. You can't read this either!

To Jesse and Justin: Thank you for being so proud of me that you told your friends what I was doing. I'm always proud of you. Oh, and thanks for telling me that writing U in a text instead of you was not cool! P.P.S. You can read this book, but you may not want to. It's not so mom-ish!

To my parents, sisters, and brothers: Thanks for always encouraging me to be the best Hilary I can be. I've always been allowed to spread my wings, and it gave me the courage to try this. You guys have my back and I know it. I love you.

And last but certainly not least—to my husband, Jack: It's hard to keep this to a few words. Your support and encouragement mean absolutely everything to me. Thanks for helping with the *research* and for sitting on the beach reading a romance novel. You'd do anything for me, and I do know it. You and the boys are my world, and I love you with all my heart.

Made in the USA
Middletown, DE
03 January 2015